EVILSpeaks

EVIL Speaks

WARRIORS and WATCHERS Saga #1

S. WOFFINGTON

Evil Speaks
Warriors and Watchers Saga, Book 1
Copyright 2015 by S. Woffington

First Edition 2017 by Red Summit Publishers
Dana Point, CA

WarriorsandWatchersSaga.com

ISBN:-13: 978-1-944650-001
ISBN-10: 1-944650-00-8

Editor: Shelley at eFrog Press
www.efrogpress.com

Cover design by Judy Bullard
www.customebookcovers.com

Interior design by Maureen Cutajar
www.gopublished.com

TO BOB

The moment I contemplated that perhaps the magic called love is best left for those younger, you magically appeared and proved me wrong. You can prove me wrong anytime!

Acknowledgements

Robert Folkenflik, distinguished professor at U.C. Irvine and my honors program mentor, I should have acknowledged you in my first novel, *Unveiling*, but failed to do so. You taught me the value and pleasure of solid research, a necessary task in daily life, in the teaching life and, especially, in the writing life.

Donna Hopson, beta-reader extraordinaire, thank you for providing critical input after reading the rough draft and for the eagle-eyed proofreading of the final draft. Without you, errors and confusion would abound.

Shelley, thank you for professionally editing and polishing this gem. I appreciate your attention to detail and your enthusiastic endorsement of the story.

Tara, Tiffany and Tiana, daughters divine, you inspire me daily with your boundless creativity, passion and love. Thank you for giving this a read, critique and thumbs up.

EVILSpeaks

Chapter One

"This is a bad idea, Benny," said Maximus, eighty bucks clenched in his hand. Maximus was one of those geeky kids. His parents, knowing full well he'd be a scrawny math and science nerd—because his father was a scrawny video game developer and his mother was a scrawny chemist—decided that a gigantic name would overcome their son's predetermined geekiness and make him a great man one day. "My parents advised me to seek a diplomatic solution to my problem."

"You tried diplomacy. Dillon stuffed your face in a toilet filled with red dye."

"I'm aware of that," said Maximus, his face an orb of red atop a white stump of a neck, like a talking fairy-tale mushroom. "But you're not mean like he is. If you get hurt, I'm resp—"

"You don't know me, Max," said Benny, aware that Maximus hated to be called Max, but he couldn't be bothered with such a long name. "I'll tell you something you don't learn in math or science. People grow mean or calloused or cynical or solitary for all kinds of reasons. Including me."

"That *is* science. It's called psychology. You wouldn't shove my face in a toilet."

Benny grabbed the money out of Maximus's hand and stuffed it down the front pocket of his black jeans. He had, at first, turned down Maximus's offer of cash for defense. He had no reason to intercede in the affairs of his newest school, but the cash was his means of escape, so he agreed. "Considering I'm about to fight Dillon on your behalf, and you're paying me for it, your theory of my kindness is less credible."

"Good point."

Benny removed his sunglasses and handed them to Maximus. "You're responsible for these. Break 'em, and it's another eighty." Stubble shaded his jawline because his mother had held him back when he flunked the eighth grade last year—he simply quit trying. She made him do it over—this he hadn't expected, so now he tried just hard enough to pass. His dark wavy hair fell to his shoulders. His black tee shirt advertised his favorite band, EpicEvil, and his favorite album, *Rise Up to Extinction*, which was also the title song. An emaciated man and woman, wailing in torment, stretched tightly across his muscular chest. A prized possession, he refused to toss the shirt, even though too small.

"Let's go, Toad Eyes!" shouted Dillon, swirling about in his old football jersey and shorts, punching the air with his fists and hopping about on expensive tennis shoes. Dillon's buzzed red head tilted to and fro. His large red lips, pursed amid large freckles and a pasty-white complexion, looked like a split plum thrown against a mud-spattered stucco wall. Dillon's "Plan A" for nearby Princeton, his father's alma mater, was to gain entry through football, but his coach, first, and then the youth football league, banned him for unnecessary roughness. Dillon switched to lacrosse, while his father worked on suing the youth football league. "Plan B" involved prodding (sometimes paying) others to help Dillon with homework. But what began as a lucrative tutoring business for Maximus had turned into demands for completing Dillon's homework and writing his papers. Profitable prods soon became demands, then threats, then physical torture.

"Awooooo! Ruff! Ruff!"

Dillon's friends howled like a pack of wolves because Benny's first nickname at his new school was Wolf Eyes, not Toad Eyes, but the girls began using it as a compliment, cooing, "Hey, Wolf Eyes" or "Wha's up, Woofy." Bree, Dillon's ex-girlfriend, even started a fad among her clique, wearing tops that she had specially printed with the green eyes of a wolf. So Dillon found a lower species with which to ridicule the "new boy."

The name "Toad Eyes" had come from an incident in the science lab involving Blaze, the fire-bellied toad who lived in a tank. Blaze had a green-and-black back with a bright red-and-black belly, the red meant to ward off predators. Likewise, Benny had unusual eyes: half green and half reddish brown around a black iris. What's weird—because sectoral heterochromia was not unheard of in humans or animals with round eyes—is that both reddish halves tilted at forty-five degree angles, exactly opposite to one another. It freaked people out. It used to freak Benny out.

Dillon waved his arms to stop the wolf howls and initiated croaking sounds. "Toad Eyes, Toad Eyes," barked Dillon.

Benny clasped his hands behind his back to stretch in preparation to fight.

"Crik! Crik! Crik!" shouted the crowd waiting for the match to begin on the basketball court of a carefully selected, remote park not far from the school

Benny had researched fire-bellied toads, and besides his discovery that they were not really toads at all, but frogs, he was pleased to find they were extremely aggressive. Voracious diurnal hunters, they searched day and night for their next meal—basically, if it moved, they ate it, which is impressive for a creature that is full grown at two inches. As Benny locked eyes with Dillon, he remembered his mistake of taunting Dillon with this information.

When Dillon entered the science room one day, he informed Mr. Shipley, the instructor, that the office needed him pronto. "It won't take long, Mr. Shipley. I'll monitor the class." Mr. Shipley believed Dillon, because he was the instructor's student assistant.

Once out of sight, Dillon boasted, "Time to test your theory, Toad Eyes. I haven't fed Blaze for two days." He then pulled Frizzy, the seven-inch, red-and-gray eastern milk snake from its habitat and dropped it into the tank with Blaze.

Before Benny could push Dillon's friends and other aghast onlookers away, Blaze had gobbled half of Frizzy, head first, and continued to swallow. Benny picked Frizzy up by the tail and slid Blaze off, much like pulling meat off of a skewer of barbequed chicken. He barely had time to toss Frizzy back in his tank before Mr. Shipley returned, and Dillon apologized for misunderstanding the office's request.

Benny had grown accustomed to taunting. His eyes made him different. And since difference was not tolerated in children beyond the age of four—that's when kids turned mean, he discovered—Benny turned mean in defense. He'd never hit anyone, but at his last school, he had pushed a kid away more forcefully than intended, and the kid fell backward, sprained his arm and gashed his brow on a desk, requiring two stitches. Benny landed in detention, not the boy who taunted him— ceaselessly, after this incident. In detention, Benny folded his arms over his chest and ignored the lecture about "sticks and stones" and "free speech."

"Crik! Crik! Toad Eyes!" chanted Dillon's followers, while Bree and her followers chanted, "Wolf Eyes! Wolf Eyes!" and howled.

4

Benny cracked his neck, one side then the other. He stepped into the imaginary circle of battle, where he and Dillon paced slowly, sizing up the other.

"Crik! Crik! Crik!" shouted the boys. "Wolfy, Wolfy," chanted Bree, while others—the fence-sitters—remained silent, awaiting a victor to hail.

Benny grinned. "Time to tutor you in manners, Dill Pickle!" Maximus and his friends exploded in laughter, the girls giggled, and even Dillon's friends cracked a smile here and there.

Dillon's face flushed red with rage. He swung at Benny, who dodged the blow with ease.

As Dillon's body twisted away, Benny tripped him, sending Dillon to the pavement.

Dillon jumped to his feet. His fists curled into steely knots.

"Crik! Crik!" shouted Dillon's friends, louder now.

"Get him, Wolf Eyes! Dill Pickle needs manners," shouted Bree. "You're the toad, Dillon!"

Dillon lunged at Benny full force. The two locked forearms. As they turned each other about, Dillon tried to throw Benny over, but he could never get his leg behind Benny's knee.

Dillon didn't play fair. He tried to head-butt Benny, but Benny dodged the blow. Dillon tried to break free, but Benny held tight.

A surge Benny'd never felt before in his life shot through every vein and artery of his body. He let out a growl and snarled in the air. Two sides warred within him, one bent on total annihilation, the other on peace. Benny set a downward blow of his head in motion but at the moment just before impact, Benny shoved Dillon away with such force, he tumbled three times before flopping to a stop at the foot of his pack of friends.

"He's insane!" shouted Dillon, pointing a menacing finger. "Fight's over!" He jumped to his feet, holding his elbow and wincing. "My father will have you expelled!"

"Been there. Done that." Benny wiped his brow with his forearm and eyed the crowd, who eyed him back in stunned silence. Bree and others averted his gaze. Benny offered a final warning. "Stay away from Maximus!"

"My father already hired a replacement—one who knows his place and follows orders." Dillon stormed off, followed by his gang. The girls dispersed, as did the nerds, all but Maximus.

Benny reached out to take his glasses from Maximus, who stammered for something to say. He didn't expect a thank you. It would have been oddly inappropriate, and they both knew it. "Back to diplomacy, Max. Your parents were right."

"Dude, your eyes, the red is so bri—" A single look from Benny shut him up.

"Gotta go, Max. Ma's waiting for me at the university." Benny headed down the tree-lined street, reliving each new start at each of the new schools he had had over the years. This was, officially, the worst ever.

Benny named each move as a new life. He had become inured to teasing by Life Number Three, calloused by Life Number Four, a loner by Life Number Six. And now, in Life Number Seven, the transformation was complete: the butterfly had devolved into a caterpillar and tucked itself back into its cocoon where it planned to remain, insulated from the outside world.

Benny couldn't remember the exact moment when he started numbering his many panicked moves from city to city or state to state, same as the proverbial cat had numbered his nine lives. He just did it. His ma said they moved to "keep Benny safe," but in fifteen years he had never figured out safe from what, and Ma never said, not really. It had something to do with his father's death, a man he'd stopped caring about a move or two ago. Gone is gone. And that made him calloused. Proudly so. Calluses thickened the skin. They could harden the heart, too.

"My father died when I was three." That fact had rolled off Benny's tongue easily. The moment he had said it, Bree glared at him like a doctor ready to bandage a wound, and, when she asked, "How did it happen?" the pat response was, "I'd rather not talk about it," after which she gushed apologies and clawed his bulging bicep, proud of herself for having found a reason for the new boy's aloof disposition. The story then flew around the school via the Galloping Gossip Girl hotline—faster than the speed of the Internet—until his story grew into an unspeakable tragedy of such horrific proportions that it rendered Benny mute on the subject. Before the day was out, it seemed like every girl in school shot googly eyes and pointy fingers at him as they passed by. Some of them, like Bree, stood willing and ready to crack his shell by salving his unspeakable wounds with tender sympathy—which he readily accepted—but really, it became a contest and he became the prize.

Who would extract the deep, dark story from his lips?

Needless to say, girls flocked to his side. He liked this very much but pushed them back with the ease of a simple response: "I'm sorry. I just can't get close," after which they gushed, "I understand, Benny. Take your time."

Benny knew that by tomorrow, the girls would peel away, uttering some new gossip about a violent past or criminal history, no doubt.

"My father died when I was three." At first, Benny didn't believe it himself. But when repeated over and over again, it became his new truth. Solid. Affirmed.

Benny gained a sense of peace by creating new truths. He stopped trying to make new friends. Funny thing though, when he let go of people, he grew more attached to his stuff, like the tee shirt of his favorite band. But he lost stuff, too.

When running away with seconds to pack, Benny and Neeve, his mother, left stuff behind. Like furniture and televisions and bicycles. "Just leave it! We'll get a new one," Ma shouted. But there was rarely money for a new one. The number of boxes dwindled. The most recent move had whittled them down to a satchel apiece, his computer, a dartboard, two potted plants and a clunker car: a rusty faded-yellow box with dull headlamps that had once been a taxi.

New starts were easier when he was the "invisible" student, the kid no one paid attention to, but his eyes made that impossible. Dudes inspected him with scrutiny the moment he stepped onto their turf. He was sure girls did the same with "new girls" on their turf. Checking out the competition. Benny had enough experience to know that if the girls ignored him, so, too, would the boys.

Invisibility became impossible the moment Bree and her chick click flocked around him. That necessitated the boys pulling him into their bro pack where they could keep tabs on him. Once a part of the pack, Benny would be bound and obliged by the unwritten "bro code" to stay away from the girls, at least the ones Dillon and his friends had identified as "theirs." As a bonus, if Benny joined one of their sports, the team could use his calloused disposition to thrash their opponents.

But, by this time, Benny was no team player. And if he wasn't with the bro pack, he was against them. Not that it mattered now. He'd done it. He'd whittled himself down to not needing anyone or anything—even Ma. He'd planned on leaving after finals, which he'd planned on passing as a final goodwill gesture. It's why he took Max's eighty bucks. To get away. Far away. To disappear. Now, he didn't care. He'd leave tonight after dark.

———

A black shark of a car turned the corner into the Chambers University campus. Luigi, the driver, rolled down his window and yanked the steering wheel hard left. The wheel grazed his pudgy belly as the car swerved to the opposite side of the road in pursuit of a slim, long-haired blonde carrying a load of books. He ignored oncoming drivers honking and shouting and maneuvering around him and lowered the tinted window.

"Hey, baby. It's a dangerous world. Let me give yous a lift?"

The girl picked up her pace, nose in the air. "You're out of your league, you maladroit, undesirable cretin."

From the passenger seat, Antonio, a simpleminded man with slicked-back hair, asked, "What did she say? Must be a foreign student."

Luigi didn't answer. He swerved back to the other side of the road, allowing a dark grin to creep across his face. He exhaled a black fog that escaped through the window and swirled toward the girl. It formed the shape of Luigi and walked alongside the blonde.

The moment the girl turned her head, and shock and horror filled her blue eyes, the foggy image grinned and shoved her into a patch of bloodroot. Her fall decapitated the last white flower of the season. Her books flew into the air. A nearby groundskeeper turned to grouse, catching what he thought was a smile in a patch of black smoke that evaporated before his eyes.

"Like I said," Luigi muttered as he pulled the car to a stop along the curb. "It's a dangerous world."

"You sure she's here, boss?"

Luigi patted some papers lying between them on the seat. "Got her class schedule." He scanned the passersby for any sign of Anna Neeve Adez. "Someone's helping her. Just keep your eyes open."

"Then what?"

"Then, she leads us to the boy. He wants Benny. He wants his grandson."

———

Inside a tiny university office, Neeve, known as Sophia Smith by her professor, shifted uncomfortably as Professor Daniel Archer Daniels III poured himself a cup of hot water to make tea.

Dark circles hung below Neeve's fiery green eyes. She ran long, graceful fingers through unruly waves of red hair, a contrast to her drab attire: a white tank top, Bermuda shorts and cheap tennis shoes.

"Sure you won't join me for a nice cup of tea?" asked Professor Daniels, who sounded English, but wasn't, due to the fact he had spent a few academic years at Harvard and the way he sharply articulated every syllable. "Earl Grey," he added as he peeled the paper from a teabag and dunked it in his Chambers University mug.

Besides tall cases crammed with books and a floor stacked with even more books and papers, the walls held a grotesque combination of tribal masks, a world map stuck with pins, and several pictures of the professor, years younger—but with the same wild brown hair and bulging, brown bug eyes—standing next to primitive tribes and mammoth cave entrances. Human bones covered his desk.

"Maybe next time, Professor Daniels. Nice pictures. You look more at ease in them than in your lectures."

Professor Daniels nestled his cup between a femur and a skull. He sat behind his desk, all the while dipping his tea bag up and down, up and down, as if counting the exact number of dips that would render the perfect brew. "Is it that obvious? I'm afraid you're right. I am more at home in the field. Please, call me Daniel."

"I mean . . . I love your lectures, too. I'm sorry if I—"

"Tut, tut, don't apologize. As a scientist, I appreciate keen observation. You may not know this, but I have a PhD in forensic

cultural anthropology and a master's in comparative mythology."
He held the tea bag over the cup to let it drain. "Until discredited,
that is, and made a laughing stock in the scientific community by
a . . . well, it doesn't matter. I'll prove her wrong, if it's the last
thing I do." He hurled the tea bag into the trash can, then sipped
his tea in gentlemanly silence. "Ah, well, I'm grateful to be here.
Teaching anatomy at the nurses' school pays the bills."

Neeve grabbed the femur and stuffed it into an unzipped
duffle bag sitting by her feet. "I really appreciate your letting me
take these home to study. I promise I'll be ready for the exam on
Friday."

"I'm sympathetic. Just an old softie, really." The professor
leaned forward. "I see the effort you're putting in, Sophia. It's not
easy to transfer to a new program—weeks before finals, no less.
Frankly, I don't know how you pulled it off. What's your secret?
Friend in the Dean's Office?"

"No time for friends." Neeve picked up the skull. "Except for
my buddy, here, but he doesn't talk much."

The professor wagged a finger of warning. "Just be careful
who sees you with those. I don't know about your neighbors, but
the lady next door to me is quite handy with a pair of binoculars."

"Why? What did she do?"

"She overreacted, that's what she did! A few months ago, I
brought Harry home and—"

Holding a spine with a rib cage attached, Neeve froze. "Harry?
The cadaver, Harry?"

"Why not? He lives on a cart with foldable wheels."

"Technically, Professor, he doesn't live at all."

"Oh, you know what I mean, Sophia. It was late. I was prep-
ping him for a midterm, and I was tired. I decided to take my
work home. You know—homework." Professor Daniels set his

cup down to free his hands for embellishing the story. "I simply rolled him into the back of my station wagon, and off we went. It was past midnight when I got him home. And there I was, minding my own business, eating my freshly delivered pizza and sticking Harry with pins with numbered flags for identification on the morning exam, when the police burst into my kitchen, guns drawn. I nearly put out Harry's eye."

"Poor Harry," said Neeve, putting the last item, a foot, into her bag and zipping it up.

"The brutes threw me up against the wall and patted me down like some kind of common criminal. The dean had to come over and straighten it all out. I nearly lost my job."

"I'll be careful, and I promise to take good care of these." Neeve stood up to leave. "I've gotta go. My son is waiting for me."

"I didn't know you had a son. A boy needs a man around. I volunteer. Those are my initials, you know. D-A-D." He laughed in a way that was harmless. "How's he taking the move? That can be hard on a child."

"It's been rough for him. We lost Benny's father when Benny was three. Since then, we've moved a lot, and . . . I don't know . . . hormones, I guess. He's fifteen. Angry a lot, mostly at me."

Professor Daniels rushed around his desk to help hoist the heavy bag onto Sophia's shoulder. "I'm here anytime you need me."

"Thanks, Professor. I mean, Daniel. You're a good man."

"What a pretty necklace . . . unusual . . . ancient markings . . . but I've never seen them together."

Neeve fingered the necklace. A circle of symbols surrounded a hand whose fingertips came together, enclosing a round red gem that floated freely in its palm.

"A gift from a friend who once gave me shelter in a storm. Well, I gotta go."

Professor Daniels backed away, blushing. "Take care of my bones. I don't give them to just anyone, you know." He laughed at his own stupid joke.

A knock upon the open door made them turn their heads. "Ready, Ma?"

"Professor Daniels, this is my son, Benedito. Benny for short." Professor Daniels blushed and extended a hand, which Benny reluctantly accepted and shook.

"A pleasure, young man. Your mother is a hardworking student, as I'm sure you are as well."

"Naturally," said Benny.

An earthquake rumbled beneath their feet. Professor Daniels gasped with the delight of a child having found a lost treasure. He raced to his computer and hit a shortcut key on his desktop screen that opened a site dedicated to seismic activity. The earthquake map showed simultaneous earthquakes around the globe. Daniels glanced at the world map on the wall—the pins coincided with the locations of the earthquakes, all but one, the one that shook his office. A news feed popped up on his screen. He opened it.

An Italian female reporter with horror and shock on her face pointed to the ruins of the Roman Forum behind her. A rocket-like column of fire shot into the sky. "Not ten minutes ago, an explosion rocked the Roman Forum, which you see behind me. There are no natural gas lines in the vicinity. Therefore, investigators suspect vandals or terrorists have set the explosion that continues to burn."

"That's awful," said Neeve, but Daniels didn't respond, so she added, "See you tomorrow, Professor." She and Benny slipped out the door.

Professor Daniels noted the epicenter. He rose from his desk and stuck a pin in upstate New York. "That's impossible. We would not have felt it this far away." He glanced at the pin stuck in Rome, Italy, and removed a postcard just below it. He stared at the image, a marble relief of Marcus Curtius, a Roman soldier upon his horse, both in full regalia, stepping downward into a chasm in the forum believed to be an entrance to Tartarus, the underworld. "What in blazes—pun intended—is going on?"

Chapter Two

Neeve drove out of the parking lot and headed home, unaware of the black car following them at an inconspicuous distance. "How was your day, Benny? Did you make some new friends?"

"Sure. I was surrounded by them."

"No need for sarcasm."

"Yeah, well, maybe you shouldn't preach what you don't practice."

"I made a new friend today. Professor Daniels."

"Teachers aren't friends, Ma."

"You're just not trying."

Benny threw up his hands. "Every friend I've had since Dad died has become a pen pal. I hate writing. Hence the D in English."

"You have a D in English?"

"D+. I'll pull it up to a C- before the term ends. Max offered free tutoring." He doubted the offer was still on the table after today, but he didn't need it now anyway. He was out of here!

"It seems like we fight all the time. Like we're growing apart. Can't we ever just talk?"

"Okay, let's talk. Tell me about Dad—the truth. Why are we on the run?"

Benny waited as his mother turned the corner in complete silence, as if the corner required superhuman concentration to maneuver.

"Let it go. Your father died trying to save us."

Crap! Another sucker punch. Wasn't he old enough to hear the truth? Why did he think another year older would make a difference? Or produce a different answer? But the moment he asked himself the question, he figured out the reason: my father died when I was three. It was his pat answer, practiced and delivered with the same pitch and tone, place to place, year after year. This was her pat answer.

"I loved your father. He loved us."

Another pat answer. "There's something you're not telling me."

Neeve parked the car at the curb. The engine sputtered to a stop. "You're imagining there's more to it. There isn't."

"Oh, yeah, that explains it. My wild imagination. Or maybe I'm nuts! Thanks, Ma. Thanks for the pep talk. I feel so much closer to you now." Benny dashed up the cracked concrete walkway of a dilapidated two-story house that sat at the farthest edge of the pristine, polished, affluent town. Its windows, covered with dust and grime, no longer glimmered. Its face had splintered and sagged. The once hopeful and gay blue paint with white trim had both faded to a ghostly gray that chipped away, leaving bare wood that had also grown gray from exposure. Not even weeds grew on the lot, despite the weedy empty lots on either side of the house and across the street.

Benny climbed the creaking steps of the front porch and yanked open the screen door, which screeched as if in pain. He unlocked the door, wondering why they bothered. They had nothing worth stealing. The door, too, creaked in complaint when he opened it. He spun to face his mother, just climbing the steps behind him and struggling with the heavy bag. But he'd run out of words.

Neeve lowered the duffle bag onto the porch and rubbed her shoulder. "I love you, Benny."

"Well, I hate you! And I barely knew my father, so it's even easier to hate him. Kind of a two-for-one deal."

"Ben—"

"Look around, Ma. We got nothin'!"

"We have each other. That's all that matters."

Benny nodded toward the two flowerpots sitting on the inside ledge of the window. Part of "her stuff." The pots had traveled with them through every move. "Water your little friends, Ma. They're dyin'." He ducked inside and raced upstairs to his room.

Neeve shouldered the bag and headed for the kitchen. The door upstairs slammed shut. She swung the bag under the aluminum dinette, picked up at a church yard sale for ten bucks since it had only three chairs, and the red vinyl on one of the chairs had cracked open, revealing orange-yellow foam. "Focus. One more year and you're a nurse." She unzipped the bag and pulled the bones out one by one, setting them on the table.

EpicEvil lyrics shook the walls of the house:

> *Endangered humans, on earth a blight,*
> *Your time has come, no way to fight.*

Across the street, Luigi parked the car, punched his cell phone and waited.

———

In a study lined with mahogany bookcases, an exceedingly tall and exceedingly bald butler answered the phone in a deep monotone voice. "Mr. Domenico H. Adez's residence." The man listened intently before saying, "One moment, please."

The butler walked the phone over to a figure seated in a tall-backed, red-leather chair, who sat before a fire that roared in a gigantic stone hearth.

Upon hearing the butler's approach, the man pulled the hood of his black fur robe over his curly red hair, stroked his beard and complained. "It's so cold here, even in summer." He warmed his wrinkled hands before the blazing fire.

"It's Mr. Luigi."

The wrinkled hand snatched the phone away. "Did you find him?" the man rasped into the mouthpiece.

"Yes, and her, too," said Luigi.

"Blow the house to kingdom come, as they say."

"I thought the plan was to nab him?" asked Luigi.

"I changed my mind. We don't need him or her."

"What about the council?"

"Fear me, Luigi, not the council."

———

Neeve set her anatomy book on the chair beside her and opened it to the skeletal section. She tried to tune out the music blasting above her:

People are weak; they will run
When they come, when darkness comes
To obliterate the sun

And we will run and run and run
And rise up to extinction.

Neeve grabbed a hand and pointed to the wrist bones. "It's my extinction if I fail the final exam." She glared at the hand. "Never Lower Tilly's Pan . . . what a stupid phrase to remember these bones. What derelict thought that up?" She thought for a moment and came up with her own: "N-L-T-P-M-M-C-H. Never Let Tall Poodles Make My Chihuahua Hide—navicular, lunate, triquetrum, pisiform . . . pisiform . . ." She scratched the top of her head with the skeleton hand.

With an exasperated sigh, she dropped the hand on the table and headed for the stairs.

———

Luigi opened the trunk and grabbed a shoebox. He opened the box and fiddled with the clock.

Antonio whined, "This is so old-world."

"I know," agreed Luigi. "But it's not time yet. We have to avoid suspicion."

"Like you did this morning with the blonde?"

"She made me mad. I could have done worse—as you know. You won't make me mad, will you, Antonio?"

"No, boss."

"Get inside. Plant the bomb and get out. Timer's set for ten minutes once activated. Don't drop it. If you blow yourself up, as amusing as that would be to me, I'll take heat from Domenico."

Antonio grabbed the box and crept across the street. He skulked alongside the house, past a tree. He heard shouting and loud music from a second-story window. The music stopped.

"Leave me alone!"

"Open the door and apologize for what you said."

"What did I say?"

"That you hated me and your father."

"Dad's dead. He won't know I said it."

"Benedito Adez, you open this door right now!"

"When hell freezes over, Ma."

Antonio snuck around back and peeked inside the window next to the kitchen door. He crept inside and waited to see if the argument had stopped, but it hadn't. He crossed the kitchen and stood at the foot of the stairs. His black forked tongue shot out and wound its way upstairs, hovering just behind Neeve's calves and flicking the air to pick up information.

Without turning from the door, Neeve swatted at her leg to shoo away the obvious fly that annoyed her.

Antonio could taste her scent in the air. His stomach growled. He snapped his tongue back and headed to the kitchen.

Neeve turned but saw nothing. She pounded on the door. "If you don't apologize, Benedito, you won't see your next birthday!"

"Birthday? Oh, you mean that day when you stick a candle in a cupcake and hand me a container of Gak?" Benny turned on his old computer and opened the *Warriors and Watchers* video game.

Downstairs, Antonio set the box on the edge of the table. His stomach growled again. His tongue shot out to taste the skull. He grimaced and yanked it back, bumping the box, which fell off the edge of the table.

Neeve slammed her fist on Benny's door. "Sometimes, you make me so mad I could explode!"

Antonio's tongue shot out of his mouth and around the box, arresting its fall just before it hit the ground.

"Permission granted. Explode," yelled Benny, battling a troll with the assistance of an Asian avatar. "Then, maybe I'd have some peace and quiet."

Antonio pushed a button. A red light flashed on the bomb. He shoved the box next to the wall under the kitchen table and arranged the duffle bag in such a way as to conceal it. Before leaving, he eyed the refrigerator. He opened the door, disappointed to find a rotisserie chicken missing a leg and a breast, two green Jell-O cups and a head of lettuce. He grabbed the plate of chicken. His jaws stretched wide and shot forward over the chicken, devouring it whole. The bulge moved slowly down his neck and disappeared. He set the plate back where he found it and reached for the two Jell-O cups. His long tongue ripped off the foil tops and sucked out the wiggly green food. He crushed the empty cups and threw them back in the fridge.

Neeve's tone softened. "Benny, I . . ."

Benny turned up the music.

Nowhere to run when darkness comes.
But to rise up to extinction.

Neeve crossed her arms over her chest and headed downstairs. She opened the fridge door. "Really, Benny? Did you have to take the whole chicken to your room?"

She plunked down on a chair and leaned over to face the skull. "You're my friend, right? You with your sexy orbits. Your inferior maxillary and superior maxillary, and those amazing zygomatic arches. Your . . ." She leaned back and ran her fingers through her red waves of hair. "I've gone insane."

———

Benny shut down his computer, too angry to play. He grabbed darts from the dartboard, stepped back, and flung them with more anger than aim. The first stabbed the wall to the right of the board with such force, it embedded itself up to the feathers. The second stabbed his duffle bag, sitting on the floor, and the third hit the bull's-eye.

He pulled the dart out of the duffle bag. How many times had he packed it? He yanked open his drawers and stuffed the bag with clothes. Time to get out and get going.

Outside, Luigi and Antonio sat in the car and waited. "Is that Gak on your cheek?"

Antonio licked it away. "Jell-O. I prefer cherry."

"I prefer blood. Yours, if that bomb don't go off soon."

———

Neeve stared at the skull. "You know this one, it's easy. It's . . ." she snapped her fingers as if that would help. "It's . . . crap!" She kicked her foot against the duffle bag, shoving the shoe box a couple of inches forward. She eyed the book. "Temporal bone. Temples. Where I have a monster headache right now. How could you forget that one, dummy?"

As she rubbed her temples, she eyed the two plants sitting on the sill in the living room. "Benny's right. You do look pretty sad." She pushed away from the table and crossed the living room to retrieve the plants.

She set them gently in the kitchen sink and turned on the faucet, directing the trickle of water to drop on the dry soil. "Some nurse I'll be. I'll do better, guys. I promise. And that's just what I'll tell Benny in the morning, when I'll tell him the truth. At least what I know of it. Could he hate me more than he does now? How would you know? You're plants."

Benny zipped his hoodie, pushed up his sleeves and opened the window. The branch of a dead tree reached out to aid him in his escape. He hoped it would hold his weight. He turned to grab his bag and leave, but froze upon seeing objects on his nightstand that he had dragged from move to move—New York, Florida, California, Texas, Tennessee and New Jersey. He had decided to leave them behind this time. Good riddance to it all! But something caused him to reconsider, some pang deep within him, some memory perhaps. All he knew was that it had a connection to his father. He didn't remember how old he was, maybe six. His mother held his hand as they walked down a street in Los Angeles, but to him, it was just another street he'd never seen before, in a town he'd never seen before. And they were, once again, "safe." Back then, he remembered feeling safe just by holding her hand. Neeve pulled him into a bakery for a cookie, and there it was, sitting atop a red velvet cake with red frosting: a castle and a knight wielding a sword, battling a fire-breathing dragon.

"I want it! It's daddy!" Benny cried and threw his cookie down. But Ma told him it was someone else's birthday cake. He wailed more, and she dug in her purse but didn't have enough money. The Latino lady behind the counter disappeared. She returned holding a plastic bag—it contained a brand-new castle and knight, untouched by frosting. Maria hired Neeve on the spot and gave Benny cookies on a regular basis. That was Life Number Four.

Benny stared at the knight, as he had each evening before closing his eyes to sleep, hoping to suddenly remember the connection. He sometimes dreamed of a knight battling a hideous dragon with red eyes, but he could never see the knight's face.

The clock ticked off the last ten seconds.

Benny climbed back inside and grabbed the knight. He shoved him in his bag, returned to the window and threw a leg out. A screech made him jump. He eyed the white heart-shaped face of the owl that routinely perched itself on an upper branch. "Why can't you hoot, like other owls?"

Neeve set the plants back on the window sill. She spotted a black car across the street. A gasp left her mouth and her heart raced. She opened the screen door but a crack to get a better look.

KA-BOOM!!!

The bomb exploded in an upheaval of force that shot Neeve forward, out the door, over the porch and into the yard, where she rolled and tumbled across the barren dirt and landed in a heap. The two flower pots shot out the window and into the air; one plopped into the soil beside Neeve's face. The other smashed over her skull. A trickle of blood oozed down her forehead.

The owl screeched and jettisoned into the air.

Benny shot into the tree.

His head slammed against an upper branch and he fell, smashing through a weak limb that broke off and hooked him under his jacket. The limb stabbed through his tee shirt and scraped his back, leaving him out cold and suspended in the tree.

Flames ignited the dry timber of the house, crackling as they raced across the rafters, the wooden floors, and the porch. Fire engulfed the old house, which creaked and groaned as it died. The roof timbers crackled and snapped. The roof fought to stay aloft. Fire shot out of Benny's bedroom window and licked at the dry tree branch, which easily caught fire. Flames crept upward toward Benny.

A few blocks away, sirens screamed, piercing the air.

The driver of the fire truck careened around a beer-bellied workman wearing a hardhat and holding a sign that read SLOW.

The workman's partner, standing in a ditch, reached up. "Joey, give me a hand, will ya?"

A charred skeleton hand suddenly fell from the sky and landed in his. He jumped upon seeing it, and threw it aside. "Wise guy! That ain't funny, Mr. Practical Joker. You're fired! Ha, ha. Are you laughing now?"

———

Luigi reacted quickly. He flipped a U-turn, jamming the front right tire over the curb. "Get her!"

Antonio jumped out. He scooped Neeve into his arms, threw her in the backseat and jumped in beside her.

Neeve opened her eyes a crack. Antonio's eyes turned to slits and then swirled. Neeve kicked and squirmed, getting her legs out the door.

Luigi yelled, "Get the amulet, dummy!"

Antonio grabbed for Neeve's necklace and ripped it off. Neeve's eyes shot open as her hand shot out to retrieve the necklace.

Antonio's eyes swirled. Neeve resisted looking into them, but Antonio pulled her hair back, and her eyes opened. "Ssssleep."

Neeve closed her eyes. Her hand fell to her side.

Antonio slammed the door shut. Luigi punched the gas just as the fire truck rounded the corner and they sped past each other.

The roof caved in and the porch collapsed. Hot flames crept across the branches of the tree and licked at Benny, heating the rubber soles of his tennis shoes and singeing the hair from his left forearm.

Chapter Three

Benny opened his eyes and tried to focus. He could see a hazy white room and a dark figure standing in the doorway. He blinked a few times and reached up, only to discover that his hands were tied down. He tried to speak, but nothing came out.

The dark figure set something down, rushed to his side and fumbled at Benny's wrists.

Benny blinked away the blurry lines until he saw a man in a black suit hunched over him. "Take it easy, kid. You were thrashing all over the place. The doc put the restraints on for your own good. Remember who you were fighting?"

The man, fortyish, had curly black hair, dark brows, deep hazel eyes, a Roman nose with a scar at the bridge, an even longer scar along his chin, and another scar across half of his neck, which disappeared under his shirt collar. He had a strong square jaw with a couple days of stubble. As if reading his mind, the man said, "I've had a few tours of duty. Earned a few battle scars. There, you're free, but take it easy."

Benny surveyed his situation: he had an IV stuck in his left arm; bandages wrapped around his head and left hand and forearm; his head ached, felt heavy, and pain shot through his back. He tried to speak, but again, nothing came out.

"I'm Michael Salvatore. FBI. Call me Mike."

Benny tried to sit up, but Mike pushed him back down.

"Take it easy, dude. Two days ago we found you hanging in a tree next to a pile of burning wood that used to be a house."

Benny mouthed the words "Ma! Ma! Ma!" but no sound came out.

Mike nodded understanding.

Benny didn't like the pained expression on the man's face.

"Look, I'm not just FBI. I'm a friend of your . . . a friend of Neeve's." He cleared his throat. "We found . . . bones . . . in the rubble. We've sent them to the lab for testing."

Benny shot forward, ignoring the pain. His mouth opened wide in a silent scream.

Mike gripped Benny by the shoulders. "I'm sorry, kid. I'm so sorry." Benny pushed back. Mike wouldn't let go, he just kept talking. "Neeve—her Irish dad picked that name. Did you know that? Some queen of the otherworld, like a utopia or something." Mike released Benny and pushed the button next to the bed to call a nurse. "I admitted you under an alias. Jake Deer. Remember that. You're Jake. Only the doc knows your real name."

Benny's mind raced. He'd asked for it—asked her to go away. He didn't mean it. Not like that!

The nurse rushed in. "Get the doc!" Mike commanded. The nurse nodded and raced out.

"You're coming home with me, Benny. I know you don't know me from Adam, but I promised Neeve that if anything ever happened . . ."

Benny stopped thrashing. He glared at Mike. Was it true? Had they really been in danger? Did this guy know? He wanted to scream. He wanted to tear something or someone apart. He slung a leg over the side of the bed and reached for his IV.

Mike pinned Benny down so hard, pain ripped through the center of his back and his forearm.

A balding, bespectacled doctor rushed to Benny's side with a nurse in tow. In a calm voice, he said, "Stop it, Jake. Or the nurse will knock you out my way and we'll restrain you again."

The nurse held a syringe next to the IV and waited for instructions.

"He can't speak," Mike interjected.

Benny stopped thrashing but seethed.

The doctor signaled the nurse to lower the syringe. "That's better."

The doctor felt around Benny's neck as he introduced himself. "I'm Dr. Simms. I'll order some tests."

"When can I take him home?" Mike handed the doctor a piece of paper.

Benny snatched it away. The doctor tried to take it back, but Mike waved him off. "It's okay. Let him read it."

To Whom It May Concern:
   In the event of my disappearance or death, I give full legal and physical custody of my son, Benedito H. Adez, to Michael Salvatore.
   Anna Neeve Adez

It was dated July 29, 2002. The day Benny lost his father. Why hadn't his mother ever mentioned this guy? More secrets!

Mike gently lifted the paper from Benny's hands and handed it to the doctor, who scanned its content before stuffing it in his pocket.

"I presume, Jake, that Mr. Salvatore gave you the shocking news of your mother's death the moment you awoke." Dr. Simms admonished Michael with sarcasm. "How kind of him. Why don't you go home, Mr. Salvatore. We can call you if there's any change. You can't possibly sleep in that chair a third night. You need some rest, too."

"I'm not leaving him," said Mike.

"Nancy, send in an orderly with a gurney, please. MRI of his head and neck, stat." The nurse nodded and left.

"And there's something wrong with his eyes," added Mike. "They're half red and half green."

The doctor examined Benny's eyes. "The red is really a shade of brown. Have you always had sectoral heterochromia?"

Benny nodded.

The doctor turned to Mike. "It's rare, but it's possible for one sector of the eye to be another color than the rest, even for one eye to be a different color than the other eye, which is called heterochromia. Nothing to worry about."

An orderly arrived to move Benny onto a gurney.

Dr. Simms added a warning. "Be good. Any trouble at all, and I'll order that sedation."

———

It was dark outside by the time Benny returned to his room. Mike helped the orderly position the gurney, and Benny slid back into bed.

Benny couldn't sleep. He tossed from side to side reliving the fight with Dillon and the fight with his mother. "I love you, Benny." He remembered his answer and every hateful word he had used to stab her. At some point, he fell asleep, only to dream that an explosion rocked him awake. Heat engulfed his room, cast a red glow over all. He shot up in bed. Sweat poured down his face. Flames danced beyond the doorway. A red-eyed dragon burst through the wall of fire, coming straight for him. A knight, sword in hand, blocked the doorway, thwarting the dragon's advance. Benny wanted the knight to turn around, so that he could see his face, but the dragon tossed the knight aside and crashed through the door frame, splintering it and punching out the wall around it. Benny struggled to get out of bed, but restraints strapped him down. The dragon stood before him. Its eyes glowed. The red half of Benny's eyes glowed too.

Benny shot upright in a sweat. His chest heaved. Mike, a dim shape slumped in the chair in the corner, didn't stir.

———

The following morning, Dr. Simms introduced his colleague, a middle-aged brunette who seemed somewhat flustered, as if caught off-guard by Mike's rugged appearance and his holstered gun that bulged beneath his crinkled jacket.

"I'm Dr. McCullough, Catherine—Kate. Just call me Kate. Um, should we step outside to discuss this?"

Mike stood next to Benny in a military stance, his feet slightly apart and his hands clasped. "Just tell him what you found."

Finally, thought Benny, someone would include him in the discussion.

"Very well," said Dr. McCullough. "Dr. Simms and I have examined Jake, and—"

"Talk to the boy," Mike interrupted. "Not to me."

Dr. McCullough stepped next to Benny. She hugged her clipboard to her chest. "The test results confirm that there's been no damage to your trachea or vocal cords or brain, although you did sustain a serious concussion. In short, there is no physical explanation for your mute condition. We feel it is more likely a psychosomatic reaction to the trauma and the news of . . . of . . . your mother. I'm so sorry."

Mike asked, "So, you mean it's all in his head? He can speak when he wants?"

"Not exactly," responded Dr. McCullough, puffing with pride to show off her expertise. "He wants to speak now but can't. I understand that he's transitioned frequently from place to place, and that his father is also . . . well, the boy has suffered a lot of emotional trauma in his early years of life. His body has reacted. Shut down, if you will. His voice might come back sooner, later, or . . ."

"Or never?" asked Mike.

"It's completely unpredictable," added Dr. Simms.

Mike asked, "Is there anything I can do to help?"

"Normally, I'd recommend . . . "

Mike implored her with a strong gaze to direct her conversation at Benny.

She dropped the clipboard to her side. "Normally, I'd recommend a psychiatrist. Jake can communicate in writing on a computer notepad, for example. It might help."

Benny put up a hand and shook his head to indicate a flat out, "No way!"

"Thank you, Kate," said Mike. "He says no, so it's no."

Dr. McCullough nodded. "Call me if you need me . . . I mean, if there are any changes in his condition, of course."

"Thank you, Kate." Dr. Simms turned to Mike. "Benny can go ho . . . I'm sorry. I mean I've released Benny from our care."

"Thanks, doc."

Once the doctors disappeared, Mike handed Benny a notepad computer. "This is yours. I know you've got questions. I can't answer them all, but I'll try."

Benny wrote, "who did this" — no caps or punctuation.

"I don't know, but I have an idea or two."

"who" Benny stabbed at the keyboard.

"I don't know, Benny. But I'm going to find out." Mike leaned in. "Your mother came into my New York office a long time ago. We both grew up in El Barrio, an old neighborhood in New York. We went to school together, hung out. Neeve's mom and mine were Puerto Rican. Friends. Everything changed when Neeve started dating your dad, Romero, a rich guy from out of the area. I can't blame—"

Benny punched the notepad. "how rich?" This time, he added a question mark.

"Filthy — and I mean filthy. Romero's father, Domenico, is like the godfather of all godfathers — into every illegal business you can think of — and not just here — international too, but the FBI has never been able to arrest him."

"what happened to my father" Benny wrote.

"I don't know. You just turned three when Neeve came to see me in Manhattan. She figured out that her father-in-law was with the mob or worse. She sounded crazy, made it sound like he had some kind of power protecting him. She was scared. She said they both wanted out—Romero, too. I have my doubts about that."

Mike continued, "It's a long story, but bottom line is this—we raided the compound, got Neeve out. Your father didn't make it. I offered Neeve witness protection, but she wouldn't take it. Said she'd handle it herself. I told her to keep in touch. Every time she moved, she'd call me and give me her new address. I'd jot it down and put the info in the computer, so that I'd be notified if any police calls came up at those addresses. Years went by, more moves, but no red flags. I began to think that whoever she was running from had quit looking.

"Three days ago, my computer flashed with the report of an explosion at your current address. I had you admitted under an alias—a takeoff on John Doe. I informed the press that you both died in the fire. I've taken a leave of absence from the FBI. I will find who did this."

Benny wrote a final note. "WE will find who did this"

Mike put a hand on Benny's shoulder. "We will. I promise." Mike dug in his pocket and handed Benny a business card. "This was your mother's first address after she ran away from your grandfather. She said a friend was helping her start a new life, someone she'd only recently met but trusted. Said she saw her in a dream the night before the raid. Then standing outside the FBI building as she left with you. It's screwy, I know, but I'm hoping Neeve kept in touch with her and that she can fill us in."

The card was odd. A golden sun burned brightly in the upper right corner, beaming down on a gilded owl in the bottom left corner. Across the band of light, it read: Minerva Pallas, PhD, One World Academy, but no address, only the words "Minerva, New York."

Chapter Four

Neeve awoke. She had a hazy memory of living in darkness for hours on end. How long had she been here? Where was she? She smelled a rank odor: musty, moldy, dank. From somewhere, a steady drip fell into a puddle in a consistent, soothing rhythm. *Tink. Tink. Tink.*

A rattling of metal against metal turned her attention to the barred cage door. Her father-in-law stepped into her cell, carrying a rolled-up newspaper.

Neeve tried to sit up, but her head reeled. She felt a bandage across her forehead. "Benny! Where is he?"

"Save your strength," said Domenico. Antonio rushed to place a chair beneath him and he sat.

The sound of his voice, deep and raspy, gave her instant willpower to disobey him and sit up. "Let me go."

"But you're home, Neeve. You're with family."

"Benny is my only family now, not you."

Domenico held out the newspaper. "Benny's dead."

Neeve grabbed it and read the article. She threw the paper at his feet. "It says I'm dead, too. You're a liar!"

"You destroyed this family, Neeve. You poisoned it. You had everything! Money. Power. Love."

"My love for your son cost him his life."

Domenico raged. "You tried to turn my son against me!" He opened his hand. Neeve's necklace dangled down from it. "You have no protectors now."

"Benny does. I made sure of that. He's all that matters."

"Beautiful Neeve. At least you were once. Romero fell in love the moment he laid eyes on you." He reached out to touch her cheek, but she turned her face away. "He plucked you out of El Barrio and made you a princess. How you loved the money, the furs, the jewels, the houses, the cars, the travel."

"Until I found out where the money came from!"

"It's just money. And no matter what color it is or what potentate or politician bears the face of it or what country it hails from, it's all the same. People don't care how they come by it. They just want it."

"I care."

Domenico rose and signaled Antonio to open the door. "Read that newspaper, Neeve. Corruption is everywhere and growing stronger every day, from the slums to the capitals of the world."

"Thanks to you."

"Even after you knew the source of my wealth, you turned a blind eye for a long time."

"I had Benny to think about."

Domenico let out a raspy laugh as he left the cell. "Now you're the liar, Neeve."

———

Mike turned from US 9 to Route 28 North in the Adirondack Mountains. His silver Mercedes four-seater convertible wound along the verdant terrain, which alternated from a woodsy forest of birch, maple, pine and fir to grassy open fields. "We're almost to Minerva, so keep your eyes open."

Benny sucked in the familiar smells of the forest. Each earthy whiff ignited flashes of memories, none of which remained long enough for close inspection: a house in the woods, a white building, other children, and a game room, where he threw balls and walked on a beam that seemed extraordinarily high off of the floor. He remembered gazing a long way down without feeling any fear. Before he could concentrate on it more, older memories flared up and burned through the game room: a roaring hearth appeared and before it his grandfather and father argued. Flashes of light and sound erupted. Guns popped off rounds. Those thoughts blew up, too, replaced by the angry words he spat at his mother and the house exploding beneath their feet. He ripped away his sunglasses and rubbed his eyes to wipe out the images, none of which he could control or piece together. They were too bright. Too blinding. Too painful. He put his glasses back on, despite the fact the day dimmed as the sun began is final descent. The trees grew darker, cast long shadows that formed a cage, trapping him in an agony of his own making. No escape in sight.

"You okay?"

Benny nodded, but he was far from okay. What a stupid question!

"We'll drop by the school first. It's late, but it's worth a try."

Mike slowed as they drove through Minerva, a quaint mountain town neatly tucked in for the night. "I checked it out. Minerva was founded in the early 1800s. Population less than a thousand. Made up of a few farms, craft and antique stores, a barber shop, cafes and inns, a bakery, and a biker bar. The town was named after the Roman goddess of wisdom, Minerva.

Athena in Greek." Seeing Benny's lack of response, he added, "Never mind."

As they exited the town, the first stars appeared.

Mike complained. "No signs in town. Let's drive up the road a ways. If nothing shows up, we'll double back and ask directions—you'll have to do it. I don't ask directions."

Benny removed his glasses and pointed to his neck, indicating the impossibility of that request.

"I repeat," said Mike. "I do not ask for directions. Hate to say the cliché that 'it's a guy thing,' but sometimes clichés become clichés because they are historically and empirically accurate."

Benny typed, "just means you're a cliché dude :("

Mike argued with him as they proceeded up the road. "Am not!"

Benny pointed at Mike's black jacket, his collared white shirt, his sunglasses and the car they drove in. He typed, "you're so *MIB*"

"And Tommy Lee Jones and Will Smith rocked it in that movie! Chicks dig black. Like you'd have a clue." Mike pulled the car to the side of the road and waved for a pickup truck behind them to pass by, which it did. "We're heading back." As he craned his neck to check for traffic, an owl swooped over their heads. They both threw arms up in defense.

Only then did Benny see it. He slapped Mike's arm and pointed to a dirt road to the right. A golden owl perched atop a golden pole held one wing up and pointed down the path.

Mike complained, "Not much of a sign."

Benny shrugged.

Mike drove down the dirt road and flashed on his high beams. The radio turned to static. Mike turned it off.

Just when Mike suggested they had gone too far or missed another turn, they spotted another owl on a stick, one wing up, pointing left. And then another pointing right.

S. Woffington

After a drive of several hours, the last hour on a dirt road seemed interminably long. Or maybe it was anxiety—soon enough, they might be face-to-face with people who had answers.

They turned another corner. There it was. A golden gate. Mike stopped the car. Benny grabbed the windshield, hauled himself up, and hopped out over the door. The gate was a massive circle with symbols all around it: a circle made of knots, a swoopy symbol like a letter *H* crossed at the top, a hand with an eye in the middle of it, a face sticking out its tongue, another eye, and a dragon-like snake thing.

"Looks like one of those New Agey, hippy-dippy places," said Mike.

Benny grabbed the notepad and punched the keys. He held it up.

Mike read it aloud as he stepped from the car. "same signs on ma's necklace"

"She probably got it here. The only sign I know is the om. My buddy has it tattooed on the side of his neck. Says people chant it. Means 'peace' or something."

Benny and Mike approached the gate and peered through it, but all they could see was a lane lined with trees, an arboreal tunnel with no end.

"I don't see a call box, a button, a camera—no way in."

Benny grabbed the gate, ready to climb over it, but the moment he latched on, the semicircular gates parted slowly and swung open.

Benny dropped to his feet, rushed back to the car and hopped over the door, sliding into the bucket seat.

Mike opened the door using the handle and slid into the driver's seat. "Could you open the door, please. Like me, this car has way too many miles."

Benny rolled his eyes.

"Hey, when you buy your first very used convertible Mercedes—the car of your dreams at a reduced price you can't pass up—and someone trashes it, you'll understand."

Mike drove through the golden gates and down the tree-lined road. Benny cast his eyes up to the vaulted leafy ceiling. He felt an overwhelming sense of protection. It was a haven, and he had been here before.

When they exited the tree tunnel, they entered a clearing. Lights illuminated a cluster of two-story neoclassical buildings. In the center, six heavy columns upheld a triangular pediment containing the same symbols as on the gate, and others. A domed rotunda behind the triangular pediment soared skyward, maybe four stories high.

Mike parked the car next to a blue VW Beetle, whose roof, hood and trunk were covered in fluffy white clouds. Wings graced its sides. A sign marking the space read PRINCIPAL. A bumper sticker read COEXIST.

"I nailed it," said Mike, approaching tall arched doors of gold. "It's a hippie-dippie-trippie New Agey school. I think your mother was right—no one would have looked for you here."

Benny typed and flashed the screen at Mike. "i know this place"

Mike didn't knock. He opened the doors, and they stepped inside. All-white modern furniture and sweeping, suspended staircases that seemed to float graced the expansive lobby. Benny only remembered the warm wooden floors. He remembered sitting on them, running along them, and falling on them.

The lobby was empty: no desk or receptionist, just white molded furniture, a free-flowing ocean of white that, while unique, did not seem practical to sit upon for any length of time.

A pair of tall arched doors swung open, and an older woman with short white hair swept through them. While fiftyish at least, she seemed youthful in the way she approached in graceful but affirmative steps, or perhaps it was her youthful attire: white yoga leggings and a white chiffon tunic that sparkled with a broach, which, upon closer inspection, was an owl. Short white hair swept back from her rosy cheeks. A stern smile formed at her lips.

"Benny. You found us. I knew you would." She reached out to hug him, but Mike intervened with a protective step forward.

"Who are you?"

"Dr. Minerva Pallas." She reached for Mike's hand and shook it, but she kept her eyes on Benny. "Call me Minnie, Mr. Salvatore."

"Mike. How did you know—"

"Neeve mentioned you long ago. Do you remember me, Benny?"

Benny rocked his hand to indicate "a little."

"Well, you were quite small when I saw you last. No matter. You're here now. It's late. Let's get you settled in. I'll introduce you to the others tomorrow. Your cabin is just as your mother left it."

Mike protested, "Hold on a minute. Benny's staying with me in Manhattan."

"All students and their guardians stay on campus." Her voice and eyes resonated in a way that forbade objection. "He's not safe in Manhattan. Neither are you, Mr. Salvatore. What do you say, Benny?"

"He can't speak. Not since the explosion. The doctors think it's from shock."

Minnie's eyes bored into the wound on Benny's forehead and then into Benny's eyes, digging too deep for his comfort, but he refused to turn away. Instead, he augured just as deeply into her eyes, nearly colorless, like diamonds in a pale blue sky.

"Some things are more horrific than a soul can bear. Follow me. See what I have to offer. Then make up your mind."

Minnie led them through the expansive lobby, around a circular hallway and out a door at the back of the building. Seven pathways shot out from the back porch and into the woods, like seven rays of the sun.

Minnie strolled down the central path that led into the forest. "Do you recognize it, Benny?" Minnie's smile became more genuine and less stern.

This time, he nodded yes. He didn't remember specific images, only that he did know the place. He searched every direction, inhaled every smell, listened to every sound—as if to find the one sight or scent that would break the dam and allow all of his memories to flood back.

At the end of the path, Benny recognized the white, thatch-roofed cottage. It had two stories, three gables, and leaded glass windows. The porch light alit a bounty of wildflowers in pink and white and lent it a softness that seemed overly sweet—like too much cotton candy. Memories flooded Benny's brain faster than he could process them. He had lived here with Ma, peaceful and happy.

"You do remember it," said Minnie. "Well, you should. You picked the design. You pointed to it in a storybook—the Seven Dwarfs' cottage." Minnie sighed. "Neeve loved these flowers, especially the spring beauties and the trillium. I gave her two pots of them when she left."

Benny approached the wooden door, turned the knob and stepped inside. It seemed much, much smaller now.

"Two bedrooms and bathrooms upstairs," Minnie said to Mike.

Benny walked to the stone hearth and picked up a framed picture of his parents, both beaming smiles. Their arms enfolded each other and a baby boy between them, smiling as widely as his parents. His father was clean-shaven and had dark short curly hair.

"We've kept it clean, but otherwise, we left it just the same," added Minnie. "Have you eaten?"

"No," said Mike. "We drove straight here."

"I'll send trays over. Get a good night's sleep. We'll talk tomorrow."

"Benny's got a bag in my car, but I've got to get back to Manhattan. I didn't think we'd be staying out here more than a night. I need to pack more clothes and get some things from my office."

"Must you go immediately?"

"Faster I go, faster I get back."

"Leave Benny here. He's safe here." It was a command.

Mike stood his ground. "That's up to Benny."

Benny set the picture back on the mantel. He nodded approval in a way that let Mike know he needed to be here, needed to dig around and unearth more memories.

"I'll send a breakfast tray in the morning, Benny. Rest well. Come to my office when you're ready." With that, she turned and left.

By the time Mike retrieved Benny's bag, two dinner trays had arrived loaded with two plates of rotini pasta, grilled vegetables, tomato and mozzarella salads topped with fresh basil, and two glasses of milk.

The small wooden table was cozy. Benny discovered the scratch he had made when he was small and had stabbed at a fly with his fork. To his shock, he struck it dead and cried.

Benny picked at his food, eating little. As good as it was, he felt guilty for eating when he should be grieving.

"No meat. I don't mean to sound ungrateful," said Mike, "but I hope they're not vegetarian."

Benny shrugged. He honestly didn't remember the meals from that long ago.

"I'll stop in Minerva on the way back. Make a beef and bacon run and pick up the usual junk food. Any requests?"

Benny shook his head. Maybe the adrenaline high of trauma had finally worn off or seeing familiar sights gave him hope—all he knew was that his eyes could barely stay open. Sleep infused every cell of his body, shut them down one by one. He pushed himself away from the table without a word and with no thought at all as to how his dish would be cleared or who would wash it. He grabbed his bag at the foot of the stairs and headed up to his room. He knew the way. He remembered crawling up these stairs, gripping the softness of the carpet one step at a time.

Chapter Five

Carrying a large black coffee strong enough to dissolve the hull of an aircraft carrier, Mike rushed past the skinny placard that read 26 FEDERAL PLAZA. Once in the elevator, he reached past several others and hit the button for the twenty-third floor. The board was lit up like a Christmas tree, so he had time to sip his coffee. Mike felt the woman next to him stare. Not at him but at his scars, probably. He rubbed the scar on his neck, from a slit to the throat that had nearly ended his life. Then he felt it. The toilet paper tab he had stuck to his neck when he nicked himself shaving. He yanked it away and saw the woman stifle an amused smile. He'd gotten to his apartment around three in the morning and tossed and turned until jolted awake by the sound of the alarm.

The elevator dinged, and the amused woman stepped out.

Mike guzzled his coffee, waiting for the caffeine to do its job and kick him into gear. The moment the elevator doors cracked open on his floor, he shot straight to his desk, nodding hello to fellow field office agents, some of whom were surprised to see him. He grabbed a handful of miniature candy bars from a jar on a coworker's desk.

"Are you havin' a midlife crisis?" Maxine complained. "You hate candy, fool." Maxine was a tough woman: African American, mid-forties, never married, former military sniper.

"It's for my cat." Mike sank into his chair.

"You don't have a cat, Mike. You need a cat. But right now, honey, you look like kitty litter."

The moment Mike sat down, tiredness struck, but he shoved it off. He didn't have time. No time for guilt. No time for tears. No time to grieve for Neeve. He set the coffee and the candy on his desk and yanked open his file drawer, extracting two files with tabs that read ANNA N. ADEZ and DOMENICO H. ADEZ. He pulled the business card from his breast pocket and set it atop the files.

"Thought you were taking time off?" Bill handed Mike a report.

"Just grabbing a few things."

"This just came in. Thought you'd want to see it. Lab results."

Mike read the report. "Cadaver bones? Is this right?" Tired as he was, he jumped to his feet. "Bill, I'd kiss you, but it would start rumors."

"Yeah. My wife would appreciate that. She still doesn't believe that you and Maxine pranked me on poker night by grabbing my face as I left and applying body glitter."

"It was Maxine's idea."

Maxine laughed. "It was your idea, Mike, and a good one. Bill, you married guys need to shake it up now and then. Let your wife think you're some sexy superspy."

"I'll tell you what she thinks, Max. She thinks you two are trouble." As Bill walked away, another agent approached Mike's desk. A bug-eyed man with a visitor's badge followed closely behind him.

"Mike, this guy's been here since we opened. I was gonna pass him to Jim, but I saw you walk by. It's regarding your case in Jersey."

"Take him to Jim," Mike said, staring at the lab report. "I gotta get outta here."

"I overheard what you said to the other agent. I can explain those cadaver bones. I'm Professor Daniel Archer Daniels III, and they are, or were, my bones."

Professor Daniels extended a hand, but Mike pointed to the chair opposite his desk. "Have a seat, Professor."

"Daniel, please. Sophia was a student of mine and—"

"Sophia?"

Daniel paused briefly. "I suspected that wasn't her real name. She didn't always answer to it during class. I read about the explosion. I met her son, Benny. I can't believe . . ." He pulled a handkerchief from his pocket, dabbed tearful eyes, and blew his nose.

"Professor? Or Daniel, I'm sorry. Can I get you a cup of coffee?"

"A cup of hot water, if you have it. I carry a bag or two of Earl Grey with me." He sniffled and gasped between words. "If it isn't any trouble."

"No trouble. I'll be right back," said Mike, rising from his chair.

Daniel blew his nose obnoxiously loud. When his eyes popped open, they fell on an odd business card with a familiar name—Minerva Pallas. He plopped his hanky onto the desk over the card and rummaged in his breast pocket for a tea bag.

Mike set an FBI mug filled with hot water in front of his guest.

Daniel scooped up his hanky along with the card and stuffed it in his breast pocket.

"The bones?" Mike asked as he sat back down, pen in hand, ready to take notes.

"What's her real name?" Daniel tore the tea bag open and bobbed it up and down, up and down.

"I can't tell you that."

"Then I'll just call her Sophia. She's been my student for a few weeks now. Chambers University nursing program. I gave her the bones to study. She had a final today. So did I. I sent a sub. I was too upset. It's not every day one of your students and her son is blown to smithereens."

Mike jotted down the professor's name.

Daniel held up the tea bag and let it drip until Mike noticed. One-handed, Mike grabbed his trash can and held it out. Daniel tossed the bag in the trash and leaned forward. Their eyes met. "But then, she isn't dead. Is she, Mike?"

Mike lowered the trash can to the floor and leaned forward, meeting his gaze. "What do you know, Daniel?"

"Simply what I observe. You're disheveled. Or, as your colleague said, you look like 'kitty litter.' You haven't had any more sleep than I have—there's a nick next to the scar on your neck. Probably showered this morning for the first time in days, scraping away heavy stubble, but you were in a hurry."

"I'm always in a hurry."

"You're fond of Sophia."

"And what makes you say that?" Mike set down his pen and leaned back to gain distance from dissection.

"Your demeanor changed when you read the lab report. It indicated surprise, shock and extreme joy, the kind of joy that indicates closeness to an individual. You suspect she's alive. So's he. But she's missing. He's not."

Maxine caught Mike's gaze and sent him a smirk.

Mike leaned in and whispered. "And how do you know that?"

"There's candy on your desk. I suspect you grabbed it for the boy."

Mike grabbed a mini Snickers bar, tore it open, shoved it in his mouth, and chewed, mumbling, "I love candy."

Daniel smiled. "Your coworker said you hate candy. And you don't have a cat."

Mike spit the candy into his trash can.

Maxine snickered.

"The file on your desk suggests that her real name is Anna N. Adez, linked, no doubt, to the name on the other file, Domenico H. Adez, an organized crime boss. As I recall, he was raided some years back. Sophia said they lost Benny's father when he was three. 'Bout the time of the raid. I can help you. Tell me what's going on."

"We're doing all we can, Professor Daniels. I'll call you if we need any more information." Mike stood up. "Thanks for coming in."

"I see." Daniel rose to his feet and paused. Mike waited.

"Mind if I keep the FBI mug? It's rather flashy."

"Sure. Keep it."

———

Benny slept soundly but not peacefully. His body crashed, shutting down from emotional exhaustion more than physical effort, but his mind refused to shut down. Shards of memories slashed at him all night long, opening gashes new and old.

In the morning, he found a basket of breakfast breads and fruits on the table, along with a jar of honey and a note explaining that butter, jam, milk and juice were in the fridge. In the hospital, he could care less about food. Didn't touch it. But here in a familiar space that he had shared with his mother, he regained hope. He'd find her killer. Renewed purpose required sustenance. He was famished. He split a blueberry muffin, doused it in honey, and shoved half in his mouth, forcing it down his gullet with full glass of milk. He shoved the second half in his mouth, grabbed his tablet, and headed out the door, still chewing.

He could not get to Minnie's office fast enough. The moment he stood in the doorway and held a fist in the air to knock, a golden owl paperweight on her desk spun its head toward him. Its eyes blinked and it made a mechanical cooing sound.

Minnie typed at lightning speed. Benny had never seen a computer screen change so fast from image to image. Like her car, her office had blue walls and faux-painted, billowing white clouds. They almost looked real. Sun poured through a skylight, washing Minnie, her desk, and the all-white furnishings in a soft ethereal glow. She shut down her computer and rose to her feet. "Half past ten, but you look ghastly. Did you sleep at all? Never mind. Did you eat?"

Benny nodded affirmatively, made a quizzical expression and pointed at the owl.

"Sensors picked up your movement. Cute, isn't it? A gift from an old friend, a smithy, more of an artisan, really."

Minnie came around her desk in a floor-length tee shirt with an owl on the chest. "I just love owls, don't you?"

He typed on his notepad. "u always wear owls?"

"Do you always wear black—and sunglasses?" Without waiting for an answer, Minnie scooped her arm through Benny's and led him out of the office and down the hall. "You'll see a lot of them around here."

Benny shrugged.

"Owls, of course. Barred owls, great horned owls, sometimes an eastern screech owl."

Benny typed, "know one with a white face, screams?"

Minnie beamed. "My favorite! The common barn owl. But they're not so common in the Adirondacks."

Minnie released Benny's arm and pushed open a pair of white arched doors. "Here's the gymnasium. Do you remember it? It's changed some, of course."

Benny followed her into the strangest gymnasium he had ever seen — clearly this was the heart of the building, the rotunda. It was a round room, four stories high with ropes dropping down from the domed roof and martial arts weapons in racks on the walls. Even stranger, ledges and rocky footholds of various sizes jutted out from the walls all the way to the ceiling. Beams and tightwires crossed the ceiling at odd heights, clearly not for architectural purposes.

"Do you remember it?"

Snippets came back. Benny remembered standing on a high beam — not as high as the beam crossing the dome — and looking down; he remembered other children. He remembered — no, not really remembered — he sensed a common sadness in their play, a lack of smiles all around. Even anger, mostly from a kid who couldn't use his legs, who tore around the place in a souped-up go-cart of sorts.

"The students will be here shortly, finished with their morning studies — Latin, Greek, mathematics, mythology and history. We encourage our students to be strong of mind and body."

Benny typed, "i don't exercise i play computer games"

"Do you still play *Warriors and Watchers*?"

Benny's face contorted into a clear question that needed no words.

"I gave it to your mother. A present for you when she left us," explained Minnie.

Benny punched his tablet. "no 1 knows it"

"Of course not. I wrote it."

A set of double doors opened on the far side of the gymnasium, and an odd group of six — three boys and three girls, about his age or a little older—crossed the floor toward them. One had a white cane and another maneuvered a motorized wheelchair of sorts—the angry kid. Benny knew them in another way—they were his avatar allies in the video game, except that in the game, they wore dorky gold jumpsuits. They crossed the floor wearing dorky white shorts with a gold stripe down the sides and dorky white tank tops and tee shirts with One World Academy in gold lettering and a dorky owl with enormous eyes, but a rather small head and body. Benny stifled a smile—they'd never get him into one of those outfits.

"Take off your—" commanded Minnie, but she didn't need to finish. Benny had already removed his glasses. "Let me reintroduce you, Benny. It's been a dozen years since you saw your playmates last."

"I don't remember him," said a beefy, slightly overweight Latin American boy whose short hair stood straight up, jelled into place. What caught Benny's attention were his eyes—with unusual eyes of his own, it was the first thing he noticed about people. The boy had one golden eye and one brown eye—heterochromia.

"Me neither," scowled a pretty Asian girl with slurred pronunciation.

Benny remembered her. Deaf girl. Lip-reader extraordinaire. And in the game, a kick-ass avatar. She actually scared him at times, but he'd never admit it. In real life, she was hot, except for a distinct coldness in her manners. She had fair skin, thin lips and black silky hair that fell just past her shoulders, straight cut like her bangs that fell to furrowed brows and angry gray eyes, soft gray in color but hard and unreachable, like two pale stones sitting on the surface of a turbulent stream. Out of reach.

"No. I expect not. You're a year younger," said Minnie. "You were both about two and Benny three when he arrived, and he only stayed a year. Benny, this is Zuma and Kami."

"Hi, Benny," chimed the boy in the motorized wheelchair. "I'm Chaz."

He seemed less angry now. His striking blue eyes reminded Benny of glacier ice. He had to be about seventeen by now. His ultra-blonde hair swirled around a thick neck and surrounded perfectly chiseled features. From the waist up, he looked like a bodybuilder or Thor's twin.

"Benny's lost his voice," said Minerva.

Benny gave a thumbs-up sign.

"Hey, Benny. What about me?" said a gorgeous girl with pouty full lips and a perfect nose with a slight arch. Her long reddish-brown hair, streaked with pure blonde highlights, fell in thick waves down to her elbows. Her well-endowed bosom stretched the limit of her tee shirt. Her lavender eyes, outlined in black, shimmered like the Burmese star sapphire, a prize to be won in the video game—and she knew just how to dip her chin to make those eyes claw at his. Even in gym clothes, she was rock-star gorgeous.

Benny typed, "layla." His mind accessed the information that he didn't even know he had. He typed "taj" and pointed to the dark-haired Indian girl. He remembered the red dot on her forehead more than her emerald-green eyes, because she kept her eyes and chin down most of the time, letting long straggly hair fall forward over her shoulders. Now, her hair was akilter—long on the right, which still draped over her face, and short on the left, which feathered inward toward her neck. There was an under layer of neon green. Benny remembered something else—the reason she kept her eyes and chin down and her hair cascading down her right cheek was to cover a birthmark, purple and angry, like a spike or a dagger that ran from her temple to her jawline.

"Close. Rajani. Raj for short," she corrected him, sweeping the long hair toward the center of her chest in an unconscious habitual motion, still hiding the birthmark as best she could.

"I'm Amir. The handsomest of the group, even if I am blind now—I could still see when you were here. A little."

"Frealz, dude," said Raj, shaking her head. "In the country of the blind the one-eyed man is king, and in our little country, the blind man thinks he's wickedly handsome."

"I'm blind. But *you* cannot see," quipped Amir. "Or, you would agree."

The others rolled their eyes. "He was just as obnoxious when he was little," added Raj. "That you might remember, Benny."

The blind boy wore sunglasses, but Benny remembered his eyes, too. Black as onyx. The iris matched the pupil. Because of their almond shape, not much white showed. His hair was short now, but Benny remembered him with wild, thick, curly hair that puffed out all around his head. His boyish face and half smile dampened the bravado by adding a touch of humor.

Benny rocked his hand to indicate that he remembered him a little.

"Oh, schad," Kami added, with an insincere pout upon the word *sad*.

"Looks like you were easily forgotten, dude," smirked Raj.

"One never forgets greatness," chided Amir. "I'm much more handsome now than I was back then. And a better dresser than all of you, when I'm not forced to wear these ridiculous PE clothes—which actually make me appreciate being blind."

"Amir, what have I told you about boasting?"

"Sorry, M," said Amir. "You're pretty, too. I can hear it in your voice."

Minnie rolled her eyes. "Do not flatter me. And don't call me M. Makes me feel like I'm in a bloody James Bond movie."

"Two shtrikes," said Kami.

"I think we should have the afternoon off to show Benny around the compound," added Zuma.

"Yeah," chimed Layla, giving Zuma a fist pump. "We want to get reacquainted."

"Totes!" shouted Raj.

"How odd. We *totes* agree," added Minnie. "I'm dismissing your classes for the remainder of the day. Lunch is ready in the dining hall. Then you can take Benny to your fort or hideout or club or whatever you call it these days. I had the cook prepare a dessert."

"Dessert?" added Zuma, rubbing his belly.

"That's righteous, Min," said Amir.

"Minnie, if you don't mind. Or I shall call you A. Or Am. Really. Are there no manners left in the world?"

"Thank you, Miss Minerva," said Zuma.

Chaz added, "Meet at the hangar in thirty. Benny, you're with me."

Chapter Six

Chaz maneuvered his wheelchair out the back door of the building using a toggle switch for direction. He veered down the path to the far right, explaining the layout of the compound to Benny. "I'm far right. Cabin one. Layla is in cabin two; Zuma, cabin three; you're in the middle; then Raj, Amir and Kami."

When the path ended, they came to a perfectly flat clearing with three buildings. All had the same simple barnlike efficient design. The outer two were bright red with white trim, and the central one was a single-story house of unadorned wood. All had high-peaked roofs. They would fit just as well in a Scandinavian fjord or among chalets snuggled in obscure mountain passes.

"Barn on the left houses Slippy, my uncle's horse, and my aunt's boars, which she treats like pets, but then she treats every animal on a personal basis—squirrels, lizards, you name it. On the right is my uncle's bike and auto shop. We live in the middle."

Chaz veered along the path that led to the auto shop. A harsh caw led Benny's eyes to the roof, where two ravens perched.

Chaz and Benny found Big O hunched over a motor, signaling Friday, who sat behind the wheel of a crazy-looking car, to rev the engine. Upon seeing Chaz, Big O yelled, "Cut it!" and made a slashing movement across his neck.

Benny didn't remember any of it. Maybe it had been built after he left, or maybe he had never ventured down the paths in the woods that led to the other houses. The barn was deceptive from the outside—he had expected a small space, but it was a massive auto shop and garage—spic-and-span with a shiny polished concrete floor, loaded with equipment, tools, a substantial four-post car lift and a smaller bike lift. The left side served as a parking garage for the coolest vehicles he'd ever seen: ten or so single-seat and two-seat off-road vehicles with roll bars. They looked like mini formula cars of various colors, except for one, which was like a mini vintage convertible with gold paint, a dainty windshield and tan leather interior. Three big custom Harleys sat at the far end: two black, one white.

The car that Chaz's aunt and uncle worked on blew Benny's mind more than any other. It was a seven-passenger street buggy, counting the jump seat in the back, with a low-profile front, roll bars, and a crazy paint job: bright yellow with black and silver bolts of lightning. The front grill incorporated a circular design: four crisscrossed spears with strange symbols on the ends formed the eight spokes of a wheel, and at its center were three interlaced triangles. The same sign was tattooed across Big O's massive bicep but added a castle-like structure and the word *Valhalla*. Big O came toward Benny wearing hard-toed boots, loose jeans and a sleeveless tee shirt with the same spear-wheel-triangle insignia but with added wings and the words *Warriors and Watchers*. He had a blue knit cap pulled down over long gray hair. His rosy cheeks swelled above a long beard and mustache, which gave him a friendly appearance, like a biker Santa Claus.

Aunt Friday was a knockout, one of those women that made you stare—even though, due to the difference in age and deference to friends, it was impolite to do so—from her black motorcycle boots that hugged her slim calves to the tight jeans that hugged her long legs and narrow hips. Long wavy blonde hair fell over her shoulders, held in place by a headband of small pink flowers. Her pale pink tank top had the same Warriors and Watchers logo but could not begin to conceal her buxom chest, despite which she carried herself in an unassuming, innocent manner. She had blue eyes—softer than Chaz's—and a lightly freckled face, free of makeup. Her smile was genuine. Benny could see it even given to her pet boars.

"Aunt Friday, Uncle O. This is Benny."

Without hesitating, Friday wrapped her arms around Benny in a tight embrace and kissed him on both cheeks. "Ya, Benny. It's good to see you again. I'm so sorry, what we hear of Neeve." She released him. "I can't believe it." She spoke with a Scandinavian accent.

Benny nodded.

"He lost his voice," Chaz explained.

Friday hugged him again. "You poor dear! Come see me. I make you an old remedy. Tea with special herbs and honey and a touch of mead, a sweet beer, but don't worry, I add just a drop. Chaz will tell you."

Big O finished wiping his hands on a rag and put out a hand to shake Benny's. He wore a gold ring with the same wheel, wing and triangle insignia as on his tee shirt. "You need anything, Benny, we are here for you. We are one big family."

Family. Benny could see it. A pang of loss impaled his chest. Why had his mother left? Taken him away from people who were willing to fill the void and call themselves his family?

"Is the cruiser done?" asked Chaz.

"Just giving her a final tune up," said Big O. "Then she's ready."

"Minnie gave us the afternoon off to show Benny around," said Chaz. "Can we take the minis to the hideout?"

"Ya" and "Sure," said Friday and Big O simultaneously.

Raj, Zuma, Layla, Kami, and Amir stepped into the hangar wearing street clothes: the girls in leggings and tank tops; Zuma in jeans and a brown tee shirt; and Amir in matching tan slacks and vest, a crisp white short-sleeved shirt and a straw hat with a white band. They greeted Big O and Friday with warm familiarity, and Benny could see that Friday hugged everyone like she had hugged him—tightly and sincerely—which Amir returned by tipping his hat, Zuma returned with polite restraint, Raj and Kami with jealous restraint, and Layla with gushy compliments. Another pang of jealousy stabbed at Benny. It was obvious that these people had history together. Even the restraint between the girls reminded him of the cliques that existed at every school he'd been too. Clique—it meant history. Shared experiences, good and bad. Bonding. Loving. Hating. Feeling for another in some way, due to some experience you'd never forget. He'd never been in one place long enough to build a history. Why had Ma dragged him from coast to coast? He hoped he was about to find out.

Kami guided Amir to the passenger side of a cobalt blue two-seater before she hopped in the driver's seat. Layla, Zuma and Raj opted for single-seaters: Layla's was covered in flames, Zuma's black and gold, and Raj's lime green and purple. Zuma stowed a small picnic basket and ice chest in the storage space behind the driver's seat, hopped in and revved the engine.

Chaz directed Benny to a red car with black trim that looked like a mini convertible Corvette with a spoiler and open spaces where doors would be. He aligned his wheelchair next to the driver's side and reached upward for a long triangular trapeze bar that dangled above his head and over the driver's seat. He gripped it easily and pulled himself up, over, and dropped into the driver's seat. He pulled his legs in after him. "Hop in. And buckle up."

Benny did as instructed, putting on the shoulder harness and snapping the seat belt. Using hand controls, Chaz backed out and shot forward, leading the way out the back barn doors and onto a well-traveled dirt road that ran alongside a fenced-in pasture. A white horse with a long mane and tail raced alongside them just inside the white fence.

"Slippy!" shouted Chaz over the roar of the engines.

Benny nodded. The horse ran so fast, it seemed like it had eight legs.

Chaz pushed the limit and the small car shot forward, but somehow, the horse kept up, even inched ahead, until Chaz veered left and roared along a winding path that careened through the trees.

Benny's eyes widened. He would prefer a slower pace, but Chaz clearly knew the road well enough to gun it to their destination.

"My uncle is a genius with engines," Chaz shouted over the high-pitched whine of the engine. "The new buggy will allow the whole gang to head to town at once. Not that they let us out much. The buggy is street legal. Of course, a few of us are not—I don't suppose you have a driver's license?"

Benny shook his head to indicate no. The air was crisp and clean, mid-seventies, maybe. The sky a cold blue with no clouds in sight. Tall trees flickered past. Here and there, Benny caught sight of vivid color: a clump of wildflowers in white or purple, or the yellow or blue blur of a passing bird. He'd never been this deep in the forest, but the scent and sight of it returned fragments of memories that fall like pine needles and floated freely before his eyes. He remembered tending the garden in the front of the cottage beside Ma. He punched the ground with a plastic red spade. When she turned her back to him, he picked a handful of flowers, tapped her back, and set them in her hands. Ma beamed a radiant smile, grabbed his hand and rushed him inside to put them in a glass vase, which she filled with water and set on the kitchen table.

Something scurried across the road, maybe a chipmunk or a squirrel. Benny was happy for the distraction. As the animal bolted under a fern, Benny sympathized. He knew what it was like to run that fast, to feel the burn of fear that put the heart in a panic.

Chaz pulled into a shaded clearing and parked beneath a green awning and another trapeze bar. He cut the engine. The others pulled in and lined up next to him.

Benny climbed out of the vehicle and grabbed his tablet, which he rarely set down nowadays. It had become a part of him, like an arm or a leg. The green canvass castle rising before him could hardly be described, as Minnie had called it, a "fort" or "club," or as Chaz had called it, a "hideout." That it was, but on a grand scale. His eyes traveled from a furnished ground area up into the trees, where triangular shade sails of green canvas overlapped one another as they rose skyward, like a spired cathedral.

Raj unfolded Chaz's wheelchair and set it next to the driver's seat. Chaz grabbed the trapeze bar and pulled himself up enough to scooch into the chair. To Benny's surprise—even though foldable—the chair was motorized.

Benny followed Chaz past a round tree-slab table surrounded by four curved benches, and toward four wicker clamshell loungers suspended from metal frames that faced a sooty fire pit. Layla and Zuma ripped away the snap-on canvas doors, meant to keep animals out. She hopped in first, taking the small picnic basket and cooler away from Zuma, who hopped in beside her.

Chaz pushed a button, and his chair lifted several inches. He reached into the clam shell and pulled his body in behind him, then turned and sat up. Benny hopped in next to him.

Benny's heart sped up. His mind filled with questions burning to be asked and answered, but he had to wait for the others to settle in. Time passed as slowly as it had the night he lay awake in the dark, waiting for his mother to rise and Maria to arrive to take him to Disneyland for his birthday. His one great birthday.

Raj and Kami directed Amir to a lounger opposite Layla and Zuma. As soon as Amir hopped in, they hopped in on either side of him.

"Anyone want water or a cookie?" asked Zuma.

"Me, me," said Amir.

Zuma spun an oatmeal cookie like a Frisbee into his waiting hands. Amir snatched it midair.

Raj scowled. "Lucky catch."

"Lucky, my gorgeous face!" said Amir. "It's knowing when to clutch at the moment of touch."

Layla nibbled a cookie, while Zuma stacked three and chomped into them hamburger style.

"More for me, then." Zuma cracked open a water bottle and washed them down.

Chaz didn't hesitate. He threw out a question that made Benny realize that they sought answers, too. "So, Benny, where have you been all these years?"

Chaz read aloud as Benny typed an answer. "'coast to coast' You are a man of few words, Benny."

Benny typed. Chaz read, "what is this place?"

"It'sh an inshane asylum for sherial-killer youth," said Kami, making a scary face. Benny noted how she pronounced s like *sh*. Other than that, he could understand her pretty well.

"A fat farm—they starve us, Benny," said Zuma. "Healthy food—all day long! Except for cookies on special occasions, like today. I guess you're special." He gobbled down two more. The others didn't seem to care that he hoarded the bulk of them for himself. It seemed common and even supported. "Oh, man, what is wrong with giving us some refined sugar once in a while? Fresh fruit cups are so not the same." Zuma stuffed the last cookie into his mouth and moaned as he chewed.

"It's a freaking boot camp!" chimed Layla. "All we do is work out in that stupid gymnasium and study stupid dead languages. It wears me out."

"You're worn out?" sniped Raj. "You have more excuses to dodge gym than anyone here."

"Not really," said Layla. "My bro, Zuma, is the king of excuses—he comes up with enough for both of us. He's my hero."

Zuma held up both hands, a cookie in each, as if having received an award. "Thank you, Layla. I'm glad that my many talents have not gone unnoticed."

Layla gave Raj a stink-eye glance. "Nor mine, obviously."

Amir spit out a random question. "So, Benny. What's the new fashion trend out there?"

Kami rolled her eyes. "Dude. Do we have to remind you that you're blind? Again?"

Amir swiped his hands down his vest. "'Tis not I for whom I dress, but you—*you* are not blind to my good looks, my little Japanese geisha."

Kami's face flushed red with anger. "Call me that again, Amir, and you won't be sho pretty. E-ver a-gain!"

Benny started to laugh, but he saw that Kami wasn't joking. The petite girl had a dark streak. Maybe she was a serial killer.

"That was so sexist, Amir," Raj added in defense.

Layla added, "I think it was racist and sexist."

Amir calmed them down. "Chillax, dudes. Just a joke—like your constant reminders that I'm blind."

Benny was no longer amused. He needed answers. Now. He typed and turned the screen toward Chaz.

Chaz nodded. "'the real story'—I think I speak for the rest when I say that we know mostly what we've been spoon-fed all of our lives, but we've suspected for some time that there's a lot more to 'the real story.' We hoped you could clue us in."

The space in the forest just shrank. The others eyed him expectantly. They seemed to hold their breath. He knew that hungry, desperate-for-answers look all too well. Benny sighed and shrugged his shoulders.

"Well then, maybe we can help each other. You're our contact to the outside," said Chaz. "What we've been told is that this is a school for special children—orphans whose parents were abducted. None of us remembers exactly what happened to our mothers, but we have bad dreams. And we have no memories whatsoever of our fathers. Although I supposedly caught a glimpse of him fleeing in the dark when I was six."

Kami jumped in. "I dream of an ugly hag that grabsh my mother away. I jump out of bed, and kick and shmack her, but she won't let go. Gramdfather Kiyoshi rushesh in, shcoops me into his armsh, and out again. He brought ush here from Japan, but he tellsh me I dreamed it all to account for how mother went misshing."

"My mother, Zaria," said Amir, quite serious, "is a model. Even prettier than me. GOR-GEE-OUS. Seriously, I have pictures, but I don't need them. I remember her face. I could see then. She's smiling, tucking me in. One minute she's there, then there is a fog between us. Like a beige cloud or duststorm. When it cleared, she was gone. Uncle Jalal moved us here right after that. No explanation—except the same line Kami got—I dreamed it."

Raj played with her hair and bit her lower lip. "Mother and I are in a shabby little room, somewhere in India. Just one room. It's Nana's home—that's what I call my grandfather Andy. We're poor and I'm hungry, but I'm happy. Mother is playing the sitar. My eyes are closed. She often played before I napped. I don't know what happened to her. I remember a foul stench, like dead beetles. When I opened my eyes, she was gone. Nana brought me here. I never saw her face again. I didn't see—I can't remember her face anymore."

"We're lucky we didn't see what happened," said Amir.

Raj jolted to her feet, fists clenched, and screamed, "No! I'm not. I want to remember her." Raj ran into the woods.

Kami pointed in Raj's direction, asking Chaz if she should go after her, but Chaz shook his head and nodded to Zuma.

Zuma didn't hesitate. "I'll make it quick. My mom, Catori—Cat for short, is Hopi. Pueblo people. All I remember is I wake up and gaze into the dream catcher that hangs beside my bed, and I see a jaguar looking back at me. It growls a warning. He has the same eyes as me: one gold, one brown. He's guarding the dream catcher. I see past him. My mother is walking away with someone. They turn. It's a skeleton. She's walking away with a skeleton. Next thing I know, I'm here with these dudes and my grandmother, Cookie, and on a strict diet."

Layla folded her arms across her chest. "I dream of snakes. Lots of them, crawling on the ground. And a giant black snake with yellow eyes. I'm on my feet but I'm frozen with fear. It coils around my mother's body and drags her away. I scream. The snake whips back around and faces me with those yellow slit eyes. I scream. It rises up. Towers over me. It opens its mouth like it's going to bite me, but I think it means to swallow me whole. It strikes. I close my eyes. Something jerks me off of my feet and into the air. Like a bird or something."

Chaz added, "And I dream of an ice palace and snake dragons. But unlike the others, I don't dream of my mother being pulled away from me or just disappearing. I was old enough to remember. I grew up with my aunt and uncle. The story is that my real mother abandoned me, and my aunt and uncle raised me. For my sixth birthday, they took me to a Viking festival where they first met. It was in Denmark, but we lived in Norway then. I wandered out of our tent and into the forest. I heard a woman's voice calling my name. I came across a white tent with weird writing on one side that I later learned were ancient Viking, runic letters. I stepped inside. Candles burned all around the place. A woman with blonde braids and her face painted half blue called to me, but I didn't understand the language. The rest is confusing, because suddenly Minnie and some other blond-haired dude rushed in, yelling. The blond-haired guy grabbed the blue-faced woman and pulled her out of the back of the tent while Minnie grabbed me and raced out the front, and we ran into my aunt and uncle, who wielded flashlights and raced toward us. The tent burned to the ground. My aunt and uncle brought me here. They told me that the blue-faced woman was Friday's sister, my mom, and the other guy was her crazy violent husband, but I know there's more they aren't telling me."

Benny typed, "bad dreams. i'm beginning to believe the serial-killer theory."

Chaz glanced at the others before responding. "Then consider this, Benny. There's another strange coincidence. We are different ages: Kami's thirteen; Zuma, fourteen; you and Raj, fifteen; Amir and Layla, sixteen; and I'm seventeen—but we're pretty sure that our parents all disappeared the exact same day. July 29, 2002."

That date! Benny pounded at the keyboard.

"how do you know?" Chaz read from Benny's notepad.

Zuma said, "Raj snuck into Minnie's office and accessed her computer a month ago. We snatched Minnie's key, duplicated it in the auto shop, and got it back unnoticed."

"I found where she keeps her password," added Layla.

Chaz explained, "Raj found our admittance records, and they all showed the same date of having been 'orphaned.' I arrived here first. The rest came within days."

"I almost got caught," added Raj. "Needed more time."

Benny hopped to his feet and paced.

"You figured it out, didn't you?" said Chaz. "That's the day your father disappeared and your mother brought you here. The only mother who got away. But your father went missing."

Benny stabbed at the keyboard. Chaz read, "and now she's dead!!!"

Amir said, "None of us remember our fathers—you're the only one. That's different."

"Benny! We all want to know the truth," urged Chaz. "I see it in you. You want to know. So do we."

Benny ran a hand through his hair. He felt like his head would explode. He typed, "i need wifi"

Chaz nodded. "We're only allowed to use the school computers to play *Warriors and Watchers*. No outside access. But we can get you into Minnie's office."

Benny typed.

Chaz eyed the others. "Benny says, 'do it.' We need a distraction. Zuma, it's your turn."

Zuma clasped his hands together, turned them inside out and stretched. His knuckles cracked. "You guys are amateurs. Making excuses for gym isn't my only talent."

"Layla, Kami, go find Raj," Chaz urged. "It's time to head back."

As Chaz gunned the engine and tore through the woods, Benny kept his eyes dead ahead. His gut twisted. He didn't feel any closer to having answers. Bad dreams—sure, he had them, too. So what? His memory was still hostage. Memory. Geez! That much he had—memories of his mother, tons of them. Until this second, he had no appreciation for them. None. He had fifteen years with his Ma that these dudes had lost. He understood why they held so tightly to the last memory, even if it was a nightmare, or stormed off, like Raj, wishing she had a bad memory rather than none at all. But she was wrong.

She was better off to have no memory, rather than a last image that would haunt him for the rest of his life.

What did he have to hold on to? A fight. Spiteful, burning words. A plan to never talk to his Ma again. Never see her again. And an explosion that forever ripped her out of his life. The answer had to be on that computer. It had to be. And when he found the person responsible, he'd rip their world apart.

Chapter Seven

Mike flew in the door and dropped his bag next to the staircase. He extracted his laptop from his briefcase, set it on the kitchen table and punched the keys. "You're kidding—no Wi-Fi?"

Benny came through the door, almost in slow motion. He saw Mike and dashed upstairs to avoid him.

Mike raced to the bottom of the steps. "Benny! She's alive. Neeve. She's alive."

Benny spun around and dropped down the steps.

Mike pointed to the sofa. Benny sat down and leaned forward.

Mike sat next to him. "The bones they found in the house were cadaver bones. A Professor Daniels gave them to your mother to study for some test."

Benny clasped his hands together in thanks. The bag. The heavy bag. So that's what was in it. Relief was soon replaced by anger and confusion. He typed, "where is she?"

"I don't know."

Benny typed, "grandfather"

Mike stalled.

Benny stabbed the keys. "TELL ME"

"It's possible. Domenico's a thug and a crook." Mike read the notepad.

"mafia"

"Something like that."

"how did my father die?"

Mike paused. "What did your mother tell you?"

Benny shook his head, indicating nothing.

Mike rubbed the scar across his neck. "I already told you that Neeve came to see me when you were about three. I've never seen her so scared—of your grandfather. She said something big was happening. Domenico wanted your father to run things, take over and manage some huge expansion plan. According to Neeve, father and son argued. The FBI wanted them and Neeve was our way in. We set a date for the raid."

Benny typed. He flashed the screen. "7.29.2002"

"Right." Mike met him square in the eyes. "It didn't go well, Benny. I wanted Domenico, and if your father was a crook, I wanted him, too. I won't lie about that. All hell broke loose. Neeve rushed out of the house with you in her arms. Your dad was just behind her and your grandfather behind him. I grabbed you from your mother's arms, and we ran toward the FBI SWAT vehicles. Bullets flew all around us—I still don't know how we didn't get hit. The next thing I know, someone grabs me from behind and slits my throat. I drop to my knees. Neeve drops down next to me. I pass you to her and point at the FBI chopper that was just landing. As soon as she runs for it, I grab my gun and turn. Domenico and your father are running toward the house. I fire at them." He paused, as if forming the right words.

Benny typed, but Mike grabbed his hand. "Let me finish! I need to get this off my chest, and you deserve to know! I hit him. I hit your dad. He slumped, but he kept running. Domenico pushed him into the house."

Benny bore his eyes into every pore of Mike's face.

"Another agent, Maxine, slid next to me. I asked, 'How bad?' She said, 'Lucky. Flesh wound.' Neeve passed you off to an officer aboard the chopper and climbed in. I watched it take off. I got to my feet and raced after Domenico and Romero. Maxine tried to stop me but I shoved her off. As soon as I got inside the house, I saw the butler run through a door. I chased him into a huge room with a fireplace. Domenico and Romero rushed through patio doors into a garden. The butler turned and tangled with me. By the time I got outside, Domenico was all alone, sitting on a black stone, warming his hands over a fire pit. It was like he was waiting for me. Your dad was nowhere in sight. The castle surrounds the garden on three sides, and there's a wall with an archway on the fourth side. I thought Romero either ducked back into the house or ran out through the archway onto the grounds and maybe into the forest. Either way, we'd find him. But, we didn't. We searched everywhere. No body. And no case. I tried to put you two in protective custody, but your mother brought you here instead."

"alive?" Benny typed.

"Your dad? Don't know. He's never reappeared, so I think . . . Look, if he'd have lived, wouldn't he be back with his father—or with your mother? One or the other? But he's not. So I wouldn't hold much hope, Benny."

Benny typed, "she came to u for help. u did this. u destroyed my family!"

Mike shot to his feet. "I did my job! And got my throat cut in the process. And let's not forget that we found you in a tree with a packed bag, clearly on your way out the door! For good, I'm guessing."

Benny lunged to his feet and swung a fist at Mike's face.

Mike ducked and put his hands up in a sign of peace. "We'll find her, Benny, but we have to work together."

Benny stormed upstairs and slammed his bedroom door. He fell back on the bed. She's alive! It's all that mattered. He needed that computer.

———

A couple of hours later, Mike called upstairs, "Benny, you comin' to dinner?" No answer. "I'll meet you there." As he headed to the door, he mumbled, "Let's see what you know, Minnie."

In the dining hall, Minnie directed Mike to a seat beside her. The students sat at a table of their own at a distance from the adults that afforded privacy. Minnie introduced Mike to the guardians. She started with an older Asian man who rose to his feet. He placed his hands together before his chest. He wore a long brown shirt that fell over loose slacks. The man smiled and bowed, and when he did so, his eyes closed into little smiles of their own. He had a perfectly round, childlike face and a perfectly round head, topped with a red knit cap. After bowing, he resumed his seat.

"This is Kami's grandfather, Kiyoshi."

Mike nodded. "My pleasure."

Next, Minnie pointed out a middle-aged man with dark curly hair and a dark well-trimmed mustache who effused energy through a wild-eyed gaze and a white toothy smile.

"This is Amir's uncle. Jalal is from Turkey."

Jalal, in a white shirt buttoned up to his neck, coiled his hands over his head with the grace of a dancer. He bowed his head. "Welcome, Mr. Mike."

"Just Mike."

Next, Minnie pointed to a gray-haired man, whose beard was so long that it curved up and over his shoulder like the trunk of an elephant, a resemblance encouraged by the man's enormous ears. The man rose, put his hands together at his chest and bowed. He wore a collarless yellow shirt with a breast pocket that had something moving about inside it. As he bowed deeper, the tiny head of a mouse peeked out, twitching its nose as if to inspect the newcomer. The man's long shirt flowed over a long yellow skirt of sorts. A red *bindi* dot was centered on his forehead just above kind hazel eyes, like a third eye. Despite the calm exterior, there was fierceness in the old man's face. Where Mike had scars, this man had deep wrinkles—both earned in battle.

"This is Raj's grandfather, Nandana, but we call him 'Andy.' He's from India."

Mike added, "Nice to meet you. And your little friend."

Andy sat back down and pinched a morsel from a roll, which he stuffed into his pocket. The creature inside wiggled with delight before stopping to feast.

"I'm Cookie, Zuma's grandmother." Two long braids, secured at the ends with leather strands, framed the woman's face. She wore a white crocheted vest. Dream catchers with blue and beige beads and feathers were worked into it.

"Lovely," said Mike.

"Thank you. I'm forever crocheting. Keeps my hands busy," she replied.

"Mona," said a woman with Nefertiti's astoundingly good looks. "Layla's aunt." Black silky bangs fell to a point over her eyes before the rest swept around her face and terminated at the jawline. Pale rose lipstick emphasized her full lips, and dark liner extended beyond the edges of her eyes, a contrast to her fair skin. She wore a heavy gold necklace, which draped over her chest just above a simple black dress.

"Mona is a doctor," added Minnie. "We're lucky to have her."

Mona laughed. "Not much doctoring to do around here, but I have the Band-Aids, should you need one, Mike."

"Nice to meet you, Mona." He pointed to his scars. "As you can see, I'm often in need of Band-Aids."

"Big O," said a friendly biker type, sitting next to a gorgeous, unadorned blonde.

Mike noted the logo on his tee shirt for some kind of bike club.

"And my wife, Friday," said Big O. "In case you wondered. I look a lot older than I am, and she looks a lot younger that she is—what can I say. Too much mileage on this old chassis, ya."

Mike laughed and pointed to his scars. "Yeah. I know all about mileage."

"Where's Benny?" asked Minnie.

"He'll be along shor—" said Mike as he saw Benny mosey in, wearing all black and sunglasses.

Servers in white set various dishes before the group: fish dishes, vegetables dishes, tofu in curry sauce, kabobs over rice, and in front of Big O, a sausage platter.

Mike sent a signal to Big O to pass the sausage when he was done. "What kind of a school is this, Minnie?"

"A school for troubled youth, in a way," said Minnie. "All of the children have lost their parents in tragic accidents."

Andy lowered his head. "We are most sorry to hear about Neeve."

Friday's eyes welled up. "She should have stayed. She would have been safe."

"Safe from what?" asked Mike.

Minnie jumped in. "Safe from harm—the world is full of it. You're in the FBI, surely you see it on a daily basis."

Mike pressed Friday. "Her tone suggested specific harm?"

The guardians kept their eyes on their plates and lifted forks to their mouths.

Minnie quipped, "It is specific, Mike. It's the kind of harm perpetrated by those who set bombs in houses where a mother resides with her son."

"Neeve is still alive," said Mike, matter-of-factly, keeping his eyes on the reactions of the others.

They all turned to one other with relieved smiles or glanced skyward and made gestures of praise or met each other's gaze with relief and joy.

But Minnie kept her eyes on Mike. "Any word on who set the bomb? Or where Neeve is?"

"I have an idea, but that leads me to the next question. Where can I get Wi-Fi?"

"In town," Minnie replied without hesitation.

"But your computer—"

"We block the outside world," Minnie said with authority. "Eat your supper. Strong mind. Strong body."

"Look, I'm trying to solve a case, and find—"

Zuma jumped to his feet with such force it knocked his chair to the floor behind him. The din caused heads to turn. Zuma spewed a mouthful of food in the middle of the student table.

"Minnie," shouted Raj. "Come quick! Zuma's sick."

Cookie and Mona rushed to Zuma's aid, followed by the others.

Zuma slumped to the floor, holding his stomach, writhing and moaning at the top of his lungs.

"We'll get towelsh! Come help me, Benny," shouted Kami, already racing out the door and into the hallway, dragging Benny behind her.

Benny glanced back to make sure no one had followed them. They rushed down the corridor, ducked into a linen closet, grabbed towels and raced to Minnie's office a few doors farther down.

Benny tried the door. Locked.

Kami whipped out a key and unlocked the door, which Benny pushed open. He raced behind the desk. The golden owl's eyes followed him.

Kami whispered, "That thing ish sho creepy."

Benny punched the keys. The screen asked for a password. The owl blinked and cooed.

Kami lifted a wing. The owl squawked a complaint but spread its other wing, revealing a sticker with a word written on it. Kami reached over Benny's shoulder and said as she typed, "CommonBarnOwl," before she rushed to the door to keep watch. "You've got five minutesh. No more."

The golden owl spun its head, following Kami, before spinning its head again, returning to Benny. Benny turned the owl's body away until it faced the door, but it spun its head back to face him and blinked.

Benny typed "Domenico H. Adez, address." He found an address in Alexandria Bay. He searched for driving directions. *No way!* The blue line ran from Minerva to his grandfather's location. He could get there in three hours.

"Hurry!" Kami scolded.

Benny hit "images," and the screen populated. His brain could not fathom what he saw. His eyes jumped from one picture to the next, but one caught his eye—of a castle-like estate, sitting atop a hill. A memory shot out of some deep crevasse and into his active mind. He had grown up in that castle. He remembered sitting at the foot of a fur-robed man, who he knew without a doubt was Domenico, his grandfather. He remembered his fascination with watching the fire blaze in the hearth, and his grandfather smiling and coaxing him to get closer to it.

He remembered crawling closer. Unafraid of the crackle, the pops, the heat. He would have crawled right into it had his mother not scooped him up into her arms. But who was the dragon and who was the knight?

"Time to go," whispered Kami.

Benny shook his head and held up one finger.

"Now."

Benny had to know. He opened the file labeled Admittance Records and scanned through all seven sheets of information. He saw the identical date under 'orphaned,' as he'd been told, but he saw something else even more striking.

"Benny," Kami whispered as loudly as she dared. "Minnie'sh coming. Shut it down."

Benny ignored her and typed "Romero H. Adez" and "images." Pictures of his father appeared. *What the hell!* Benny clicked on an image of his mother and father and Mike standing together. It was a wedding picture—Neeve's and Romero's. Both men had their arms around his mother's waist. Mike didn't look forward at the camera—he had his eyes on Neeve, and in a way that Benny didn't like. When he shot his father, was he protecting his mother? Or protecting his interests?

"Benny!" Kami whispered, louder this time. She rushed away from the doorframe and ducked under the desk.

Benny typed furiously. He didn't care if Minnie caught him or not. He found a newspaper report of the raid. As he read it, images of knights fighting fire-breathing dragons came to mind, only they transformed into FBI agents and gunfire and explosions and his own terrified cries. He remembered reaching over his mother's shoulder, seeing his father, and crying, "Daddy, Daddy," but she kept running farther away. She jumped into a big bird, at least that's how he saw it long ago. Now, he saw it for what it was: a helicopter. And they flew into the sky.

The doorknob turned, and the sound slammed sense into Benny's brain. He shut down the computer and ducked under the desk. Kami gave him the stink-eye. The door cracked open.

"Minnie, come quick!" shouted Raj from down the hallway. At the same time, the golden owl jabbered.

Benny grabbed the owl from the desk and wrapped it in the towel to muffle the sound.

"What now?" asked Minnie.

"Zuma's puking blood!" shouted Raj.

"Blood! Good heavens! I'll call 9-1-1," said Minnie, opening the door full swing.

"Wait!" said Raj.

The owl's warning grew more insistent, but Benny muted it by sitting on the towel, after which it made hardly any sound at all.

"He's okay! I misunderstood Amir—he shouted 'Zuma's looking good.' My bad!" yelled Raj. "He's getting up! Come see!"

Minnie closed the door and retreated down the hall.

Kami and Benny let out a sigh of relief. Benny unwrapped the owl and set it back on the desk. It went crazy. It flapped its wings, blinked its eyes and chattered. Benny raised the towel before the owl's eyes and scowled, a clear threat to do greater damage. The owl stopped chattering and lowered its wings.

"Come on," said Kami, peeking out the door. "All clear." They entered the cafeteria carrying towels and rushed to the scene.

Benny knelt down next to Chaz's wheelchair. He typed on his notepad. "need wheels. got someplace to go."

"Then we all go," whispered Chaz.

Benny typed, "too risky. they'll notice"

"We go. Or it's a no-go," whispered Chaz.

Benny typed, "OK i might be in need of serial killers"

The students stepped out the back door and into the black

night. They hung back as if to say good-night to one another and let the adults pass them by.

When it was clear, Chaz gave instructions. "Tomorrow's Saturday, but Andy, Kiyoshi and Jalal rise with the sun. That's about five fifteen a.m. We'll roll the buggy out of the shop at four thirty and get her down the road before starting her up. Meet by the back pasture."

Before everyone dispersed, Benny typed. He seemed reluctant to show it to the others, but at last he did. Chaz read aloud. "1 more thing. saw our records. i'm the only one with a birthdate. your records have 'found on' and then a date. no two dates the same."

"Found?" said Zuma. "What the hell does that mean? Like a toy in a box of cereal kinda found?"

Amir could barely contain himself. "Not possible."

After an uncomfortable pause, Chaz added flatly. "Perfect! So, our mothers aren't even our mothers. They found us?"

"Raj, how did you missh that?" reprimanded Kami.

"I told you—I almost got caught! You couldn't have done any better."

Benny typed. "get info tonight if possible. tell them Neeve told me and i told you."

Chaz shut down any further discussion. "Back pasture. Four thirty sharp."

As Benny headed home, he realized that tonight would drag on slower and far more painfully than any other night. Tomorrow, he would find his mother. He was sure of it. He hoped his voice would return, so that he could beg her for forgiveness. In any case, he'd hug her. He'd hug her so hard, she would know how much she meant to him—a hug so big it screamed everything he felt but couldn't say: Thank you. I'm sorry. I love you, Ma.

Chapter Eight

Kami wasted no time. She flew into the house, found Kiyoshi
trimming a bonsai tree on the kitchen table and confronted
him. "Who am I?"

Kiyoshi's scissors froze, saving a tiny branch from death.
"You are Miko's daughter and my granddaughter." Snip. The
tiny branch fell.

Kami pulled out a chair, allowing the legs to scrape the
wooden floor. She straddled the chair backwards. "I am a shtray
cat."

Kiyoshi's lips formed a tight line of contemplation. He
snipped some buds and grunted. "When my dear Kyo departed,
leaving me with your mother Miko, just a baby, we too became
stray cats."

Kami paused, not due to patience but due to exasperation.
She wanted to scream, explode . . .

"You floated into Miko's arms and then into mine," added
Kiyoshi with another snip.

"What? Like shupernatural kinda floating?"

"'Like' on a river 'kinda' floating. During the Obon festival in June, your mother wandered away from me, away from the singer on the platform, and away from the dancing crowd. I did not worry. I knew that she headed to the river as she had each year. She was seventeen. So much like Kyo. She found a solitary stretch of shore, lit her paper lantern with a wish upon it for her mother and set it afloat upon the water. As she watched it leave the shore and catch a tide that carried it downstream, a boat-shaped lantern drifted to shore and landed at her feet. And there you were, a gift from the river. A gift that healed the cleft in Miko's heart and mine."

"You should have told me."

"This tree is partially shaped by me, but it also has a life force of its own. Too much interference from me, and it may wither. Too little and it goes astray. The river shaped you. It brought you to us. And when it brought your question to my feet, I answered. I have shaped you, Miko has shaped you, but it is you who must know who you are, Kami. You who must decide if you are a stray cat or Miko's daughter and my granddaughter."

Kami rose to her feet and let out a sound near a growl. "I am all three, grandfather."

———

Even in turmoil, Zuma showed deep respect for his grandmother. He found her in the living room listening to her favorite Native American flutist, R. Carlos Nakai, and crocheting. He sat down in the wide chair, whose woven pattern of reds, golds and browns usually brought him peace—it had become *his* chair, a place where he rested after a hard day, but his unrest could not be abated tonight. He could not find the right words. They seemed too unbearable to say aloud. Instead, he locked his gaze on one of the many Katsina dolls—nothing irritated Cookie more than when people called them Kachina, which was not a Hopi word—that lined the room. Zuma stared at Buffalo Dancer's horned and feathered head; he was a protector capable of erasing evil thoughts. Cookie had quite the collection—dolls that brought rain, healed the sick, and nudged children to do their chores—but were they for heritage sake or because Zuma needed so much protection?

"You're troubled, Zuma. My ancestors said, 'Don't be afraid to cry. It will free your mind of sorrowful thoughts.'"

"Sorrowful thoughts doesn't even begin to cover it. I just found out I wasn't born, I was found. Care to explain that?"

Cookie set her crocheting in the intricately woven basket at her feet and removed her reading glasses. "Benny?" Cookie didn't wait for confirmation. "Well, good. It's time that you all know just how special you are. But, this story starts with your mother Catori. I did the best I could to raise her as I've raised you—with the stories of our Hopi people—the *Hopituh Shi-nu-mu,* 'the peaceful little people.' But Cat was hardly ever peaceful. She tried. But her smile left the day her father left us. Children sometimes believe the adult who remained did something wrong or was to blame. Or they blame themselves. Cat talked of leaving, of hating me and of hating herself. I . . ."

"Take your time. I need to know this."

Cookie nodded. "Cat spent years searching for something to fill the hole left by her father: participating in tribal functions or ignoring them, donning tribal clothing or wearing styles from outside the reservation, trying to fit in or rebelling against it. One year, her plan was to seek the ancient ones, to learn the secrets of the ancient Puebloans. She drove to Mesa Verde, met the guide at Cliff Palace, and followed others along a path. Cat did not do well with following paths chosen for her. She slipped away from the group to discover the site for herself, which was easy because not all visitors can hike at over 6,000 feet, and an elderly man had fainted, keeping the rangers occupied. At one point, Cat climbed down a ladder and into a sacred kiva. Each clan had its own kiva. There were many kivas at Cliff Palace. Cat said that for once she felt at peace, which was not surprising: the kiva is round, meant to represent the womb and the world below from whence the Hopi people came through to the Fourth World where we live now.

"Cat was ready to leave when something blocked the entrance. Light disappeared, leaving her in the dark. She panicked and rushed to the base of the ladder, waving her arms before her. She had climbed the first rung, when light not only returned, a beam of light shot through the opening, blinding her and alighting the fire pit. Cat climbed upward, but she heard a sound in the kiva, like the faint growling of a baby animal. She climbed back down, entered the pit and found you, Zuma. We never discovered who left you there. Had Cat not found you, who knows how long you would have survived."

"If mom was so messed up, why did she keep me and bring me home to you?"

"I wondered the same, when she arrived home with you in her arms. Her face and heart had changed. I could see it. You filled her heart. I thought it auspicious that you were found on Winter Solstice, a sacred day for the Hopi. The sun leaves our people for a long, long time. Each year the Hopi perform the Soyal ceremony to cajole the sun into returning to us. Only the strongest warriors of the tribe can bring the sun back."

"Nice bedtime story. Is that it?"

"No." Cookie dumped her crochet basket onto the floor and handed it to Zuma. "You were found in this basket."

Zuma observed the markings more carefully than ever before. There was a crudely styled blue face woven into the bottom of the basket, and a pattern radiated out from the blue face. "What is it? A katsina?"

"It's the Blue Star Katsina."

"I don't know that one."

"We are in the Fourth World, but the Blue Star Katsina represents the start of the next world. There are many signs of the coming of this time, some of which appear to have already occurred. What's important is that the Blue Star Katsina is the ninth sign, the last. Its appearance initiates the coming of another, the True White Brother, who will search the world for the pure of heart. If none are found, the world will be destroyed."

"In this little scenario, if I'm the Blue Star, what? Is Benny the True White Brother?"

Cookie shrugged her shoulders.

"For the record, Grandma, I much prefer your story about the Spider Grandmother. Way perkier."

"Zuma, Cat and I could not love you any more than we do. Sleep well."

Zuma clutched the basket as if it were a lifeline to his mysterious past. "I'll try. Can I keep this?"

"The basket is yours. It belongs to you."

———

Layla did not take disappointment well. She meekly entered the house, the interior of which seemed too richly gilded for such a small space. The striped silk furnishings affronted her eyes. She could not bear such brilliance right now.

Mona had her feet tucked under her on the sofa, as she read a book on ancient Egyptian medicine. Layla plunked down next to her and sank her head into Mona's lap as she had many a day when the world pressed too hard on her shoulders.

Mona set her book aside. Without a word, she ran her hands through Layla's long tresses, moving them aside enough to massage the base of her neck as she had done many times.

Layla popped up. "I can't do it. Go on like nothing has changed. It's all changed. It's all gone."

"Layla, slow down. What are you talking about? What's wrong?"

"Am I Tahira's daughter or not?"

Mona's fingers rushed to her lips. "Oh, dear. Isis, help us now," she beseeched the healer goddess. "I'm here. You're here. Nothing has changed between us, Layla, but I will tell you what you want to know, if you want to hear it."

Layla's lips pouted; her violet eyes fell in uncertainty. She let her hair fall forward with no strength to move it back from her face. Her heart beat faster, unsure if she could stomach the truth. Once spoken, she could not erase it. She would be forced to deal with it, and she'd made an art of dodging rather than confronting, like the day she lured Chaz to the woods. She knew he had a crush on her, but when he tried to kiss her—he was only fourteen and she only twelve—she freaked out, slapped him and let everyone think it was all his idea. Worse, yet, she only did it because Kami and Raj had been so mean to her. She knew they both liked Chaz, but Chaz liked her. She did it to hurt the girls, but she hurt Chaz, who had always been kind to her. She never had the guts to tell him the truth. She just let him apologize, and she accepted it. At least she learned a lesson that day: love wasn't something you experimented with, and it wasn't to be used as a weapon either. She couldn't take that back, and if she asked Mona to speak, she couldn't take that back either. Reluctantly, she nodded.

"It is true that my younger sister Tahira found you. Do you want to know more?" asked Mona, like a surgeon careful to cut away the cancer and not the healthy tissue.

Layla nodded.

"Two sisters had been born into a slew of brothers. Tahira was a decade away from me, her clostest sibling. It put her in a tiny boat upon a vast sea. I coped by pouring myself into books and dreaming of becoming a doctor one day. Tahira coped by idolizing my father. She was the jewel of his world. Quiet, obedient and very spoiled by him. She allowed my boat to sail away unnoticed. When father faltered about sending me to medical school, it was Tahira who convinced him how noble his act would be, saying Mona would save lives. He could not say 'no' to her. Father passed away shortly after I'd landed a job as a surgeon. That's when Tahira's boat sprung a leak.

"She didn't know how to live without father doting on her. She and mother fought constantly, mostly over mother's insistence that Tahira marry, but Tahira was grieving. She wasn't ready. I interceded. I moved out and took Tahira with me. My brothers were furious, but what could they do? I suggested that Tahira find a hobby, like exploring ancient landmarks and writing about them. She seemed romantic enough to write ten novels, I told her. This inspired her. She set out for a day trip to the Giza pyramids. We'd been before but she was too terrified of taking the tour to the interior chamber, which required a hunched walk downward along a stone corridor. She promised to overcome her fear and write about her journey. But she did not come home that day, nor the day after. She called periodically to say she was fine. She arrived home six months later—with you in her arms. She told me a wild story about finding you in that chamber in a basket lined with a blanket, under which were gold coins and jewelry, like some story from the Arabian tales. She said she had to break free and be on her own for a while. Besides, she didn't think her brothers or I would let her keep you, and she could not bear the loss if we took you away. She was right. I hate to admit it, but I would have been practical. However, I took you both in when she came home. I felt responsible. Wait here. Don't move."

Mona retrieved a woven basket and a blanket from her bedroom. "These are yours. Along with this." She held out a golden bracelet, a snake encrusted with emerald eyes, and carnelian and blue lapis lazuli. "This made me a believer. It's real and it's old. Very old."

"I hate snakes," said Layla, sliding the bracelet onto her forearm so that the snake crawled upward toward her elbow. She turned her arm this way and that to watch its emerald eyes sparkle. "Is there more?"

"That's the last one. Tahira spent the rest traveling and doting on herself and you, but it's worth a small fortune."

Layla held up the blanket, disappointed. "More snakes?" the soft blue background could not soften the black, gold and white snake that formed a crazy eight across its length. "Well, at least mother didn't leave us destitute."

"I was in surgery the night she disappeared from the house. But she's out there somewhere, Layla. We'll find her."

Layla signaled for Aunt Mona to sit beside her, and when she did, she plopped her head in Mona's lap. "We will."

———————

Amir found his uncle waiting for him. He could sense the heavy silence the moment he entered the living room, crossed the soft silk carpet and sank into the sofa. "You've been waiting for me."

"What you seek . . ." Jalal rubbed his fingers down the sides of his mustache. His chin boasted a day's dark stubble.

"Is seeking you," added Amir, completing one of the many Rumi quotes in his uncle's repertoire. "Your sister is not my mother."

"Zaria raised you. She is your mother. She also found you, and now, you need to know of that time."

Jalal spoke in a matter-of-fact tone that Amir recognized as no lack of emotion for the subject but a strong sense of duty toward it. Amir could pick up the subtlety of tones and inflections that few others monitored in another's speech. "I'm all ears."

"Our parents died when Zaria was only fourteen. I was twice as old. It's difficult for a girl when her older brother suddenly takes the place of her father. She fought my authority. Within a couple of years, she had flunked out of secondary school, but she found work in modeling. I supported it. I thought that it would provide her with a strong sense of her own power, but it did the opposite. It numbed her. That world is full of dolls. When one is tossed on the heap as too old, five more eagerly take its place. One day, when Zaria was about to leave for a photo shoot in Derinkuyu, she came to me and apologized for her behavior, saying it was because she ached so deeply that she lashed out at me and everyone else around her. I was stunned. I told her, 'The wound is the place—"

"Where light enters," finished Amir.

"Just so. I felt she had turned a corner. At the end of the shoot in the underground city, the crew packed up the equipment, and Zaria climbed the steps on her way to the surface four stories up. The lights began to flicker, and as Zaria hurried her pace, the tunnel system went black. She fell and slid down an incline into the arms of a stranger. He calmed her, took her hand in his and led her upward again in the dark. Zaria heard what sounded like rock grating against rock. The man let go of her hand. The lights sparked to life and illuminated the room. Zaria was overjoyed, until she saw before her a round stone door rolling to a stop, sealing off the tunnel. She found an airshaft and screamed for help, fearing that if she continued through the tunnel system, she would never find her way out. From somewhere, she heard a response that help was on the way and to stay calm. She paced the room as she waited. She was in a room with vats or tubs, which she was later told was an ancient winery room. One cracked vat had a woven mat over it. Zaria moved it aside, and simply put, there you were."

"That's it? I was found in a cracked wine vat in some old ruins?"

"That's it, except that you saved your mother's life. By the time the workers came to free her, she could care less. They offered her sweet, repeated apologies as they grumbled at the oddity of how the door could close, as it could only be sealed or opened from one side, which meant someone had intentionally sealed her in. She didn't hear a word of it. She became a top model, a proud woman, and a loving mother. You had captured her heart."

"Well, of course. I can't even imagine how cute I was as a baby, given how I look today. Adorable, for sure." Amir headed off any reprimand from Jalal by quoting Rumi: "Shine like the whole universe is yours! Goodnight, Uncle."

———◆———

Raj stormed through the door and rudely confronted her grandfather, but was careful to add an affectionate term of endearment. "Nana! You lied to me! I can't believe you lied to me!"

Andy jumped out of Lotus position, out of mediation and into the air. His long beard seemed to jump too. Once standing on bare feet, he ran a hand down his beard as if to recenter his composure. "I've never lied to you, Rajani. But, I have omitted a considerable amount of information that I did not think you needed at the time."

"Well, I need it now," she barked.

"Come, my old bones need to sit." He directed her to a group of pillows on a low red divan in an arched plaster alcove. As they sat, Raj hugged a small beaded pillow, smothering it against her chest.

"Let's start with your mother, Amala. She was never my daughter, as I never married. I found her and she found you." Andy paused to allow Raj time to take in the hard truths. "Amala was a street urchin with no parents, until I gave her a parent—me. I had no intention of it, but my heart knew better than my head. Amala's bright disposition and smiles soon cracked my heart wide open, and she rushed insde. In return, she gifted me with a father's love for his child. Never did I see a gentler spirit, not only satisfied with what little we had but so eager to show kindness to others. I surprised her with an old sitar one day. She learned to play it on her own, convincing musicians to giver her a free lesson here or there. She eanred a little money playing, which she dutifully spent on food or surprised her old father with a new pair of sandals or perhaps a sweet treat, which we split upon my insistence. I worried for Amala's future. But she seemed without worry, caring only to comfort others. One day, she left home to visit a sick friend. She came home with you. I could not turn you away. She did not explain where she found you, except that it had nothing to do with the sick friend. She simply said that you had no parents, and that as of this day, 'I, Amala, am her mother.' I never doubted her. And I've never doubted you, Raj."

Raj hugged the pillow. "I remember her face, Nana. I remember her smile."

———

Chaz had spent so much time in his youth in anger over the abandonment of his mother and the waning strength of his legs that he had little anger left, even with the newest morsel of knowledge. But he still had plenty of fight left with which to unearth buried secrets.

Chaz wheeled himself into the house and found Friday and Big O conversing over mugs of coffee at the kitchen table. The conversation stopped the moment he crossed the threshold.

"How about a nice game of Tofl?" asked Big O, speaking of a Viking board game akin to chess, except that the enemy's army, which had no king, far outnumbered the defender's army, which surrounded and protected its king.

Chaz wheeled himself to the table. "How about some answers?"

A wall of silence descended between them, soon broken when Big O reached out to squeeze Chaz's shoulder. "Answers ye shall have, boy."

Friday kept her hands around her mug, as if needing the comfort of the warm ceramic. She took a sip and set the mug down. "It wasn't my sister who gave you to us, Chaz. We're not really your aunt and uncle. We could not have children, and when—"

Big O set a big hand over Friday's delicate forearm. His voice dropped to a whisper. "I'll start, then just tell him what you told me, and I'll tell him the rest." Friday nodded. After a pause and a swig of coffee, Big O jumped right in. "Every year, a friend and I hauled our horses from Alesund, Norway, to Aurhus, Denmark to go to the Moesgaard Viking Moot Festival. Nothing seemed like more fun back then than joining the cast reenacting Viking battles and galloping around on horseback, wearing a helmet, wielding my sword and grunting. But the moment I saw Friday in the crowd, that all changed. Literally. I wasn't watching the battle, and my friend smacked me in the helmet, and I fell off my horse."

"You never told me that," said Chaz.

"Corse not. I got my pride. Anyway, it was the best smack of my life, because when I found Friday after the battle, she had no trouble remembering me. I took her for a night ride on the beach. After that, my friend still hauled my horse, but Friday and I biked and ferried to the festival, a two day ride through some of the prettiest scenery in Norway." Big O gave Friday's arm an affectionate squeeze. "We not only met at the festival, we married there in full Viking regalia." This made Friday smile, and she let go of the mug to place her hand over his.

"About eight or nine years later; while I was riding my new horse, Slippy, and waging mock war, Friday walked around the festival." A nod of his bearded chin let Friday know it was her turn.

Friday's blue eyes met Chaz's. "Ya, well, I liked visiting the crafts tents. Over the years, the artists had become our friends. After I left the tents, I strolled along the beach and into the forest that edged it. I came across a white tent. It was odd that it was so far removed from the others. Rune letters covered the entrance. That wasn't unusual at a Viking festival. I began to walk past when I heard a baby cry. I waited, expecting a mother to calm the child, but the cries grew louder. I called out, but no one answered back, so I stepped inside. You were swaddled in white fur and nestled in animal pelts that lined a basket made of ice, of all things. That was weird. I picked you up and held you until the sun began to fall, hoping someone would come back. But I couldn't wait any longer, and I couldn't leave you there alone. I took you with me and found Big O in our tent. I told him the story. Flashlights in hand, we headed back to the tent in the forest. It was gone, except for the pelts that had lined the basket that had melted into a puddle of water.

Big O interjected, "We spent days looking for that tent. I couldn't figure out how a parent could up and disappear on a kid, but then, I've seen some strange things. You gotta understand that Friday and I wanted a child. Still, we didn't want to take a child belonging to another. We searched long and hard. No one even remembered seeing such a tent. We brought you home and told friends that Friday's sister had passed you to us. After that, Friday stayed home with you, and I went to the festival each year with my friend, not to play act, but to search for that tent. Never saw it. When you were turning six, we took you with us for your birthday."

"That's when I wandered away from camp and found the tent in the forest," said Chaz.

"Ya, that's right," said Big O. "By the time Friday and I realized you were missing from our tent, we grabbed flashlights and ran into the forest. There it was—the white tent with runes. Burning. We caught a glimpse of two people running away from it, but all we cared about was that a woman darted out of the entrance of the tent with you in her arms. Friday took you from her, and we all went back to our camp. Minnie said you were in danger, but she could keep us, and you, safe."

"And you believed her because?"

Friday added, "When I unswaddled you from the fur, I found a rectangular stone."

Big O plopped the stone on the table. Chaz scooped it up and examined the carvings. "What does it mean?"

Friday explained, "Ragnarok is the Viking end of the world. A great battle, which causes the demise of many gods of the Aesir, the unleashing of natural disasters, and a flood that wipes out all life. It's said renewal will then take place."

"Guys, you've been to too many Viking festivals. I get that some crazy mother abandoned me, and I'm glad—really glad—you found me. You've been mother and father, not aunt and uncle to me. But the Ragnarok thing is a bit out there. As you said, there were many craftsmen at the festival who could have made a rune stone. And let's face it, a woman who abandons her son at a festival and hangs out with a violent lunatic would be the type to tuck a foreboding rock in his swaddling."

"Ya, ya, of course, Chaz," agreed Big O. "It's way, way out there."

"Don't worry any more about it," added Friday. "I'm glad you know the truth now."

"See you in the morning," said Chaz, already wheeling his way to his bedroom.

When the door shut, Friday whispered, "We should have told him the museum tested a sample of the pelt and it's from 500 AD."

"He'll just think his crazy mother stole a hide from the museum to further the prank. That's what we thought."

"Ya, we did, but we came here anyway. Just to be sure."

Chapter Nine

Too tired to travel farther in the dark, Professor Daniels slowed his station wagon and searched for vacancy signs. Spotting one, he pulled into the gravel and dirt lot of the Blue Birch Motel. In the morning, he would head the rest of the way to Minerva and find Dr. Pallas.

Daniel tossed and turned. Nightmares of his last lecture at the Smithsonian in Washington, D.C., flooded his mind. In the midst of a sentence, a voice from the audience shouted, "Rubbish! Nonsense!" He could barely make out the white-clad figure until she stepped forward into the light—Dr. Minerva Pallas. "Caves? Ancient myths connected to modern-day earthquakes? Throw in gods and fairies and you'll have a best seller, Dr. Daniels."

"I don't know the cause, obviously, just that they are occurring at locations believed to be—"

"Is California an entrance to the underworld, Doctor? Because they have earthquakes all the time."

Laughter erupted and reverberated throughout the hall.

"Yes, yes, I know. I've sorted those out and focused on these specific locations, and the statistics show a striking anomaly that cannot be ig—"

"That can be considered coincidence. Pure coincidence. Nothing more. Sometimes the best minds overlook the simplest explanations. You wouldn't be the first. Good day, Doctor. Thanks for the chuckle." With that she turned to leave and others followed, sniggering and snickering, mocking and belittling.

A ruckus and banging caused Daniel to bolt upright in bed. He heard it again, outside his window. He checked the clock. Three a.m. He turned on the bedside lamp.

Peeking outside, Daniel eyed a raccoon, who, having knocked over a trash can and pried off the lid, munched on scraps. The animal's eye glowed in the light from his room, giving it an eerie appearance.

Daniel packed up, checked out and drove through Minerva, all the while looking for One World Academy. He drove slowly in the dark. Outside of town, he spotted an illuminated golden owl on a stick. He followed it to another and another and finally to a golden gate. He looped back around and pulled his car onto a little-used side lane where it would not be seen and doubled back on foot.

As he eyed the gate, his heart raced. He knew the symbols well. They were on Sophie's—or Neeve's—necklace, but more than that, each ancient symbols had the same purpose: protection. They came from societies spread all over the world: a Celtic cross; a Shinto torii; a *hamsa*, or hand, with an eye in the center of it meant to ward off the "evil eye"; an om, a Sanskrit word; the face of Tonatiuh, the Aztec sun god of the fifth world; the *Wedjat* or eye of Horus; and the snake dragon, associated with Marduk of Babylon.

Daniel searched around the gate, but he saw no way to enter, no way to call inside. Just as he decided to circle round the fence line for a way to climb over it, he heard a motor approaching from within. He hid in a clump of bushes. The dark afforded him a hideout.

The gate clicked and swung open. A bizarre buggy of sorts drove out, filled with adolescents, three rows of two, and a black-and-green-haired girl in a jump seat in the back. A blond-haired boy drove down the path toward the main road with a dark-haired boy next to him—Benny!

With a click, the gate began to close. Daniel rushed in and skulked from tree to tree, inching down the arboreal tunnel, staying out of sight should another vehicle or a security guard cross his path.

He soon reached the end of the road and came upon a well-lit neoclassical building with a dome-like structure that reminded him of Rome's Pantheon. Rather than cross the open expanse, he hugged the tree line and inched around back, where he found small houses. The first, a single-level wooden structure that sat between two red barns. A horse stared at him from a pasture, and ravens cawed from the peak of a roof, as if warning him to come no closer.

The next home was a mini Egyptian palace, fronted by four pillars under a triangular pediment with a relief of a kneeling woman, spreading long wings, painted in blue, green, red and gold: Isis, the Egyptian goddess of nature and magic, the protector of the dead and of children.

So far, no sign of people. Daniel crept along, coming upon an adobe home with exposed vigas, beams of Pueblo construction. The sun began to lighten the sky and leave him without cover as he crept past an English cottage.

A little farther along, he heard a soothing, melodic chanting.

He approached the back garden of a white stucco home with a golden domed roof topped with a spire. A bare-chested man, muscular and fit in his advanced age, draped his excessively long beard over his bare shoulder as he knelt before a small shrine of Ganesh, the Hindu deity with an elephant face. Incense burned. The man offered the statue small plates of food as he chanted. He laid a garland over the statue's head.

Daniel ducked when he saw a flash of white in his peripheral vision. A dark-skinned and mustached man wearing a white shirt and skirt and a tall beige cap swirled past him, arms in the air, like a ballerina. "A Whirling Dervish?" Daniel muttered, suspecting that One World Academy was some kind of spiritual retreat. A rattling noise just behind him caused him to spin on crouched knees and throw his hands up. He'd been caught.

Daniel stood upright, towering over a short Asian man in drab attire and a red knit cap, shaking a walking stick with six rings looped through the top.

"Enemies crouch and hide. Friends stand tall. Show their faces."

"I'm no enemy," sputtered Daniel, standing upright. "I don't even know you."

Jalal whirled to a stop beside them. His white circular skirt fell gracefully until it rested around his legs. "Then you hide in fear?"

"Don't be silly," said Daniel.

Kiyoshi added, "Men take the crouching posture for many reasons: fear, spying, hunting—"

"Curiosity," said Daniel. He did not see that the long-bearded man had snuck up behind him.

"That would be spying," said Andy.

Despite the man's age, his muscular tone and hairy visage made an ominous presence. Daniel stammered, "I come in peace."

Kiyoshi laughed. "What are we, aliens?" He put out his hand to shake. "I'm Kiyoshi."

"Daniel," he said, reaching out to shake hands. "I'm looking for Minerva Pallas."

Andy pulled a red tee shirt over his head. "Come then. Join us for breakfast, Daniel."

Daniel followed the men along a path and into the main building. As they strolled down the corridor toward the cafeteria, shouting emanated from up ahead.

"The buggy is gone! So are the kids," shouted Big O. "Chaz left a note, saying they were headed to town."

"I don't buy it!" Mike argued.

Minnie stepped out of her office and into the hallway.

Daniel could not contain himself. He rushed forward, wagging a finger, his face scrunched with accusation. But before he could say a word, Mike cut him off and jumped in between him and Minerva. "Daniel? What are you doing here? Did you follow me?"

"She . . . that woman . . ." Daniel wagged his finger. "You made me a laughing stock! Turned my life upside down."

Minerva gently nudged Mike aside. "I'm sorry, Daniel. Truly, I am. I had to discredit you. You were getting too close to the truth."

"What in hell's bells is going on here?" shouted Mike.

Minnie kept her eyes on Daniel. "While I'd love to explain, it seems we have some missing children to attend to first."

Cookie and Mona sauntered through the back door. Their laughing ceased the moment they heard the words *missing children*.

"I saw them leave," offered Daniel. "Over an hour ago."

Mike interjected, "I know where they went. Benny is looking for his grandfather. I'm calling in the FBI."

"I'll call the WWs out," said Big O, referring to the Warriors and Watchers bike club. "They can get there a hell of a lot faster than the Feds." He added for Mike's benefit, "No offense."

"Use my office, Mike," Minnie instructed. "Give me your keys, Daniel. Where's your car?"

"Down the road, I'm afraid, but I can—"

"No time. Well take mine." Minnie turned to the guardians. "Pack up."

"Minnie," whispered Cookie. "They're not ready. Are they?"

Mona gripped Cookie's arm, waiting for the answer.

Daniel stammered, "Ready? For what? What's going on? What did you mean? Exactly what truth am I close to?"

Minnie ignored him. "Prepared or not is irrelevant. The time has come."

Chaz pulled into the quaint village of Alexandria Bay—not so quaint in the summertime when tourists abounded—and parked along the curb. Raj jumped out and dashed into a donut shop. The smell of sugary breads mixed with the scent of sea air and fish. The normally quiet life of local residents gave way to a constant influx of thousands of summer visitors, who clogged the sidewalks and packed the ferries, or sailed their yachts or chartered boats across the bay, headed to Boldt Castle or other destinations up and down the Saint Lawrence River, which ran from the Great Lakes to the Atlantic, forming the Thousand Islands archipelago, where some of the wealthiest families built monolithic homes on private islands. The seabirds, too, seemed to know they lived in opulent surroundings and swooped noisily overhead, demanding to be fed.

A man clad in a pirate's outfit—eye patch and all—rushed up to Benny and shoved a flyer in his hand announcing the upcoming Bill Johnston's Pirate Days in August.

"Dude, personal space," said Layla, two seats behind Benny.

"And hygiene," added Amir, sitting right behind Benny. He sniffed the air and waved a hand before his nose. "I smell booze and BO."

Chaz asked, "Which way to Domenico Adez's place?"

"That nut in the fur cape! Don't go there," the pirate spat through missing teeth.

Raj emerged from the bakery holding a pink box and climbed into the jump seat.

"Which way?" Chaz repeated.

"Dead ahead a ways. Turn off on Basso Loco Place," said the pirate.

Chaz hit the hand control. The buggy shot forward, merged with traffic and headed out of town.

Zuma reached for the box, but Raj pulled it away. "Chillax, dude."

"I'm starving!" Zuma complained.

"Oh, like that's a news flash!" sneered Raj, as she cracked open the box and withdrew a sticky chocolate éclair. "You're obsesh with food." She passed the box to Zuma, who snatched it from her hands. Zuma wiggled his fingers as if warming them up while making his selection.

"And you're a grumpy twig," Zuma retorted. "Maybe if you ate more, you'd be chillax instead of cray-cray." He grabbed two huge bear claws and an apple fritter. Layla took a simple glazed donut and passed the box forward to Kami.

"You're the crazy one, Zuma," said Raj, taking a bite of her éclair. "Crazy for food."

"Whatevs, green goddess," said Zuma, sandwiching the apple fritter between the bear claws and chomping into his sugary burger, moaning audibly.

Benny typed. At a red light, he held it up for Chaz to read. "drop me off & leave. grandpa is mafia. i'm not sweet on u guys but don't want u hurt."

Kami, leaning over the seat to read it, shot back, "Shorry, Benny boy. We want anshwers, too."

"Check," said Layla, giving Zuma a fist pump.

"Mate," said Zuma, completing the saying that had evolved from their many chess games.

"And you are sweet on us," said Chaz. "We're the only family you've got right now."

"We're a seriously disturbed family," said Amir. "But that's normal, I think."

———

By the time Mike arrived in the parking lot, Minnie was slamming the trunk of the VW shut. She hopped in the backseat while commanding, "You drive."

Mike had no choice, as his silver convertible idled at the entrance to the arboreal tunnel, fully loaded with passengers. "FBI is on the way."

Once on the main road, he sped down Route 3 headed west with Big O in the passenger seat, and Daniel in the backseat, sandwiched between Minnie and Friday. The tiny engine whined as Mike put the pedal to the floor. He was surprised at the speed, considering the drag of passenger weight in the tiny car. Behind them, Jalal drove Daniel's car, filled with Kiyoshi, Andy, Mona and Cookie.

"Need your phone, Mike," said Big O.

Mike handed it over and Big O punched the buttons. Over the speaker, it rang and rang and abruptly stopped. Big O hit redial. It rang and rang and stopped again. He punched redial again, and a sleepy, irritated voice shouted in a Latino accent, "Michael, whoever you are, you are no friend of mine. Nor are you a friend of a friend, because it's Saturday morning and people are sleep—"

"Raphael. It's Big O. Got an emergency. Need the WWs."

Raphael's tone changed. "What up, O?"

"The kids snuck out. They're headed to Domenico's place. We're about an hour behind them."

"On our way, dude."

"One more thing?"

"There's more? What's worse than that?" Raphael sputtered.

"The FBI is headed there, too."

Raphael exploded. "Not the Freakin' Boobs of Idiocracy!"

"Uh, Raphael," said Big O. "You're on speaker phone. FBI at the wheel."

"I'm sorry. I meant the Followers and Bumblers of Institutions."

"Raphael!"

"The Foolish Brainless—"

Big O hung up. "Sorry, Mike, my friends . . . well, they—"

Mike finished for him. "Don't like big government, I take it."

"Oh, no," said Big O. "They don't like any government. But they're good souls."

"That's just what we need," said Minnie from the backseat, staring straight ahead. "I like Raphael immensely."

Mike interjected, "I placed a call to a friend after dinner last night. There's no record of the Warriors and Watchers bike club."

Big O turned at an angle to see Minnie. "Minnie started it 'bout the time we all moved out here. Kinda exclusive. Her chopper's at my place. It's a beauty. All white and chrome."

"With an owl?" Mike guessed.

"Not on the bike," said Big O. "On her helmet."

"Don't dawdle with idle conversation, if you please," Minnie scolded. "Faces forward."

"Pardon me for interrupting, but exactly what is going on here?" asked Daniel.

"Do you believe in fate?" asked Minnie. "The Greek kind. Destiny."

"Well, I . . . I don't know," Daniel stuttered. "I haven't given it much thought. Why?"

"Because I tried to keep you out of this. That's why I discredited you. But here you are, sitting right beside me," said Minnie. "Fate, Dr. Daniels. It's why you're here. It's why we're all here. Now, our fate lies ahead. None of us knows the future, not even the gods."

Chapter Ten

Chaz turned onto Basso Loco Place and began a slow incline along a black paver-stone road. The forest, an airy, green expanse, changed shape and hue as they drove ahead. The tree trunks twisted and bent. Roots erupted into tangles that strangled one another. Knobby limbs of bare branches reached out for them, like spindly arms with bony fingers. Green disappeared, replaced by ashen limbs, and dense fog blocked out the sun.

Sounds, too, disappeared. Neither a bird nor an insect made a peep.

Benny removed his glasses.

Chaz flipped on the headlights.

Benny and Chaz both flinched as the lights illuminated two statues, one on each side of the road: a three-headed beast with the heads of a lion, a leopard, and a wolf.

When they emerged from the foggy woods, a black castle sat atop a hill, awash in a pink and orange sky—an angry sunset sky, but it wasn't sunset. The black road, lined with gargoyles with bat-like wings, led up a grassy knoll and straight to the castle.

"Looksh like crime paysh," said Kami.

"But it's black. Someone needs a decorator," sniped Raj.

"Right," said Layla. "Like you'd say 'no' to living in a castle like that."

"I'd paint it pink,'" Raj countered. "Benny, is this where you grew up?"

Benny nodded. He remembered the castle, the hearth, the courtyard garden. He remembered rolling down this very hill with his father and mother, laughing as they tumbled. It was as if the picture on the mantel came to life and rolled down the hill with him this very minute.

Chaz drove into a square flanked by more gargoyles with bat-like wings. Chaz cut the engine. "Amir and I will wait here. Raj and Kami, walk around the left; Layla and Zuma, around the right. We'll meet back here in thirty minutes."

Benny typed, "if I'm not back. leave. get help."

Benny climbed a set of steps two at a time and stood before an enormous door crisscrossed with iron. He reached for the head of a gargoyle sticking out its tongue and pounded the knocker. The sound echoed inside. The massive door opened.

A super tall, bald man with emaciated features grinned. He reminded Benny of the man on his *Rise Up to Extinction* tee shirt.

"Welcome home, Master Benedito. He's expecting you."

Benny stepped inside. The door shut behind him with a loud thud that echoed in the dark foyer with a massively high vaulted ceiling. Strange tapestries and paintings lined the walls. One showed stacked layers of creatures and humans with faces in torment; others showed people running from fiery destruction.

"This way," said the butler. Benny followed.

———

"What a handsome young man!"

Chaz whipped his head toward the voice beside him. He'd been so busy keeping his eyes on the castle, he hadn't seen that a woman had slipped into the passenger seat beside him. She wore sheer red, including a veil and what looked like a genie outfit.

"Thank you," Amir responded from the seat directly behind her. He whiffed the air. "She smells fine."

"She looks fine, Amir."

"How fine?" the woman teased. "Describe me to your friend." She removed her veil.

Chaz nodded in submission. "As you wish. Amir, she's even prettier than Layla and her Aunt Mona combined. She has almond-shaped eyes that shimmer like gold, long dark lashes. Gold jewelry dangles over her forehead, at her wrists, and fingers and ears."

"And ankles," the woman added, sticking a foot in the air, before bending her knee and setting it down on Chaz's seat. "Tell him more."

Chaz moved to set his hand on her foot, but she withdrew it. "Her nose is slim, her lips full and red, and her dark, silky hair is pulled back, but it falls in a twist over her shoulder. She's wearing red, sheer red. She's . . . twenty?" He paused to allow her to answer.

The woman laughed. "A little older. Tell me your name," said the woman. "I command it."

"Amir. If anyone cares."

"Chaz. You?"

"Nope. No one cares," said Amir. "Ignore the blind boy."

"Inanna."

"I'm guessing you're a belly dancer?"

Inanna laughed harder. "I'll dance for you anytime." She patted his leg.

"I . . . I can't feel your hand. My legs—"

"Feel what?" Amir said in an irritated voice. "What am I missing? Deets, pa-lease!"

Inanna pouted. "I must go. I'm late to the party. But I'm sure we'll see each other again. After all, I owe you a dance. Close your eyes."

"Hey, don't worry about me. You all do your thing," Amir said with caustic sarcasm, folding his arms over his chest.

Chaz closed his eyes, but opened them a split second later. "Wait."

She was gone, all but her veil, which he stuffed into the glove compartment to retrieve later.

"FYI, I am way better looking than him. I'm just sayin'."

"She's gone, Amir."

"What happened?"

"Nothing happened."

"It didn't sound like nothing."

"Duck," said Chaz, and Amir complied.

Chaz peeked at the front of the house. Two men, one tall, one short, both in dark suits, came out the front door. They split up, one going left and one going right.

"Two guys just came out. They're walking the perimeter."

———

The butler led Benny into a library with a roaring fire that licked at the edges of an enormous hearth and closed the door on his way out.

Benny saw fur-covered legs protruding from a high-backed red leather chair before the blazing fire. Benny stepped around the chair to face him.

The old man pushed back his hood. Benny recognized the wild shock of curly red hair and beard, and his red eyes, the whites of which were yellowed. The heads and tails of dead creatures that composed his hooded cape hung over his shoulders, chest and legs. The black beads of their eyes glistened as if they lived. Their sharp teeth bit into one another, head to tail, willingly obeying their master and keeping him warm. Benny remembered more. Flash after flash of images hurled themselves toward him. Mostly, he remembered his father's face, sometimes smiling, sometimes twisted with rage. He welcomed both, no longer willing to forget, no longer pushing them away.

"Benedito. I've been searching for you for years. You're home." Domenico reached out to take Benny's hand.

Benny pulled his hand away and typed on his notepad, "this is not my home."

"Have you no voice? Ah, well. Then let me speak freely. This is all yours, Benny. This and more. I'm your family, especially now that your mother is dead." He said it matter-of-factly.

Benny punched the keys. His eyes narrowed as he flashed the screen at the old man. "i'm not dead. she's not dead. no thanks to you. bring her to me."

The old man laughed, deep and raspy. "Defiant like her, I see."

The butler opened the door and stepped inside. "Sorry to interrupt, Lord, but the council is here. They demand your immediate presence."

Domenico rose to his feet. "Come, Benny. Meet the rest of your family. Then decide if you stay or go."

"my mother!" Benny typed.

Domenico's eyes raged. "Do not order me! Do not defy me. Your mother will wait. She's not going anywhere."

———

Layla and Zuma snuck along the side of the castle without incident. They passed by a door, checked it, and found it locked. At the corner, Zuma sneaked a peek around to see if the way held surprises.

Layla shoved him forward, nearly knocking him down. "Someone's coming."

Zuma regained his balance. "Look." He pointed to Raj and Kami, just turning the far corner and heading their way. He signaled for them to hurry, and he and Layla raced to meet them. They paused, standing on opposite sides of an arched opening leading into a courtyard, where they heard voices.

Raj signaled for Zuma and Layla to wait. She peered through the archway. When she waved forward, Layla, on hands and knees, crawled across. When she waved again, Zuma followed.

Zuma jumped to his feet. "There's a guy behind us."

Kami whispered, "Shame here, but we passhed a shtorm cellar. Come on."

They raced back to the cellar door that sat at a shallow angle to the ground. Zuma pulled it open and waited for the girls to enter first. He clambered down the ladder, pulling the door closed behind him. Just before it closed, a short guy in a black suit stepped around the corner, heading their way.

"I think he saw me," reported Zuma.

A beam of light from an open grate at ground level stabbed through the darkness and into a room cluttered with junk stacked against every wall. It reeked of dust and mildew. Zuma sneezed.

"Look for a way out," snapped Raj.

Cobwebs broke against them as they rushed to the far end of the room.

"This way," said Layla, as loud as she dared.

As they gathered around a door, a creak filled their ears. Light poured into the room. The cellar door had swung open.

"Hurry," Zuma whispered, panic in his voice.

"It'sh locked," said Kami, pushing on the latch.

Footfalls descended the rickety ladder.

"Look around," said Layla, already digging through paraphernalia and dust-covered debris stacked on nearby shelves.

"Here." Raj dug two keys out of an ornamental box. She shoved one key into the lock. It didn't turn.

"Did you hear that?" said a distant voice.

Kami whipped her hands in circles, telling Raj to speed up.

Raj shoved the other key into the lock and turned the key. It clicked, a sound that while not loud seemed like a gong. Raj depressed the latch and swung the door open. She rushed through, followed by the others. They found themselves in a long stone corridor with alcoves to the right and left.

"I feel like we're being herded," said Layla.

"Help!" said a voice down the corridor. "Who's there?"

Zuma crept forward, extending a hand to keep the others close behind him. He peered into the first alcove. In the corner, a woman gripped the bars of a cell. Layla rushed to her. "Neeve?"

"Yes."

"It's me, Layla."

Raj shoved the other key in the lock. The door opened and Neeve rushed out.

"Kami, Raj. Zuma. Layla. You were all so small when I saw you last. Is Benny with you?"

"By now, he's with his grandfather," said Zuma, "and we've got some goons in suits behind us."

"And more goons in the garden," added Raj.

"Follow me." Neeve ran down the corridor only stopping to make sure the side alcoves held no surprises.

Chapter Eleven

Benny followed Domenico through a great hall and out tall glass doors that led into a courtyard garden at the heart of the castle.

Benny remembered the garden fondly, despite the enormous monster statues—six of them—that stood guard: a fierce crocodile; a frog creature wielding a spear; a two-headed ogre with pink pig faces, hoisting a shield in one hand, a dagger in the other; a skinny, snarling wolf; a demented cat, and a mosquito woman with a long hollow tongue. Benny could never climb their bases. But his grandfather gave him lifts up, after which he proceeded to smash his play sword against the foe's legs but not in malice. Even in battle, these were his only playmates, and he adored them, much like other boys played war with friends. When you grow up with ogres and beasts instead of trucks and sandboxes, you grow fond of monsters—except the mosquito woman. She creeped him out with her bug-like antennae, oversized glossy eyes, skinny bug legs, narrow wings and, especially, her hollow whip-like tongue, ready to suck the life out of her next victim.

Domenico strolled along a black stone path, past planters filled with black flowers. Benny had thought nothing of them back then. He hadn't realized flowers grew in other colors until moving to the school. No wonder his mother had loved the pink and white blooms at the foot of their cottage and cared for them with such zeal after having lived in this den of darkness.

As they reached the center of the court, Benny eyed a strangely attired group. Six men and one woman sat on rough-hewn, volcanic-rock benches that ringed a fire pit. From the flat pit that offered no wall of protection, a fire shot skyward, ravaging the air with unusual force and height.

Benny typed a message. Domenico read it aloud: "what is this? a cult?"

The men's faces grew menacing, but the woman shouted, "Why not. We've been called far worse."

The men broke into laughter—all but one. Domenico introduced him as Lord Izanagi. The Asian man was clean-shaven and had a sharp chin and cheekbones, made all the sharper by his stern expression. His fine black hair, parted down the middle, hung well past his shoulders. He wore a knee-length, purple silk robe covered in spiderlike red flowers—partially obscured by a black leather breastplate and shoulder pads—draped over dark purple pants and black boots. His hands rested upon the hilts of two katana swords that hung on each hip, but "rested" was not exactly right. His hands seemed poised, ready to unsheathe the blades. The man never blinked, giving Benny the impression that if he closed his eyes, but for a second, a sword would sever his head from his shoulders before he could open them again. So, Benny didn't blink.

"Lord Nergal," said Domenico, continuing the introductions.

A man with shoulder-length flaxen hair, a goatee, and ice-blue eyes dropped his chin but a fraction. He wore no shirt over his smooth muscular chest, just a midnight-blue wraparound skirt of sorts and a black-and-blue sleeveless robe and sandals. He held a spear whose blade glistened with inlaid copper and silver, etched with leaf designs, all somehow far too artistic for a device intended to drive straight through a man and take his life. The freakiest of them all Domenico introduced as Mac-tan-too-cutey, or something, Lord of Mictlan, another no-shirt guy. Black-and-white paint on his chest and face formed the ribs and skull of a skeleton. He wore a headdress of white and green feathers that made him look like a crazed peacock and a square of leather that just barely kept his private parts private. The man gripped the hilt of a broadsword and let out a screech that Benny could not differentiate between a warm welcome and a threat. It seemed like more of a threat.

A black-skinned man sat at a distance on the base of the ogre statue. Long braids swept back from his face, giving him the look of a bulky lion. He opened his mouth and stuck out his tongue, which, incredibly, reached to the bottom of his chin. A sword hung from a sheath strapped to his back.

"Lord Kali," said Domenico. "And Lord Apep."

Lord Apep had a long neck, a long body, and a long face with long nostrils. He could have been eight feet tall if he stood up, but he had his legs tucked up under a black-and-gold kaftan with interwoven patterns of crazy eights. Dark slick hair swept back from his face, illuminating a deep widow's peak, an extremely square jaw and a deeply cleft chin. Benny wondered if he had a nervous disorder the way his head swayed from side to side.

The last man had a shaved head and bronze complexion. He could have been an evil twin of Mr. Clean. Symbols and swirls tattooed in black ran across his forehead, under his left eye, down his left cheek and down his neck. Gold loops pierced his ears. He wore a golden kaftan and a jewel encrusted belt from which dangled a khanjar, its curved blade ready to sing when ripped from its sheath.

"Lord Sharjinn, and this is Lady Inanna," said Domenico. "Benny, besides money, we wield a great deal of power. It's all yours if you join us."

———

Neeve and the others reached the end of the corridor. They climbed the steps. At the foot of the courtyard, they froze, hearing voices. A statue of a two-headed ogre blocked their view.

Before the others could stop her, Neeve crouched low and ran behind the base of the statue. The others followed. An overpowering, foul stench greeted their noses. It was like fish rotting in a sewer.

The group all held their breath, covered their noses, made faces and gasped in search of clean air.

Raj cowered and trembled. She whispered to Chaz and Benny. "That smell. The night my mother . . ."

Benny peeked over the rim. A broad-shouldered man with thick, dark braids sat on the base they had crouched behind. It was him—he stunk!

Antonio and Luigi reached the top of the steps. Upon seeing Neeve and the four youths, Luigi pointed back down the steps and made a circular motion. Antonio's eyes turned to slits as he descended the stairs to circle around.

Luigi snuck up behind Neeve, nudging her with the tip of a gun. "Let's join the reunion, shall we?"

As soon as Neeve stepped around the base of the statue, she spotted Benny. She raced across the paver stones and into his outstretched arms. "Benny! I'm so sorry. This is all my fault."

Benny tried to speak, harder than ever before. He tried to say, "Ma," but even that simple syllable stayed stuck in his throat. "Benny? What's wrong?" Neeve asked before turning menacing eyes on Domenico. "What have you done to him?"

"It's what you have done to him that I cannot abide by," said Domenico, nodding toward the open arch. "And here come the rest. Together at last."

Chaz motored through the archway in his wheelchair. Amir held one hand grip of the chair for direction and a cane that could become a weapon in the other. Antonio followed behind, aiming a gun at Amir's back.

"Let's go, Domenico," said Inanna, keeping her eyes on Chaz. "We have them."

"I quite agree, Inanna." Domenico grabbed Neeve by her arm and jerked her toward the fire pit. "You first."

Benny latched on to Neeve's other arm and yanked, but his grandfather's strength overwhelmed him. Neeve, pulling with all her might, slipped forward toward the fire.

A rumbling thunder drew closer and louder. It surrounded the outer walls, buzzing like mechanical bees in search of someone to sting. All heads turned skyward or scanned the walls.

A motley gang spilled through the archway, gunning their choppers, circling and swarming in both directions. The men and woman of the Warriors and Watchers formed a ring of protection before halting and simultaneously aiming their weapons at the group in the center.

A man with a dark mustache that dripped down each side of his chin, shouted in a Latino accent, "Warriors and Watchers taxi service. You kids need a lift?"

Zuma raised his hands overhead in praise. "Oh, hell yes, we do!"

The skeleton with the peacock headdress squawked in discontent and jabbed his broadsword at the sky.

"Another time, Domenico," said Neeve, trying to pull free of his grasp.

"Not so fast, Princess Neeve." Domenico raised his voice. It boomed louder than anything Benny had ever heard. "Step forth. Do my bidding!"

The ground shook. The creatures on Domenico's fur cape stirred to life. They yipped and snarled and snapped. They dropped to the ground and scurried toward the bikers, who shot at them or tried to knock them away. Shrieks erupted as the ferret-like animals climbed the bikers' legs and torsos and bit at their throats and faces.

The gargoyles with bats' wings that had lined the black road flew into the square and attacked.

The WWs fired volleys of shots at them. Once hit, they shrieked and plummeted to the ground.

The statues cracked like eggshells, giving birth to living beasts that jumped down from their bases and bellowed and snorted and grumbled, ready to kill.

Raj, Kami, Layla and Zuma raced away from the pit, but the lords chased after them.

As Domenico dragged Neeve closer to the fire, she let out a cry of pain.

Benny pulled harder, gaining back some of the distance lost. He stared into his mother's face. Was this the secret she'd kept for so long? No wonder she never said anything—he'd never have believed her! But his mother's face twisted with excruciating horror and disbelief.

Benny had witnessed his mother's fear many times. He'd felt her arms tremble, heard her voice quiver, but the look on her face now depicted terror like he'd never seen before. She had no clue. Her knees buckled.

Domenico yanked her forward. Benny tried in vain to pull her back.

"Who are you? What are you?" Neeve ranted.

A sadistic smile crossed Domenico's face. "I'm your father-in-law. Benny's grandfather. Domenico H. Adez." Domenico met Benny eye to eye. "H. Adez. Get it? Hades. Lord Hades."

Benny struggled to comprehend his grandfather's confession. He had no time to consider his words. His only thought and action entailed setting his mother free.

The two-headed ogre, demented cat, wolf and frog grabbed one biker after the other and tossed them into the air, crushing their bikes underfoot or with heavy weapons. Mosquito woman snapped her mandibles, flashed her big black eyes, and extended her tongue, looking for tasty targets.

The crocodile creature stood guard at the open archway, snapping at those who stepped too close.

The bikers fired upon them, but the bullets had no effect.

Benny's face contorted with effort, but Neeve slipped closer to the pit.

Mike aimed at the archway and floored the gas pedal of Minnie's VW. A tail flopped through the opening. It was too late to hit the brakes. Mike gripped the steering wheel.

Big O let out a warning, "Grab ass and hold tight!"

The little VW careened up the crocodile's back. Mike stared at Big O with an expression that said, quite plainly, "What the hell is this?!"

As the croc bent forward with the weight on its back, the car launched off of its head and into the air. It flew over Raphael and a group of WWs in battle with the two-headed ogre. "Need to go higher," Mike shouted, instinctively punching the gas pedal but realizing that an airborne car had no traction. As they flew over the pit, the fire flared up to incinerate them.

Mike grabbed the steering wheel tighter.

Big O reached for the dashboard to brace himself.

Friday screamed.

Daniel gasped.

Minnie remained stoic.

The car shot through the fiery red-and-orange tongues that singed it on all sides. It emerged and descended, headed straight for the frog creature wielding a spear. The creature seemed quite unprepared for the attack. The car rammed into its chest, knocking it off of its amphibian feet. As it flopped backward, its head crashed through the patio doors and landed just inside the great room. It oozed green blood; its mouth fell open. Quite dead.

The VW came to a rest upon the frog's slick white belly.

Stunned yet pumped with enough adrenaline to take on an army, Mike leaped out of the car and waved his gun in the air, eyes wide and wild, seeking a target.

Big O kicked out his door, hopped out and shoved his seat forward. He helped his wife, a shaken Daniel, and Minnie to slide out. Minnie popped the trunk and grabbed a sword, raising it in the air just in time to thwart the downward thrust of the demented cat's claws, which threatened to split Daniel in half.

Daniel screamed as Big O yanked him out of the way.

"Daniel," said Minnie, as she sliced a curved nail clean off. "I suggest you sit this one out."

Daniel wasted no time. He dove into the backseat of the VW and peered through the back window.

Big O grabbed a shield, a spear and a tire iron from the trunk. He handed the tire iron to Friday. "Let's get these to Chaz and Amir!" They ran into the courtyard.

Chaz and Amir waited, helpless, as a hungry wolf snarled and drooled, stalking toward them.

"Sounds bad. Big and bad," said Amir.

"It gets worse, my friend. Two creepy dudes are headed for us, too."

"Maybe the snarling thing will eat them."

"Not likely," said Chaz. "But our uncles and my aunt are on the way with weapons. If Fido doesn't gobble us up first, we stand a chance. Zuma, I recognize the blonde guy. He's the one who yanked my mother from the tent. I think he's my father."

"The crazy dude?"

Chaz didn't answer.

The crocodile creature at the archway recovered. It shook it's short arms with rage and bared its teeth. It opened its jaws, ready to chomp into Raphael, who threw an instinctive arm of protection upward. As the croc lunged for Raphael, Jalal drove Mike's convertible Mercedes through the archway and up its back.

Jalal yelled, "Hold your heinies!"

Andy chanted.

Kiyoshi put his hands together and bowed his head.

Mona and Cookie squeezed each other's hands.

The weight of the car shoved the crocodile's snout into the ground. Raphael curled into a ball as the drooling jaws fell over him; teeth impaled the ground around him. When Raphael finally peeked, realizing that he was still alive and the croc was dead, he whispered thanks and crawled out of his toothy cage.

Jalal braked. The car came to a stop but teetered on the croc's skull.

From across the courtyard, Mike watched, helpless. "My car!" He let out a sigh of relief as the car stopped rocking and settled itself, intact.

Jalal, Andy, Kiyoshi, Mona and Cookie bolted out of the vehicle. Cookie popped the trunk, which held a cache of weapons.

The bikers fought the enemy with renewed zeal. Shots filled the air. The bat creatures fell like rain.

The guardians grabbed weapons and raced to get them into the hands of the children. The council of lords raced to intercept them.

Minnie shouted a command that reverberated throughout the courtyard, "Children, fight them! Use what you have learned."

Zuma shouted back, "Are you crazy, woman? You fight them!" The skeleton with the peacock headdress ranted gibberish as he raised his sword and came at Zuma. It took a while before reality struck Zuma froze in place and watched his attacker approach. "A skeleton man! Where is my mother, you creepozoid?"

The skeleton slammed his blade down. Zuma jumped back just before it sliced him in two. "Grandma!" Zuma zigged and zagged to avoid the blade.

Lord Apep slithered off of a bench and toward Layla. Layla ran screaming toward her aunt Mona, who was just pulling a scimitar from the trunk of Mike's car.

Raj bolted past Layla to reach Andy, but she spotted Lord Kali lumbering to intercept.

Raj braked hard as Lord Kali jumped between her and her grandfather. "Oh, man. Why did I have to get the stinky one?"

Andy threw a club. It hit Kali in the head. Kali snorted, rubbed his head and turned to find the source of his pain. Andy threw a lathi, a fighting stick with a metal tip, in an arch over Lord Kali's head. It fell into Raj's hands, and she wasted no time in slapping and prodding Kali, who didn't flinch. Instead, Kali slowly reached behind his head and grabbed the hilt of the broadsword strapped to his back and unsheathed it.

"Nana!" yelled Raj. "Lathi not the best choice here! He'll make toothpicks out of this."

Lord Izanagi unsheathed both katanas and swirled them to show off his prowess while staring into Kami's eyes.

Kami blurted, "Sshow off."

As Izanagi swung both blades, attempting to sever her legs, Kami leaped atop a volcanic bench and bounded from one to another. She flipped over Inanna's head and landed in a crouch on the stone courtyard directly in front of Kiyoshi, who bowed as he held out a katana, hilt first. Kami grabbed the hilt and swiped the blade through the air, forcing Izanagi—just running up behind her—back.

Mike pleaded with Minnie, "Benny's not trained for this!"

"Neither are you," said Minnie. "But the fight is here and now. We fight. Or die."

Chapter Twelve

Benny and his grandfather had Neeve in a tug-of-war near the fire pit.

Mike made a move to rush in to help, but he needed a weapon. He spotted the frog's spear lying in the creature's dead amphibious hand.

The cat swiped its claws at Mike to stop him, but Minnie's sword sliced through the air to intercept, severing another pair of nails. Mike dove for the weapon, grabbed its shaft, and sprang to his feet.

The cat's claws gashed through the roof of the VW, narrowly missing Daniel who screamed aloud.

Mike stabbed at the cat, sinking the blade into its paw. The cat hissed.

This gave Minnie an opportunity. She stabbed the beast in the heart, and it sunk to its death with a final shrill cry.

Daniel waved his hand through a narrow opening where the back window used to be, signaling that he was okay.

Mike ripped off his jacket and ran for the pit, but the two-headed ogre with pink pig-like faces intercepted. The beast raised its shield to stop Mike's jabs, while it returned jabs of its own, which Mike dodged.

Minnie scaled the roof of her dilapidated car and swung her blade, which bit into the ogre's shield.

Zuma reached his grandmother, who was dragging a heavy sword behind her. Upon sight of Zuma, she dropped it. Out of breath, she said, "Take it."

"Grandma, I can barely swing that thing in the gym."

"Try. I know you can do it," Cookie urged.

"Are you kidding? It's not like you're asking me to finish my spinach." He had no sooner spoken these words than the wacky skeleton guy flung his sword through the air.

"Watch out!" Zuma shouted as he ducked.

Cookie dove to the ground. The blade sailed toward Cookie.

Zuma dropped to his knees, grabbed the sword, and with both hands he swung the blade. He knocked the tip of the enemy's sword away just enough that it stabbed the ground, impaling Cookie's dream catcher vest but leaving her unharmed.

As the peacock gripped the hilt of his weapon and wrested it from the ground, Zuma jumped to his feet and raised his sword. "Prepare to get poked, plucked, pinioned and pierced!"

The skeleton man spouted jibberish, but he was clearly pleased with himself.

Zuma helped Cookie to her feet. "Get out o' here, Grandma."

Cookie ran.

Zuma swung his broadsword.

The peacock-man ducked. The blade ripped across his headdress, severing the green and white feathers, which rained down around his shoulders. The crazed man blathered more gibberish and swung wildly.

"Bring it on, you peacock freak," said Zuma, mocking his

opponent by squawking gibberish and dancing around, flailing awkward arms and legs. "Caw, caw, zeep, ra!"

Not far off, Kali swung his heavy sword and severed Raj's lathi with a single blow.

"Rajani!" Andy threw a sword in her direction. It spun through the air and stabbed the ground at her feet.

Raj grabbed the hilt and raised the blade just in time to thwart Kali's downward blow.

"Thanks, Nana!" Raj flipped in the air to avoid Kali's next swipe across her legs. As Kali's blade swept beneath her feet and her opponent twisted away from her, Raj wasted no time, already seeing a path before her on his body. She stepped atop Kali's bent knee, onto his forearm, then shoulder. She smashed the hilt of her sword into the top of his head, flipped off of his shoulders, twisted midair and landed just behind the lumbering hulk, poking him in the buttocks. "Hey, I'm over here. You're big but slow, stinky."

Kali bellowed and grabbed his butt. On slow, heavy feet, he turned and swung his sword so fast it caught Raj off guard. She ducked to avoid it. His blade met hers with greater force, a force she could not withstand for long. He may be slower, but he was far stronger.

Layla fell into Mona's arms.

Mona pushed her back and held out the scimitar. "Here, take it. I have to help the wounded."

"I'll help you," offered Andy, taking her medical bag from the trunk.

Layla shook her head, refusing the scimitar. She slunk down next to the back wheel of Mike's car. She folded her arms over her knees. "I'm staying here. Go."

Mona hesitated, but people needed help. She and Andy bolted away.

Izanagi crouched into a fighting stance before Kami, who pursed her lips, narrowed her gray eyes and poised her katana, ready to strike back.

"You are no match for me, little girl."

Kami read his lips and smiled. "Then why do you need two weaponsh, and I only one to defeat you?"

Her enemy's face erupted in wrath. He swung his blades, as if to cut her in quarters.

Kami sprang up over his blades and landed a double kick to his shoulder and head. As her opponent's head turned away but for a second, she landed on her feet, scooped her blade under one of his and whipped it out of his hand with a blind rage that erupted within her and gave her strength she didn't know she had. Her nostrils flared. "Need a third weapon, little boy in the red-flowered jacket?"

Neither of their eyes blinked as they eyed each miniscule movement of the other, studying strength, agility, ability, courage.

"Ahhh, you like red spider lilies. Me, too. Beautiful and poisonous. I'll send some for your funeral, little girl who talks funny."

Kami's face flushed red. She swung her katana, fueled by unstoppable rage, and the two danced, blade to blade, past Lord Sharjinn, who approached Amir and Chaz.

Amir tilted his head from side to side, listening. He let go of Chaz's wheelchair and stepped away.

"Amir, come back," urged Chaz, seeing the man approach.

"Dude, I'm saving your life," said Amir. "Thank me later."

"This is no time to joke around!" shouted Chaz.

Amir tilted his head this way and that. "Shut up, Chaz. I need my ears, not my eyes, or I will be dead."

A bald man with tattoos on his head and half of his face stood before Amir. "You can't see? It's not a fair fight. But then, who cares? I'm not one for fighting fair anyhow."

"I figured," said Amir. "I don't suppose you'd shake my hand first. You know, make it sportsmanlike."

"When you feel my hand, it will be around your scrawny throat, squeezing the life out of you."

"Good tip." Amir swiped his cane through the air, smacking his opponent's legs, arms, and head before Sharjinn ripped it from his hands.

Amir slid one foot forward, one back, and he raised his hands into position. "You're ugly! Ug-ly! I can hear it in your voice."

Lord Sharjinn rushed forward, gripping Amir by the throat, but Amir stood ready. He gripped the brute's arm, felt his weight and bulk, and twisted his body to swing him off balance, using the man's own weight against him. Amir flipped him onto his stomach, crashed his knee into the small of his back, and twisted his arm in the air in a way that forbid the man from making another move against him.

Lord Sharjinn grimaced. "You think you can hold me?"

Amir twisted his opponent's arm, and Sharjinn grimaced again. "Pretty sure. Another quarter inch and your shoulder pops out of the socket."

Wielding his spear, fair-haired, blue-robed, bare-chested Lord Nergal approached Chaz, just as Friday and Big O ran up behind his wheelchair and handed him the spear and shield. Friday handed the tire iron to Big O.

Nergal stroked his goatee. "Step away from him!"

"Back off, blondie," said Friday.

"Or I'll remount your pretty face. Ya!" added Big O.

"Nicely put, honey," said Friday.

Nergal jettisoned his spear at Chaz's chest. Friday screamed.

Chaz raised his shield a second's breath before the spear sank into his heart. It hit the heart of the shield instead. "Missed. My turn." Chaz tossed the shield aside, raised his spear and threw it.

Lord Nergal knocked it from the air with one hand. "My turn." He nodded to the snarling wolf that had snuck up behind Friday.

The wolf bit into Friday's jacket and lifted her into the air, shaking her from side to side. She screamed and kicked her boots in the air as the beast trotted away.

Big O dropped the tire iron in Chaz's lap, grabbed a fistful of the wolf's neck hair and hurled himself onto its back. As the wolf trotted away, Big O pounded its neck with his fists and clenched his muscular thighs against its ribs to hold on for the ride of his life.

Lord Nergal tried to approach Chaz, but each time he came too close, Chaz swung the tire iron, keeping him at bay. "Fight me. No weapons. Just the strength of your arms against mine."

After several swings, Lord Nergal stepped in, caught the tire iron and ripped it from Chaz's grip. He grabbed Chaz by the neck and tipped the chair over in his attempt to strangle him. Chaz sprawled to the ground but managed to grip Nergal by the neck, too. As they rolled, they squeezed, neither willing to let go of the other. "I know who you are," said Chaz. "My mother's crazy husband. My father."

Nergal squeezed Chaz's neck. "No son of mine would be so pathetic."

Layla cowered, eyes closed, until a shadow blocked the sun. She glanced up, seeing a long-faced man before her in a cowl-necked kaftan of black and gold. Lord Apep. His head swayed side to side.

"Come," he commanded. "I'll keep you ssssafe." His yellow eyes turned to slits. She felt sleepy. She reached around her for the scimitar.

Lord Apep arched his body into a curve and lowered his head until he came face-to-face with Layla. She met his gaze. Apep's head swayed from side to side; his eyes of black and gold turned from slits to swirls. His snake-like tail swung forward. It caressed Layla's leg and blocked her escape.

Layla's lips parted. Her eyes grew heavy. She felt the grip of the scimitar and clasped it in her hand. In a single chopping motion, she raised the curved blade and swung it downward, lopping off the tip of Apep's tail.

Lord Apep hissed, withdrew his head, and bared his fangs; his forked tongue whipped the air.

Layla scampered to her feet and ran. The thing slithered after her, flicking its tongue.

"You die too easily," said Lord Nergal, squeezing the life out of Chaz, who struggled to break the man's grasp but couldn't. Chaz's hands slipped from Nergal's neck. His eyelids lowered.

Hearing those words, Amir released Sharjinn, and he flung himself in the direction of Nergal's voice. He ripped the man off of Chaz's chest. They both rolled to the ground onto their backs.

A weight dropped on Amir's chest with such force that it knocked the wind out of him.

"Did you think you held me?" scolded Lord Sharjinn. "I let you hold me to test you. In saving your friend, you released your enemy. Poor choice—a weak man's choice."

Jalal twirled and leaped into the air. As he floated down on Sharjinn's head, his white circular skirt flared out and draped over Sharjinn's face, blinding him and making it a fair fight. "Strike!" Jalal commanded Amir, just as they had done in practice.

Amir's fist shot forward. With lightning speed, it rammed into Lord Sharjinn's neck. Sharjinn flung Jalal away and struggled to his feet, gasping.

Benny couldn't hold Neeve much longer. He lost ground fast. He could feel the heat of the fire pit. Neeve screamed as they reached the edge of it.

Mike heard this. He had to get there, and fast. As the two-headed ogre lunged forward with the dagger, Mike grimaced and jabbed the spear into one neck. That head drooped, as did half of its body. The ogre fell to the ground, half dead. The living pig face grunted displeasure; its arm and leg flailed the air. It was as unable to rise up and fight as a bug on its back.

Minnie rushed to Mike's side. "Help Neeve! I'll finish him."

Mike ran past the crocodile as it chomped into a biker. He would have stopped to help, but WWs rushed over. Mike faced forward unprepared—the mosquito woman stood in his path. She stabbed at him with her hollow tongue, which shot forward approaching his chest. At the very moment the tip of her tongue should have impaled Mike's heart, a WW biker woman slashed the mosquito's leg. The monster whipped her head around and unleashed her tongue at her new attacker. Mike veered toward the woman to help, but it was too late. The mosquito's tongue plunged into the woman's chest, sucked out the victim's blood and tossed the lifeless body aside.

Neeve screamed, as one foot slipped into the pit.

Mike leaped into action.

Hades's foot entered the fire pit, but the fire didn't seem to hurt him or Neeve. Mike grabbed Neeve around the waist. Benny and Mike pulled together.

Domenico head-butted Mike. Mike's head reeled back, but he didn't let go. Benny howled and gripped Neeve's arm tighter, pulling her toward him.

Hades's foot stepped out of the pit as Benny gained ground. Benny tried to speak. A sound emerged: "Agh." He tried again. "I . . ."

Hades bellowed, "Return!" The sound echoed in the court-yard. His eyes glowed red, and he yanked Neeve off her feet with a force so strong, they plunged into the fire.

Mike and Benny hit the deck, grabbing on to Neeve's wrists.

Hades dangled, his arms wrapped around Neeve's waist. Mike tried to pull his face away from the fire, until he realized it didn't burn.

Neeve pleaded, "Mike, let me go. Save Benny!" She stopped fighting to hold on and opened her hands to let go.

Mike shouted, "No!" Neeve began to slip from his grasp.

Benny let out a guttural roar.

All at once, the flames disappeared and a black void took its place.

Benny struggled to speak. He struggled to hold on.

Neeve's body dangled. Her eyes seemed locked on Benny's and a faint smile crossed her face as she slipped from Mike's grasp. Benny held tighter, his eyes locked on Hades' who smiled broadly.

Mike tried to re-grasp Neeve's hand, but she would not offer it.

Apep had chased Layla in a circle back to Mike's car. Layla reached in the trunk and grabbed her bow and arrow. She panted. Her hand trembled as she loaded the arrow.

Apep came at her, ready to strike. He froze the moment Layla drew back the bow. Layla's chest heaved. Apep smirked. He brought his face up to the tip of the arrow. "Shhhhoot."

Layla heard a scream. Her eyes turned. The wolf tossed Friday into the air and opened its mouth to receive her. Layla redirected her aim and let the arrow fly.

The arrow hit the wolf in the chest, and the beast dropped to its death. Big O rolled off its back as Kiyoshi and Jalal caught Friday's fall.

Layla awaited her fate, facing Lord Apep as she lowered her bow. To her surprise, Lord Apep slithered away and dove into the pit.

Lord Nergal released Chaz. "We'll meet again. Be better prepared." He, too, raced toward the pit, leaving Chaz weak, coughing and wheezing.

With a swipe of his sword, Izanagi disarmed Kami and rushed in. He pointed the tip of his sword at her throat.

Kami seethed but did not move a muscle. Their eyes locked on one another's, both cold and gray and full of rage. Izanagi bolted away, yelling as he headed toward the pit, "Kali! Come!" Kali disarmed Raj and knocked her to the ground. As she sprawled and tumbled, he lumbered toward the pit and jumped in.

The crazed peacock blasted Zuma—who struggled to raise his sword one more time—with a final blather of gibberish, before he, too, ran toward the pit.

"Oh, thank God!" Zuma dropped the sword, fell to his knees, and onto his back. "Takin' five, guys."

"Benny, let go!" Neeve pleaded.

Benny peered into his mother's eyes. He leaned over the pit, prepared to go with her. He would not let her go. Ever again. But as he tipped forward to follow her, Mike grabbed his shoulders and yanked him back. The force pulled her from his grasp.

"Ma!" shouted Benny, uttering the first word that finally broke his mute silence. He hugged the rim and watched them fall, acceptance on her face, sinister satisfaction on his.

Before Benny could make another dive and go after her, Mike threw him aside like a sack of grain. Benny sprang to his feet and swung wild fists at Mike, who blocked his entry to the pit.

Mike swung, too, landing blows in Benny's sore spots, whatever it took to keep Benny away.

The sheared peacock leaped into the pit and disappeared.

Benny raged. He clenched his fists, let out a feral howl and charged Mike, prepared to push him, too, into the pit, if that's what it took to reach his mother.

Just reaching the pit, Minnie shouted, "Benny! No!"

Inanna jumped in the void. The pit closed just as Benny shoved

Mike backward. Mike grimaced as he smashed into the volcanic rocks. Benny fell on top of him. The ground began to roll and rumble. Mike grabbed Benny's shoulders and rolled both of them off the volcanic rocks a second before a rocket-sized column of flame shot into the air from the pit. This fire burned red hot.

"Get out! Everyone!" shouted Minnie.

The bikers started the engines of the bikes that still functioned. Others piled unconscious friends over them before hopping on and peeling out through the archway.

Friday and Big O helped set Chaz on the back of Raphael's bike. As Raphael peeled away, Friday and Big O flanked Amir, grabbed his hands and raced away on foot.

Benny knelt beside the roaring fire and shoved his hand into it. It burned his flesh, flesh that had already been burned by the explosion days earlier. He yanked his hand back.

Mike tried to pull him away, but Benny threw his hands off.

Minnie dropped beside Benny. "Get the others to safety, Mike. I'll stay with Benny."

He hesitated.

"Go!" she commanded.

Mike raced to help free Daniel, who was trapped in the VW with mosquito woman standing over it, sticking her tongue into every open crevasse, trying to suck the blood out of one more victim. Mosquito woman ran her tongue over the driver's side door, gripped the handle and ripped the door away, exposing Daniel.

"Hey," called Mike, to get her attention. "O negative. Right here, lady. Universal donor. I know you want it!" He spotted a sword, lying beside Zuma. "Hang on, Daniel! I'm coming!"

The mosquito woman scurried toward Mike on her bent bug legs, one wounded leg dragging the ground behind her. She zapped and snapped her tongue as the distance closed, as if in practice or already tasting her next meal. Mike ran toward her, tucked and rolled. He gripped the sword, just as mosquito woman came within feeding distance. She hurled her tongue at Mike's chest, but he rolled away. It just missed him.

Mike had one shot. He dove beneath the creature and raised the hilt of his sword. As she fired her tongue at where he'd been seconds earlier, he impaled her, shoving the blade upward into her heart, if she had one. She crumpled down, driving the blade clear through her back. As she collapsed, Mike rolled out from under her, watching her black shiny eyes grow dull; her head fell to her chest and her wings sagged.

Daniel had already wriggled out of the VW. He rushed to help Mike to his feet. "What about Benny?"

"Minnie's got him. Let's get out of here." They ran toward the archway.

Benny stuck his hand in the fire and burned it again.

Minnie softened her voice. "You can't help her that way."

"I'm going after her."

"This entrance is closed. But there are others."

Benny bore his eyes into hers. "Entrance? To where?"

"To the underworlds." Minnie put a gentle hand over his reddened flesh. "There isn't time. Come, Benny." She rose to her feet. "I promise. You'll have the answers you seek."

An explosion rocked the courtyard. The fire pit sank into the ground, pulling everything around it down too. Benny jumped to his feet and backed away, watching Daniel and Mike exit the archway. Only he and Minnie were left.

"This way!" shouted Minnie, already racing toward a downed black Harley. She and Benny tipped it up, and Minnie hopped in the driver's seat. Benny hopped on the back.

"Hold tight!" said Minnie, revving the engine. "Time to twist the wick and rip it up!"

"Twist what?" asked Benny, as Minnie turned the throttle and the bike shot forward toward the archway. The fire pit exploded behind them with such force the volcanic benches blew apart and flames and debris shot into the sky and rained down around them.

Minnie dodged the debris, and Benny held on with an iron grip.

They bolted past Mike's convertible, which still rested atop the dragon that had already sunk into the ground, and now the car sank, too. The ground beneath them cracked and split and rumbled. Minnie dodged newly opened fissures.

Rising to his feet and standing in the archway, the butler interposed and wielded a sword that seemed to be waiting for them.

"Keep straight!" said Benny, as he gripped the seat frame and leaned over until he could touch the ground. He had one chance to get a grip on the hilt of a katana, resting on the belly of a fallen fighter. He reached out, scooped the hilt into his hand and swept it into the air, pulling himself upright at the same time. "Pass him on the left."

A fissure opened up and raced toward the back tire, threatening to swallow them whole. Minnie hit the gas so hard the front tire left the ground before slamming back to earth. The bike accelerated.

As they approached the butler, Minnie ducked. The sword swept over her head. Benny swung the katana with such force that the moment it struck the opposing sword, it spun the butler off of his feet and knocked the blade from his hand. The archway split and crumbled down, just missing them and burying the butler as they shot out of the courtyard and into the open expanse.

Minnie and Benny raced to the front of the crumbling castle and down the black road amid screams and shouts and people running and tumbling down the hill. Sirens wailed in the distance. At the bottom of the hill, Minnie pulled a Mad Max spin on the front tire before setting the bike down and turning off the engine. "Good work, Tail Gunner."

Getting off the bike, Benny glanced over his shoulder. The castle sank into a pit of flames until no longer visible. The sky, a swirl of red and yellow and black, formed a vortex over the site. It sucked in the forest fog and whipped and lashed the survivors, threatening to pull them into it. Without needing instructions, everyone hit the ground, letting the evil winds wash over them.

When the winds calmed and the vortex grew to its widest, hovering over the castle, they rose to their feet. The swirling tornado was sucked down into the pit and disappeared.

The new sky was clear blue. Birds chirped.

"My car," Mike whined.

"You must have insurance," Minnie scolded. "I lost my car, too."

"That's not the point," said Mike. "*That* little baby was my first convertible Mercedes."

Daniel put a hand on his shoulder. "Women don't get it, Mike. But I do. I feel the same way about my station wagon. Oh, we've had some adventures, I can tell you."

"The WWs will get you home," assured Raphael.

Sirens blared, growing nearer. A row of black cars poured through the tree line like army ants on a mission. They braked just behind the crowd. Men in black suits jumped out of their vehicles and aimed their guns at the bikers. A man with a bullhorn shouted, "FBI. Drop your weapons! Hit the ground. Face down!"

"Oh, good heavens," said Daniel. "Not again! I'll tell them everything."

Minnie whispered, "Daniel, you can't tell them what you saw."

"I will," he retorted. "I'll be vindicated. My reputation restored."

Raphael sneered, "You'll be carted off to the looney bin, amigo. The Fibbing Boobs and Idiots are the kings of cover up. Remember JFK?"

Mike raised his arms and took a step forward as those around him hit the ground. "I'm FBI agent Mike Salvatore. My badge is in my pocket."

"Help us, Daniel," Minnie implored. "We need you."

"Who is we?" blurted Benny.

"You'll find out soon enough," said Minnie. "I'm so glad your voice is back."

Chapter Thirteen

Back at One World Academy, Minnie gathered the weary group in a room that she normally kept locked. She pressed a button on a remote. A wall panel lifted, revealing a television screen. She punched another button, and the screen lit up.

Zuma whined, "No way! All this time, we had television?"

"Totes unfair," added Raj.

"Hush," scolded Minnie.

"BREAKING NEWS" flashed across the bottom of the screen. Over the shoulder of a reporter, fire trucks maneuvered into place and arcs of water shot across roaring flames. Clouds of black smoke billowed into the blue sky. "As you can see behind me, the home of Domenico H. Adez has been engulfed. Nothing is left. Investigators suspect arson, even high explosives, given the damage. The possibility of mob retaliation has not been ruled out. The FBI is here, as Mr. Adez has been under investigation for illegal activities for some time. As you may remember, this home was the site of a 2002 FBI raid, after which Mr. Adez's son, Romero, disappeared. Authorities suspect—" Minnie turned off the television.

Daniel broached the first question. "You said this morning that you had discredited me because I was too close to the truth. The seismic events?"

"At very precise locations, according to your research," added Minnie. "We did not need the scrutiny of the scientific community."

"The caves and other entrances? But Domenico's place isn't a known entry point," argued Daniel.

"Yes," said Minnie. "That's because—"

"Wait," said Benny. "You said the entrance was closed at Domenico's. You said it was an entrance to the underworld."

Before Minnie could respond, Daniel fell into a seat, grabbed his kerchief and daubed his brow. "I was right? I was right all along? But that's crazy."

Amir burst out laughing. "Is anyone buying this crapola?"

Chaz reached over and put a hand on his shoulder. "Amir, if you saw what we saw today, you'd believe anything."

"Well I saw it, and I still don't believe it," argued Mike. "Dr. Pallas—"

"Call me Minnie, for Pete's sake. Battling underworld creatures should give us some familiarity."

"Everyone shut up and let her speak!" said Benny.

The room quieted.

"Thank you, Benny," said Minnie. "In short, there has always been a balance of good and evil in the world. The scales tip one way, then the other, but balance is preserved. Until now. The lords of the underworlds have done the unthinkable. They've joined forces. When they were busy fighting good but also fighting each other, balance stayed in check. But together? They have one purpose—to create seven gates, exits to the underworld, and to tip the scales. Oh, heavens, who am I kidding? If that happens, there are no scales left. They will rule the earth. It's the oldest prophecy in the world, but even the gods didn't see it coming. Or saw it coming and could do nothing to stop it. All we know is that the seven gates have either been built or are under construction and that there is a key for each: capable of opening them or keeping them locked. One underworld at a time, we have to find those keys. I mean, you have to find them."

"Minnie," said Benny. "What prophesy?"

"Various cultures around the globe have predicted the end of the world, the day where chaos and evil rule on earth. Daniel, name a few please. Only a few. We've no time to waste."

Daniel cleared his throat. "Well, um, sure. The Norse called it Ragnarok; the Hindus, the age of Kali Yuga; the Christians, the Apocalypse; the Aztecs—"

"Thank you, Daniel."

"The Blue Star Katsina," added Zuma.

"Quite right," confirmed Daniel.

Minnie continued, "There are many immortals—some good, some not. Most of the evil ones have, at one time or another, tried to rule the earth, and we fought them, pushed them back. Humans fought, too. We never imagined or truly believed they would work together—until today."

Kami asked, "What do they want with ush?"

"Other than to kill us," added Zuma.

"If they wanted you dead," snapped Minnie. "You'd be dead."

Kiyoshi removed his red cap. "Minnie came to each of us the night your mothers disappeared in what we thought was a dream. She spoke of the danger you were in and instructed us to bring you here. I bolted upright in the dead of night. I didn't want to believe it, but, Miko was gone, and I knew it was real. We hoped this day would never come. Until today, I'm not sure I believed it ever would."

Mona added, "We decided that it was our job to give you

some good memories of childhood, for as long as possible. When we arrived here, I heard the same story from the others, of how our loved ones disappeared . . . But still, I had doubts. Until today."

Minnie defended the guardians. "Your watchers only knew what I chose to tell them. I take full responsibility."

"Watchers?" asked Benny.

"Daniel, tell them about watchers," instructed Minnie.

Daniel stuttered. "Watcher? I don't have any idea—"

"Oh, yes you do. Watcher—go on, explain."

"You can't mean . . ." Daniel stuttered.

Minnie glared at him with an "of course I mean just that" expression.

"I don't understand the significance," said Daniel, "but she's referring . . . well, the term is used to describe . . . Minnie?"

"Tell them," she admonished. "They won't believe it coming from me."

Daniel huffed. "She refers to several world mythologies that record stories of immortals mingling with mortals and producing earthly heirs. Watchers are human. But they have insight or some other ability stemming from their immortal ancestors. They were the heroes of the past. Am I a watcher?"

"No, Daniel," said Minnie. "Neither is Mike. Although you should be. Both of you. You see, Watchers have a sixth sense about things. Nothing blatant. A few have gifts that make them strange to others. They typically feel a connection to the gods, a strong bond that they can't explain. Some ancients called them 'star people.' They've been depicted in ancient cave art. Others thought of them as divine in their own right, demi-gods, but they are more human than immortal. They live. They die. They pass on the connection through their genes."

"Our mothers are watchers?" asked Chaz.

Minnie beamed, "Yes. And your guardians. Not that it will help you any. As I said, watchers are mostly human."

"Let's stick to the facts. *Exactly* who are we fighting?" asked Mike.

Benny answered, "Domenico H. Adez, for one. He told my mother and I that H. Adez stood for Hades—as in Lord Hades."

"H. Adez is Hades," said Zuma. "Can't he spell?"

Minnie snapped. "Oh, please, you young people have names spelled b-x-y, and you say 'Hi, my name is Becky.' And don't get me started on the lingo that Raj uses that isn't even close to proper English."

Raj rolled her eyes. "Chillax, M. This is totes awks. Spill the deets."

"Daniel? Can you translate that please?" asked Minnie.

"Sorry," said Daniel. "I speak several languages. Adolescent isn't one of them."

"She said to chill," said Amir. "That this is totally awkward."

"And to give us the details," added Layla.

Minnie huffed. "How you young people have slaughtered Greek and Latin is unforgivable."

"The deets," repeated Mike. "What do you know?"

Minnie raised her chin, not in a haughty manner but a must-do-the-right-thing-even-if-difficult one. "The days following your mother's disappearance, your watchers all brought you here, except for Neeve. She's not a watcher. I located her in New York—caught her as she left the FBI office. She was going to stay with Mike temporarily—until I offered her a safe haven here. I convinced her that no one would ever find her and Benny. A year later, she wanted to leave. I tried to stop her. I . . . I made a mistake. I told her the truth about Domenico. She said I was crazy."

"Hold on. Back it up," said Mike. "You're saying Hades, as in Greek mythology underworld Hades? You're saying he's alive and well and living in upstate New York?"

"Well, not anymore," quipped Minnie.

"Who's Inanna," asked Chaz.

"She flirted with my man," added Amir.

Raj rolled her eyes. "That figures. We're fighting, he's flirting." Chaz and the others ignored the jab.

"Did you say Inanna?" stammered Daniel. "She's also knows as Ishtar, the Babylonian goddess of love."

"Dude! Score!" said Amir, holding a hand in the air for a high five which never came, so he sheepishly put it down.

"Be careful, Chaz. When King Gilgamesh spurned her advances, she convinced her father, the sky god, to release the Bull of Heaven to destroy the crops and kill humankind. But Gilgamesh and his friend, Enkidu, fought and killed the bull, which led to Enkidu's slow and extremely painful demise."

Daniel rose to his feet, as if thunder and lighting had propelled him to stand. "The others. Oh, heavens. The others! They're real!"

"What's he stammering about?" asked Benny.

"He figured it out," said Minnie. "The other Lords. Tell them, Daniel. Tell them who they are fighting."

Daniel waved a hand, as if to calm his racing brain enough to pose answers. "Kami . . .Kami fought Lord Izanagi. He and his wife are creators, but his wife, Izanami, died, and became a hag who dwells in Yomi, the World of Darkness. Raj fought Kali, the Lord of Kali Yuga, which is the last of the four yuga stages and the one called the Dark Age of Destruction; Layla fought Lord Apep, the Lord of Chaos in Egyptian mythology; Chaz fought Lord Nergal, the lord of disease and death in ancient Mesopotamia, and Amir fought Lord Sharjinn, the name simply means Black Jinn or Black spirit, one who rules darkness, and Zuma fought Mictlantecuhtli—"

"Wow! Time out—name change," said Zuma. "He shall now be known to all as MacNutty. Continue."

Daniel nodded, "Good idea. It's a mouthful. MacNutty is the lord of Mictlan, the Aztec land of the dead."

Benny jumped to his feet. "We're wasting time! I'm going after my mother! Where's the first entrance?"

Minnie shouted with indignation. "Foolish boy! This isn't about Neeve!" Her eyes roamed to each of the children. "It isn't about any of your mothers—this is a battle for the human race. If those gates open, there will be nothing left. No mothers. No place to call home. No world as you know it!"

Benny confronted her. "You act like you know a great deal, but you don't seem to know much at all!"

Minnie shot back. "It's not like the lords of the underworld are going to invite us to the table and divulge their plans to us, now is it? Our spies only recently informed us of the collusion and told us about the gates and keys."

"What does this have to do with us? They're the watchers," Zuma pointed. "Not us. And—no offense, Grandma—but her best talent is crochet."

Minnie searched his face and the others, too. "It's you, children, who must locate the seven keys and keep those gates locked. They are your watchers, but you—well, you are the warriors."

"Okay. Now I'm with Amir," said Chaz. "Are you missing the fact that I'm sitting in a wheelchair? Seems kinda lame anyone would choose us instead of heavyweight boxers or the guys and gals in Special Forces."

"Normally, Minnie," said Amir, "I'd be grateful for such an honor. And as you know, I refuse to let the fact that I'm totally *blind* interfere with my life. I don't use it as an excuse to duck gym like Zuma or Layla—sorry dudes."

"No offense, bro," said Zuma.

Layla shot him a thumbs up. "None."

"But," continued Amir, "sending a blind boy into the under-world to search for a missing anything? You might as well send me for an afternoon stroll through a minefield to look for an elephant. Same result."

"Why us?" asked Benny. "Hades said he's my grandfather. Is he?"

"You were right, Benny," said Minnie. "We don't have all of the answers. But yes, we believe that might be true. What we don't know is the origin of your father—in other words, who is your grandmother?"

"I can't do this," cried Layla. "I'm not tough like these guys." She yelled at Minnie and at the watchers. "You knew! You didn't tell us! You should have told us. I'm not going."

"Blame me, Layla, if you must blame someone. And the other immortals, who tried to stop this. We had hoped to keep it a battle between us and leave humans out of it. But fate dragged you in—every last one of you!"

"I'll go," said Benny. "Show me where to find the first entrance. Show me now."

Minnie laughed. "After that appalling display this morning? Not one of you worked together. No teamwork. And you, Benny, other than a video game, what preparations have you made? You'll train first. All of you. And if, in the end, you stay behind, that is your decision to make. No one will force any of you to accept this quest. You must choose for yourselves. You'll do that much, won't you, Layla? Train with your friends?"

Layla shrugged her shoulders.

Benny put a hand on Layla's shoulder. "Help me train, Layla. You're leagues ahead of me."

"Okay," she said in a barely audible whisper.

Benny addressed Minnie, "We need to know what you know. All of it."

"If the immortals had all of the answers," Minnie scoffed, "Hera would not have needed hundred-eyed Argus to keep a watchful eye on Zeus's passion for Io. The truth is I don't know who you are any more than I know why your mothers were taken. I do know, however, that it doesn't matter. The only thing that matters is that you train your best and try your hardest. No matter who you are—you're this world's only hope. No more questions." Minnie headed to the door. "We'll eat lunch. Training begins precisely at one in the gymnasium."

"But it's Saturday," whined Zuma.

Minnie continued walking. "Evil does not wait for Monday. Neither shall we."

Chapter Fourteen

As Minnie, Daniel, and the watchers waited in the gymnasium for the children to arrive, Minnie kept an eye on the clock. Her lips became more rigid and her eyes narrower with each minute that ticked past one o'clock, signaling a further laxness in punctuality.

At twenty past, the group strolled in, but they were not wearing the white-and-gold gym attire assigned to them.

Benny led the pack in baggy shorts and his EpicEvil tee shirt. Amir wore a fashionable tennis ensemble of tan, cream and turquoise; Zuma, baggy brown shorts and an extra-large tee shirt; Chaz, navy blue running pants and a tight white tank top from which his muscles bulged. And if that wasn't bad enough, the girls were scandalous.

Kami strode forward wearing cheetah-print leggings and a matching strappy bra top; Raj, similar apparel, except blooming in neon flowers; and Layla, a red, rather low-cut, backless, hooded, shorts onesie.

"Where are your uniforms?" commanded Minnie. "Go change."

Benny spoke for the group. "We decided that if we're training to save the world—"

"Or to die," said Amir. "As in my case."

"We will wear whatever we pleashe," said Kami.

"And we want dessert with every meal," said Zuma.

"And we want out of here," said Raj.

"Once a week," added Chaz.

"No," said Minnie. "It's not safe outside the compound."

"You're kidding," said Benny. "Safe? Does that even apply to us anymore?"

Minnie huffed, "Fine. Wear what you want, and I'll make *some* food allowances. Dessert with lunch only, but no sharing," she eyed Zuma as she said it. "The rest I have to think about. Now, can we begin?"

Benny checked for a consensus among them. All agreed.

"Quite frankly," said Minnie, eyeing Benny's attire, "I'm not sure at all of your lifespan either. These children have studied martial arts, languages, mythology and played games to sharpen their mental and physical acuity for years." She shook her head and added a tsk-tsk. "Let's start with a demonstration. Raj, parkour."

Raj nodded. She raced across the room, jumped atop the balance beam, flipped and ran to the end of it, dove in the air, caught the lower of the uneven parallel bars, flipped this way and that, from high to low, low to high, dismounted, and raced to the wall picking up speed. She bounced off one ledge, hopped to the next, and another, working her way upward, higher and higher, crossing midair beams with flips and dips, and flying from rope to rope, and across wires until she reached the dome roof, where she stood upon a ledge, breathing hard.

Benny now understood why there were platforms, rocks, ropes and beams all around the room.

Raj called down, "Come on up, Benny. The air is fine." Before waiting for an answer, she grabbed a rope and swung down, rope to rope, until she reached the floor.

"You should see her outside in the trees," added Zuma. "I swear, she's part monkey. Kami, too."

Minnie explained for Benny's benefit. "Kami is adept with the katana, a sword, but she is also an expert with mixed martial arts, or *vale tudo*—anything goes—so don't sneak up on her or make her angry. Amir is proficient in jujitsu, close battle, where he uses an opponent's body weight against him. Layla is an expert with the bow."

Minnie waved a hand toward the weapons lining the walls. "They've all learned to use the lathi—or bamboo stick—axes, maces, javelins, discs, spears; they even skydive and rock climb—"

"Mind you, Benny, we didn't know we were training to save the world," interrupted Chaz.

Zuma added, "We thought—silly us—this is just PE. That other kids out there do the same thing."

Benny glanced at Layla. "No wonder you worked so hard to dodge PE."

"Right?" said Layla.

"Raj, you're amazing," said Benny, genuinely impressed.

"Thanks." Raj beamed.

Kami smirked. "Raj ish amazing, Benny. The last time we went shkydiving, she almost went bonsai. I shwore I'd tell if she did."

Minnie scowled, "What's that? What did you do this time, Raj?"

Chaz, Zuma and Layla sent Kami a warning glare, which she didn't heed it.

"No way, girl!" said Amir. "You were going to throw the parachute out of the plane and jump after it?" As he sat there with a full grin on his face and his hand in the air, waiting for a high five, he noticed an overwhelming silence. "I wasn't supposed to say that, was I?"

"She hash a death wish," scowled Kami.

"Actually, Kami threatened to throw my chute out and make me chase after it," corrected Raj. "Get it straight, Little Miss two-for-three." Raj held up two fingers.

Kami's face burned bright red.

"What does that mean? Two-for-three?" demanded Minnie. She poked Amir's arm.

"My lips are sealed," said Amir.

"Never mind, Minnie. Just an inside joke," said Layla.

Minnie was unrelenting. "Zuma, tell me what that means or you'll miss dinner."

"Oh, dude. Not fair," said Zuma.

"Did you just call me 'dude'?" asked Minnie, consternation in her voice. "Digging a deeper hole, Zuma."

Zuma blurted, "It means she's deaf and dumb but not blind."

"And what's wrong with being blind?" Amir shot back.

Benny burst out laughing.

Kami erupted. She sprang into the air and kicked Benny square in the chest, knocking him off of his feet. She pounced like a cat atop of him and held two fingers over his eyes. "I can make you four-for-four. Deaf, dumb, blind, and dead."

Benny sputtered, trying to catch his breath.

Kiyoshi raced to Kami's side and yelled, "Wrath is not the answer! Control your anger!"

Benny stared into the fingertips hovering over his eyeballs. "Uh, sorry."

Kami let him up. She stuck her tongue out at Raj as she took her former place.

"Stop it, you two! I'm sick of your petty squabbles," said Layla. "Just get along."

Raj folded her arms over her chest and snapped, "And Layla's talent, Benny, is getting out of work. La-zy!"

Kami laughed. "Oh, no, she's good at being a princessh. Can you help me with thish? Can you help me with that? I'm too pretty to break a nail. And Zuma'sh talent is eating."

"Hey! What did I ever do to you?" asked Zuma.

"That wash for the Geisha comment," retorted Kami.

"Kami!" said Minnie. "Raj!"

"Layla's a coward!" blasted Raj. "She hid while we fought. Did you miss that, Minnie?"

"Yeah," said Kami. "A lot of help she'll be."

Chaz broke in, "Cut her some slack, guys. Did she expect to see some snake-man chasing her this morning? Or creepy, enormous monsters?"

"And she lopped off the snake-thing's tail," said Mona with pride.

"She saved my life with that arrow," added Friday. "She set aside her own safety to save me."

Big O wrapped an arm around his wife. "Ya, for sure! We be beholdin', Layla."

"Man, what is it with chicks? *Rraaar*," said Zuma, clawing like a cat.

"If Layla's in, I'm out." Raj headed to the door with a final sneer at Kami. "TTYN."

"Shame here," shouted Kami, heading for the other door. "Talk to you never!"

"Mankind is doomed," said Amir.

"Not again!" said Chaz. "Can't they just duke it out like guys? Crack a rib or a get a bloody nose or something and move on? I can't stand girl drama."

"Oh, no," said Layla. "They moved past girl 'drama' years ago. They push it until they hurt everyone around them. That is girl 'trauma.'"

"Stop!" said Minnie. "Get back here this minute!"

"Or else what?" Raj said as she continued toward the door. "You'll ground us?"

"Or take away the computer or cell phone—which we don't have anyway. There'sh nothing to take away, M," said Kami.

"Duke it out. Good idea, Chaz," said Minnie.

"What? What did I say," asked Chaz.

A rope fell from the ceiling. Quick as a cobra strike, one end grabbed Kami by the ankle, and the other grabbed Raj. The girls screamed. The boys laughed as the rope knocked them to the ground and dragged them to Minnie's feet. "Hmmm. Or else what? Good question," Minnie pondered. "Glad you asked. You'll train together. Every step you take must be a joint effort. You will stay that way until you can learn to get along. A day. A week. A month. As long as it takes. You'll eat and sleep together. Duke it out."

Kami stuck her tongue out at Raj, and Raj returned a raspberry. They both crossed their arms over their chests.

Zuma scratched his head. "And pee together? That's not cool."

"Don't be silly," said Minnie, rolling her eyes. "The rope will loosen, giving them just enough privacy when they need it."

"You said we had a choice," Benny added.

"To accept the quest, yes. To train, no," said Minnie. "I'll train you until the underworld seems like a bloody beach holiday."

"Thanks, girls," said Amir.

"Yeah, nice work," added Zuma.

"Benny, for today, observe the others," said Minnie, "Choose a weapon or a skill to start with. Watchers, spot them. Daniel, stay with me."

"Minnie," said Cookie. "We've been talking, and we want to train, too."

"We were useless this morning," added Friday.

"It's not your fight," said Minnie. "Your job is to train them. Get them strong of mind and body."

A heavy silence made Minnie reconsider. "Is everyone in cahoots against me?" She didn't wait for an answer. "Fine, fine. You're right. Even though it's not your fight, being prepared mentally and physically is important for all. The children are our focus, but today, you were put in danger, too. It may happen again, who knows. Mona, I think it's also imperative that you teach everyone first aid."

"Of course," Mona replied.

"Good. Let's begin," said Minnie.

Benny followed Kami and Raj to a large square floor mat. The girls grabbed lathi sticks from the wall and stepped onto the mat. As they crouched into position, the rope relaxed, allowing a distance to grow between them. The girls leaped, flipped, slashed and relished every strike that resulted in pain to the other. Every strike to the knee, the ribs, the shoulders, or the legs sent a crack and a howl and a satisfied grunt that seemed to say "take that."

Benny, Kiyoshi and Andy flinched with each blow.

Kiyoshi observed, "Perhaps they will beat some sense into each other."

"Before they kill each other? They're both stubborn," said Andy. "I'll take them tonight? You tomorrow?"

Kiyoshi bowed his head in agreement. "I recommend extra ice and liniment."

Another crack of stick to bone made the three onlookers flinch again. Kami gave Raj a smack across her forehead, and Raj landed a fist in Kami's eye.

"That'sh cheating," barked Kami, holding her eye.

"That's warfare," sneered Raj.

Benny had fought Dillon, but he shoved him away before doing real harm. He could not watch the girls tear each other apart for another second. He wandered over to Chaz, who sat next to a control panel on the wall.

Chaz pushed a button, and the ropes that dangled from the ceiling moved into a new position. Chaz wheeled himself beneath a center rope. As he pulled himself upward, arm over arm, his biceps bulged into round, hard boulders. He made it seem effortless, the way he dragged the dead part of his body skyward, until he reached a beam. He lowered himself on top of it and rested before swinging to a ledge, grabbing another rope, swinging again, and working his way back to the floor and into his chair.

"I'll never be able to do that," said Benny.

"Come on. Maybe this will work for you." Chaz wheeled himself over to the wall. He took the lid off of a container and chalked his hands. He locked the brakes on his chair and pushed a button that raised his chair a few feet. He reached for a thick white belt on a hook against the wall. The belt was attached to a rope that fell beside a wallboard. Chaz fastened the belt around his waist and slid out of the chair. He hung, suspended. His shoulders were even with the bottom of the board, and his toes dangled inches from the floor. The board leaned out from the wall at about twenty degrees. Chaz explained, "This is a campus board. It strengthens the fingers and forearms for climbing. Some holds on a wall are no more than an eighth of an inch. It's knowing how to place the hands and how to use them that gives a climber the most friction. And it's friction that glues you to the wall, not just muscle strength. On a rock wall, you use various holds: the crimp, open grip, pinch grip, friction grip, and monkey hook. The board is for finger work. Don't try it until you've climbed a while. Don't make a sound—I need to concentrate." Chaz reached up and curled his fingertips over the bottom edge of the board.

Benny noticed that the rungs changed shape. Some were flat, some round.

Chaz started with a controlled set of pull-ups. He climbed the board like the rungs of a ladder, hand over hand, sometimes skipping a rung. He worked his way to the top then back down again, stopping at times to count to three or five.

As Benny watched, he disbelieved the "not just muscle strength" part of Chaz's speech. Benny squeezed his own bicep, feeling somewhat inadequate.

At the bottom, Chaz repositioned his fingers, using two to four fingers on each hand. He climbed strategically. When he reached the top, he attempted a single finger hold, using the middle finger of his right hand. Benny counted to himself, one . . . two—

Chaz fell, but the belt caught him with a jerk. "Still haven't mastered the monodigit." Chaz reached for the arm of his wheelchair and positioned himself into the seat before removing the safety belt and returning it to the hook on the wall. "Wanna try it?"

"I'm observing, remember?" said Benny, already walking away, looking for a simpler task to attempt first. "I'm gonna go see what Amir is up to."

"Suit yourself," said Chaz.

Amir stood in the middle of a mat, hands ready for a fight, legs crouched, listening intently.

Uncle Jalal, barefoot, moved around him, testing Amir's acute hearing.

Amir waited for the strike.

Jalal leaped at him.

The second his feet left the ground, Amir's head turned toward his assailant.

Jalal grabbed Amir's arm and twisted it back behind him, but before he could lock it in, Amir spun until his arm was in front again. Amir bent his leg, hooked it around Jalal's and whipped it forward, dropping Jalal onto his back. Amir straddled his uncle's chest.

Jalal formed a fist and landed three quick blows to Amir's ribs, neck and jaw. The blows were hard enough to be felt, not hard enough to inflict damage.

Upon the third blow to the jaw, Amir swept Jalal's arm in a circular motion. His next move would have been to pop the elbow, breaking the joint, but, instead, he wrenched the arm into a lock. Jalal cried, "Release!" And release Amir did.

They rose to their feet and bowed. Jalal then passed Amir the *gatka* equipment, a sword and a shield.

"What's that for?" asked Benny.

Jalal explained, "How can I explain *gatka*? Think of it as training for combat in two realms. I sometimes use two swords: one represents worldly battles, the other, spiritual." Jalal handed Amir a sword.

Amir added, "That never made more sense than today, Uncle."

Jalal moved in precise, smooth steps. "*Gatka* hones the body, trains the mind, and forges a fearless soul. The three unite, and like braided rope, form the strongest bond of all."

Jalal and Amir maneuvered body and weapon: strike and recoil, leap, strike and recoil, leap and strike, in a rhythmic dance of harmony and grace and contemplation. It was a tap here, a tap there, in precisely calculated movements that required super concentration as well as trust. Benny saw *gatka* as more of a rehearsed performance, a ritual between them, rather than a fight, but their precision of blade to body—especially given Amir's lack of sight—moved him to silent awe.

"Possible," Benny mumbled to himself. "I can do that. Maybe." Minnie signaled for him to join her. As he headed over, clashing metal echoed throughout the room. Kami and Raj had moved on to swords.

Minnie and Daniel stood with Layla, Zuma, Mona and Cookie. They waited for Benny.

Layla whined, "I'm no fighter. Look at Raj and Kami—I'll never be like them. They're so competitive."

Minnie admonished her. "With thoughts like those, you're quite right. You'll never be a warrior. But look at them. They fight to destroy each other, and that may be their downfall. This fight will take into account far more than physical strength."

"Oh, goodie," added Benny. "I'm not exactly the brain of the group either."

Minnie scolded, "You all have individual talents. Focus on what you can do well and perfect it. Dwelling on what you're not good at is an anchor that will hold you down all of your life."

"I remember numbers pretty good," said Zuma. "I like math. Not sure that will help."

"And you play soccer," added Minnie.

"I suck at soccer," said Zuma.

"Practice, Zuma. That's all it takes," said Minnie. "And Layla, you're extraordinary at archery and dance."

"And she rocks crossword puzzles and riddles," added Zuma, giving Layla a fist pump.

"Riddles and crosswords will hardly save our lives," Layla scoffed. "Minnie, can't you just, like, zap us or something?"

"No, Layla. I can't 'like' zap you," said Minnie.

Mona added, "You can zap yourselves. It all starts with a positive attitude."

Cookie agreed. "Start small. Work together. Build each other up, not down."

Zuma said, "If you mention *The Little Engine That Could*, I'll puke. Again."

Layla sighed. "I'll try. Mona, let's start with *tahtib*. I'm still shaking and that always calms me." Layla referred to the ancient Egyptian martial art using sticks.

"And you, Zuma?" asked Minnie.

"I'll work with Layla and learn the sticks. Then we'll teach Benny archery, although Layla is the star, not me."

"Thanks," said Benny. "Gotta start somewhere, and the girls would kill me."

"Later, I'll show you guys the battle axe," said Zuma. "And I can teach you to draw more than a stick figure. Not sure how that will help though."

"I can't draw, Zuma. You've tried to teach me before. But we can teach Benny chess," added Layla. "He might be totes brill. Oh, crap. I sound like Raj. Shoot me."

Minnie curved the edges of her lips into the slightest smile. "Good. Get on with it then. Don't dillydally." She and Daniel walked over to Kami and Raj just as Kami lunged forward and swept her sword upward, dislodging Raj's sword from her hand. As Raj's eyes flew upward, following her sword, Kami planted a fist in her eye. In retaliation, Raj kicked Kami in the ribs, knocking the wind out of her. Kami dropped her sword, bent over and held her side.

"Wait," said Kami, doubled over.

Raj stood beside her, bent at the hips, chest heaving. She put her hands on her knees and whispered, "I've got an idea." Raj leaned in and whispered again. Kami nodded her understanding.

They squared off, throwing a few air punches and kicks, as if preparing to kickbox, but instead, Raj did a series of roundoffs, and with each one, Kami hopped back and forth through the loop of rope formed as Raj's ankle flew in a circle. Turn after turn, hop after hop, back and forth.

"What are they doing?" asked Benny.

"I've no idea," said Minnie, but after a few more turns, she could see exactly what they were up to. The rope was in knots. They sat on the mat wearing triumphant grins and high-fiving each other.

Minnie said, "Good. You finally worked together."

"Right," said Kami. "Sho let ush go."

"Yeah. We're like besties now," said Raj, attempting a sincere smile and pointing back and forth between them.

Minnie's brows lifted. "Rubbish! I was not born in a box."

"No, she had a rather unusual birth," said Daniel. "Athena in the Greek, Minerva in the Roman, popped out of her father's head—in full armor."

"Quite right," affirmed Minnie. She eyed the girls. "So, do not trifle with me."

"Nevs," said Raj.

"Right," said Kami. "Like we'd be that shtupid."

"Ever again," mumbled Raj, tugging on the rope around their ankles.

"Never ever again," said Kami.

———◆———

Layla and Zuma showed Benny how to use the short cane: how to grip it, move with it, and how to strike. He faced Layla, but he had a hard time striking at her, so Zuma stepped in and took her place. Zuma moved slowly, yet he was far more nimble than Benny expected. And each time Benny faltered, Zuma whacked his arm, knee, thigh, ribs, and even slapped the side of his head.

Benny took smack after smack. He finally blocked several blows, but he only landed one, which barely grazed Zuma's thigh.

Layla led them to an adjoining room. Targets covered the cork wall at the far end. Layla demonstrated the longbow. She relaxed as she pulled her hand back to her ear. With an easy release, the arrow flew across the room and hit the bull's-eye dead in the center.

Layla set the bow in Benny's hands and instructed him in the proper grip. The bow was as tall as Layla. She maneuvered Benny's feet into position and showed him how to stand, how to pull, how to eye the target and release.

Benny pulled back, which was not as easy as he had expected after watching her. He let the arrow fly. It sank to the ground long before it ever reached the wall. "Practice," assured Layla. "Try again."

Benny fired arrow after arrow. He eventually hit the wall but not the target. Layla dutifully encouraged him or repositioned him.

Zuma fired arrow after arrow at another target. Sometimes the arrow drove into the target, and sometimes it hit the cork wall, but none ever hit the bull's-eye.

"Don't worry," said Layla. "If I can do it, so can you. Once you can get better, we'll try aiming at moving targets."

"How long did it take you?" asked Benny.

"To hit the wall from here? Years," she said. "But I was pretty little when I started."

"I'm pretty sure we don't have years," said Benny.

Chapter Fifteen

Some hours later, Minnie led the bedraggled group into a classroom.

Zuma plopped into the first desk he came upon, just inside the door, and he lowered his head onto folded arms. Layla and Benny took seats beside him. Raj and Kami sat side by side, the rope still around their ankles. Chaz rolled in with Amir in tow. The watchers sat behind them.

Maps covered the walls, as did images of locales around the world: fiery magma flows, ancient Greek ruins, the pyramids, mountaintop shrines, snow-covered peaks, caves, the Roman Forum. A bank of computers lined the back wall.

"I thought there were no computers," Benny said to Layla.

"We play games on these, like *Warriors and Watchers*, but they don't have Wi-Fi," Layla replied.

"They have Internet now," said Minnie. "The cat is out of the bag. You'll need them for research."

"Research?" asked Benny. "What research?"

"You'll spend some time learning what we think you may

need to know," said Minnie. "Very few humans have entered the underworld and come back to tell about it. But some have. Then, you'll train physically and mentally."

Daniel's eyes widened. "Hercules, Dante, Odysseus, Aeneas."

Zuma laughed. "Dude, did you say what I think you said?"

"Zuma," Minnie reproached. "This is no time for jokes."

Zuma put his hands up to indicate surrender. "Sounded like he said anu—"

"Zuma! Enough," Minnie scolded again. "Daniel knows more about the underworlds and the ancient entrances that lead to them than any scholar on earth. He will tutor you with what facts we have. You'll learn all you can."

"What do the keys look like?" asked Kami.

"We've no idea," said Minnie. "Just that they open the seven gates."

"Where do we start?" asked Raj.

"We thought it would be the Roman Forum, until it blew up," said Minnie.

Daniel blurted, "The Lacus Curtius!"

"The what?" asked Benny.

Minnie nodded, giving Daniel the floor. "The story comes from Livy, a Roman historian who lived a couple thousand years ago. He wrote that a strange chasm of unimaginable depth opened in the middle of the Roman Forum, a chasm which could not be filled, despite all who threw earth into it. People feared that unnatural causes were to blame. Soothsayers said that the gods had instructed the Roman people to sacrifice its strength, the thing it held most dear. If it did not, the Roman Republic would not survive. A young soldier, Marcus Curtius, strode forth and declared that nothing constituted the strength of Rome more so than her courageous soldiers. In full splendor of man and horse, Livy wrote, Marcus shouted to the gods above and the gods below before riding his horse into the chasm, sacrificing the both of them to seal the entrance. The place is called Lacus Curtius—Lake of Curtius—as there was, at one time, a lake or swamp there."

"We think Hades has been trying to either open or seal the entrances to the underworld to prevent your access. That's the seismic activity Daniel has been tracking," said Minnie.

"But didn't he open a gate at his castle? A way out of the underworld," asked Chaz.

"Yes and no," explained Minnie. "He created a tiny portal that allowed a few creatures to pass through, but they could not go beyond the woods. And Hades could not sustain it, which is why it collapsed. All we know is that someone or something is building seven gates, or exits. Once opened with the keys, the creatures of the underworld will escape and flood the world with chaos and mayhem. It will be the end of mankind."

"Why would Hades seal the entrances?" asked Layla.

"Never presume he plays fair," said Minnie. "He might be leaving us with fewer choices."

"Where do we start?" asked Benny.

"You start by preparing." Minnie's eyes focused on each and every one of the children's faces. "These enemies will do everything in their power to win. Everything. Even turn you against one another."

Zuma asked, "Why didn't they kill us when they had the chance?"

"I don't know," said Minnie. "And that bothers me most of all. Maybe they think they can turn one of you. Maybe they need one of you for a reason to which I am not privy." Her eyes shot at Benny. "You are Hades' grandson, after all. That much we do know."

"He has destroyed my life. I'll destroy him," affirmed Benny.

"Unto death," said Amir. "I'm in."

"Death?" Minnie laughed. "Death would be a gift compared to what they are capable of doing to you. They will find your weaknesses. Every defect. And exploit them."

The room fell silent.

"From this day forward, you are warriors. And I expect you to act as such. Train hard. Learn well. Your watchers will help you, test you. They will, like me, push you to your limits and then push you more. Do as they ask of you. Daniel, they're all yours."

Minnie left the room, and Daniel passed out computer pads and stylus's as he began his lecture. "You can write on these or type, as you wish. Amir and Kami, your tablets have voice recognition software that will translate my lecture in real time, so you can replay it or read it for review later. We'll start with Dante Alighieri, an Italian poet who lived in the fourteenth century. He wrote *The Divine Comedy* in three parts. In fact, the numbers three, seven and nine are prominent in mythology, but we'll cover that later. We'll just concern ourselves with one section, titled *Inferno*, Dante's descent to the underworld. He initially came upon three beasts who tried to stop him: a she-wolf, a leopard, and a lion, just like the statues at the entrance to Hades' castle. Should have been a clue," Daniel chastised himself. "And the street named Basso Loco— means 'low place'—Hades has a dark sense of humor."

"That might help us," said Benny. "Right."

Daniel stuttered. "I . . . I don't know, Benny. I hadn't thought of it. Maybe. Anyways, Dante invented the terza rima, the triple rhyme, but let's focus on the descent . . ."

———

After an agonizing lecture, during which Zuma fell asleep more than once, and Layla knuckled him into wakefulness, Daniel allowed them to play *Warriors and Watchers* on the computers.

Only now did Benny see the resemblances between the nine circles of the underworld described by Dante and the game world created by Minnie. Benny wondered how accurately the images captured the real place, if they did at all. Hades' avatar, with curly red hair and beard, portrayed his nemesis perfectly.

When the game loaded, a new cast of enemies appeared. Minnie had uploaded a new version of the game. Hades remained the same, except now other avatars joined the game — the six other lords of the underworld.

But this was no longer a game. Minnie might want to save mankind, but, for Benny, a personal war had begun.

His ally avatars had new meaning for him, too — cartoonish figures, dressed in battle gear. He glanced down the line of computers: Chaz, Amir, Zuma, Layla, Kami and Raj. He'd been interacting with them all along and never knew it. He rubbed his eyes, unable to focus on the game. All he could see was Ma's hand slipping away from him and her scared eyes as she plummeted downward in Hades' grasp.

Raj shouted, "Zuma, stop button-mashing!"

Zuma pressed the buttons even faster and harder. "Brawn over brains, baby. I do what it takes to win. Ooo, did you see that? Score!"

For Benny, the game suddenly became pointless. It could not reveal the keys to the gates, the strategies needed to win, or the dangers posed. He shut down the computer.

Minnie entered the room. "Dinner is ready. Zuma, dessert is blueberry pie. Small portions."

"Dessert? For real — not a fruit cup?" Zuma pushed back from his computer. "Righteous!"

"For real," said Minnie. "And I have one more surprise, for Benny."

Benny crossed the room. "Can't it wait for tomorrow? This day has been a little too full of surprises."

"Then what's one more?" said Minnie, without waiting for an answer. "I just received word from Mr. Adez's attorney. You have inherited fifty million dollars from your grandfather's estate."

Amir shrieked. "Fifty million dolla's!" He stuck out his hand. "Alms for the blind. I take checks, dude."

"Shopping shpree," said Kami.

"Deffo," said Raj.

Benny walked past Minnie and out the door. Money! It's all he had wanted a few days ago. All that mattered. Had it begun? Hades' first sick joke at his expense? A way to turn the knife in his gut? Or was it a bribe?

"Maybe he thinks you'll take the money and run," Minnie called after him.

"I might." Benny glanced over his shoulder and smirked. "After I kick his curly red ass straight into the sun. Use the money any way we need it."

———

After dinner, Kami followed Raj home and up to her bedroom, a round room with a red-and-gold patterned dome of geometric circles that resembled a flower. Yards of colorful fabric covered the walls, some bloomed with gold or white flowers; others had delicate golden embroidery. Raj cracked the window open, letting the fresh summer breeze wash through the space.

"Pretty," said Kami, touching the fabric-lined walls. "You've redecorated shince I wash here last."

Throughout the years, the triad of girls had shifted alliances: Layla and Kami, then Layla and Raj, and for a time, Kami and Raj. Eventually, the three just pretended to be friends each day —

with moments of sincere fondness in between moments of sheer dislike.

Raj faced Kami, so that she could read her lips. "These saris belonged to my mother. A few months back, I was having a bad day. Andy brought these in and helped me hang them. It's a little like having my mother here. This pink one stands out the most. I don't know why."

"Maybe she wore it a lot. Could be her favorite."

Raj nodded. "Maybe."

"My mother wore her hair up. That's a shilly thing to remember." Kami put a hand next to her cheek. "Her skin wash shoft against my cheek."

"That's a good memory. That's no sillier than a fondness for a pink piece of cloth on a wall." Raj sat gently on her bed, giving her sore spots time to adapt. Kami did the same, taking a spot on the other twin bed.

There was a knock on the door.

"Come in. I can't move," said Raj.

"Nor I," said Kami.

Andy came in carrying a brass tray, which he set on the teak desk in the corner. He handed each girl an ice pack wrapped in cotton cloth. "One for your eye, and the other for Kami's. I made an herbal liniment, and Mona delivered medication to reduce swelling. One tablet before bed, and one in the morning. No refusals."

The girls thanked him, and he left. Raj put a pack over her eye and forehead. "How did we get this way? When did it happen?"

"I don't know," said Kami, applying her pack to her eye. "But if we ever want to go our own waysh again, we should figure that out. Minnie knows when we're lying."

"Deffo."

"Urg! That drives me crazy—and I'm not shaying cray-cray. I

think you do that to fit in, to shound cool. It shounds shtupid! Where did you find that language, anyway?"

"A teen magazine Mona bought in town. And yes, I want to fit in—is that so wrong? But since you want to chat about it. Know what drives me crazy? You constantly compete with me. Parkour, swords—"

"Wrong! You compete with me!" Kami jumped to her feet, but regretted it the moment pain shot through her limbs.

"You're jealous!" Raj jumped to her feet and grimaced, holding her ribs. "Oh my gosh that hurts. Thanks for the warning."

Kami grinned. "I alwaysh share with my friend. Even pain."

The rope pulled them together, until they stood in the middle of the room.

"I have to sit down or I'll fall down," said Raj.

"Me, too," said Kami. "Let's try moving together."

"This way," said Raj. The girls shuffled toward Raj's bed and gently sat down.

"Admit it. You hate the attention the boysh give me, eshpecially Chaz," goaded Kami.

"Ha! Chaz wouldn't come near you for fear you'd gouge his eyes out."

"He won't come near you either, Raj. He likes Layla."

"Not anymore!" defended Raj.

"Yesh, he doesh. She just doeshn't like him."

"Exactly. Layla likes Zuma."

"They're just friendsh," said Kami.

"Now we're getting somewhere! You're jealous of Layla because she's got big boobs, is prettier, and nicer—way, way nicer than you! You don't stand a chance with Chaz."

Kami shook with anger. "You wish you *were* Layla and that Chaz had tried to kissh you!"

"That's what you wish! I'm taking a shower. Rope, let me go!"

The rope relaxed. Raj grabbed a white cotton nightshirt from a dresser drawer and headed toward the bathroom at a snail's pace. She slammed the door behind her. "Ouch! That hurt!"

When Raj emerged from the steamy room, Kami waddled past her and into the bathroom, also slamming the door. "Crap! That does hurt!" She emerged some time later, wearing pajamas covered with yellow Pikachu creatures. Raj was already in bed with the lights out. Kami slid into the other bed, but the rope tightened, pulling her across the floor to Raj's bed.

"Hey, rope. Privacy," said Kami, but the rope didn't budge. "Raj, the rope won't let me leave. Shorry, but ya gotta move over."

Raj slid closer to the wall. Kami climbed into bed beside her. "Shtupid rope!"

The silence widened between them. Neither of them closed their eyes. Finally, Raj turned on the light and sat up. "When did we get so mean?"

Kami sat up beside her and shrugged. "Jusht happened."

"You take my punches, and I take yours, but I was thinking about Layla in the shower. We used to be her friend. She used to be tougher. Didn't she?"

"She got in the middle. Between us," admitted Kami. "Became our punching bag."

"Some people are easier to tear down," said Raj.

"Or tear apart," agreed Kami.

"It's true, Kami."

"What'sh true?"

"I envy you. I always have. I've got this birthmark on my face. And you're so pretty. No one will—"

"O-M-G. I'm pretty all right—pretty mean. I get sho angry. I don't know why. I hear myshelf, but I can't shtop. The things I've done to you, to my grandfather, to Layla—"

"Me, too. Did we make Layla afraid?"

Kami shrugged. "Maybe."

"She quit fighting a long time ago. 'Bout the time she became friends with Zuma."

Kami sighed. "It didn't shtop ush. We taunted her more."

"Especially when we thought Chaz liked her and not us."

"Minnie will talk her into going with ush."

"She's gonna die," said Raj.

"Unlessh, we help her."

"Like totes—I mean totally toughen her up. Together."

"Together. We shtart tomorrow."

Kami rubbed her neck. "He could have killed me. Lord Izanagi. He had the point of his sword at my throat. But he didn't."

"That," Raj smiled, "was his first mistake."

"Totesh," added Kami.

They both laughed and lay back down. The rope released their ankles and slid out the open window.

"Hey, we're free." Kami sat up and swung a leg over the side to move to the other bed, but Raj grabbed her arm, "Don't go. Please."

Kami smiled as she shoved her legs under the covers and Raj turned out the light.

Chapter Sixteen

Benny's eyes shot open with the sound of the alarm. He slid his legs over the side of the bed. Excruciating pain ripped through his body. With each movement, he discovered a new injury. It hurt to walk. He shuffled his feet, and headed to the bathroom. He faced himself in the mirror. "Dude, I didn't think you could look worse than being blown up. Congrats!" His singed flesh, red as a stop sign, throbbed.

He managed to squeeze toothpaste onto his toothbrush, spilling some onto the sink. He could barely lift the brush to his mouth, and once there, it hurt to brush. He glanced at his hairbrush, "Forget it. Not worth the pain."

He lifted his shirt and winced. The mirror reflected long, skinny bruises and welts all over his torso. He hadn't been this physical in a long time. Ever, in fact. He lowered his shirt and pulled on a new pair of shorts and a tee shirt, moaning and groaning with each movement. Putting on his shoes and socks was almost more torture than he could take. He descended the stairs, taking it one at a time. He spotted Mike on the sofa, tapping the keys on his computer.

"Looks like you got your Wi-Fi." Benny learned that it also hurt to breathe and speak.

Mike closed his laptop and rose to his feet. "You look like crap. Reminds me of my boot camp days."

Benny preferred silence. It hurt less.

Mike added, "I'm packin' in the ice today. And I'll get some muscle rub and cold packs and tape."

"Good. You can tape me back together tonight."

Mike ran a hand through his short curly hair. Look, Benny, I didn't sleep last night. I still can't believe it. It's crazy. But, Neeve . . . you guys were in danger all that time. Had I—"

"You couldn't know, Mike. Let's go to breakfast."

"Wait. I thought about it, and I'm going with you. To the underworld. Chosen or not. I'll get Neeve back or I'll die trying."

Benny glared at him. Could he possibly feel any worse? Yes, he could. "For me, Mike, or for you?"

"What are you talking about?"

"The way you looked at her in the wedding photo."

"It's not what you think. Sure, Neeve and I hung out a lot when we were young. And I admit, I had feelings for her. But she chose your father. I just wanted her to be happy. You gotta believe me."

"Can we not discuss this anymore, because I have so many people slamming their ideas of what I should believe and do into my skull right now that it's about to go Willy Wonka."

"Sure. Sure. I get it." Mike held his hands up. "Whatever you need. Tape. Food."

Benny walked past him and out the door. "Right now, breakfast and pain-killer."

—————

171

At breakfast, Kami and Raj smothered Layla with apologies for the way they had acted, which she received with reticence. After that, the students spent the morning in the classroom, listening to Daniel lecture, then they trained in the gym or outdoors. And when good and tired, Minnie insisted they return to the classroom where they played strategic games, saying that anyone could solve problems when rested but they would not have that luxury. She forced them to think their hardest when wiped out physically.

Initially, the same groups formed: Layla and Zuma paired up to play games—chess, scrabble or riddles. Kami and Raj played shogi—Japanese chess. Chaz taught Benny how to play 3-D chess on a board with seven platforms. And Amir played a verbal word game on the computer that had speech-recognition software.

But Minnie and Daniel mixed them up, pairing Amir and Chaz in a verbal sparring game; Benny and Zuma in a game involving memory or math; and the three girls played French tarot, an old-time European card game, later adopted by mystics and fortune-tellers to divine the future.

The seven would-be warriors also played against one another in vast games of Magic the Gathering, pitting their unique card decks against their opponents' until all but one of them—each a powerful wizard called a plainswalker—had suffered enough spells and damage to have lost their life points and perished. Amir had marked his deck with raised symbols, a Braille-like identification of his own making, while the others informed him of the cards being played. Curious, Daniel joined in, and shortly thereafter, he set his own deck before them in challenge. Daniel played with the enthusiasm of a kid, but occasionally had to be shushed when he drifted into some archaic bit of history dislodged from his memory by a spell or enchantment or artifact.

At times, the would-be warriors played musical instruments. Kami played the flute, Amir the saxophone, Raj the sitar, Zuma the drums, Layla the piano, and Chaz the guitar.

"This is training?" Benny complained to Minnie.

Minnie shot back, "Music is a language. Orpheus charmed living creatures and even moved stones with his song. What do you play?"

"My iPod," said Benny.

"Grab that harmonica," Minnie ordered. "It's that or the tambourine—we've no time for anything else with you."

"I'm not really a tambourine kind of guy." Benny picked up the harmonica and blew a sour note.

After that came languages. All but Benny had studied Greek and Latin and they enjoyed some humor at Benny's expense.

"*Veni, vidi, dormivi,*" said Zuma. "I came, I saw, I slept."

"*Docendo discimus,*" said Layla. "We learn by teaching."

"*Dum spiro spero,*" said Chaz. "While I breathe, I hope."

"*Semper paratus,*" said Kami. "Always prepared."

Benny repeated the words. Amir whispered in his ear. Benny said, "*Cave canem.* Enter the caves."

They all burst into laughter. "Dude," said Raj, "that means 'beware of the dog.'"

Besides Latin, Amir and Layla both knew Arabic; Layla, basic hieroglyphs; Chaz, French; Zuma, basic Spanish and some Hopi words; Raj, a little Sanskrit; Kami, Japanese and some Chinese. None of them felt they knew much of anything they had studied very well, except for Chaz, an avid reader. When he had idle time, he had a book in his hands: French poetry, the classics, and his latest—Dante's *The Divine Comedy.*

Day after day, week after week, they trained.

Benny grew more proficient, but not without further bruising of his body and his ego. He even sounded decent on the harmonica. He did whatever Minnie asked him to do.

The group ceased complaining—even Zuma and Layla.

Raj and Kami devoted themselves to Layla, and Layla helped Zuma, and they all helped Amir or Chaz to do as much as they could. They ran farther and faster through the woods, or bounced parkour-style from branch to branch. They rode on Slippy's back, swam across lakes. They learned hang gliding and spent time inside of caves, spelunking. Amir and Chaz joined in every activity, finding ways to overcome challenges. One such challenge came when a helicopter picked them up at the school midafternoon. It lifted off and shot across the Adirondacks, settling atop a slab cliff face. Minnie jumped out first.

"I thought you said we were climbing. Sun's almost down," said Benny, wearing a harness, helmet and gear.

"Descending." Minnie lifted her chin and stiffened her back. "This time in the dark. Just halfway down, then back up."

Zuma howled, "A wolf descent! Yeah! Let's do it."

Another day, they entered Daniel's classroom and discovered a female dummy sprawled on a table.

"CPR: cardiopulmonary resuscitation," said Mona. "Meet Resusci-Anne. Do I have a volunteer?"

"I volunteer," said Chaz. "As the dummy. The girls can practice on me as much as they want."

"Thanksh, Chaz. But I'll take the female dummy," said Kami.

"Me too," said Layla.

"How about you, Raj?" asked Chaz. "You'd resuscitate me, wouldn't you?"

"Sure," said Raj. "The moment your hot little heart stops beating, and you turn cold and blue, I'm there, dude. Until then, dream about it."

Daniel stifled a smile. "Looks like Anne wins. You know, her face is supposedly modeled from the death mask of a young girl who drowned in the Seine River in the 1880s."

"She is kinda pretty," said Chaz. "I volunteer to go first. If the girls ever need resuscitation, I want to make sure I know just what to do."

"Somehow, Chaz," said Kami, "that'sh not reassuring, but I'll go next."

To unwind, the group played basketball or stick hockey. To make it fair, they all jumped into wheelchairs, which made it a different game altogether. Amir sat in Chaz's lap, and Chaz directed him when to shoot the basketball or when to swing the hockey stick and on which side. No one cared who won. Their game wasn't meant to save the human race; it was just for laughs. Maybe the last laughs they and the rest of the people of the world would have. Minnie and the watchers hovered over them, observing and cheering.

It was during a morning game of stick hockey in the gym with Minnie, Daniel, Mike and the watchers gathered around to cheer the boys facing off against the girls that the ground beneath their feet shook. It brought a sudden end to their merriment.

Benny said, "They're kicking us from below."

Minnie confirmed, "Yes. It's time." She proceeded to hand out instructions in her usual nonnegotiable tone. "Daniel will go with you. He'll get you to the first entrance to the underworld. Then, you're on your own."

Benny asked, "Where is the first entrance?"

"Haven't a clue," said Minnie. "But I know who does."

Mike argued, "I go where Benny goes."

"You can keep Daniel company, if you wish, but you cannot enter the underworld. You'll be as useless as a one-armed monkey hanging from a limb with an itchy arse—I do love that one. Saw it on the Internet. You mortals can be quite funny."

"I am not useless. I'm a Marine, and a damn good marksman," said Mike. "I know my way around a battlefield."

"As do I, Mike," snapped Minnie. "And I'm in charge. If and when you are called upon, stand ready. That goes for all of you, watchers included." She eyed Mike. "Until then, you'll follow orders, soldier."

Benny asked, "When do we leave?"

"Straight away. You need to be in Delphi tomorrow," said Minnie. "You'll land in Athens in the morning."

"Why tomorrow?" asked Benny.

"Because the oracle of Delphi only sees consultants once a month on the seventh. Used to be the first, which I preferred. Anyway, thanks to Benny's money, I've purchased a jet for us. A small one."

Amir shouted, "Oh, man, some things this boy would like to see!"

"This is not for your pleasure, Amir," Minnie explained. "This is for the safety and protection of others. You are targets. Put you on a commercial plane and we endanger innocents."

"Zuma, go grab the chest from my office," instructed Minnie. "They just arrived."

Zuma nodded. He kept his head down and wrung his hands together as he left. It wasn't long before he returned, toting a golden chest. He plopped the chest on the ground next to Minnie and waited for her instructions.

"Don't dawdle, Zuma," said Minnie in a huff. "You'll have to dole them out. How do I know whose is whose and which is which?"

"Benny," said Zuma, handing out black-and-silver clothes, folded neatly.

Benny accepted the bundle but asked, "What's this?"

"Uniforms," said Minnie.

"You're kidding, right?" said Raj.

"They're of a special fabric. Nearly indestructible."

"Nearly?" asked Benny.

"Well, we don't know for sure, but the silver mesh is as strong as chain mail," said Minnie. "They're flexible and heat resistant. Go put them on, I want to see them."

Before Benny left, he said, "If these have a golden owl on the chest, I'd rather scorch."

Minnie rolled her eyes. "After you rebelled with wearing the PE clothes, I figured as much. Zuma is highly artistic. I asked him to design them for you."

"And I gave him some magazines," added Mona. "Latest fashions."

"Dude," said Kami, "thish better be good."

The adults chatted lightly while they waited. Cookie asked, "What do they look like, Minnie?"

"How should I know?" She played with her owl necklace. "I was too terrified to peek."

The far doors opened and the band of seven strolled or rolled in: Kami and Raj wore strappy midriff tops and hip-hugger leggings, overlaid in silver mesh. Mesh sleeves and a hood were attached by suspender fastenings. Layla wore a zipper-front shorts onesie with mesh arms and hood; the shorts were attached to mesh leggings with suspender fastenings. Benny and Zuma wore loose pants, where Amir's and Chaz's were more fitted. Their tops and vests gave them the appearance of modern-day knights ready for a rumble in an alley.

"Oh, good heavens!" said Minnie. "You look like a troop of hip-hop dancers."

"I love it!" said Friday, and the others cooed as well, congratulating Zuma on his designs.

"They will have to do," said Minnie, circling about them and poking at various metal loops and straps sewn in here and there. "I do like the combat boots."

"There's a climbing harness built in," explained Zuma. "And look, carabineers are attached, but they unclip, see? And I designed a skinny climbing backpack as a separate piece." He held one up.

Minnie reached for a black-and-silver owl broach on the hip of Raj's uniform. There was an owl on each uniform in various locations. "While I appreciate the owls, Zuma, this is no time for ornamentation."

"Well, I like it." Benny tapped the owl pinned to the pocket of his vest. "It stays."

"Me, too," agreed Kami, and the others added their approvals.

"You're dismissed," ordered Minnie, already turning to leave. "The helicopter departs in thirty minutes to fly you to the jet in New York."

Big O slapped Zuma on the back. "She's proud of you kids. So are we."

"The owls were the one part I thought she'd like," said Zuma, somewhat dejected.

"Oh, ya, she liked them a lot," said Friday. "She had to leave or get weepy in front of you."

"She doesn't do weepy," added Benny. "Neither do I."

Chapter Seventeen

The moment they landed in Athens, a white minivan with wheelchair access drove up to the plane. The driver moved the bags from the plane to the van while the steward assisted with the customs officer who had boarded the plane to clear the private passengers.

Mike drove the van, Daniel rode next to him, and the others settled in the back.

"How long 'til we get to Delphi?" asked Benny.

"Daniel has us on the scenic route, so it's about six or seven hours of drive time, but we'll stop for lunch and refuel somewhere. We'll edge around Athens to the north, westward to the coast, skirt along the Peloponnese and the Gulf of Corinth, cross over the Rion-Antirion Bridge, and up into the hills to Delphi."

Daniel added, "It's a lovely drive. I remember my first visit here as a grad student. I could just picture Odysseus landing on island after island, battling the Cyclops, and—oh, my!—you don't suppose that was real, too, do you?"

Mike weaved around traffic. "Daniel, right now, I'd believe just about anything."

Once out of town, the scenery opened up: rocky hills stretched out, dotted with sheep and olive trees and scrub brushes, occasionally speckled with pink or yellow or red wildflowers. Small white stucco villages with red-tiled roofs flitted in and out of view, its church usually rising above all other buildings.

The waters in the gulf lapped at the rocky shoreline, which weaved gently along the coast.

The Rion-Antirion Bridge came into view—an elegant white dragon leaping from one shoreline to the other. Four support pylons, like four diaphanous white wings, rose across the back of the dragon, which spanned the gulf in an impressive arc of beauty. As they moved with the traffic across the bridge, they noticed blue accents against the white: simple blue lamps hung overhead that in the night would cast a mysterious glow over the back of the beast.

Midbridge, the gulf waters frothed into choppy waves.

Mike cautiously maneuvered through the narrow streets of the small village on the other side. Three-story apartment buildings with balconies on every level walled them in and kept their eyes forward.

They stopped and ate at a gyro shop. Zuma, in particular, relished the multitude of food choices, settling for two pork gyro sandwiches while others savored lamb, fish, beef, and salads or meat-filled pastries laced with olive oil, oregano, mint and garlic.

Back on the road, the van quickly ascended the mountain, winding its way up, past scrub brush on either side and past decorative boxes, faced with glass, which held candles, pictures, and mementos of those who had died along the road to Delphi. From up above, the gulf appeared calm and serene, and across the gulf, layers of land formations rose and fell in shades of blue or gray, layered one behind the other, until the last was but a shadow of white.

Daniel called the group to attention. "Everyone, listen up! I don't know what to expect, since the Temple of Apollo is in ruins, but let me tell you what I know. Maybe it will help. Delphi became 'the place' to go to seek prophesy in the Greek heyday. According to mythology, Python, the serpent, first ruled over the priestess or oracle of Delphi—called the Pythia. Python guarded the omphalos, or navel—a carved stone that marked the center of the earth. Due to a family squabble that I won't get into, Apollo, avenging the suffering of his mother, slew Python and ruled over Delphi and the oracle. The Pythia, or priestess, was said to communicate directly with Apollo. Besides being a renowned place for prophesy, Delphi held the Pythian Games every four years, just like the Olympics, but since Apollo was, oops sorry—is—the god of light, truth, healing, music and poetry, to name a few, they added art and dance to their celebrations."

"How do we find the oracle?" Benny asked.

"How do I know?" said Daniel. "The priestess only consulted once a month after a week of preparation and rituals involving fasting and a bath in the Castalian Spring and a drink from another sacred spring."

Raj asked, "What do we do when we meet her?"

"According to various accounts," said Daniel, "the visit starts with an interview by the priest, who helps you frame your question, and then you walk along Sacred Way—"

"Bogus," blurted Kami. "You tell the priest what you're going to ashk in advance. Then he tellsh her. Bam!"

"Totally," said Raj. "Like those television psychics."

"Let him finish," said Benny.

Daniel waited but a moment before jumping in. "As I was saying, the consultant—one who seeks counsel—walks along

Sacred Way, presents an animal, often a goat, for sacrifice, pays a fee, and—"

"Back it up," said Raj. "We are not going to sacrifice an animal."

"I would hope not," said Daniel. "I'm simply telling you the old-time ritual, so you'll be prepared. Once the consultant enters the Temple of Apollo, he is led to a room where the Pythia sits on a tall stool, a tripod. She is said to be holding laurel and a dish of sacred water. You ask your question. She answers. You leave."

The car ascended into the mountains, and the gulf grew smaller and farther away.

"Shounds pretty easy, except for finding her in a ruined city," said Kami. "And the animal shacrifice part."

"There is one other thing," said Daniel.

"What?" asked Benny.

"There are multiple stories. Some say the oracle spoke gibberish, others not. Plutarch, a former priest, wrote that vapors emerged from a spring or a fissure that ran under the temple. Some scientists speculate that these gases gave her hallucinations. We know that the temple lies over a bituminous layer and two fault lines. Earthquake damage has been recorded in the past."

Raj complained, "So, let me get this straight. You give the priest your question; slaughter a poor, defenseless animal; pay a fee; see a crazed psycho woman; ask your question, she babbles and you leave."

"Umm, yes," said Daniel. "That pretty much sums it up."

The domiciles and shops of the village of Delphi climbed the side of Mount Parnassus; its roads, none flat, either rose or fell to match the mountain. Cars lined one side of the road, such that Mike's mouth twisted with each car that zipped by, apparently unconcerned by the narrow passage.

"Delphi, here we come," added Mike. "You kids ready?"

Benny, sitting just behind Mike, gathered a consensus of headshakes, thumbs up or down and whispers before saying, "Let's do it."

"As the saying goes, 'we'll rest when we're dead,'" said Zuma.

The others fell silent.

"Sorry, guys. Poor choice of words," said Zuma.

They bought visitor's tickets at the tourist kiosk, passed through the gate and headed up Sacred Way, initially walking on a dirt road but later on square paver stones. Daniel led the group, playing tour guide, pointing out treasury buildings, patrons' names carved into the stones, or showing where statues once stood, or explaining the difference between the dark stone, local gray limestone, and lighter stone, marble.

Pointy dark-green trees, bushes and pine trees surrounded the ruins. Mount Parnassus rose in craggy formations behind it. Delphi faced outward on the side of the mountain, offering them a breathtaking view of slopes and valleys.

Zuma helped push and maneuver Chaz's wheelchair over the rocky, uphill road. Layla guided Amir, and Benny, Kami, Raj, and Mike followed behind. They passed by a row of columns standing alone and a structure of white bricks with a triangular pediment and roofline.

Peering down at the ruins behind them, neat rectangles and squares outlined where buildings once stood. It was like a tornado had whisked away the buildings, leaving their foundations behind. An old tree with striated bark offered a small patch of shade from the warm sun. They cupped their hands and sipped water that dripped from a small spout into a square marble basin before pushing on up the road.

"That's the Temple of Apollo," said Daniel, pointing downward, "where the six columns stand. I had hoped we'd see something by now. A sign. The site closes in an hour. Let's go to the top, and we'll work our way back down to the temple."

Daniel led them past the semicircular amphitheater that sat empty, as if waiting for actors, spectators and applause. They wound upward until they reached a long plot of land where athletes once competed in the Pythian Games. Stone bleachers covered the hillside. Stairs led upward to the seats, where spectators once shouted, argued, or wagered. The seating extended the length of the field on one side. Pine trees rose skyward behind the stands, now mere onlookers with nothing left to watch but tourists and children running races with their siblings.

"Nothing," said Daniel. "Let's head back."

"Buy my rose?" said a voice. "I've only one left."

A young gypsy girl stood before them. A flowered scarf, rimmed in gold coins, covered the top of her head. The coins dangled over the palest of blue-green eyes, like a calm sea with the power to turn wild. Thick dark curls poured down each side of her face. As she swung her narrow hips back and forth, her flowered skirt—a mismatch to the flowers on her scarf—swished this way and that. A white cotton blouse fell off of one shoulder.

"No, thank you," said Daniel.

Without warning, she threw her lone rose into the air. It drifted toward Benny, who reached up and caught it.

"Come." She grabbed Benny's free hand and dragged him away.

Benny shrugged and let her pull him along. How was he supposed to know if she was a sign or a crazy gypsy?

She pulled him fast, perhaps to distance him from the others. She twirled about him, again and again as she pulled him forward. Tourists stared. Others snapped pictures. She thanked them and bowed and pulled Benny along some more, reeling into him and then away, making quite a display.

Mike, Daniel and the others kept a close watch and followed behind at a short distance. Chaz pleaded with Zuma to push him faster to keep up. Kami and Amir fell back, too, but Kami described what she could see.

"Who are you?" Benny asked.

The gypsy plucked leaves from a bush and climbed atop a rock. She threw the leaves, and they rained down on Benny. "Don't you know?"

A female security guard approached. "American?"

"Yes," said Benny.

"Your girlfriend cannot climb the rock. Get her down."

"She's not my—"

Throwing her arms skyward, the gypsy shouted, "I love Apollo!" before leaping off the rock, straight at Benny and the guard. The guard ducked to the side.

Benny's eyes widened. He caught the gypsy girl in his arms and somehow still held on to the rose. She flipped her head back and kicked her feet in the air and laughed. Tourists walked around them at a greater distance, showing scowls and sneers of disdain. As the guard complained in a flurry of condemnation, Benny set the girl on her feet. The gypsy lunged for Benny's hand and raced away with him, dashing toward the Athenian Treasury.

The guard chased after them, squawking into her shoulder microphone.

Benny and the gypsy raced between the pillars of the treasury. The gypsy grabbed a ring of vines from a marble stump and set it on Benny's head. "Herophile must leave you now."

The Delphic guard raced into the treasury. Daniel rushed forward to catch up to her, but he smacked into her as she exited.

He said in Greek, "I should sue you people, letting crazy gypsies accost tourists!"

She answered in Greek, huffing and puffing, "Where did they go? They're not in the building."

"There she is!" shouted Layla, pointing to the gate. The gypsy turned toward them, blew a kiss and danced out. Benny was nowhere in sight. The guard barked into her shoulder microphone and raced down Sacred Way.

"Where's Benny?" asked Mike.

Daniel gazed at the ruins where the grand Temple of Apollo once stood. "Let's hope he's with the oracle."

"What do we do?" asked Amir.

"We wait," said Mike.

"Aren't we all in this together?" asked Kami. "I shuck at waiting patiently."

"Kami," said Daniel, using the tone he used with whiny students who complained about too much homework, even though Kami had complained about not having enough to do. "Benny may be in danger for all we know. Do not wish for the unknown— you just might get it. The girl threw the rose into the air. The Greeks believed in fate—one chosen for a task. It fell to Benny— this time. Apollo's choice, perhaps, but certainly not yours."

"We close soon. Please head to the exits," shouted a guard.

"Let's head down to the temple," suggested Daniel, already taking steps in that direction.

A small, speckled owl landed on the peak of the treasury building and stared down at the group with enormous yellow eyes.

Chapter Eighteen

Benny found himself at the entrance to a grand temple encircled by a row of pillars.

A large golden door opened and a keen-eyed old man, wearing a white chiton belted at the waist and a brown outer robe, strolled out. "There you are. Come. Come. She'll see you now." His white mustache and beard bobbed as he spoke. He waved Benny forward with urgency. "Even I, Plutarch, never keep the oracle waiting."

As Benny took a step, he felt material swipe his ankles. Peering down, he saw that he, too, wore a chiton of white and an outer robe of saffron yellow and sandals. The rose he held had turned to pure gold. He still wore the crown of laurel upon his head. Benny entered the temple doors, following his guide. They crossed the marble floor and passed by statues of Poseidon and Zeus with full beards, a clean-shaven Apollo, and past others he didn't recognize.

"Come, come." Plutarch descended a set of steps. Benny followed. They entered a chamber, where a dark-haired girl dressed in red welcomed them.

"Leave us," she commanded.

Plutarch did as instructed.

Behind the girl rose a statue of Apollo, flanked by two golden eagles. Benny remembered Daniel's lecture about how Zeus sent two eagles out to circle the world, and they met here—at the navel of the world. Before Apollo's statue sat a tall, bronze tripod. There was a hole in the floor directly under the tripod, and in front of it, in the center of the small round room, sat an egg-shaped pinkish stone, the navel of the world.

The girl approached two basins of water on either side of Apollo. She dipped a silver chalice into the one, then another chalice into the other. "Begin your journey with refreshing drink."

"I'm not thirsty."

"You must choose," she insisted.

Benny reached for the chalice that had been dipped into the basin on the right.

"Drink."

Benny took only a sip before turning his face away. He no sooner swallowed the sweet water than the room swirled about him. He stumbled back, guided by the girl, until he fell upon a couch. His last clearheaded thought was that perhaps the "consultant," and not the oracle, was the one put into a trance of sorts.

"What do you seek?" asked the girl.

"I . . . I . . . I don't remember. Where am I?" The golden rose dropped to the floor.

"You have returned home after a long battle. And now, you will stay with me. Forever in love and comfort."

Benny struggled to remember. "I was in a battle? Yes, I was. . . fighting a dragon. Was that the one?"

Bronze-faced Apollo glared down. Benny thought he saw Apollo's eyes move, but then everything in the room moved.

The girl sat beside Benny. "Yes, a dragon. Now, drink. Refresh yourself. Forget all problems."

The girl lifted the chalice to Benny's lips.

Benny pushed the cup back. "A problem. I had a problem. That sounds familiar."

"Drink and you'll have no more problems ever again. You want that, don't you?"

The cold metal touched his bottom lip. Apollo's eyes moved again, darting away from

Benny.

"No more questions." She tipped the chalice.

The moment the water touched his lips, he sealed them shut and shoved the chalice away. The chalice and its contents flew across the small cell. The chalice hit the wall and bounced to the floor.

"Questions. I'm here to ask a question." Benny scrambled to his feet and staggered to the other basin. He cupped his hand and drank. The moment the bitter water slid down his throat, he shouted, "I remember!"

The red-clad girl pouted as she left the room. "Remember later that I gave you the opportunity to forget."

White vapor flooded the room through the hole in the stone under the tripod. It filled the small space with swirls, oddly transparent and well defined, more like white flames than cloudy smoke. They congealed and took shape, forming a woman whose hair floated in the air behind her. She glided to the tripod and sat. Although only white flames covered her flesh, there was innocence about her bare shoulders, midriff, arms and long legs. Her eyes opened—hollow, like a statue's—yet piercing, knowing. Her lips parted.

King, sage, scribe, soldier, senator or common man,
Ask the question of greatest portent and demand.

"I'm not a king. Just a common kid," said Benny.

Before he could ask his question, she rose and floated around him. As she did so, she inhaled the vapors that continued to seep through the hole beneath the tripod. Her arms swayed over her head and her head swayed as she approached. She stood inches before his face and bore her hollow eyes into his. Her lips parted.

Common, because unaware of affairs that bind.
Common, because unaware of your fate that blinds.

"Okay. Not sure what that means, but I do have a question. My question is, where can I find the first entrance to the underworld?"

The woman's face turned angry. She shouted a response that reverberated in the small space, causing Benny to reach for his ears:

Blind to the question needed above all the rest!
'Tis not a path but a key that is thy true quest!

Realizing the truth of it, Benny recanted. "Right. So, where is the first key?"

The oracle floated before him.

'Tis but one question and no more you are allowed.
I'll answer the first, by duty bound and avowed.

As she answered, her arms swept around him, embracing him in a circle of smoke.

At Hades command, one path is sealed forever.
The path you seek lies at the foot of my sister.

The smoky woman withdrew her arms and began to dissipate and retreat to the hole through which she had arrived. Benny reached out to stop her from leaving, but his hand swept right through her. "Wait, I don't understand."

Only her face remained above the tripod.

The knowledge you seek is in clefts ancient and deep.
Know thyself. Follow the signs, where e'er they may lead.

Benny turned to leave. He scooped up the golden rose and set it on the tripod. He headed back up the steps of the cell, across the floor lined with statues and out the front door. The moment he crossed between two of the front pillars, the temple dissolved into ruins and his clothing changed back to shorts, a tee shirt and tennis shoes. He spotted Daniel, lecturing the girls and Mike, who gathered in the center of the ruined temple, on the same spot where he had met with the oracle.

Upon seeing him, Chaz wheeled his chair along the path to the front of the temple to catch up to Benny, and Amir held on, careful of his footing. The others soon spotted him, too, and rushed to greet him.

"Closing time. Please move to the exits," shouted another guard.

"Dude," said Zuma, reaching him first. "You're wearing a vine thingy."

Benny hadn't noticed. He pulled the laurel wreath off of his head and tossed it onto what remained of an altar.

"Was it the gypsy girl? Was she the oracle?" asked Daniel.

"No. The gypsy said her name was Hero something," said Benny.

"Herophile?" asked Daniel.

"Maybe."

"Move to the exit!" shouted the guard, more insistent this time.

Mike interjected, "Let's get into town, get a bite to eat and figure out our next move."

"Yeah! Food! Hiking old ruins makes me hungry," said Zuma.

They shuffled down Sacred Way and back to the van. Daniel forced them to stop at the museum first so they could see a replica of Delphi as it would have looked in antiquity, to see the famous bronze charioteer and other pieces of a bygone time—not so bygone to Benny. As they drove to the museum, Daniel told them the story of Herophile. "She's one of the earliest Sibylla or sibyls—a word that simply means prophetess. Herophile was more, actually; she was said to be the daughter of Zeus and Lamia, a Lybian queen born of Poseidon, which granted her powers over water and sea creatures. Pausanias, a Greek geographer, wrote that the Delphians considered her the first sibyl. In fact, the rock your gypsy climbed upon is called the Rock of the Sibyl. From the rock, Herophile was said to chant oracles, one of which predicted the birth of Helen and the ruin she brought to Troy when the Greeks engaged them in war on her behalf. Herophile was not a Pythia. *Herophile* simply means hero admirer or one who loves the gods, and—"

"Dude, never mind the history lesson. What did she look like?" asked Amir.

"Smoke," answered Benny. "Beautiful smoke."

Chaz blurted, "I knew it!"

"Never mind all that. What did she say?" asked Mike.

"It wasn't gibberish, but she spoke in rhymes," said Benny.

"Hexameter," said Daniel. "Twelve syllables, probably heroic couplets, but exactly what did she say?"

"Let him start from the beginning," said Mike. "Don't leave anything out. It could be important."

"A guy named Plutarch led me to the oracle," Benny began, "and—"

"Oh, what I would have given to meet Plutarch!" said Daniel, biting his knuckle. "He was a priest at Delphi, but also a historian and—"

"Daniel, please," said Mike.

Daniel sputtered, "Right. Sorry."

Benny continued, "A pretty girl in red gave me some water to drink and things got hazy. I couldn't remember why I was there. I drank from another basin and remembered."

"Odd," said Daniel. "That's never been mentioned of Delphi. However, the underworld has several rivers. Pausanias wrote of one ritual, prior to seeing an oracle, where a consultant drinks from Lethe to forget the past and from Mnemosyne, from which we get the word *memory*, to retain the information given by the oracle."

"Well, it seemed more like a trap," said Benny. "Like I was supposed to forget all about why I was there. She tried to get me to drink more, forget more, but I saw the statue of Apollo looking at the other basin. At least, I thought I did. I can't be sure, since everything in the room was spinning. I knocked the cup from her hand and somehow made it to the other basin to drink."

"It's possible the first girl worked for the bad guys," said Mike. "Or that it was just a test of your willpower?"

"I do remember that the oracle said I had asked the wrong question—I asked where to find the entrance to the underworld, but she said I should have asked about the first key. She's right. I blew it, guys."

"Sho, where ish it?" asked Kami. "The entrance."

"The oracle said it's at her sister's feet," said Benny.

"Anything else?" asked Daniel.

"She said 'know thyself.'"

"'Know thyself,'" Daniel repeated, "That phrase is inscribed at the entrance to the temple, along with 'nothing in excess' and a mysterious E, which no one can figure out. Not sure of the significance. Means to know your strengths and faults, as they, more than anything external, will determine a person's destiny."

"Where do we go from here?" asked Mike.

"I don't know," said Daniel. "There were several sibyls—they all considered one another sisters. Let me give it some thought. After dinner, I'll call Minnie and get her opinion, too."

At the café next to their hotel, the food arrived hot and savory: bread, olives, a garlicky cucumber and yogurt dip, gyro-stuffed pitas, moussaka, meat-and-spinach-filled pastries in a flaky crust, sausage stew and plenty more. Daniel sipped red wine, and Mike, a beer.

They ate with gusto, tired but happy over a successful meeting with the oracle. Benny described the event in detail, and his friends laughed as he described his robe and sandals, the golden rose, the omphalos, Apollo's eyes and the smoky girl.

While Mike and the others enjoyed dessert—baklava, custards, almond cookies and ice cream—Daniel stepped outside to call Minnie. The setting sun lit Parnassus with a divine red glow.

When he returned to the table, Daniel sat amidst anxious ears, waiting to hear an answer. "As I thought, and Minnie concurs, the oracle must have referred to the Sibyl of Cumae. She was even more famous than her sister here in Delphi. Virgil wrote of Aeneas's descent—"

Zuma erupted in laughter. "He said it again."

The girls rolled their eyes. "Go on," said Kami.

"After Troy fell to the Greeks, some Trojans escaped. Aeneas, it was prophesied, would found a great empire. His wife was dead, but Aeneas carried his old father on his back and held his son by the hand as they left Troy. During his quest, he met the Sibyl of Cumae, not far from Naples, Italy. The oracle resided in caves through which Aeneas descended to the underworld to confer with his then-dead father. Eventually, Aeneas founded the city of Rome, and the Roman Empire."

"Is it the first entrance?" asked Benny.

"We think so," Daniel confirmed. "Virgil wrote his epic poem about Aeneas's journey around 19 BCE, but another famous story dates the sibyl back to 500 BCE. Actual caves, as described by Virgil, were discovered in 1932. A second city, Baiae, along the Bay of Naples, was a playground for wealthy Romans, much like Pompeii. Baiae also has underground caves, boiling rivers, gasses and volcanic activity, indicative of the underworld. Both Baiae and Cumae were part of the caldera of Vesuvius. But most of Baiae is underwater in the bay. We'll drive back to Athens tomorrow and board the jet for Naples, then drive to Cumae. Minnie will meet us there."

The table fell quiet. Smiles became serious straight lines.

Benny put his hand over the middle of the table. "This is it, guys."

Zuma put his hand over Benny's, followed by Chaz, who whispered to Amir, "Put your hand in," which he did. Kami and Raj followed, then Mike and Daniel.

Layla sucked in a deep breath and blew it out. She reached her hand up and placed it atop the others.

"You don't have to," said Benny.

"This is for realz, Benny. That snake thingy took my mom. If it had taken me, mom would have come after me," said Layla. "Daniel, was Aeneas afraid?"

As they all broke hands, Daniel clutched Layla's hand and gripped it tightly. "I think so. Most heroes—the best ones—were either reluctant or afraid to heed the call. Odysseus, the hero of the Trojan War, didn't want to go. When they came to get him, he pretended he was crazy, hoping they'd go away and leave him in peace, but they found him out, so he went. And he was a king. Achilles, on the other hand, knew of a prophesy—he would either stay home and live a long life in obscurity, not having made a name for himself—or he would go to Troy, die and become famous. He chose to go to Troy and die a hero."

"You guys are my family," Layla said, gazing around the table and pausing at each face. I'd rather die trying to protect you, and these people, too, I guess, rather than wait at home for the end to come."

Benny put his hand over hers and Daniel's. "Now that's a warrior." The others piled their hands on again. Benny added, "We're all scared, Layla. And that's no lie."

Chapter Nineteen

As the plane descended, Daniel pointed to a city of beige-and-white dwellings with red roofs, sitting on land that jutted out from the shoreline. "That's Naples."

The coastline of highs and lows stretched from the Bay of Naples southward, as far as their eyes could see. One prominence rose above the miniscule houses that surrounded it. "And that volcano is the famous Mount Vesuvius."

"But it's dormant, right?" asked Zuma. "Or they wouldn't build so close to it."

"Not at all," said Daniel. "Its last eruption was in 1944. It's not even six miles away from Naples. It's considered the most dangerous volcano in the world by the density of population living near it. About three million people are in harm's way. Ironically, it's thermal hot springs and the Roman baths built over them is what drew wealthy visitors to Herculaneum, Pompeii and Baiae, all known as scandalous seaside resorts, until the famous eruption in 79 CE buried them in ash, but it also preserved exquisite mosaic floors, colorful fresco paintings and numerous bodies caught in the midst of death. In fact, Julius Caesar, Nero and others had villas in Baiae—the richest of the three resorts. It sits directly adjacent to the *Campi Flegrei*, or Fields of Fire, highly active volcanic fields. Roman engineers even cut channels, some large enough to drive a chariot through, from Cumae and surrounding lakes to Baiae. They built cold, moderate and hot baths, mineral baths, saunas—even built a casino."

"The first Las Vegas," added Mike.

"The rich man's Vegas—entirely exclusive," corrected Daniel.

When they landed, Mike offered to drive again, but when he hit the tight curves and narrow streets of old Naples, he blurted a series euphemisms. His favorite was "Blanketly blank," which he repeated over and over with increasing volume, sometimes slapping the wheel or horn.

Tiny cars, often dented on the driver's side, whipped past. Parked cars sat with two wheels on the sidewalk, edging away from the street as best as possible. Those had dents, too. When a tour bus came at him, Mike panicked and stopped, waiting for a crash. Cars behind him honked. As the bus passed by, they all pulled their feet up, expecting a crash that never came. As they lowered their feet back to the floor, Mike put his foot down on the gas pedal and they inched forward once again on the windy streets. To this, Mike simply yelled, "Blank! Blank! And blank!"

As soon as the van stopped and they all piled out, the warm, muggy air and a clear blue sky could not deter their enjoyment of the cliff-top city and the view of the bay and the Amalfi Coast. They settled into their hotel, agreeing to meet in the lobby at seven for dinner. Daniel and Mike had rooms of their own. The girls shared a room, and the boys had two rooms: Chaz and Amir, Zuma and Benny.

The group met in the lobby and headed out the door. Daniel led the way along several streets to the funicular station. They bought tickets and boarded the tram. They reached the bottom of the hill long before they ran out of conversation. Enjoying the cooler temperature of evening, they strolled along a seaside street that smelled of wood-burning ovens, garlic and salty sea air. The sun, which had no more than an hour of life left, cast a warm pink glow over the sailboats and yachts that bobbed in the bay.

Benny paused at a pizza place. "I know you had a fancier restaurant in mind, Daniel, but how about pizza?"

"Totally!" said Raj. Kami and Layla agreed.

Chaz said, "Doesn't matter to me." Amir and Zuma gave a thumbs-up.

"Whatever the kids want is fine by me," said Mike.

"Napoli is known for pizza. It's a good choice," said Daniel. "It's also known for pickpockets, so be careful."

———

Over large pizzas, orange Fantas and other drinks, the group relaxed. The warriors laughed about training mishaps or past events, as if flipping through mental photo albums. Benny shared the events of his life—the good times. Mike shared the moments of combat that led to his decision to join the FBI after his tour of duty, and Daniel shared humorous stories of his most unusual tribal studies—odd foods, scary rituals, and the one time he had to leave an expensive camera behind to appease an irate tribal chief after Daniel declined the offer of marriage to his daughter.

Raj and Kami showered Layla with hugs and humor, assuring her that they were no longer odd twos but, in every way, a triad again.

"And triangles are the strongest polygon," added Zuma with pride. "It's why bridges are made of them."

Chaz, Amir and Zuma did much the same, ensuring Benny of his place among them.

No one spoke of the next day. It was if they all pretended, for a short time, they were in Italy for a vacation. The funicular closed by ten, but no one rushed. They boarded the last car up the hill, and Daniel kept the night alive by insisting they stop for gelato, promising a taste on their tongue that rose far above the best ice cream they'd ever eaten.

Metal pans loaded with wavy mounds of raspberry or pomegranate red, pistachio green, white coconut, smooth beige hazelnut or *dulce de leche* caramel, banana and lemon yellows and a horde of other choices, dotted with decorative fruit or nuts, satisfied their eyes long before reaching their tongues. Gelato cups or cones in hand, they strolled back to the hotel between wide yawns. For a moment, no adrenaline stormed their veins. For a moment, they could just be kids. Not warriors. They turned in and slept hard.

———————

Daniel and Mike rose early to meet Minnie in the hotel lobby to organize the day.

"I couldn't stay away, you know," said Minnie. "Should have come with you in the first place, but my father is always telling me to delegate more."

Mike added, "Now you know why I fought so hard to be here."

"The children need a proper send off," added Daniel. "It's the least we can do. They'll be happy to see you."

The students joined them for breakfast, wearing the black-and-silver clothing that Zuma had designed for them. The staff of the hotel believed they were actors filming a commercial, so no one batted an eye over the duffle bags that, had they looked, were filled with weapons, not cameras. Their backpacks contained a couple of water bottles, trail mix bars, a compass, a first-aid kit, lighters, binoculars, a map of sorts that Daniel had constructed from historians of the past, climbing racks and climbing rope. Each added personal items. For Benny, it was the picture of him with his mother and father. No one, not even Minnie, really knew what to pack for a trip to the underworld.

Over breakfast, Mike initiated the briefing. "We'll be here when you get back."

"If we get back," added Amir.

Mike reached his hand over to Amir's and gripped it tightly. "*When* you get back, Amir." He released Amir's hand and eyed the others. "When you *all* get back. Daniel, fill them in."

Daniel cleared his throat. "First of all, keep in mind that the world has changed, and so, too, I imagine, has the underworld described by the few travelers who entered it long ago. Also, Hades' realm was not all bad. Those related to the gods, favored by the gods, or heroes, rested in this peaceful land after death with the same comforts they had in life."

"The Elysian Fields," said Chaz.

"Quite," said Daniel. "I don't know what to expect when you meet the Sibyl of Cumae, but here's what I know. Virgil described her cave just as it was discovered in 1932:

> *A spacious cave, within its farmost part,*
> *Was hew'd and fashion'd by laborious art*
> *Thro' the hill's hollow sides: before the place,*
> *A hundred doors a hundred entries grace."*

Daniel continued, "Virgil described the sibyl as a crazed woman, making hollow groans and with hair standing on end, a convulsive rage, shaking limbs, and foaming when she spoke. But Ovid's description is much kinder. He relates a tragic tale. She was once beautiful. So stunning, she caught the eye of Apollo. To ensnare her heart, he offered her any wish, if she would only love him in return. She pointed to a heap of sand and asked for as many birthdays as there were grains of sand. Apollo promised her this—and more—reminding her that she had only asked for a long life, not youth. But she refused him her love and remained unmarried, which ignited Apollo's anger—tip for the future—do not anger the gods. Apollo kept his promise and granted her wish— but no more—he gave her one thousand years but not youth. When she met Aeneas," Daniel paused, glancing at Zuma.

"What? I got your point yesterday," Zuma defended.

"Go on, Daniel," Minnie directed.

Daniel complied. "When she met Aeneas, the sybil was seven hundred years old and withering away, but she said that no matter how small she became, her voice would never die. One of her prophesies foretold the coming of a hero or savior. That's all I can tell you. I hope it helps."

"What about our weapons?" asked Benny. "How do we get them past security at Cumae?"

Mike jumped in. "They think we're a film crew shooting a commercial."

"Let me guess," said Benny. "A commercial for the *Warriors and Watchers* video game?"

Mike and Daniel nodded to confirm, while Minnie remained stoic.

Daniel spared Mike by driving the half hour or so due west, although the drive was much easier than in town. Time passed quickly and quietly. They drove by Lake Avernus. The sky of azure blue and the Tyrrhenian Sea in the distance held no special charm. The frivolity of a beautiful day meant nothing more than a snapshot of a sight they hoped to see again if they made it back.

Daniel drove into the archaeological site and parked. He purchased tickets but, for once, he had no interest in touring the ancient rubble, where Christian edifices replaced earlier Roman ones, which replaced earlier Greek ones, which replaced cave-dwelling Iron Age Cimmerians, the first to settle the region. The others felt the same way. They had one destination, and no acropolis nor necropolis, no temple to Zeus nor Apollo, no myth nor historical point of interest could turn their attention away from the sunless world that came closer with each footfall taken in the direction of the Cave of the Sibyl.

Minnie and Benny took the lead. Kami, Layla, Raj and Zuma followed, side by side like an impenetrable wall, loaded with duffle bags. Mike and Daniel lagged behind, helping maneuver Chaz's wheelchair down stone steps and guiding Amir.

At the bottom of the steps, they came into view of the trapezoidal opening, carved into yellow tufa limestone. Numerous slits cut into the sides of the long shaft cast slices of light that pierced the tunnel and alit the dirt floor. It was easy to see why Virgil had described it as having a hundred doors.

Their hearts sped up but their feet slowed down to ensure Chaz's and Amir's presence among them. It was as if, from this point forward, they huddled together, not in fear, but in strength of will.

At the entrance to the shaft, Chaz said to Daniel and Mike, "You can let go. I got it." The words emerged as more figurative than literal—Chaz meant to let go, not of his chair, but to let go of *him*. Amir put a hand on Chaz's shoulder. "Lead on, bro." Mike and Daniel followed close behind.

The angled walls of the long shaft reached deep into the throat of the cliff. The ceiling rose above their heads, three times their height. The far end loomed larger, while behind them the shaft of light at the entrance grew smaller—already it felt like a descent into a dark abyss.

At the end of the tunnel, they spilled into a square room with three vaulted recesses whose walls were mottled in sickly greens, yellows and blacks. A smaller recess had hewn benches on either side of a double-arched alcove; perhaps it served as the waiting area for those wishing an audience with the sibyl. Tourists milled about, but the guards began to herd them toward the shaft, explaining they were closed for the afternoon due to a commercial shoot.

Minnie and Benny waited for a young American couple to exit the alcove. The girl spoke with a Southern accent. "What idiots, thinking this was some kinda entrance to hell." Her husband added, "Well, not today. No. But people back then were superstitious."

Benny wished that he still had their innocence and ignorance.

The warriors entered the alcove. Minnie put up a hand to stop Daniel and Mike from following. "You two stay here. Keep watch." Before Mike could argue, she added, "That's an order, soldier."

Benny saw the difficulty of obeying that order in Mike's eyes. But Benny got it. Minnie didn't want to tempt Mike. The closer they got to the entrance, the more likely Mike would fight to tag along. Mike marched to the shaft opening and assumed an on-duty stance to guard the entrance and ensure privacy.

Daniel's face showed disappointment and obedience.

As Minnie stepped into the alcove, Benny eyed the others in the dim light, taking comfort in being pressed together, bumping an arm here, a leg there.

The ground shook and rumbled. Sand and small rocks rained down. All light disappeared. They threw their hands up over their heads. Just as suddenly, the shaking stopped.

A shimmering light of gold, pale green and violet swarmed around them, like a living aurora borealis. Benny sensed it was living and friendly. As it spilled out of the alcove, he knew they were to follow.

They stepped into a chamber quite unlike the one they had left and crossed over a mosaic-tiled floor, black and white, patterned in swirls and florals. Fresco paintings of Apollo admiring a fair-haired woman covered every wall as well as the ceiling. At the center of the room stood a marble pedestal upon which sat an urn of gold.

The group dropped their bags.

A melodic voice sang to them. If voice alone could carry unforetold beauty, this was it, alluring, sonorous, seductive:

> *Sister of Delphi bespoke of youthful athletes*
> *Chosen and chaste, in Hades games shall you compete*
> *Warriors seven, the only hope for mankind*
> *Keys to seven gates, 'tis your fated quest to find.*

Benny called out, "We seek the entrance to the underworld. Can you help us?'

The aurora borealis dove into the fair-haired girl in the fresco and disappeared. The girl turned her face away from Apollo's and gazed at the visitors. She stepped out of the fresco and strode toward them. A chiton of white sheer cloth draped over her petite figure; a sheer scarf adorned her head, held in place by a delicate gold band of flowers; a long twisting coil of blonde hair fell over one shoulder. Her face, stunning even though unadorned, carried innocence and torment. "If you help me."

Benny asked, "How?"

She paced among them. "A foolish and greedy sister sold our books of prophecy to the last king of Rome, Tarquin the Proud.

She offered him nine volumes at a rich price. He refused. She burned three and offered him the remaining six at the same price. Again he refused. She burned three more. He bought the three that survived for the original price. Hades stole our books."

Layla asked, "What do the books have to do with us? We're after keys."

"Take pity on me. I was young, foolish. Prideful even." She gazed at Apollo. "He loved me so, and I spurned him for a thousand years. I . . . I feared his love. Distrusted him. And when I turned old, withered, and then to ashes, he loved me still. He forged this chamber and set my urn in the middle. Every day, he speaks to me and watches my ashes disappear. I finally confessed my love to him. The Sibylline books contain a prophecy. It will not restore my life, but once read, it will restore my sense of touch for as long as I have left. My time is nearly gone. I will be nothing but a voice. I can accept that if I could but touch Apollo's hand one time, and in that touch, return the love that he has shown to me."

Minnie's brows knitted in consternation. "Selfish girl! You can't ask this of them. You know what is at stake."

"It's knowing what is at stake, what will be lost, that has driven me to ask," she replied. "Have mercy. I beg you."

"Lead them to the entrance at once!" ordered Minnie. "Recant your selfish desires."

"Just swear you'll try," pleaded the sibyl, ignoring Minnie and pleading with the others. "Please. That's all I ask. No more."

Benny thought of how he had spurned his mother, and how he'd do anything to get her back. "I'm in."

Zuma added, "Let's face it. It's crazy anyway—why not make it crazier." The others agreed.

"The key, the books and our mothers," said Raj. "Piece of cake." All consented.

Benny added, "Lead the way."

"You'll need my golden urn," said the ghostly figure.

"For what?" asked Benny.

"You'll know when the time comes. Pour my ashes on the pedestal."

Benny picked up the urn and tipped it.

"Wait!" Layla pulled off her backpack and unzipped it. She withdrew a sheer red scarf. She spread it out on the pedestal.

Benny poured the contents, a sprinkling of ashes, onto the scarf.

Layla neatly tied the corners. "This was my mother's scarf. She'd approve. She enjoyed a good love story."

The sybil bowed her head in thanks. As she disappeared, her light danced around them and she sang:

Nine circles deep and dark, for Hades' realm thou start
In search of treasures: one of hope and one of heart.

With a sound of stone grinding against stone, the back wall slid aside. A blast of heat swept through the room.

The warriors stepped through the portal entrance.

"Be strong," said Minnie. The entrance closed before any of the warriors could turn or respond. "And keep safe," she added, too late for their ears to hear it.

Chapter Twenty

Puddles and sprays of lava shot into an inky black sky over which hung a red moon. Zuma pushed Chaz's chair.

"Wait," said Chaz. "Amir, sit on my lap. I don't want you tripping into a puddle of lava."

"Is that why it's so hot?" Amir sat in Chaz's lap, tossing out a joke to lighten the mood. "You're my hero!"

"Ahh, it'sh a bromance," said Kami.

"So adorbs," said Raj.

"This must be what it's like to walk on Venus," said Benny, stepping on a purple stone. A flare of fire shot up between his legs. Benny jumped out of its way. "Warning. Do not step on purple rocks."

Layla said, "There's something glowing up ahead."

"I see it." Benny headed straight for what looked like a small sun on the horizon.

They reached a ramp leading up to a donut-shaped black granite object filled with fire so hot it burned white at the center. Red neon signs encircled the granite: ABANDON ALL HOPE, YE WHO ENTER HERE, TURN BACK, DO NOT ENTER, DANGER, and MIND THE GAP.

"Gotta love Hades' sense of humor," said Zuma.

"No, we don't," said Raj.

"I'll go firsht," said Kami. "Check out the other shide."

"I'll go with her," said Zuma. As they walked into the white fire, Zuma screamed, writhed and waved his arms about. Kami stood motionless.

Benny and Layla lunged to reach for Zuma.

Zuma stood still. "Just kidding, dudes. Can't feel a thing."

"So not funny, Zuma!" scolded Layla. "Next time, I'm not coming after you and you'll fry because I'll think you're messing around."

"You'll come. You're my bestie," said Zuma. "See ya." He and Kami took another step and disappeared.

Raj and Layla went next, then Chaz, who wheeled himself up the small ramp and over the edge.

Benny set Amir before the fiery portal. "Just walk straight ahead." Once Amir disappeared, Benny shouldered his bag, clutched the urn and stepped into the ring of fire. He plunged headlong into dark space. He heard Amir let out a high-pitched scream, so innocent and authentic of him, that Benny could not hold back a short smile. It meant he was still alive. By now, he knew Amir's screams well, and this one did not pose fright so much as surprise.

The strap of the duffle bag slid down his arm and ripped it away from the urn. Both the bag and urn flew into space. He didn't mind losing the bag, but he had to have that urn. He wasn't great at diving after things in midair, not like the others who had better skydiving skills, but he had to try. He put his body into a dive and chased after the golden spinning object.

The fall pushed his cheeks back. As he tumbled freely, he remembered Daniel's lecture, which now seemed true: "Hesiod wrote that an anvil falling for nine days from the upperworld would hit the ground on the tenth. So, too, would an anvil fall for nine days from earth before it hit Tartarus." The urn was within reach, but shifted right or left just as he grabbed for it. "Steady," he said to himself, getting the hang of it. His best chance was to hit it, not grab it. He picked up speed and aimed for it. The moment it slammed into his chest, he wrapped his arms around it. He curled into a ball around it, knowing it was the worst possible position in which to land, but he had no choice.

Benny didn't mind the fall. It brought him all the closer to his mother, and he figured Hades didn't want him dead just yet. He hoped. Whether they found the keys or books or not, whether they saved humanity or not, if he had a little more time with his mother, a chance to apologize, he would—like the Sibyl of Cumae—be satisfied in death. He shook the thought away. Death was not a thought he could afford to entertain.

The black sky lightened to yellow orange. Benny saw a pile of sand below him and braced for a crash. The sand shot into the air, forming spindly fingers and a palm that caught his fall. "Not bad," he said all too soon. The hand hurled him down the sand hill.

Benny tumbled down the hill, over and over, clutching the urn, until he flopped to the bottom.

Benny felt a hand reach for his and yank him to his feet.

"None of our weapons made it. Hades must have snatched them in the fall," said Zuma. "Chaz's chair didn't make it either."

A pile of twisted leather and melted metal sat in a heap nearby. Benny eyed the landscape in all directions: mound after mound of sand dunes stretched before them. "We still have the urn and our backpacks. We can use the rope and tie a hammock to carry him."

Layla helped Amir to his feet. Amir wiped sand from his eyes and opened them.

Layla and Amir screamed at the same time. "His eyes!" said Layla. "They're black."

"And I can see. I can see! I can see!" Amir jumped up and down. "Layla, girl, you are stunning!"

Raj and Kami huffed.

"Are they pretty? My eyes?" asked Amir. "Exactly how black are they? Does anyone have a mirror?"

"Bees' eyes black, dude," said Raj.

"Creepy and shiny," said Kami.

Kami's hands rushed to her ears, "O-M-G! I think I heard that. I did. I can hear myshelf. Ooo, I shound funny."

"Only your *s*," said Layla. "They sound like *shhhh*. Should be *sssss*."

Kami tried to correct herself. "*Shhhh. Shhhh.* I don't get it."

"Give it time," said Raj.

Amir waved his hands in the air. "Oh, never mind. Kami can hear and I can see and Chaz can walk! When did you go green, Raj? Benny, you have stubble—makes you look mean, like your voice. Kami, you're so little. Zuma, you're so big!"

"I'm skin and bones." Zuma complained, "Thanks to Minnie and her fruit cups."

The group huddled around Chaz. Chaz stared at his legs, as if willing them to move. The group waited and held their breath.

Chaz concentrated and concentrated. Finally, he wiggled one foot then the other. "I don't know about walk, but I can move my toes. Help me up."

Even though two assistants would have been sufficient, all of the boys rushed to get a hand on Chaz and prop him on his feet. "I got it," said Chaz.

They let him go. "I'm standing! I'll try a step." Chaz slid one awkward foot before the other.

"That's one small step for mankind, a giant leap for the Chaz-man," said Zuma, altering Neil Armstrong's words when the astronaut took the first step on the moon.

Chaz took a second step. "I can walk." The moment he said it, he wobbled and fell on his face.

"Or not," said Raj.

"He'll get it," said Benny. Without waiting, the boys lifted him to his feet again.

"Baby steps," reminded Layla.

Raj tapped Kami on the shoulder and whispered, "Is it gone?" She pushed her hair aside to reveal her birthmark.

Kami shook her head. "Maybe it will fade the longer we're here."

"Maybe," said Raj. "I'll scout around."

"I'm coming, too," added Amir. "I'll protect you!"

"Protect yourself, bug boy!" Raj let out an angry huff.

"Okay. You'll protect me then," scoffed Amir as he followed her.

"No, I won't," she said.

"Yes, you will" and "No, I won't" continued back and forth, fading as the pair climbed the tallest dune.

By the time they returned, Chaz was sliding his feet in slow circles, dancing with Layla. He spun her into his chest, *"Mon amour."*

Layla rebuked his "my love" with "And me armed and danger-ous," after which she shoved him off with "Don't make me break your brand new legs."

"In case anyone cares," said Amir, "the dunes end over this next hill."

Raj added, "Then it's flat desert all around. But we see people in the distance and what looks like a signpost."

"Lead the way," said Benny.

Zuma flanked Chaz. "I'll keep an eye on Dancing Dude."

They trekked together, laughing as if back at the forest compound. Amir could not stop pointing and describing everything—everything—down to the laces on his tennis shoes. His newfound wonderment and excitement made for a hilarious walk.

Chaz enjoyed his new talent in silence. Zuma gave him pointers. "You're shuffling. Lift your feet. Like this."

Chaz copied Zuma's demonstration.

"Now you look like you belong in a marching band playing the piccolo. Not so high," said Zuma.

Upon reaching the strange swarm of people, the group halted and tensed, ready for a fight.

"What the heck?" said Zuma.

People wearing plain white underwear milled about, heading in all directions and yet, it seemed, in no particular direction at all. Others laughed and bounced up and down on seesaws. Others sat upon fences, gazing first to one side, then to the other. Others stared down at the ground, putting one foot carefully before the other, following a yellow line that wound this way and that, in loops and twists and crazy eights that eventually connected back to the beginning.

And some people had no mouths.

Benny stopped a short, middle-aged man. "Where do we find Hades?"

The man's face contorted with anxiety. He ran both hands over his short gray hair and down his chest as if calming himself long enough to pose an answer. He puffed out his cheeks as he thought, which seemed to take great effort. Finally, he stuttered, "I-d-d-d-d-don't n-n-n-know." With that, he rushed off to continue his meandering.

Chaz stopped a rather pretty redhead, early thirties, with a shapely figure and asked, "Where is Hades'?"

Her eyes brightened, she smiled and sucked in a breath, then let it out as if giving an answer as erudite as one of Daniel's, and said, "Om-to-see-on-the-uh-over-where-the-maybe-next."

Chaz and the group eyed one another.

Raj repeated the question. "Didn't catch that. Which way?"

This time, the pretty lady bobbed her head up and down and put a hand over her heart as if to say, *Of course, silly me. I get it now.* Again, she sucked in a breath and let it out, saying, "Over-that-is-on-where-you-go-to-something-something-and-again."

"No good," said Benny.

"Neither is the sign," said Layla. One marker pointed left and read THIS WAY, and the other pointed right and read THAT WAY. Below which, two more signs read, NO, THIS WAY, and the other read NO, THAT WAY, and below that read OVER THERE, and the opposing one read NO, OVER THERE.

Chaz added, "Dante described a desert that he called *limbo*. This may be it."

An old couple approached the sign, read it and headed THIS WAY. A younger couple read it and headed THAT WAY. Both headed off in opposite directions into the barren landscape.

Just then, a man and a woman walked by, carrying on a conversation between them. He said, "Let's go that way," and she said, "Let's go that way," and then she said, "My turn to lead," and he said, "My turn to lead," and then he said, "It's a fine day," and she said, "It's a fine day." And off they went, passing right through the newcomers and back toward the dunes.

As if that wasn't weird enough, the strangest creature of all approached—it had two heads, one male, one female, but only one body, half male, half female. Its fingers were interlaced over its chest. "We hear you have a question," said the man, adjusting dark-rimmed glasses. "We'd like to help," said the woman.

"Thank you," gushed Zuma. "Finally!"

Benny asked, "Where can we find Hades'?"

They both smiled and threw their heads back in laughter. "Simple," he said.

"So simple," she said.

"Come with us," he said.

"We'll take you there," she said.

"We appreciate it," said Amir.

"Totes," added Raj.

The creature proceeded to take a step, but he put a foot left and she crossed over it, taking a step right, after which they eyed each other with disdain. "It's this way," he said pointing.

"You're wrong, it's that way," she said, crossing her arm over his and pointing in the opposite direction.

"I'm always wrong," he said.

"Well, that's right. You're always wrong."

"Which means I'm not always wrong! Got you!"

She huffed, "Let's try this again."

He said, "Fine!" They each took another step, this time in opposite directions, after which they argued more.

"What did I ever see in you?" she said.

"My superior intelligence," he said.

"Thinking you're superior does not make you superior."

"I outsmarted you, didn't I?" With smug satisfaction, he put his hand on his hip.

"I'm done," she said.

"I'm done," he said, and with that they began pulling and tugging in opposite directions. Their faces strained with the effort. Their cheeks puffed with consternation and turned fuchsia, until quite suddenly, *Rip!* Right down the middle. After which they each hopped about on one leg, wagging a finger, before hopping away.

"Wow!" said Kami. "Ish . . . issss that how people divorce down here?"

"Extreme!" said Zuma.

"What do we do now?" asked Amir.

"Beats me," said Benny. "You guys are the scholars—come up with something."

"I have an idea," said Layla. "Benny's right. We have to use logic. The direction we came from is behind us, so we know what's there. The signposts tell us to go this way and that way, so I don't think we should go in either of those. We go straight ahead. Right through these people."

Zuma wrapped an arm around her shoulder. "Check!"

"Mate!" said Layla.

"Let's do it," said Chaz.

"What if she's wrong?" asked Raj.

"Would you rather split up, Raj?" asked Zuma.

"Maybe that'sh what they want," said Kami.

"I say we stick together," said Amir.

"I agree. We can always double back," said Benny.

"The sages have spoken. Let's go," agreed Raj.

They crossed through the odd menagerie of people. No one paid any attention to them, except the one-legged man hopping after them surprisingly fast, but not quite fast enough to catch up to them, at which point, he bent over and walked, like an inch worm, from hand-to-foot, hand-to-foot.

They walked and walked with the man sidling along behind them, until the strange people became ant sized.

"Look!" said Amir, pointing dead ahead and wagging a finger.

No one saw anything.

"You guys are blind!" said Amir. "There is a guy, right there, sitting in a chair with an umbrella attached. His chair is next to a boat."

"Could be Charon?" said Chaz. "The ferryman who takes us across the Acheron, the River of Woe, that leads to Hades' realm."

"But I don't see any river," said Amir. "He's sitting in the middle of more desert."

"Those black eyes seem to be getting stronger," said Raj. "Hope that's not a bad thing."

Layla put a hand on Chaz's arm, then let it fall away. "I hate to admit this, but it's nice to see you with your swag back."

"I got my legs back." Chaz tipped his chin down to meet her eye to eye. "I never lost my swag."

Layla laughed, slapping his arm in an affectionate way.

Raj rolled her eyes. "Now, I'm going to puke."

Benny nodded. "I see him! He's wearing a blue shirt."

"Actually," said Amir. "It's a Polynesian shirt with palm trees and coconuts, and he's wearing baggy beige shorts, sandals with an anchor clasp, and he's holding a drink with a teensy-tiny umbrella stuck in it."

"Show off," said Kami.

"Not really," said Amir. "Showing off would be to tell you that there are girls in bikinis on the teensy-tiny umbrella."

Benny added, "From now on, Amir, you're our eyes."

Chapter Twenty-One

The group approached the man sprawled on the lounge chair. His excessively hairy legs and one hairy arm hung over the sides of the chair. In his other hand, which rested on his rotund belly, he gripped a fruity drink.

"Is he awake?" asked Raj.

"Ish he alive?" asked Kami.

The man belched and sat upright. As he did so, his drink sloshed on his shirt, which he wiped onto his shorts. "Shoot. I just washed this shirt a millennium ago." He rose to his feet, towering over them.

"Is that for me?" the man asked.

Benny handed over the urn. "You Charon?"

"If this is legit, I am." The boatman bit one of the urn's handles, raised his hairy brows and nodded approval. He led them to the boat, a silver-and-orange semi-rigid inflatable with four rows of seats and a stern-drive console with a steering wheel suited for a pirate, complete with a skull and crossbones at its center. "All aboard!" Charon climbed in and stood behind the console.

Kami stepped into the front seat and sat next to Raj. "Don't we need water? Like, a river, maybe?"

"What we need," Charon spat back, "is for the dead to remember they're dead."

Layla sat just behind the girls. "I like your boat."

"Well, I hate it!" grumbled Charon. "Hades complained that I couldn't row fast enough with all of the crowds piling up these days, so he gave me this contraption. Just look at me. I used to be fit!"

"May I join you," asked the half-man, who had caught up to them. He'd grown a leg but still didn't have a second arm.

Charon shrugged. "Your call. Urn's good for a few more."

"Have a seat." Layla scooted over and the man sat beside her.

"Can I have a life vest?" the newcomer asked Charon.

Charon let out a gut-wrenching bout of laughter, spilling his drink down his shirt again. "Look what you made me do." He wiped his wet shirt. "What's the matter? Afraid you're gonna die?"

"I guess that was a silly question." The man pushed his glasses back on his nose. He introduced himself. "I'm Wendell." He gave her his left hand to shake, as it was the only one he had.

"Layla."

Zuma and Chaz occupied the last seat, and Amir and Benny piled in behind Layla and Wendell.

Charon set a black-and-gold captain's hat upon his curly head. He immediately transformed into a skeleton. His Polynesian shirt and shorts shredded to tatters. Winds blew in torrents and gusts and howls. "Hold on for dear death."

Charon turned the key. The engines sparked to life, only instead of a rumble, it sounded like moaning and groaning. The ground beneath them rocked, forming a channel of sand on each side of the boat. A long purple stream snaked its way toward them from somewhere ahead. The moment it touched the hull of the boat, the sand shot up beneath them, forming a chute filled with roaring purple water.

Benny peered over the side. Faces in the water stretched and elongated and twisted in the currents of the River of Woe.

Charon pushed the throttle forward. The boat plunged ahead, throwing back the heads of the passengers. Everyone's hands gripped the rope along the rim of the hull or the very benches on which they sat.

The landscape changed as the boat shot forward down the chute. They left the flat desert behind and entered a canyon of coal, a charred, barren landscape, like an abandoned planet devoid of life. Craggy cliffs and knife-sharp spires stabbed at an angry orange sky.

The boat careened around twists and turns, nearing the edge and threatening to fly out of the chute at any moment. Downward and downward they plunged.

Amir screamed like Benny had never heard anyone scream before. He closed his eyes and dropped his head.

Benny realized that this sight would be overwhelming to Amir's new eyes. Amir had grown accustomed to coping with the feelings of life but he had been protected, until now, from the sights of it. How terrifying it must be.

"Don't peek," shouted Benny.

"No duh!" shouted Amir.

The river-like chute did loop-de-loops and spirals and shot nearly straight up into the air. A time or two, they became airborne until landing in the chute again.

The sky turned an angry mix of orange, black and purple. Wendell screamed. Charon laughed as he peeked over his shoulder directly at Benny and pushed the throttle full forward.

Benny saw a curve ahead. He knew they couldn't make it.

The boat hit the curve, climbed the edge of the chute, plummeted over the edge and plunged downward.

Everyone screamed, Layla, Wendell and Amir most of all.

The bow of the boat plunged into a wide body of water, where black mingled with purple. A wave shot over the helm, over Charon, and downward, drenching Kami and Raj.

The boat bobbed upright and slowed down as it crossed the watery expanse, headed for land.

Suddenly, Raj yelled, "I hate you!"

"It washn't my fault!" said Kami. "I hate you more!"

"You talk funny!"

"You're ugly!" Kami grabbed Raj's shoulders and yanked her to the floor of the boat.

"Stop it!" screamed Layla.

Benny watched the girls reach for each other's hair and scratch at each other's faces.

"It's the water!" yelled Chaz. "The Acheron crosses the River Styx, the River of Hate. They must have swallowed some."

"What do we do?" said Layla. "They'll kill each other."

Benny hopped over the seats and shoved between Layla and Wendell to reach the girls. He tried to pull them apart, but they fought around him and jabbed at him.

Charon's eyes glowed red, as if he enjoyed the spectacle. Benny spotted Charon's drink sitting in a cup holder on the helm. He lunged for it.

"Hey, give that back!" Charon complained, swiping at Benny with a bony skeletal hand but missing.

Benny tried to steady the cup over the moving mouths of the girls. Kami kicked him in the shin.

"Ow! That hurt!" Benny poured the drink into their mouths as they shouted curses and complaints.

"Serves you right, Benny," shouted Raj. "I hate you more than I hate—" Gurgle. Cough.

"Yeah, get out of the way, sho I can tear her—" Cough. Gurgle.

Benny poured the entire drink in both of their faces. They gasped in shock that he would do such a thing.

Benny watched for signs of improvement. He had reacted hastily, not knowing what else to do. He didn't know if the drink would help or hurt them, but then they already had scratches and strands of hair twisted in their hands.

"What happened?" asked Raj, her fingers tracing over scratches on her cheek.

"Ouch," said Kami, dabbing her fingers gently to her swollen lower lip.

Benny helped them up. "You two tried to kill each other. We think you drank some Styx water."

"The gods swore oaths on Styx," said Chaz. "And the goddess of the river gave birth to other gods and goddesses: Nike, goddess of victory; Bia, goddess of force; Kratos, god of strength or power and Zelos, god of zeal, energy. Some say the water makes a person invulnerable. Achilles's mom held him by the heel and dipped him in it, which is why he was a great warrior—until he was shot in the heel and died, that is."

"Sounds powerful," said Benny.

"You saw what it did to the girls, and they swallowed a few drops. It's pure hate."

The boat glided onto a shoreline and came to a stop. In the near distance was an impressive red granite wall, veined in black. A sprawling staircase led up to a landing and an imposing gate, whose black doors slowly swung open. Black flowers in golden urns lined each side of it.

Chaz helped Kami and Raj out of the boat. Raj burped. Kami followed with an even longer belch.

Charon removed his hat and returned to his pudgy self. He offered a hand to help the others out of the craft.

Benny knelt down. He pulled a water bottle out of his backpack, emptied the contents and filled it with black Styx water. As soon as he capped it, the water turned clear. He scratched the label to mark it and tucked it back in his pack.

"It's beautiful," said Amir, as they climbed the staircase, keeping an eye out for danger. "For a creepy underworld place."

The group scurried up the staircase to the landing but halted when a small dog appeared in the entranceway and barked at them. It was the size of a Chihuahua, beige, but with three heads with black faces, bulging black eyes, and a spiked collar. It wagged a small scaly tail, which zigzagged in the air like a small bolt of lightning.

"Oh, how cute," said Wendell, rushing up to greet it. Before the others could stop him, he dashed forward, extending his one and only hand. "Nice puppy."

Quick as a school of piranha, the dog leaped on Wendell, devouring him so fast that no one saw even a drop of blood, just his shredded clothes flying in the air, until nothing was left but shredded cloth.

All three heads swiped their tongues across their lips, and even tried swiping the face next to them, which received growls of complaint and a gentle nip.

An old man standing behind the small dog and just inside the gate, pointed to a large burlap bag that he let down from his shoulder. He signaled for the group to wait. He untied the opening. A blue boar with a long snout and long tusks charged toward them on clawed feet.

Before it reached the warriors, the small dog chased after it and pounced. The old man waved his arms frantically. "Run for it!"

Benny and the others rushed forward, while the dog devoured its meal. The warriors crossed the threshold one after the other.

Amir tripped over Wendell's glasses and sprawled on the ground a few feet short of the threshold.

Cerberus swallowed the last of the blue boar by sucking down his spiraled blue tail, spaghetti-like, until it disappeared.

"Hurry, young lad," shouted the old man.

Benny lunged for the threshold, but the old man stopped him. "Do not throw away two lives, for one. We need you!"

Benny yelled, "Amir, get u—"

Before he could finish his sentence, the dog perked up its ears, licked its chops and shot toward Amir. It pounced on his chest, bared his teeth and growled. As it sniffed him, its spiked collar pricked Amir's neck.

The old man shook his head. "Oh, dear. He's a goner."

"Don't say that," said Zuma. "We've got to do something."

"Wait and hope," said the old man. "But if he isn't dead, he's as good as dead."

The center head sniffed Amir's face.

"Nice doggy." Amir's voice became high-pitched and whiny.

Each head sniffed again. The one in the middle peered into Amir's eyes and cocked his head. The other two heads growled, dripping saliva onto Amir's neck. The one in the middle licked Amir's face.

"Blech," said Amir. "Right? I taste horrible. Like turkey butt. Or . . . or worse . . . like fish butt. Yeah, stinky fish butt. That's me."

The head in the middle yipped and nipped at the other two. All at once, the three tongues licked Amir's face again and again. Amir had to put up a hand up to stop them, and they licked his hand, too, and wagged the stubby bent tail.

Amir sat up and scratched behind the ears of the center head, then moved on to the outside heads, all the while rising to his feet, slowly, in case he saw a change in the dog's demeanor. He bent over, scratching ears and backing up toward the threshold.

The dog followed him to the entrance, jumping at his feet as if wanting to play or begging him to throw out another blue boar for it to hunt down and gobble up.

Amir raised a foot and slid it back and over the threshold.

The heads snarled, snapped, gnashed their teeth and stood on Amir's remaining foot. Amir froze. "One chomp, and I'm footless guys. This is so *not* how I saw my life ending."

All at once, Benny and Zuma grabbed the straps of Amir's backpack and ripped him off of his feet, yanking him over the threshold so fast they all flew back and fell to the ground. Amir landed on top of them, and Cerberus did a flip in the air before standing guard again.

Cerberus cocked his heads to the side in unison and whimpered, as if asking Amir to scratch it behind the ears again.

Raj and Kami gave Amir a hand up.

The old man sighed. "You're in, so we're safe from Cerberus. But that poor man. He didn't know any better."

The three-headed dog plopped down on its belly, keeping all six eyes on Amir while wrinkling its brows. It lowered its three heads onto its single pair of legs and sighed.

The old man led the group to a red granite bench. "Let me catch my breath a moment. I haven't seen battle for quite some time. A broggie bag is the only way to get past that little beast short of rendering him unconscious. Cerberus loves a good brog. Of course, he'll eat anything."

"Or anyone," added Zuma.

"He likes me." Amir grinned from ear to ear. "I can tell."

"Maybe he was full," suggested Chaz.

"He's never full," said the old man. "I once watched him eat an army."

"Maybe you taste like caca," said Zuma.

"Or with those creepy eyes, you look like one of the dead," added Benny.

"Well, I think he's cute," said Amir.

"Cuter than his father, Typhon," said the old man. "Even the gods fear that one. He is as tall as the stars." The old man wiped his face with the sleeve of his sooty robe, which seemed to put more soot on his face than to remove it. Soot covered him from head to toe.

"A giant gave birth to that little runt?" asked Benny.

"Do not be fooled by Cerberus's size." The old man had a wildness in his eyes.

"Who are you?" asked Benny.

"A friend. The Sibyl of Cumae asked for my help. I left the Elysian Fields to meet you. I'll take you as far as I can. The sibyl helped my son, Aeneas, long ago." The man rose to his feet. "I'm called Anchises."

"Aeneas," said Zuma, pronouncing the name slowly. "We've heard of your son, Aeneas." Zuma repeated. "Aeneas founded Rome."

The girls rolled their eyes and shook their heads. The boys chuckled under their breath. "Mind if we just call you 'Pops'? It's easier," asked Benny.

"If you like," said Anchises. "Let's move on."

Benny walked alongside the old man as they crossed the palatial square. "We saw some strange beings before we crossed the rivers. Who were they?"

"The inhabitants of limbo," said Pops. "They are a strange group indeed: see-sawers, fence-sitters, I-don't-knows, line-walkers, mumblers, mimics, crowd-followers and two-headed flip-floppers. They went through life letting others tell them what to think, copying what others said or did, following the crowd, not making decisions for themselves, and they suffer the same fate now. A few occasionally make it out of limbo, but they are not welcome in Hades' realm. Most do as they did in life, mill about without direction or purpose, following others and repeating what they hear."

"Besides the keys, we need to find the sibyl's books," said Benny.

"She told me. I have spies asking around," he paused. "Ah, the sibyl. She was a beautiful creature once. Oh, but weren't we all. I was chased by a woman in my younger years." He winked at Layla. "One caught me. And Aeneas was the result."

Raj and Kami chuckled under their breath.

Not knowing quite how to respond, Layla stammered, "Who's his mother?"

"Aphrodite," smirked the old man.

"No way!' said Chaz, impressed. "You, and the goddess of love?"

"I didn't know it at the time. She disguised herself as a Phrygian princess. I only found out her true identity nine months later when she brought my son to me. She swore to strike me with Zeus's thunderbolt if I told anyone about it."

Chaz said, "And . . . did you?"

Pop's eyes twinkled and the corners of his mouth turned upward. "Why do you think I'm covered in soot?"

Zuma rollicked with laughter. Layla knuckled his arm.

"Hey," said Chaz. "It's a guy thing."

Raj snarled, "So is being proud of every fart and burp, but that isn't necessarily a good thing."

"Hey, don't get me started on girl things," warned Zuma.

"Here it is," said the old man. "The First Circle."

They stood before a wall of metal. Once liquid, molten and fluid, it had hardened into rivulets and splashes as it descended and froze in place. Its shiny surface shimmered in gold, silver, copper, and metals tinged green or pink. The longer they stared at it, the more pronounced became the faces and hands trapped within.

All at once, the section of wall before them liquefied and parted to allow them access. It had to be twenty feet across, cutting a channel that could easily close and trap them.

"Pops, what stops the wall from solidifying while we're crossing through?" asked Chaz.

"This wall traps flatterers," said Pops. "Those obsessed with their own good looks and dress."

Amir let out a high-pitched squeak. "What's so wrong with having good fashion sense?"

Pops added, "Nothing. As long as you put others before yourself, that is."

"I do," said Amir. "Right guys? Am I right? Oh, crap. I'm doomed."

Benny responded, "We're about to find out, handsome."

Chapter Twenty-Two

Benny said, "Let's stay in a huddle. We stand a better chance. Put Amir in the middle."

"I'm not selfish," defended Amir. "It's not my fault my mother was a model! You can't blame me for good genes."

"Shut up," said Kami.

"I love you guys," said Amir. "Honest. The wall knows."

Raj added, "Amir, when you're in a hole, stop digging."

The group huddled around Amir. They inched through the molten metal pathway. As they entered, the metal swirled, closing the exit behind them. It closed in front, too, trapping them.

Benny and the others inched their feet forward as the molten wall danced and dripped. A long arm and mechanical hand punched out of the wall and arched overhead. Amir ducked and crouched, mumbling, "I love you guys. I mean it. I do. More than life it—a lot. I love you lots." The claw centered over Amir. The mechanical fingers twitched and tapped.

Benny inched forward, the others at his back. The claw reached down and snapped shut, but Amir ducked out of its way. Up ahead, the exit narrowed such that only one person at a time could pass through.

The clawed fingers, like the claws that grip prizes in vending machines, dove down, forming bars that poked into the clutch of humans separating them and leaving Amir huddled in the center in a cage of his own. A moment later, the fingers rose, as if to set the captive free.

"See, I told you guys," added Amir. "I passed."

With sudden force, the fingers pinched Amir's backpack and hoisted him into the air. It carried him toward the molten wall, as if preparing to shove him in with the others that could now squirm and move and plead but not escape.

Benny made a grab for Amir's boot, but he only managed to untie the laces rather than get a good grip, and Amir slipped away from him, just as Neeve had.

Running on instinct from practice sessions in teamwork, Layla formed a stirrup with her hands. Raj stepped into it and leaped into the air, arms wide open, and she grabbed Amir by the legs.

The hand shook Amir, side to side, attempting to dislodge the newcomer, but Raj held on tight, her legs swinging beneath her.

"Sorry, my friends!" shouted Amir. "I will never boast again. Never. I love you, dudes! That's a fact! You're way prettier than I am. All of you!"

The molten wall parted. The claw tossed Amir and Raj out. He screamed, in glee not fear. Benny and the others rushed out too. The wall solidified behind them, and the pleading faces and waving hands froze once more.

Amir hopped to his feet. Layla gave him a hug. Pops slapped him on the back. "Good man."

The group surveyed their new surroundings. They had entered a rocky landscape veined with ores: gold, silver, copper and other precious metals. Even in its rough, natural form, the veins glittered and sparkled.

In an open square of marble that sat before a golden palace, a bizarre horde of metal egg-like creatures with little arms and legs sat in groups polishing one another. A silver-toned statue of an egg wearing a crown smiled down on the creatures. Two eggs on ladders rubbed it with polishing cloths.

The egg people rubbed and blew and rubbed and wiped, all the while complaining, "You missed a spot" or "Right there, you dolt!" or "You've made it worse! Now I have a smudge." Or praising, "You positively glitter!" or "That's a killer shine, dude! Start digging the graves," or "You're glowiculous, girl!" They spoke through extra-large, pouty lips that took up most of their round faces that sat above quadruple chins. They had no ears.

A skinny silver-toned girl, who bent awkwardly at the hips and at knobby knees, raced around handing out polishing cloths or complimenting the eggs. Her metal hair was swept up in an untidy bun at the top of her head, and her torso, legs and arms stretched extra long. She was twice as tall as the egg people and slightly taller than the egg king on the pedestal, but she made a concerted effort to duck below the height of the king's statue when she was near it. The king wore only a crown and had the fattest lips of all.

"Don't you shine!" she told one egg. "You'll glow for eternity," she told another. "Stop, you're blinding me," she said to yet another. She spotted the new arrivals and rushed over to greet them. "Welcome! You must be passing through. You don't look like you belong here."

"If I may be so bold, dear," said Pops. "You don't look like you belong here either."

The girl dropped her polishing cloths and brought her hands up to her face and sobbed into her hands. "I know. I try and try, but I'll never fit in. They've tried to smelt me and add metal, but it won't stick. I picked titanium, because I thought it sounded cool. Everyone else wanted a precious metal."

Raj picked up the cloths and reached up to dab the girl's eyes. "It's okay. It's not always a bad thing when you don't fit in. I'm Raj. What's your name?"

"They call me Itsy, because I'm so . . ." She sobbed again. Her head tilted back and her elbows jutted out.

"That'sh a pretty name," added Kami.

"We're trying to get to the Second Circle," said Benny. "Do you know where it is?"

"It's just beyond the land of the Flatterers," said Itsy, gasping between whimpers. "They're called Flatterers because they never have enough. They used to be nothing but hot air bubbles, but when they tried to polish one another, they popped. A smelter arrived. He showed them how to purify the ore and melt it. He coated everyone in the metal of their choice, but only King Plat can use platinum, and by royal decree, no one can be fatter or shinier or taller that he is, or the king has them smelted and stuck to the wall for eternity."

Zuma sniffled, wiggled his nose and sucked in air. Before he could stop it, he sneezed, and the spray flew into the air and over the Flatterers.

"Oh, no," said Itsy.

The eggs turned toward them. King Plat jumped down from the pedestal and shouted, "Kill the intruders who besmirched us!"

With that, the metal arms transformed into rotating saws, jabbing spears and thundering hammers.

"Which way out?" asked Benny.

"I'll show you if you'll take me with you," said Itsy.

"Deal," said Raj.

"Promise?" asked Itsy.

A hammer struck down next to Amir's foot. He screamed and jumped out of the way. "Promise!"

"That way. Across the square," said Itsy, pointing directly at the massive metal horde.

"Oh, no, girl. That's not fair," said Amir, backing up.

Zuma stood his ground. "Bring it!" he shouted.

"Zuma! Get back here," shouted Layla. "What are you doing?"

Zuma pumped his arms together and made a manly-man, bodybuilder grunt. "Doing what I do best. Getting down and dirty." With that, he sucked his cheeks in and spit.

The globule flew through the air and struck King Plat in the eye. King Plat cried out, "You barbarian! That's disgusting!" The king rushed up to Zuma on tottering legs that could barely hold his weight. His saw blades rotated even faster. His eyes narrowed, and his lips formed a hideous smile, showing off his pointy teeth.

Zuma sucked in his cheeks and spit again, this time a globule flew into the king's other eye. The eggs didn't wait. They crowded forward, saws buzzing, hammers pounding, spears thrusting.

Benny, Kami, Raj, Chaz, Layla—and even Pops—all moved forward, shooting spitballs, parting the crowd. Amir tried and tried but nothing came out but sprays of mist.

"How do you spit? Can someone teach—" He screamed again as a saw blade struck down, just missing his toes. Amir reached out and plopped both his hands all over the metal head. "Take that! Fingerprints!"

The creature flew into a rage and waved his saw blades left and right. Amir jumped back and forth to avoid them.

Raj pushed forward with Itsy at her side, spitting and keeping Itsy safe, as Itsy could not spit.

"Traitor!" yelled King Plat. "When I get my hands on you, I'll melt you down personally! Stop them! I command you."

"We're outnumbered," yelled Kami.

"Outnumbered and surrounded," said Chaz. "Good plan, Zuma!"

"At least I had a plan!" Zuma shot back.

Itsy turned to Raj. "Take my hand."

"Why?" asked Raj.

The horde closed in on all sides. *Thunk! Thunk! Buzz! Buzz! Thrust! Thrust!*

"Hurry!" said Itsy.

Raj grabbed Itsy's hand, and Itsy reshaped herself into a sword with her face on the hilt. Raj wasted no time. With all of her might, she swung the sword. Metal bit into metal, and the eggs retreated with wails and sobs of "I'm chinked!" or "What have you done!" or "Cruel, vicious creatures!"

Raj had only to swing the blade through the air in front of them to get the eggs to part, but they followed close behind, waiting for an opportunity to strike. Everyone kept the spit flying in a gentle rain behind them to keep the eggs back.

Itsy shouted, "The new arrivals are up ahead. They're just hot air waiting to be coated. A net holds them down. Do you have some rope?"

While Benny, Kami, Zuma, Raj and Pops spit furiously, Layla, Chaz, and Amir dug into their backpacks and pulled out long lengths of cord.

"Tie a bunch of new arrivals together," instructed Itsy. "Let me know when you're ready."

Layla, Chaz, Pops and Amir grabbed the corners of the net and pulled them together, meeting in the middle. The oval-faced balloons grumbled and complained as the group tied them up and smashed them together.

"Fight! Fight cowards," shouted King Plat, but most eggs stayed back just enough to be counted as helping but not close enough to be chinked.

Raj swung Itsy through the air, smacking the more daring ones who charged up in spurts. "Hurry!" said Raj. "We're losing ground."

"Don't make me pee on you!" Zuma shouted at the horde as he reached for his zipper.

"You will not!" shouted Layla.

"Would you rather lose a foot?" asked Benny, reaching for his zipper.

"Yes," shouted Layla. "I would!"

"Last resort!" shouted Benny. "Promise."

Amir tried and tried to get one globule of spit to fly, but they all vaporized in the air.

Kami bristled. "Shtop that, Amir—you're shpraying ush not them."

"Ready!" shouted Kami, tying off the last of the new arrivals that now formed a pack of fifty or so balloons.

Itsy transformed into a basket large enough to hold them all. She grabbed the rope ends in her hands and toes and shouted, "Get in!"

Everyone but Zuma jumped in.

"Can you hold all of us?" asked Zuma.

"I'm titanium," said Itsy. "Stronger than I look."

With that, Zuma jumped in just as a saw blade pounded the basket where Zuma had stood moments before. Itsy grunted. The basket floated into the air. The eggs converged beneath it, raising their weapons and buzzing and swinging and jabbing, but the basket had already floated out of their reach.

"Itsy," said Benny. "You're quite a girl! Where's the Second Circle?"

"Straight up," said Itsy. "You go up to go down."

They floated for a time in peace, checking to see if anyone had injuries. Over the edge of the basket, Zuma tried to teach Amir how to spit, but to no avail. They soon tired and sat down with the others.

"I don't know about you," said Raj, "but I expected something different than eggs down here."

"What? You expected to die and you're still alive?" Pops grumbled. "Ah, youth new to battle. Those silly creatures could have cut us into pea-sized bits. If not for Itsy, where would we be?"

Raj nodded. "You're right. Sorry."

"I remember my first battle," said Pops. "I was ready. I thirsted for it. I was disappointed and agitated when having to wait. And I wondered, would I be brave enough? Did I train hard enough? Worse, I was disappointed if I won too easily. Disappointed . . . at having lived! Foolish."

"I wanted to go to the first gate the moment my mother disappeared. No training at all," said Benny. "Still not sure it's enough."

Pops' face turned serious. He peered into the yellow sky as if seeing an enemy of long ago. "It all changes when you face your first real enemy—an equal or better—and that's when fear strikes—the fear of death, which brings with it the knowledge that maybe you weren't good enough, hadn't trained hard enough or fought wisely enough or that even if you had, you could not stop fate. You could not save your own life, and because of it, those you love will suffer." His eyes scanned their faces. "But if you live, never again will you wish for a faster, bigger battle or a grander enemy. You'll just fight to stay alive and to keep the friend next to you alive. Because in the end—regardless of duty or glory or purpose—it all comes down to survival. To who makes it home and who remains behind on the battlefield."

Layla added, "We're all going to make it home."

Pops said, "Good, because it's fighting to preserve life—yours and your fellow soldiers'—that keeps the ones back home alive. Every life counts. Do not give yours up easily."

Pops had no sooner said the last word than a rocket whistled through the air. The balloon faces shrieked as the rocket punched through the net, causing a *rat-a-tat-tat-tat* of pops. The shriveled ones drooped downward like raisins. Some dangled, holding fast to the net. Others fell back to the land of the eggs.

Everyone inside the basket jumped to their feet.

"Itsy," shouted Raj. "Are you okay?"

"I'm okay," she said. "And we're still going up."

The balloon floated into gray smoke plumes. The group coughed and sputtered as Itsy maneuvered into clear air beside the plume. On the ground above them, armies of gruesome humans, beasts and six-headed monsters clashed with lion and eagle creatures, some on foot, others riding horses, elephants and tigers.

Explosions shot dirt and fire into the sky.

A barrage of bullets shot at the cage. With an enormous grunt of effort, Itsy closed the bottom of the cage, forming a shield of protection just before they hit. *Rat-a-tat-tat.* More balloons popped.

"There isn't enough of me to spread any thinner," Itsy shouted.

Raj patted the shield. "Hey, you just saved our lives."

Benny added, "Right. Don't apologize."

"Just a little farther," said Itsy. "Then we'll rotate. Otherwise, we'll fall back to the Flatterers."

Rat-a-tat-tat. They nearly stopped, hovering in midair, but slowly they rose again.

On the ground, a black beast with a human body and a bull's head aimed a shoulder-fired rocket launcher at them.

"Trouble at six o'clock," shouted Chaz.

"That's not good," said Itsy.

A six-armed giant dropped a rocket into the launcher's chamber. With a blast of fire from the end of the weapon, the rocket roared toward them.

"Hang on!" Itsy yanked the ropes to maneuver. The basket and its occupants tipped to one side. The rocket shot past, barely missing them. "Sorry."

Before anyone could settle back into place, the basket flipped upside down with a cacophony of grunts and moans from the occupants.

Rather than rising, it now fell toward the battlefield. "We're safe," said Itsy. "We won't fall back to the Flatterers now."

"You call this safe?" shouted Amir.

The six-armed giant dropped another rocket into the chamber. The bull-headed creature fired. The rocket blazed upward and into the balloons. *Rat-a-tat-tat.*

"Sorry," shouted Itsy. "Crash landing!"

The basket plummeted to the ground with deadly speed. Amir screamed. This time, he was not alone.

Chapter Twenty-Three

As the basket surged toward the blanket of fighters below, Itsy reshaped herself into a cage ball. Everyone inside gripped it and prepared for impact.

Amir closed his black eyes. "Some things—like my own death—are not worth seeing."

The ball crashed into a pack of bull-headed creatures. Hairy hands with hooves for fingernails reached inside to grab them.

Two giant winged animals swooped down, gripped the cage and lifted it into the air. One had a lion's head, torso and front paws and an eagle's wings and legs; the other had an eagle's head, torso and wings and a lion's legs. They beat their powerful wings. The cage rose higher and higher. A rocket whistled past them.

Two bull-headed creatures held on to the cage and rose in the air with them. They gripped the cage in one hand while unsheathing their swords with the other.

Benny, Chaz, Amir and Raj stomped and kicked the knuckles of one creature. Kami, Layla, Zuma and Pops stomped on the other.

Chaz stomped on the knuckles of the creature as the beast thrust its sword inside the cage, just missing Chaz's leg. Benny stomped, too, then Raj. The creature stabbed nothing but air as it broke away, bellowing to its death.

Layla screamed as the other creature thrust its sword at them. The blade flew under Pop's robe, and he winced. With all her might, Layla smashed the fingers with the heel of her boot, and the creature broke free.

"Are you okay?" asked Kami.

Pops pulled up his robe. A gash an inch and a half long cut across his outer ankle. "A nick. I've had worse."

The lion-headed beast roared, and the eagle-headed one cawed as the cage rose higher and higher.

The battlefield stretched for miles beneath them and in all directions.

They flew toward a rocky mountain, where giant nests nestled in fissures and upon outcroppings. At the precipice, the winged creatures lowered the cage into the largest nest and flanked either side of it.

"Welcome to my temporary home," cawed Gryphon.

The beasts folded their wings, but even then, they exuded majesty and power. They both wore crowns.

Itsy changed back into her tall, scrawny self. Everyone gasped. Her arms and legs, even her hair, had chinks.

Raj put a hand to a gouge on Itsy's arm. "I'm so sorry, Itsy."

Pops showed off his ankle. "Battle scars. They give you character."

Itsy smiled. "It's better than spending all day polishing myself."

Raj pulled her hair aside, showing Itsy her purple birthmark. "I'm chinked, too."

"We're all chinked," said Benny. And all agreed. Amir pointed to his eyes, Zuma to his belly, Kami to her scratched cheek, and even Layla pointed to a small mole on her neck, as she had no other imperfection.

The lion-headed one roared. "A noble truth. Beloved father of Aeneas, Anchises the Famed, it's good to see you again. Warriors, welcome, we've been expecting you."

Anchises bowed. "Mighty Leonidas, king of the Lionagles, and keen-eyed Gryphon, king of the Griffins, we are grateful for your assistance and honored by your presence."

Benny added, "Super grateful, but I don't know about the 'warriors' part. So far, it looks like the true warriors are saving us."

"Hey," said Zuma. "I came up with the spitting idea."

Layla faked a sneeze and mumbled, "Accident."

Leonidas cocked his head. "Warriors are not born. They are made. Forged by battle."

Gryphon cawed a laugh. "You're barely out of the nest, young ones. Trained. But not tested—that will change."

"What ish going on down there?" asked Kami.

Gryphon cawed. "The Minotaurs and Gegenees, bull men and six-armed giants, rose up from the depths of Tartarus. So, too, did the most despicable and wretched of humans from the Ninth Circle. They prepare for the moment when Hades and the lords of the underworlds unlock the gates. They will flood the world and destroy it."

"We were sent to hold them back," roared Leonidas. "But they've reached the Second Circle."

"We'll bring you weapons then carry you to the Third Circle," roared Leonidas.

"I can go no farther," said Pops. "Can you take me back to the Elysian Fields? And Itsy, you must come with me. What you did was heroic. That's where you belong."

Itsy's eyes widened. "Why, I suddenly feel very shiny. Chinks and all. How strange." A tear slid down her cheek.

"Don't do that," said Raj. "You'll rust."

"It's a very good thing that titanium won't rust," said Itsy. "Well, not easily."

While they waited, Layla ripped the hem from Pop's robe and used it to wrap the wound on the old man's ankle.

Leonidas and Gryphon returned, dropping an arsenal in the nest. Raj and Kami strapped katanas on their backs and grabbed stiletto knives that opened in a flash.

Zuma grabbed a rocket launcher and a single shell. "Now, we're talkin'. Hello, mama."

Layla grabbed a quiver of arrows, a cross bow and a high-powered rifle. Chaz and Benny grabbed rifles and stuffed their backpacks with grenades, high-powered explosives, and fuse cord.

Amir searched the pile. "I never trained with guns, nothing that required eyesight. But I can swing a blade or stick." He grabbed a scimitar and a pair of small fighting sticks.

"Grab another shell, Amir, would ya?" asked Zuma.

"Stuff your packs," said Chaz. "Whatever they'll hold."

"Itsy," asked Gryphon. "Would you gather them all in a ball again? It was easy for us to carry."

"With honor," said Itsy.

Leonidas roared, "Now you look like warriors."

Kami roared to match him. "Now I feel like one!"

Raj cawed, than added, "Let's kick some monster butt!"

Leonidas and Gryphon beat their enormous wings. Their talons clutched the ball, and away they flew, over the mountain and down, gliding over a field through which a milky white river wound. Large blue lotus flowers and a blanket of green leaves stretched along the banks of the river, making it seem like a snake, floating belly up. People lolled at the banks, as if dazed. "There's the Lethe. The River of Forgetfulness," shouted Pops.

"I've had a taste," said Benny. "Not recommended."

"Those who come here," said Pops, "usually have memories they wish to forget. They lay round the banks, wallowing at its edge, but they never seem happy in their oblivion. I think the memories fade, but the heart still bears the burden of guilt or some other pain. It just no longer knows why it hurts."

They left the plain behind, soared higher, and crossed over the summit of a red volcano spewing mud, before sailing through a gorge dotted with houses made of bones.

The gorge became a canyon, whipped by strong winds. Below them a mud river bubbled and sputtered, forming eerie shapes along its banks. Human-like mud figures stood immobile at the shore, giving it the appearance of an eerie graveyard. Twisted mud arches reached from one cliff face to another over the mud river. The howling winds whipped through mud tunnels making high pitched sounds, a requiem of sorts.

As they emerged from the canyon, Leonidas and Gryphon began their descent. They landed at the edge of an abyss.

Itsy returned to her knobby self. The warriors stepped to the edge and peered over. The chasm grew darker and more impenetrable with each yard, until nothing could be seen at all. No light. No bottom.

"Elevator, please," said Amir.

"We must leave you here and return to the battlefront," explained Leonidas. "If not for Apollo's magic—preparing a potion that made the Griffins and the Lionagles and our warrior beasts a troop of walking dead for a short duration—we would never have gotten past Cerberus to fight on the Plains of Asphodel."

Leonidas added, "Our spies tell us the first gate is nearly complete. You must steal the key that will open it."

"How do we get down?" asked Layla.

"We climb down," said Benny.

"Good thing we packed lots of rope," said Raj. "Still, we'll have to retrieve it as we go and re-anchor."

Leonidas roared, "The abyss is the Third Circle. Spies tell us that a river is the Fourth. Cross it to reach the Fifth Circle. May the gods keep you safe."

Gryphon cawed. "Good journey, warriors."

Layla continued to stare downward. Fret creased her brows. Pops stood beside her. "I prefer when I can't see what's ahead. Leaves me with less to worry about."

Layla forced a smile. "You mean, worry when I see a problem. Not before."

Pops nodded. "Not a moment before. It's a waste of energy."

She sucked in a breath. "Thanks."

He hugged her with genuine warmth. "You remind me of Aphrodite. I'll bet you can throw a bolt of lightning or two."

"Maybe so," said Layla. "Maybe so."

Itsy waved. "Shine on, you guys! Be safe." She transformed into a chair with a long bar grip at the top. Pops sat in the chair and held tight.

Leonidas and Gryphon beat their wings, clutched the bar and flew away.

"Wee!" shouted Pops. "I haven't had this much fun since the Trojan War!"

"What's the plan?" asked Raj.

Chaz kicked a boulder off the ledge and waited to hear it crash. It never did. "I think, like Pops said, the plan is staying alive. But then, I only learned to walk a few hours ago."

Kami crouched down to examine the crevasse. "Looksh . . .

looksss like we're on-sight free-soloing." She pulled a headlamp from her backpack, set it on her head and buckled the strap under her chin.

Benny argued, "Chaz, Amir and I don't have the skills to descend without equipment," argued Benny.

"Agreed," said Layla. "We're free-climbing."

Zuma held up a spring-loaded cam. "I always carry protection."

"This thing seems to go for miles," said Layla.

"She's got a point," said Raj, while searching for suitable cracks along the top of the cliff face in which to set a vector of nuts on wires, slings and carabiners for a dropline. "We'll tether together."

"No. If shomeone fallsh, whoever ish tethered to him might be ripped off the wall," argued Kami. "Seven craters at the bottom instead of one. No offense, guys."

"None taken," said Chaz. "Safety first, but we need to reuse the rope. This thing could go for miles."

Benny overrode her. "I haven't had much more practice than Chaz or Amir. But I'm willing to tether to them. Let's make two teams. Fewer craters, right Kami?"

"Amir can tether to me," said Raj. "Just stay calm, Amir."

Raj moved to the edge. "I'll set a dropline. We can climb in two groups. When we run out of rope, we secure to the wall, pull the rope through and set a new spot to anchor the dropline."

Kami used a tone that was near a command. "Fine. Raj and I are the best climbers. We'll split up. I'll go with Amir, Layla and Zuma. Raj, you take Chaz and Benny. And remember—No Panic Bears or Sloppy Plopping. One foot at a time. Secure holds." Kami stepped before Amir and stood face-to-face. She reached down and pulled a stiletto knife out of her boot and popped it open. "If you shcream, Amir, I'll cut your rope."

"No you won't. You *love* me," said Amir. Silence passed. "I'll try."

"Gear up," said Zuma.

"Remind me why we didn't bring parachutes or wing suits?" asked Amir.

Raj answered, "Uh, because we may jump into a pool of tar or blood or lava."

Amir added, "Right. We don't know what's down there. Plus we didn't know I'd be able to see or Chaz to walk. We only practiced tandem jumps. Risky."

Zuma agreed. "Not to mention, we need fall time to gain velocity before pulling a chute. For all we know, that might be fifty feet or three thousand feet."

Raj formed a plan. "Zuma's group goes first. Get a solid lock and hold. We'll go over one by one, each locking in. I'll go last and pull up the gear. If someone slips, we're secured by the others."

Layla stared into the void. "We're so not ready for this."

"For descending an abyss in the underworld?" chaffed Raj. "When would we be? It's not like you wake up one day and say— yup, I'm ready. Today's the big day. Let's go to the underworld."

Layla let out a blip of sound, then another and another, until she bent over in raucous laughter. The others joined in.

"Raj, dude, you crack me up. I needed that. Let's do this," said Layla.

"Don't look down." Kami reminded Amir. "Keep your black peeps on the wall or on ush."

"I figured that out flying in the ball cage thingy," said Amir. "This sight thing—it has definite disadvantages."

"Do you notice that we're not hungry?" asked Benny.

"I know. We should be hungry and thirsty but we're not," said Zuma. "Even me."

Amir patted his front pocket. "Still, we've got gorp and trail mix bars if we need them."

"I hate trail mix." Kami made a face. "Sssweet and sssalty—what moron put them together?" She emphasized her "s" sounds for practice.

"Your *s* is better," said Layla. "Keep trying."

"Thanksss," said Kami.

Geared up, they edged over the cliff one at a time. They moved slowly and steadily. Chaz began whistling. No one complained. It gave them a rhythm. The rock wall, jagged and coarse, provided easy handholds, footholds and ledges and good crevices and cracks where they could lock in. They descended at a steady rate.

The plan worked. When tired, they hangdogged or found a ledge wide enough where three or four could sit comfortably. Hours passed, but the bottom seemed no closer.

There was a time when they recognized a middle of sorts—it was black above and black below. The light from their head-lamps made their shadows dance. Chaz had stopped whistling. In fact, no one spoke, as reserving every shred of thought—staying honed in—and preserving every muscle—using them only when and as much as needed—consumed their minds. If they got too pumped, lactic acid would make their muscles worthless, their hands would freeze, unable to pinch fingers together or grip the wall.

There was a term for going up a grand height like the Hima-layas—an *eight-thousander*—but none of the lingo for rock-climbing or cave-diving came close to a down climb in a sound-less, starless sky where gravity became the ultimate enemy.

The group hit a particularly challenging patch of wall. Benny set a spring-loaded cam. "Secure."

At the call, Chaz moved downward and sunk a nut into a

crevice while he held the wall with two feet and one hand. "Raj, descend and secure. Not sure about this one."

Raj pulled her cam out of the wall and maneuvered downward in search of a place to set the cam. "I see a spot, but it's a reach."

Without warning, the top rope flew past them and plummeted downward. "Loose rope!" yelled Benny.

"It's in two pieces!" shouted Layla. "Cut!"

"It's okay," said Chaz, trying to calm her. "We're locked in. Only one of us untethers and moves at a time. The others act as anchors."

They heard rumbling.

"Is that rushing water? A riv—" asked Raj, but the moment she said it, the wall shook under her hands. She screamed and fell, slapping against the wall.

"Earthquake!" shouted Amir.

"Hades!" yelled Benny.

"Uber grip!" shouted Zuma.

Loose rock rained down on their heads. Rumbles and cracking filled their ears.

Benny watched his cam move. He shoved his left hand in a large crack, scraping his knuckles as he wedged it as deeply as it would go. If it closed, he'd be trapped. But he had to take the chance and secure as best he could. "Chaz, Raj—you okay?" No answer.

Below him, Chaz struggled. The nut popped out of the wall, smacking him just above his right eye. He grunted as one foot slipped off the wall. He only had a good finger hold and one secure foot. As Raj's weight pulled on him, his loose hand searched for an edge, a pocket, a flake, a sloper, anything. His loose foot scraped the wall, yearning for a landing—even one just big enough for his toes. Raj was light, but he couldn't hold her forever.

Raj reached for her stiletto knife.

"Don't do it, Raj!" shouted Amir from the other group.

Zuma had good holds—jugs—at his hands and feet. He pressed his face to the rumbling wall. Layla was below him, then Amir, then Kami.

Kami was loose, as she, too, had been descending. She had a spring-loaded cam in her hand but nowhere to shove it. She dropped it to her side and used friction to hold on. Her foot slipped with each vibration. "I'm slip—!" As she said it, she fell, tugging Amir away from the wall. Kami's weight, along with the shaking, yanked Amir's cam free, leaving the weight of two people on Layla's cam and, if that went, all on Zuma.

Zuma saw the strain and horror in Layla's eyes. "Is your cam holding?"

Layla saw her cam move. "It's slipping, Zuma."

"Kami! Amir!" yelled Zuma. "Lock in a cam or nut! Anything! Now!"

The shaking stopped.

Amir ran his hands over the face of the wall. "It's smooth here! Like glass! I got nothin'."

Kami found a grip on the wall. She set her feet and grabbed a cam, all the while desperately searching for a crevice where she could set it. She reached full might to her right. "I shee a crevice to my right. But I can't get there."

Layla's cam slipped more. "Zuma!"

"Hurry, Kami," shouted Amir.

Zuma met Layla's terrified eyes. "Keep it real, girl. I need you to do something."

Layla shook her head. "I can't."

"Swing the rope," said Zuma.

"No," said Layla. "It will pull on the cam."

Zuma kept a calm voice. "I know, but it's all we've got. The cam is already slipping. If Kami can lock us in—"

"Aghh," Layla grunted, as her cam slipped again. "Okay." She felt for the rope. With her full might, she pulled, inching it slightly and letting it go. "It's not moving."

"Amir," shouted Zuma. "When Layla pulls, swing your legs to the right. Kami, we'll swing you to the crevice. How far away is it?"

"Couple feet out of my reach," Kami yelled back. "You're crazy! It won't work!"

"Got a better idea?" shouted Zuma.

"Alright. Do it," said Kami, ready to swing freely.

Zuma signaled Layla with a nod to try again. Layla pulled. This time Amir swung his legs, and Kami pushed against the wall to start a gentle swing.

In the other group, Raj put her blade to her rope.

Chaz's foot slipped. He held the wall with a single handhold. He whispered to himself, "Hone in."

Benny grimaced as the rock cut into his hand. His cam slipped again. "Cam's not holding!" He wished he'd opted to wear gloves instead of bringing liquid chalk.

"Raj!" said Chaz. "If I go, Benny goes, too. You're all we've got!" A rock fell from up above, smashing his hand. He grunted. His fingers slipped away, until he held the wall by his middle finger alone. He counted aloud so that Raj could hear him. "One . . ."

Raj pulled the blade away from her rope and tossed it into the void. Her hands reached for the wall and searched.

"Two . . ."

Raj saw a tiny ledge just above her head and a bigger crack just above that. She gripped the ledge and pulled herself up. Her feet searched for a hold.

"Three . . ."

Benny let go of the hold he had with his free hand. His full weight shifted onto the hand stuck in the crevice. Grimacing, he grabbed a new cam. He locked it to the line and held it over the slipping cam. The moment it yanked free, he'd jam a larger one in its place. He'd have seconds. Once the cam shot out of the wall, Chaz's weight would yank his hand out of the crevice or severe it at the wrist—he wasn't sure which—and they would fall. Even if Raj sank her cam, it wouldn't hold Benny's and Chaz's weight together. It was their only hope.

Raj found a foothold. She grabbed a cam and sprang it open.

"Fo—" Chaz's finger gave way, and he fell.

Raj sank the cam. "Locked in!"

Benny's cam flew out of the crack. He jammed a new one in, deep as it would go. It held.

Chaz jerked to a stop beside Raj. He cupped his good hand—the strained one was useless—beside Raj's and found strong footholds. Raj searched around for another place to lock in. She found one and secured a nut. She helped Chaz secure his line.

Layla's cam slipped as the rope rocked. Zuma's held.

Kami stabbed at the crevice in the wall, but she missed and swung back the other way.

Amir shifted his feet to help, but Layla's cam slipped farther.

"It's gonna give!" shouted Layla.

Kami and Amir swung with their full might. They swayed in unison in a gentle motion like a pair of trapeze artists. Kami reached the crevice. She planted the cam. "Secure!" She found a foothold, then a handhold and secured a nut.

Layla smiled, relieved, but all too soon. Layla's cam broke free. She screamed. Amir's weight pulled her off the wall. The pair dangled between Zuma above and Kami below.

Zuma had good holds, but his cam wouldn't hold the weight for long. Amir dropped beside Kami, leaving Layla dangling over the smooth patch.

"Secure another cam!" shouted Zuma. He reached down and

pulled on the rope. He couldn't lift Layla, but he could try to hold her weight and ease the strain on his cam until another was in place.

Amir saw a crack. He sank a cam. "Secure."

Zuma had no choice. He had to move downward to give Layla a chance to lock in. "Layla, lock in as soon as you can. I'm heading down."

"Okay!" she shouted back.

Zuma pulled his cam free. With Layla's weight on his rope, he lowered himself, choosing the best grips with precision, one, then the next. He could not afford to fall.

Chaz shouted, "Go, Zuma. You're ubergrippen."

Layla found a crack. She set a nut. "Secure!"

"There's a ledge down a ways to the right," shouted Raj. "Big enough for all of us, I think."

———

Kami, the last to step onto the ledge, apologized. "Sorry, guys. I had nothing to grip but nubs. Thanks, Zuma."

Zuma put an arm around her shoulder, pulled her into his chest and kissed the top of her head. "You're still a wallerina with ninja feet to me."

Chaz opened and closed his hand. "Anyone else hurt?"

Benny raised his hand, showing a loose tear of flesh across the back of it.

"You got a flapper," said Layla, rubbing her shaking legs. "I'm okay, except for Elvis legs."

Benny shook it off. "I'm getting used to pain. Chaz, you passed the mono-dig test."

"I can't believe you held the two of us," added Raj.

"Nothin' like knowing your life depends on hanging on to get a good count," said Chaz. "Something I hope *never* to repeat."

"If you think about it," added Zuma while yawning. "You practiced with a lot of dead weight."

"My legs," said Chaz. "Maybe."

"I'm draggin'. Let's lock in and get a couple hours of sleep." Amir set a cam and clipped in.

Kami, Chaz and Layla removed their packs and set them aside.

Zuma was too tired to care. He clipped in, laid the rocket launcher beside him, leaned against his pack and closed his eyes.

Benny, Raj and Amir did the same, leaning back on their packs and laying their weapons beside them, too tired to fuss more than that.

"That was epic!" said Zuma, his eyes closing.

"It's only epic because we lived to tell about it," said Raj, closing her eyes. "So far."

Adrenaline gave way to fatigue. The absence of sound and time made it more pronounced. Benny thought soldiers, like Mike, must experience such feelings in battle: unsure of how long they'd been fighting, because time no longer had relevance, a new enemy crept in—the need to sleep. One could fight off the enemy for a while, but eventually, even in the midst of war, when tired enough, reason and clear thought gave way to the oncoming fog of sleep.

Their eyelids slammed shut. Their limbs sagged to their sides, and Zuma let out gentle, rhythmic snores.

There was no telling how long they had slept in the eternal night of the abyss when Kami felt an icy breath against her cheek. She swatted it away and raised one eye a crack. Her backpack moved upward. Her eyes shot open. "Wake up! Sssomething's wrong. Sssomething's here!"

Chapter Twenty-Four

Headlamps flashed on. Beams searched about. "My pack isss gone!" said Kami.

"So's mine," said Raj.

Layla screamed, grabbing for her pack as something invisible tried to yank it upward. Her fighter instincts erupted in thrusts and jabs. "Something's there, but I can't see it."

Zuma dove into his backpack and fished out a white plastic bottle. He poured baby powder into his hand and blew it into the air. The powder outlined an elongated creature with eyes but no nose or mouth. It had long spiderlike legs and feet that stuck to the wall.

Layla punched it in the face, and it fell from the rock down into the abyss.

Zuma sprayed the powder in all directions as fast as he could pour it into his hands. The creatures surrounded them. Kami unsheathed a katana and swung, knocking two of the things from the wall. The creatures fell in silence. The rest scurried away.

"I think they're gone," said Zuma. "What's missing?"

"More importantly," said Amir. "What's left?"

"Does it matter?" asked Benny. "Whatever is missing is gone. Whatever is left is all we have."

"Let's get out of here," said Kami.

Amir stretched. "I feel rested, considering."

"Me, too," said Chaz, yawning.

"I can't believe you brought baby powder to the underworld!" scoffed Raj. "Although, I'm glad you did."

Zuma cocked his head. "If you'd ever had chafed nuts, you'd understand."

Chaz chuckled. He elbowed Amir and nodded toward Kami. Everyone stared and chuckled, too.

"What's wrong?" Kami put her hands to her face.

Benny informed her, "Uh, your face is covered in baby powder."

"Now you really look like a geisha. Let me help you." Zuma reached for her face.

Kami grabbed for the stiletto she'd stuck in her boot, but it was missing. "Don't touch me!" She rubbed her cheeks and forehead. Layla helped her.

Zuma threw his hands up. "No touchy. Or geisha slicey dicey Zuma. Ah-so."

The boys cracked up, angering Kami all the more—something they knew they should never do, but sometimes they just couldn't resist.

"That's not funny! In fact, it is wrong on multiple levels," said Layla. Her motherly, protective tone worked, and the boys ceased instantly and even apologized.

"I'm sorry, Kami. Old habits," said Zuma.

"At least," sneered Kami, "you got the slicey-dicey part right. Apology accepted."

They took inventory. Benny lost the rifle, but he still had his pack filled with grenades and explosives; Raj had one katana; Kami, two katanas; Zuma had his pack but no rocket launcher; Layla and Chaz lost rifles; Amir had lost nothing.

"So," said Benny. "We've got three swords, two shells but no launcher, high-powered explosives, fuse cord, grenades, a cross-bow but no quiver, a scimitar and a pair of fighting sticks."

"And our brains and skills." Amir made a judo pass with his hands.

Back on the wall, they descended at a quicker pace. After a few hours, they spotted a red glow—the bottom. It fired their strength and their will. They pressed on.

The glow stretched in a long line, becoming better defined with each yard descended: it was a river of fire. The landscape lightened from black to shades of dark red and gray to yellow.

At the bottom, the fire raged and roared, towering several stories over them, licking the yellow sky.

"Leonidas said we had to cross a river to get to the Fourth Circle," said Chaz. "He forgot to mention it was the Phlegethon, the river of fire that Daniel told us about."

"I don't think he knew," said Benny. "Should we split up? Scout in both directions for a way across?"

"Worth a try," said Chaz. "Meet back here in one hour tops."

Zuma stuck with the girls, and the boys headed the other way.

An hour later, Benny reported for the boys. "The river winds away from the cliff face, and there's no way across. It doesn't seem to narrow."

Raj reported for the girls. "We didn't get far. Up ahead, the river abuts the wall of the abyss. We climbed the wall and got a good view."

"We threw a few things into the fire—they disintegrated," said Kami. "But there's flat land on the other side. And what looks like a city."

Zuma added, "No matter how high we got on the wall, there's no way to angle a rope down and secure it to the other side."

"You said the river abuts the cliff," said Amir. "What if we blow the cliff face, bury the river?"

"Avalanche?" said Benny. "That's going to take a big explosion. We need a lot of rock to bury the river."

"That might work," said Layla. "We found a rift, one side pushing up, the other down. Lots of pressure."

"Let's take a look," said Chaz.

As they headed to the rift in the wall, Raj showed them another spot where the wall formed an overhang above an indentation just large enough for the group to hide under it. "We can hide here when it blows."

They walked around the overhang and examined the rift.

"We've got rocketsss but no launcher," Kami complained.

Zuma shook his head. "Wouldn't work even if we had a launcher. No angle, and the rocket would explode on the wall, not in the rift. But, we've got two shells. We should wedge them in the rift with the plastics and the grenades. Everything we've got. Too shallow, not enough wall will come down. Too deep, none will come down. The wall will absorb the shock. I estimate you need to set them back about ten feet."

"Let's go take a closer look," said Benny.

Zuma and Kami climbed in one group and Benny and Raj in another. They found two spots where the rift opened in a space large enough for Raj and Kami to crawl into. The girls crawled inside, Kami taking the cleft higher up. They packed each with a rocket shell, grenades, and plastics, sticking a fuse line into the plastic.

Benny and Zuma climbed down, leaving the girls to light the fuse, as they climbed faster.

Emerging from the crawl space, Kami shouted down. "Ready, Raj?"

Kami waited by the end of the fuse, lighter in hand. Raj readied her lighter next to the other fuse. "Ready," shouted Raj. "Give a count."

Benny, Zuma and Chaz waited anxiously at the bottom, ready to lend a hand. Layla and Amir hunkered down under the overhang, occasionally popping their heads up to see the progress being made.

"Light it on three!" shouted Kami. "One, two, three!!"

Kami and Raj lit the fuses before scurrying down in a free solo. There was no time for cams or equipment, just bare fingertips, toeholds and grit.

As the girls darted down, the fuses sparked and rushed upward.

"The fuses are burning too fast," said Benny.

"I know," said Chaz.

"Hurry!" shouted Zuma.

The girls dropped from one point to the next, breaking every safety rule to move faster.

The fuses reached the fissure and ducked inside.

"You'll have to jump!" shouted Benny. "The fuse is gone!"

Raj, still twenty feet in the air, and Kami another ten above her, quickened their pace. At fifteen feet, Raj turned and jumped. Zuma hurried to get beneath her, if not to catch her, at least to break her fall.

Raj hurled into Zuma's arms, and the two hit the ground rolling. Layla and Amir rushed to help. Amir pulled a winded Zuma to his feet, and Layla helped Raj. They ran for cover.

"Kami!" shouted Chaz. "Jump!"

"Now!" shouted Benny.

Kami turned away from the wall and dove at Chaz and Benny. The uppermost charges exploded. Benny caught Kami and they rolled. Rocks the size of cars rained down. Zuma rushed out and grabbed Benny, yanking him onto his feet as a boulder plowed into the dirt where Benny had rested moments before. The second set of charges exploded. The wall rumbled. Chaz yanked Kami to her feet and they all ran for cover.

They ducked under the overhang and huddled together. With a deafening roar, the wall cracked. The ground beneath their feet shook violently.

Kami threw her hands over her ears, overpowered by the deafening roar of colliding rocks. The sky at the edge of the protrusion changed from yellow-orange to sickly brown as plumes of dirt blocked their sight.

With a crack, the wall at the back of their small shelter separated. A fissure opened. Crushed rock rained down. They threw protective arms over their heads and coughed.

Benny shouted, "Time to get out of here! Wall's giving way!"

As the group tumbled out, the rumbling stopped but the overhang collapsed. Debris tumbled down. Here and there, erratic cracks continued, like the last few kernels of popcorn to blossom. They distanced themselves from the cliff face. Coughing and sputtering, they waited for the eventual silence that brought a sense of peace.

They checked arms and legs. Raj had scraped her nose and cheek. Kami had a small gash on her forehead. Zuma had a bloody nose from an impact with Raj's elbow. Other than that, everyone had all their parts.

"You didn't scream, Amir," observed Layla.

"I was too busy trying to breathe," he retorted.

When they marched around the corner, they could not believe their eyes. It worked!

A wall of rock had tumbled down and sprawled across the river like a dam. Small flames here and there emerged between the rocks.

"Let's get across fast," said Benny. "We don't know how long it will hold."

"Ssstay together," barked Kami.

They climbed the large, irregularly hewn stones, careful to test the stability of the next step before applying full pressure. Flames danced here and there. Unlike the heat of the lava flows at the entrance that produced a harmless heat, these flames occasionally shot high enough to emit scorching heat.

One such flame leaped up beside Zuma. "Yeow!" he screamed. "This stuff is hot—I mean hot! It singed the hair right off my fingers."

Raj snickered, "It's for the best, Zuma. I don't think you're supposed to have hair on your fingers."

They reached the middle before hearing the first groan of rocks moving and grinding as the river spread and built up pressure where they had dammed it. The river fought to regain its course and flush the intruders downstream.

"Hurry," shouted Zuma. "Pressure's building!"

The rocks shuddered and shifted beneath their feet. The warriors quickened their pace, hopping from rock to rock to hop across.

Benny touched down on a stone, which began to sink. He leaped to another as the first one disappeared beneath the fiery flow. The shoreline was just ahead. He could make it.

Raj and Kami, lighter on their feet, had made it to the edge first, but, oddly, they remained on the rocks rather than stepping on to shore.

"Look!" said Raj. They pointed to an expanse of sand between them and a marble landing at the edge of a palatial city. "Now what?"

Humans, horses, strange beasts and a sole elephant dotted the sand, sinking down into it. An ogre struggled and sank from his waist to his chest. Like the river trying to swallow them, the sand devoured, too.

The rest of the group reached the shore's edge. "So not fair!" shouted Layla. "I hate this place!"

"We can't go back," said Chaz. "No time."

Benny said, "And we can't go forward."

The rocks groaned and shifted. Raj tipped into Chaz, who caught and righted her.

The flaming river erupted in pockets. Small geysers punched the air. Like a hissing cobra waiting to strike, the fire maneuvered toward the intruders, blocking their escape, eager to consume them.

Chapter Twenty-Five

"Tie your ropess together," shouted Kami. "Hurry!"

"Why?" asked Chaz.

"No time for why—jusst do it." Kami tied the end of her rope around her waist. Benny tied his rope to the end of hers, keeping it coiled as the others tied off, too, until they had one long coil.

Zuma ran numbers in his head. "If you're doing what I think you're doing, you've got just enough rope to get the job done."

"That'ss comforting, Zuma," said Kami. "I'd hate to get ten feet from the landing and find out I'm short."

A column of fire shot up next to Raj; she ducked out of its path and jumped to another rock closer to shore.

"Keep the rope away from the fire!" shouted Chaz.

"I'm trying," said Benny.

"I'm running across," said Kami. "Keep the rope slack. If it binds, I'm in sand soup. Hey guys, I did it. I said 'sand soup!'"

"You did. So it's no time to die," said Amir.

"If you get in trouble, we'll pull you back," said Zuma.

"No time," said Layla.

Benny added, "She either makes it across or none of us do. The only choice left is do you want to die by sand or fire?"

The flow formed an arch that had nearly reached across the rock dam. It seeped forward by inches, filling one crevice at a time. Every surge forward reduced the bottlenecked tension, until new surges again increased pressure. The river could explode at any moment, break free and run its course. A sudden release would sweep everything and everyone downstream, moving boulders as if mere marshmallows, people like grains of sand.

Parkour style, Kami leaped from a horse's back to the elephant's back, atop its head, to an ogre's shoulder and off again; she touched down on the back of a man, bent at the waist, belly on the sand, and onto stepping stones made of the tops of bald heads; the last sank beneath the surface just as she leaped onto a tiger's back, who reared its head and growled; she zigged and zagged, calculating three footfalls ahead, sometimes more, leaping between the big gaps with the agility of a lynx: from blue boar, to winged giant bat, to more humans, until she ran out of stepping stones. Rushing forward, her brain calculated height, speed and chances of success. An ogre's head, her desperately needed stepping stone, disappeared under the sand. No choice. She committed to the path. She flew through the air, knowing her foot would plunge into the sand, perhaps ensnaring her, sucking her down and ending her life.

A fist shot straight up—the ogre fought to grasp on to life— little knowing his action would save hers. The hand sprawled open, a final desperate cry for help. Her foot bounced into its palm and out. The hand clutched to grab her, but she had already departed.

Her legs kicked in the air, as if peddling to gain momentum that would allow her to touch down on the marble landing still several paces away. Fearing she was short, she reached her toes forward, legs straight, like a long jumper. Her toes touched down at the edge of the marble; her body flew forward to catch up, but her momentum slowed; she wobbled at the edge, leaning forward then backward, tottering like an off-balance ballerina trying with all her might to stay over her toe shoes. By sheer will alone, Kami stopped her backward fall and shot her hands into the air, a gymnast sticking the landing.

The sound of smashing rocks, followed by screams and shouts, caught Kami's attention. She ran alongside a marble wall and up a staircase to a colonnade of pillars. She swung a loop of rope around the base of a column, then planted her feet against it and inched the rope up, climbing as if coconuts or better treasure waited at the top for her to pick. But it was life—not coconuts—that drove her upward.

Kami climbed over the finial with four gargoyle heads to reach the topcap. She untied the rope from her waist, looped it around the necks of the gargoyles, and pulled it tight, garroting them.

Kami stood atop the column and waved her friends forward. The rope sloped downward over the sinking sands to her friends on the rocks.

The group had already devised an order of ascent. They had wrapped a few coils of rope around a fairly steady rock that leaned back, like an obelisk giving way to time. Zuma, Chaz and Benny held fast to the end of the rope, even though it had no way to slip. Raj raced across the sand, using the same footfalls as Kami from horse to elephant, where she jumped up and grabbed the sloping rope. She swung her feet over it, crossed her legs and pulled hand over hand, gliding up the rope, over the sand and toward the pillar on the other side. As soon as she pulled herself over the hardscape, Amir dashed along the same path and sprung onto the rope, likewise turning, gripping and pulling himself over the sand and the creatures below.

Raj secured a dropline by looping a new rope through a locking carabiner. She dangled on the rope with a grip in front and one behind and released the rope gradually to control her rate of descent. She moved as quickly as possible without burning her hands, until her feet touched the marble.

As Amir descended to meet her, Layla started to cross.

The river encroached, narrowing the jetty of safety for Chaz, Benny and Zuma. The river rocks slammed together in a cacophony of destruction. The obelisk tilted, pushed by the force of the downward current.

When Layla reached safety, Zuma ran. By now, the horse's back became ever smaller as the animal sank. Zuma slid off the elephant's back but grabbed an ear to stop his fall into the sand. He leaped for the rope, barely catching it. The rope sagged under his weight. His backside dipped down and slapped the sand. "Crap! If you live, no more triple donut burgers!" he scolded himself.

Benny and Chaz gripped the rope end and tugged, if not to take up slack, to ensure that the rope sagged no further. Zuma had wanted to go last, for this very reason, but Benny and Chaz knew it would mean sure death with no one to keep tension.

Zuma scooched up the rope as quickly as possible. While his weight caused him one problem, his arm strength worked to compensate. When he made it to the other side, Chaz dashed the course. The horse's back was no larger than a serving plate for a turkey dinner when he set foot on it. Chaz's powerful arms hauled his body up the rope with ease.

Benny eyed the obelisk, watching it tilt farther. The fiery river oozed around its base. The rocks under Benny's feet moved with a sudden jerk. He feared the river had broken free at last. Behind him, the fires reached higher and higher, inched closer and closer. They reminded Benny of his grandfather's flaming hearth that he had crawled toward as if drawn by the heat. Now, the heat inflamed his desire to survive. He would find Hades and destroy him.

The horse's back disappeared. All that was left was the top of its head. Even though Chaz was not yet over the hardscape, if Benny waited any longer, it would be too late. Flames licked at the obelisk and the rope tied around it.

The horse neighed loudly and shook its head as if urging Benny forward. It lay its head down toward him. It was on his side. Benny ran. He planted a foot between the horse's ears and sprang onto the elephant's back—or what was left of it, as it, too, had sunk to the size of a platter. The horse let out a final neigh of victory as it sank.

Benny stood up and jumped. He could not reach the rope. He jumped again. His eyes searched for another foothold. He stood atop the elephant's head and jumped. Still he could not reach the rope.

On the landing, the others shouted for him to jump. To try again.

The elephant beneath him let out a shrill blare, a last defiant cry. It raised its nose and tusks. Benny sensed the animal was as angry about dying as he was.

"You can do it, friend!" said Benny, crouching down and stroking it between its eyes. The elephant beneath him moved. It struggled as it surged upward, lifting its neck several inches out of the sand.

It was enough. Just enough.

Benny leaped straight up in the air. Straining, he hooked the fingers of his right around the rope.

A crunching sound shifted his gaze to the obelisk, which tilted toward the flames that had now crossed the river and begun to sweep the stones along the banks into the fiery stream.

Benny grasped the rope with both hands and flung his legs over it. He pulled with his full might, letting out a grunt of effort. At this downward angle, he could see the river. The center gave way. The dam broke. Benny knew the rocks along the shoreline would quickly follow.

His friends screamed for him to hurry, but he knew that already. The obelisk leaned, pulling the rope beneath his hands so taut it seemed like it would snap in the middle and drag him back into the flames or drop him in the middle of the sand. He pulled hand over hand, watching the obelisk lean down into the fire. The rope caught fire and snapped.

Benny fell, but held tightly to the rope. His body slammed into the sand a dozen feet from the marble landing. He began to sink.

Chaz, Zuma, Layla, Amir and Raj grabbed the slack line and grimaced as they pulled, full force. Still atop the pillar, Kami rappelled down the sagging line to help out.

Benny whipped across the surface and flew onto the marble, striking the edge with a knee, but relishing the pain that signaled his safety.

Benny rubbed his knee as he struggled to his feet. He stared at the expanse of sand, and the only surviving creature still alive in it—the elephant—the majestic beast that had rescued him. He would not divert his eyes. He would stay with it until the end.

"Thank you!" Benny shouted. "You saved my life!"

The elephant blared a response.

Chaz slapped Benny on the shoulder. "He saved all of our lives. The horse did too. What are animals doing in the underworld? And why would they be here in the sands?"

Benny shook his head. "They fought against Hades. And now, they're suffering the consequences. They were clearly on our side."

As they watched, Kami asked Zuma, "How did you know we had enough rope?"

Zuma smirked. "The Pythagorean theorem. The sand is a couple hundred feet across; the column is about fifty feet high, the staircase another dozen. Forms a right triangle. The angle from the top of the pillar to the obelisk is the hypotenuse: $a^2 + b^2$ equals c^2. You needed two hundred and ten feet of rope to get across, plus extra for tie offs, approximately."

"I should pay more attention in math class," said Benny.

"Why?" said Raj. "We've got Zuma."

As the elephant's trunk disappeared, Benny and the others turned their backs on the sand and toward the marble walls.

"The City of Dis, I suspect," said Chaz. The group eyed the ramparts atop the wall and the towers that rose behind it, searching for signs of danger.

"Didn't Daniel tell us that Dante described a moat around Dis?" asked Layla.

"I think the sand is the moat," said Amir.

Benny eyed the city. Its enormous Medieval-like gates swung open.

Zuma said, "We just blew up every piece of plastic and every grenade. I got zip."

"Same here," said Benny.

Kami handed one of her katanas to Zuma, but he passed it to Layla. Raj raised her katana, ready to strike. Amir passed his fighting sticks to Zuma, and Amir raised his scimitar.

"I got these," said Benny, holding up his fists.

"Me too," added Chaz.

The group ascended the staircase, strolled through the colonnade and passed between the medieval gates.

"I could use a rest," said Amir. "I'm actually hoping for a city of slow-moving zombies."

"Don't count on it," said Benny.

Inside the walls, a square opened up, leading to a marble hall in the distance. Upon sight of the newcomers, people in the square shouted and scrambled into the buildings on either side. Others ogled them from the windows of houses and buildings. The people had scratched faces, arms and legs, dark dreary eyes and tattered clothes that seemed clawed rather than worn.

"Looks like they're more afraid of us than we are of them," said Kami.

"Or maybe," said Benny, pointing skyward. "They are afraid of them."

Three giant, black-winged birds flew over the wall. They had humanlike bodies with dark skin. Long tresses of red hair on one and green hair on another whipped the air as they dipped for a closer inspection of the newly arrived ones. The third wore a crown of black loops, and long braids that draped over her shoulders. They screeched as they circled overhead, blood-curdling screams, all-too-human screams.

The warriors raised their weapons, ready for a fight.

The red-haired one swooped down. Zuma swung his sticks but missed.

The green-haired one swooped at Kami and Raj. They swung their swords but the creature evaded their passes.

The dark one beat her wings, hovering in place. She tilted her head back and screamed louder than the other two. "Trap them!

Angry citizens poured from the buildings, wielding clubs, cleavers, axes, bottles and brooms. They surrounded the new-comers. It forced the warriors back to back in a circle of protection.

The creatures landed before them. Only then did the warriors see that what they thought were long tresses of hair were actually skinny snakes of red, green, and black. Their solid white eyes were set in coal-black orbits. Red tears, green tears and black tears ran from their eyes and down their cheeks and necks. They wore tattered dresses the same color as their snakelike hair. They clawed the air with silver razor-sharp talons.

The dark-haired one spoke in words that reverberated in the air. "Surrender. Drop your weapons."

The warriors ignored her and raised their weapons.

The dark one screamed again. "Drop them or die." The crowd inched forward, brandishing their weapons.

"Guys, we're outnumbered," said Zuma.

"We seek Hades," bellowed Benny.

Zuma laid down his sticks, and the others did the same.

"My sisters and I seek atonement for your crimes," said the dark one.

"What crimes?" asked Amir. "We just got here."

The dark one flared her wings. "Follow us to Dis Pater. He will hear your plea and judge your fate."

"Dis Pater?" asked Benny.

Kami said, "Latin. Means father of Dis."

The three marched forward. The crowd collected their weapons and followed close behind, prodding the accused.

They marched down a wide cobbled street. The thoroughfare seemed to lead to the heart of the city. They crossed over bridges that arched over sand canals that presumably dumped into the moat encircling the walls of the city.

They passed by a man rolling a boulder up a hill, only to have it roll down again. He rushed down and rolled it to the top again and again.

"Sisyphus," said Chaz. "Doomed to roll that boulder for eternity."

They passed by another man reaching into a tree burgeoning with ripe fruit—fat grapes, luscious apples, golden pears. Every time the man reached up, the bough moved the fruit out of his reach. As he lowered his hand, the fruit dropped back down. He circled the tree, reaching up again and again.

"And there's Tantalus," said Raj, turning to Benny.

"What did they do?" asked Benny.

"They didn't heed Minnie's tip," said Chaz. "They angered the gods."

As they drew closer to the square, they observed men and women in stocks with their heads and hands protruding out. Others raced in circles, chased by giant green-winged wasps. Another group, in shredded designer clothes and suits, milled about, picking each other's pockets of money and jewels, just to have another pluck it from them. Still others sat in recliners facing a big black screen, pushing remotes that didn't work.

The three black-winged creatures stood before a marble judge's bench and waited. A hooded black-robed man climbed the steps and sat upon the bench.

"Dis Pater looks like the grim reaper," said Zuma.

"Yeah, except I suspect these people would prefer death over being tormented for an eternity," said Layla.

The black-robed judge sat at the desk and slammed a red gavel. He removed his hood.

"Hades!" shouted Benny.

Hades smiled. "Welcome to Dis, the Sixth Circle."

"Did we miss the Fifth?" asked Benny.

"No, the Fifth Circle is the Abominable Sands—as you can imagine, there's just no way to put up a sign that will remain there for long. No one, before you, has ever crossed the river successfully, let alone the sands. No matter, the Furies have brought you, the accused, before my court." His voice bellowed over the square. "State your accusations, oh beings of vengeance and justice!"

"This one," the red Fury pointed to Benny, "abandoned his mother! No crime is greater than injustice to a parent."

"That he did, Alecto," said Hades.

Benny shouted, "No! I—"

Hades slammed the gavel. "Silence!"

The green Fury clawed at Amir. "This one is full of vanity." She moved to Kami. "And this one is full of wrath!"

"Uh, so are you butch!" said Kami.

"And this one with the nascent mark upon her cheek is full of envy," continued the green Fury. "She disdains one friend for her talents and the other for her beauty."

Hades slammed his gavel. "Wise Megaera. It is true."

"And this one." The dark Fury cupped Layla's chin in one set of talons and ran the other dangerously close to her face. "Lazy! She stands back and lets the others fight for her. Let me scratch her!"

"I'm here fighting you, aren't I!" taunted Layla.

"No, Tisiphone, do not mar her yet," ordered Hades.

The dark one rasped in anger. She left Layla and approached Zuma and pointed to his protruding belly, which Zuma tried to suck in. "Glutton!"

"And the last?" asked Hades. "What is his crime?"

The red Fury pressed herself against Chaz. Her lips nearly touched his. "This one is full of lust, Dis Pater!"

"I'm eighteen, raging with hormones and still a virgin! That's called 'normal' where I come from," shouted Chaz.

"What is it with you and women in red?" sneered Raj.

"Hell if I know," said Chaz. "But if we live, I'm switching to blondes."

Hades slammed his gavel. "Guilty! All!"

"That's it?" yelled Benny. "Not much of a trial."

Hades swung his gavel about in the air. "It's more for show. I've haven't spared a soul yet." He pointed the gavel at the warriors. "But you thought you had a chance, didn't you? Admit it."

"Dude, that's one twisted sense of humor," said Zuma.

"I try," said Hades before bellowing, "commit the guilty to the Abominable Sands!"

"Wait!" shouted Benny. "Let them go! It's me you want."

"Hmmm." Hades stroked his red beard. "That is tempting. How ironic. I'm usually the one doing the tempting. Tell you what, Benny. I'll give you a choice. You can either save Neeve—or your friends."

The Furies howled in laughter.

Benny rushed forward but the red and green Furies each grabbed an arm, and the dark one flew ahead and alighted, intercepting him with outspread wings that forbid progress.

"Take me instead!" shouted Benny. "Take me!"

Hades pounded the gavel. "Out of order!" He tsked, clicking his tongue. "Benny—such behavior in a court of law. Which will it be? Save your mother? Or save your friends?"

Benny lowered his eyes. He would have sacrificed himself for either. His friends stood a better chance than he did of saving the world anyway, a world that his mother, too, had fought to save by letting go of him. He could hear his mother whispering to him even now. He knew what she would want. He raised his head and met Hades' gaze. "Spare my friends."

Hades laughed and laughed. "Oh, Benny. It's hard to believe that you are my grandson. I had hoped for better. That day, when you crawled toward the fire, I thought you had it in you, well . . . no matter."

Benny rushed forward, but the dark Fury spread her wings to stop him again. "Take me on. Right now! I'll not disappoint you!"

Hades smiled. "Maybe another time—if you survive—which you won't. I've got a council meeting to attend and a gate to open. Furies! Commit them to the Abominable Sands!" Hades tossed the gavel aside and descended the stairs.

Benny struggled to break free but to no avail.

The Furies beat their wings and flew overhead, screaming and clawing the air as a warning. The townspeople surrounded the warriors and herded them in the direction of the gate and the landing beyond. The warriors huddled together as they walked.

At the edge of the marble landing, the red Fury swooped down and clutched Benny and Chaz in her talons. She dropped Benny over the Abominable Sands in the very place where he was destined to rejoin his elephant friend. Benny's feet plunged into the softscape and stuck. If he wiggled or pulled, he slipped downward faster.

Chaz, still in the Fury's grip, pleaded with the enemy. "Alecto—right? You're prettier than your sisters. Red is my favorite color? If you save—"

The Fury cast Chaz into the sands.

The green Fury clutched Raj and Kami. Kami kicked furiously, trying to break free.

The Fury dropped Raj, and her feet stabbed the sand. Kami bit into the Fury's knuckle. The creature screamed in pain and hurled her downward. Kami hit the sand, feet kicking.

The dark one struggled to lift Layla and Zuma. She set Layla down, grabbed Zuma in both clawed hands and beat her wings. She dropped Zuma not far from Kami.

The red Fury returned and reached out for Amir and Layla. She gripped Amir, but Layla ducked out of her reach. This angered the Fury. She clawed at Layla, grasping her by the hair. She whisked them both over the Abominable Sands and hurled them down.

Their duty done, the townspeople retreated, chased back inside the walls of Dis by the swoops and sweeping talons and screams of the Furies.

Amir, up to his waist, shouted, "Don't struggle. You'll sink faster!"

"Great choice," said Benny. "Die slow or die fast."

Chapter Twenty-Six

Kami thrashed about, exploding in a fit of anger. "It can't end here!" Each movement caused her to sink.

"Kami!" shouted Raj. "Stop moving!"

"And what? Die?" The more Kami lifted one leg, the more the other sank, until she was waist deep.

Chaz added, "Struggle, and you'll just die faster, Kami!"

Zuma, just within reach, wrapped his big arms around Kami and held her tight.

Unable to raise her arms, Kami beat her fists against his sides. "Let go of me! I can't breathe!" Her rage shifted from the sand to the hulk that bound her.

In a calm voice, Zuma said, "Not until you can hold still, Ninja."

Kami howled like a caged animal, but it soon became one log wail and her hands fell to her sides.

Zuma squeezed her again and whispered, "We need you calm." He started to let go.

"Don't let go," Kami pleaded.

"Afraid?" Zuma asked.

"Yes, of me," said Kami. "Of what I'll do if you let go."

"Then I won't let go. No matter what." He placed a gentle kiss on her forehead.

Chest deep, Benny raised his hands above the sand. "Any ideas, guys? Now's the time."

They lacked equipment. They lacked weapons. And the silence explained that they also lacked brilliant ideas.

"Please, dudes," said Amir. "Do not let this be the last thing I see."

"There's nothing here! Nothing to grab on to." Chaz raised his arms high in the air. Sand spilled over his shoulders.

Raj, down to her chest, shouted, "Benny, I gotta know. Why didn't you choose your mother? Why us?"

Sand touched the bottom of Benny's ears. He tilted his face upward. "She wouldn't have wanted me to pick her. You guys stand a chance of stopping Hades. If I'm Hades grandson, then my father is his . . ."

"Did you see that!" shouted Amir. "A rainbow just shot over our heads."

"I saw something," said Layla, chest-deep. "I'm not sure what."

Benny sputtered as sand reached his lips. He puffed out to push it away, then gasped in another quick breath.

"Benny!" screamed Layla, up to her shoulders.

The sand covered Benny's mouth. His nostrils flared. He couldn't even bend his hands down to wipe the sand away. His head sank beneath the sand. His hands waved the air in search of something to grab.

Raj let out a scream of disbelief. "Benny!" Her shoulders dipped beneath the sand as Benny's fingertips, wiggling in panic and disappeared.

Chaz's face disappeared next. His hands shot into the air.

Something gripped Chaz's outstretched hands and lifted him

up. When his face cleared the sand, he sputtered and coughed. "Leonidas!"

Leonidas roared, dropped Chaz on the marble landing and turned to help the others.

A rainbow shot overhead and touched down beside Chaz. Its colorful bands spilled into the shape of a translucent woman with rainbow hair and golden wings; she carried a staff with two snakes wound round its top.

Leonidas reached for Layla, sunk neck deep. Layla reached out for him, but the Furies returned, cawing and scratching.

Leonidas flapped his wings and shot skyward to fight them. He roared and clawed the air.

The red Fury slashed his flank and it bled.

Leonidas smacked her from the air. Down she fell, into the sand, next to Zuma and Kami.

Chest deep in sand, Kami and Zuma grabbed her wings and pinned her down.

Leonidas dove down, plucked Layla from the sand, and dropped her on the landing beside Chaz.

The green and black Furies swooped through the air and chased after Leonidas. The red Fury shook her head, recovering her wits. Kami slugged the side of her face so hard it knocked her out again. "I go down," said Kami. "You go down."

"My Kami girl is back!" said Zuma. He shouted to the others flying in the sky. "You guys are toast now! Burnt toast!"

Leonidas batted a strong, swift paw at the green Fury, slashing one of her black wings. Her white eyes sprang open. Green tears ran down her face. She screeched in pain and flew in a hobbled manner away from Dis.

Midair, Leonidas and the black Fury faced off. She screeched. He roared. She swiped at him with razor-sharp talons. He swiped at her with razor-sharp claws. She slashed his shoulder.

He slashed her hip. She screamed. He roared. Black tears trickled down her cheeks. Leonidas wasted no time. He slashed her neck with one paw, her wing with the other.

She made a sound as shrill as death and dove to retrieve her green sister.

Up to their ears in sand and unable to fight her off, Zuma and Kami let go of their prisoner and let the black Fury carry her away.

Leonidas pulled Kami free.

"Get the others first!" shouted Zuma, as Leonidas hoisted Kami in the air.

Leonidas retrieved Raj, Amir, and lastly, Zuma. He set Zuma on the landing, and lowered his wings.

Layla sank to her knees on the landing. "Save Benny, Leonidas."

Leonidas lowered his head and eyes. "That is not in my power. Nor is it in Iris's."

The rainbow woman nodded before shooting skyward, forming a rainbow over the Abominable Sands as she exited.

"Iris is one of the few messengers who can enter the underworld. She came to me on the battlefield and informed me of your distress. I'm sorry. I dare not stay here longer."

"Benny can't be dead!" Layla crumpled into a heap.

Zuma moved toward her, but Chaz reached her side first and wrapped his arms around her. No one uttered a word—no words could bring comfort.

"Look!" shouted Amir, pointing at the sand.

Benny's hands shot out of the sand. First one, then the other. Then his head, his torso, his legs. Then the elephant's head.

"It's rearing up! Standing on its back legs!" shouted Layla, rising to her feet.

Leonidas beat his wings and flew over the sand. He clutched Benny, flew into the air and set him on the landing. He flew back to the elephant and roared as he pulled with all his might to free the creature from the sand. Exhausted and with his flank and shoulder dripping blood, he set the elephant down on the landing.

"You're hurt," said Kami.

"And it will fester if I stay longer. Fight well, warriors." Leonidas licked the blood oozing from the gashes in his flank. He beat his wings, rose into the air and flew over the fire river and up the wall of the abyss.

Layla hugged Benny in a bear squeeze, while the others gave him heartfelt slaps.

"Don't you ever die again!" scolded Amir, slapping his arm full force. "My heart can't take it."

"I'll do my best," said Benny. "I guess neither one of us was ready to die just yet. I could feel my friend here shake as it reared up beneath me."

The elephant reared up and blared again.

"What about the Furies?" asked Amir.

"Feathers will fly!" said Kami.

"Got that right," added Benny. "I've got a score to settle."

"Until death do us part—their death! Not ours," agreed Raj.

Chaz said, "I don't think we'll see them."

Zuma added, "They looked hurt. Hurt bad."

A renewed sense of purpose filled Benny's chest. He had faced death, tasted it, overcome it. Life Number Seven ended in the sand. He was beginning Life Number Eight.

The elephant blared and bent its right leg, forming a step.

Benny climbed up and sat behind its ears. "All aboard! I think our friend here wants payback, too."

The elephant climbed the steps and strode between the pillars toward the gate of Dis. It trumpeted a warning as it entered the city with its seven passengers. This time, the motley inhabitants in shredded clothing scurried like rats to the nearest hiding hole. There was no sign of the Furies.

The elephant lumbered down the cobblestone thoroughfare. As the warriors approached the square with the court and judge's bench, they heard a cacophony of sinister sounds: growls and screeches, animal and human. As soon as the elephant passed by the square where Hades held court, the warriors spied a merry-go-round at the heart of Dis. But it was no ordinary carnival ride. As it slowed to a stop, the sounds died too, leaving an eerie silence.

Starting with Benny, the warriors dismounted from the elephant.

On top of the roof of the merry-go-round, a man with long flowing hair and a beard, a broad muscular chest, and a snake body and fingers, grasped a beautiful woman with dark long hair. She, too, had a snake body. Their serpentine coils entwined, forming an elaborate roof of coils and twists that formed the top of the merry-go-round.

The sign next to the apparatus read, "The Seventh Circle."

"Great," said Benny. "A monster-go-round."

Instead of horses and swan chariots and giant lollipops— monsters and giants, beasts and gorgons ringed the platform.

"Let's see what we're up against," said Kami, already heading counterclockwise to inspect the enemy.

"I think I already know," said Chaz, following close behind. "The man and woman on the roof, if I'm not mistaken, are Typhon and Echidna—the father and mother of the most bad-ass monsters in Greek mythology. I suspect the ones below are their children. Some I recognize, some I don't."

"Wait! Those are Cerberus's parents? They're so big. He's so tiny," said Amir.

"You heard Pops. Cerberus can eat an army," Zuma reminded him.

"So what can these do?" asked Layla.

Kami stopped before a beast with a lion's bosom and hind-quarters, but it had three heads—a lion's in front, a goat's in the middle, and a snake's head for a tail.

"What is it with snakes in this place!" sneered Raj. "So unoriginal."

"It's a Chimera," said Zuma.

"Impressive," said Chaz. "A lecture you didn't sleep through."

"It's mine," said Kami. "Choose one to fight. Each of you."

The group moved on, coming to a two-headed dog with sharp canine teeth. "I'll take him," said Amir. "Dogs like me."

A beast with a lion's body, wings, and a woman's head came next. She had hollow eyes that allowed the warriors to peer inside her hollow skull. She wore a crown.

"Layla, you should take the Sphinx," prodded Chaz. "You're good with riddles."

"I'll take the one next to her—the giant Nemean lion," said Zuma. "I'll keep an eye on Layla."

Layla gave him a fist pump to say thanks.

Next, they came to a beautiful woman wearing a flowing soft white gown. Everything about her seemed innocent: her fair skin, white hair, white brows and thick white lashes. Only her lips shone bright red. She sat in a golden chariot made for two. "Mine!" shouted Chaz.

Raj shook her head. "Have you learned nothing, Chaz? She'll probably eat your face."

Chaz shrugged. "Have too learned. She's blonde and she's not wearing red. You want her?"

"You called her. You deal with her," sneered Raj.

"Does anyone know who she is?" asked Chaz.

"If she's on this toy," said Benny. "You can bet she's nothing but trouble."

"I'll take Medusa," said Raj.

"That leaves me with the pretty one," said Benny, eyeing the creature with a dragon's body and nine heads.

"That would be Hydra," said Chaz. "Careful. If you cut off one head, it grows two more."

"Good to know. In fact, we should share what we know about each of these guys," said Benny. "Huddle up."

"We need a plan," said Amir.

"We need weapons," said Zuma. "Big ones. The Furies took ours."

"Check out the center of the monster-go-round," said Benny. "It's loaded."

Swords, shields, spears, daggers, maces, kali sticks and more dotted the console.

"That's fair," said Kami.

"Don't count on it," snapped Layla. "Nothing here is fair."

"You guys keep your eyes on my monster," said Raj. "I'll go for the weapons."

The group huddled and whispered in a flurry of ideas: Medusa could turn a person to stone in one glance but Perseus used a mirrored shield against her; the Nemean lion's hide is impenetrable; failing to answer the Sphinx's riddle leads to death. They shared and whispered before straightening up. No one had any information about the white-haired young woman and very little about the Chimera.

"Be quick, Raj, a few minutes, tops," said Benny. "I don't like the idea of tangling with Hydra and Medusa at once."

"I'm on your right. I'll help with Hydra," promised Kami.

"And I'll help with Medusa," said Chaz.

Benny stepped over to the elephant and ran the palm of his hand down the elephant's trunk. He gazed into its large eyes. "Bye, my friend. Go in peace. And stay out of the sand."

The beast blared a final good-bye before lumbering toward the courtyard.

As the warriors prepared to board the contraption, they heard crashing sounds. The elephant rammed its head into a pillar which crashed down on the judge's bench and smashed it to pieces.

Benny shouted, "All aboard the monster-go-round. Seventh Circle, here we come!"

Chapter Twenty-Seven

The warriors jumped aboard, taking their stations and eyeing their targets. The platform rotated counterclockwise, slowly at first, then picking up speed. The beasts and creatures stirred to life with each rotation.

Dis became a blur of beige at the rim of their vision. Raj leaped onto the narrow platform that ringed the inner console. It turned in opposition to the main platform. At least, it seemed to. The space grew between the landing of the inner console and the ground. The entire monster-go-round lifted into the air. A swirl of beige dust spun between the platform under Raj's feet and the main platform, chest high. If Raj fell, she would fly into the void.

Black, scaly hands held the weapons in tight grips. Raj tried to pull a dagger free, yanking with full might. It edged ever so slightly away from the wall, until the hand gripped it tighter and yanked it back into place.

Amir's two-headed dog rose to its feet. Its two heads arched over him and snapped in slow motion, eager to tear him apart.

The lion's head of Kami's Chimera twisted and roared. Its snake tail hissed and rose up, spreading its cobra hood to strike. The goat's head bleated—the least menacing sound of all.

The Sphinx, lounging on all fours, turned up the corners of her lips in a sinister smile. Her lips parted as if to speak. The inside of her mouth, like her eyes, was hollow. Her lion's mane of flaxen hair framed the feline features of her face. Her hollow eyes roamed up and down Layla's form, and she spoke:

> *Answer my riddles, you must try*
> *Answer my riddles, or you die.*

Layla shot a worried look at Zuma, but he was too busy to return it.

The Nemean lion roared, adding to the cacophony of animal sounds. Its gigantic paw rose into the air, poised to swipe and shred.

Chaz wasted no time in plucking a mirrored disk from the chariot that held his fair lady. He shone the mirror on Medusa and watched her from the safety of the mirror's reflection. Medusa's orange snakes writhed upon her head and slithered down over her bare, scaly shoulders. Orange lips and fiery eyes gleamed in what, otherwise, was a lovely face. Chaz glanced at his fair lady, too, back and forth, doing his best to keep his eyes on both, as they awakened.

The white-haired girl dipped her chin and smiled sweetly. Her eyelids opened to a halfway point, to show sleepy eyes filled with spinning starlight.

With his eyes entranced by hers, Chaz did not see her reach out. The lady ran her hand over Chaz's as it rested on the rim of her chariot.

The warm, soft touch lulled Chaz like some wonderful, seductive poison. He let out a sigh of pleasure and dismay. The mirror fell from his hand and wobbled like a top before coming to a rest. Medusa smiled, nodded at the white-haired girl, and turned her attention to Benny.

Chaz's knees buckled. The fair lady reached out and pulled him into her brass chariot. Powerless, Chaz slumped beside her. She stroked his face and batted her long white lashes.

Chaz grunted, fighting the strong desire to sleep. His chin dropped. She gently pushed his chin up to keep his eyes locked onto hers. She licked her red lips.

The Hydra's many heads shot forward, one after the other. Benny dodged one, and then another as he eyed Raj, spinning past him, again and again, struggling to pull weapons free. He kept his eyes on Medusa, too. "Raj, hurry!"

Raj slammed her fist into one of the scaly hands gripping a dagger. The scales sliced her knuckles. She yanked her hand back and winced in pain. Her foot slipped from the platform, but she regained her balance by gripping the end of a fighting stick. She hoped the hand would set it free, but it held tight. Blood dripped down her fingers and onto her owl pin. Of course! She unclasped the pin and jammed it into the knuckle of the black fist.

The scaly hand shot open. Raj caught the dagger by the hilt as it fell. She stabbed at other hands, which opened. She grabbed weapons and heaved them onto the main platform without taking aim as to who or what she threw them toward: a sword, another sword, a dagger, a shield, an axe, a pair of short fighting sticks, a scimitar. Hands reached up from below, gripping her by the ankles. She swung the blade of the scimitar, severing the hands that held her captive.

The platform reached full speed. The creatures moved about, snapping and clawing, testing their opponents' strengths.

Benny grabbed a sword that slid to his feet. He hoisted it, and as one of Hydra's heads lunged at him, jaws open, he swung the blade. Instinct had overruled good judgment. The Hydra's head fell to the ground.

"Oh, no!" Benny said to himself. Immediately, two more heads sprouted, giving him ten enemies to face.

Amir shouted as he grabbed the fighting sticks, which he swung at the two-headed dog. "Not the sword, Benny."

"I know. I know," shouted Benny. "I forgot."

Kami swung an axe at the Chimera, keeping it at bay.

"Kami, trade!" said Benny, holding up the sword and hoping that an axe would do damage without lopping off another of Hydra's heads.

Gripping an axe and shield, Kami nodded, and in a flash, the axe and sword flew through the air.

Medusa slithered toward Benny and rose up. Benny leaped into the air. They both reached for the axe, but Benny snatched it away from Medusa's waiting palm. She clutched at air.

Kami jabbed at Chimera and Hydra to force them back, but they encroached anyway. Their jaws snapped. "Raj! We need you!"

Scimitar in hand, Raj jumped back onto the main platform, with no concept of where she would land. The blade of her weapon hit an object, perhaps an inner pole, and spun away from her. She dangled over the void. With a grunt, she flung one leg up, then the other. The platform tilted. She rolled across the platform and landed at the feet of the two-headed dog. Both jaws lunged at her flailing arms, ready to tear at the soft skin covering them.

Two fast and loud cracks, followed by a barrage of others, kept the heads up and the dogs yelping in pain. Amir swung the fighting sticks into their skulls, their jaws, their forelegs, again and again, giving Raj enough time to roll away.

"Nice, doggy—or I'll kill you," said Amir.

"Thanks, bro," said Raj before diving for her scimitar, grabbing the hilt in a tuck and roll and springing to her feet to join Kami in fighting the Chimera. As Kami swung her blade at the lion's head, chopping into the side of its massive neck, her arm landed within striking distance of the Chimera's cobra tail. It wasted no time in lunging for Kami's wrist, its mouth agape, sharp fangs dripping yellow venom.

Raj swung her blade, severing the poisonous head just before its teeth plunged into Kami's forearm.

"Little close there," said Kami, as the blade flashed down beside her arm.

Raj shrugged. "My bad."

The goat's head shot flames from its mouth. Raj dove for cover. Kami raised her shield just in time to deflect the fire, which struck the Hydra, igniting four of its heads. It wailed in pain and anger and revenge.

Medusa and Benny pushed against one another, chest to chest. Her sword locked in a stalemate with his axe. Medusa rattled her tail. Her eyes glowed orange, waiting for her opponent to glance just once into them and turn to stone.

Raj raced to help Benny, trapped between Hydra and Medusa. She swung her scimitar in a downward stroke, so hard the blade sliced the rattler off Medusa's tail and bit into the wooden platform. Medusa whipped about, bellowing in pain. She swiped her sword at Raj.

"I got her! Fight Hydra!" Raj ducked into a squat position and swung her scimitar overhead. Their weapons struck and gouged and bit and slammed together. Raj eyed a shiny object on the ground. A mirror! She plucked it up and sprang to her feet. Raj stumbled, intentionally, to draw her opponent closer to her. When their blades locked, she flashed the mirror at Medusa. But Medusa averted her gaze, which caught the eyes of three of

Hydra's heads. They turned to stone and crumbled, clattering against the platform. Benny bowed his thanks, which enraged Medusa. She scowled and set her flaming eyes on Raj, who averted her gaze between swipes of her scimitar and flashes of the mirror.

Long orange snakes writhed across Medusa's bare shoulders and bit into the back of Raj's hand, while others knocked the mirror loose from her grasp. Raj's eyes popped open and she watched the mirror fall to the ground and shatter into pieces.

"Old trick," said Medusa in a sickly sweet voice. "You'll not turn me to stone."

Raj battled the creature more on instinct than strategy, as she dared not meet her gaze.

Benny drove his axe into the skull of one of Hydra's heads, leaving only two left to battle.

The Sphinx's voice echoed:

> *The more you take of them,*
> *The more you have.*

"That's all you've got?" chided Layla. "I learned that one in my diapers. Footsteps."

The Sphinx shot back a threat:

> *'Tis but to warm up your heart, mind and ears*
> *I shall eat not cold, but hot human meals.*
> *If you answer me truly, as we spin,*
> *When we stop, 'tis your own life you win.*

The Sphinx added:

> *I always run but never walk,*
> *Often murmur but never talk;*

Have a bed but never sleep,
Have a mouth but never eat.

"Duh!" said Layla. "A river. Looks like you're not eating me—hot or cold."

At this effrontery, the Sphinx hissed like a cornered wildcat. Her hollow eyes narrowed:

You use it each day, but it never runs out.

Layla fidgeted and fretted. She knew the answer, but it remained glued in her mind.

Zuma shouted, "Time!" He jabbed the sword at the chest of the lion, but it failed to even scratch his hide. Zuma threw down the useless weapon.

Layla grabbed it. She stabbed the Sphinx through the hollow eye. The blade dangled eerily from her face but inflicted no harm.

Layla shouted the answer, "Time!"

The Nemean lion swung its paw, catching Zuma off guard. Razor-sharp claws cut across Zuma's chest, leaving his uniform in shreds. Zuma cried out in pain as blood seeped through the material.

"Zuma!" yelled Layla.

You hold me most dear, but if you give me away,
The moment you do so, I forever disappear.

"I don't know!" shouted Layla. "I don't care!" She threw her hands over her ears. "Leave me alone!"

Chaz had heard the question, and he knew the answer, but he could not move. His eyes pleaded with the pretty girl. His lips moved but he could not speak.

She smiled and stroked his face. "Shhhh. Sleep. It's better for you if you do not to see the other form I take."

The lion swiped again. This time, Zuma grabbed hold of its paw. He grunted as he used a wrestling move to maintain the force of the blow but direct it forward toward the enemy. His arm muscles shuddered and he grunted as he sustained the drive.

The lion roared in defiance.

With a final yell of victory, Zuma forced the lion's paw into its other front leg. Its claw slashed the leg, cutting through hide, muscle, and bone, severing the forepaw on which it stood. The lion slumped, smacking its head on the platform.

Dizzy from the effort, or maybe his wounds, Zuma shook his head to clear it. He grabbed the severed paw as the lion fought to balance on one foreleg.

"So that's it," said Zuma. "Your hide is impenetrable to my weapons but not to yours." Zuma swung the severed paw, missing the animal, which reared up before him and waved a deadly paw and a bloody stump. Zuma fought back, landing strikes that slashed and gashed the lion's flank, its chest, its neck.

Chaz's lady scratched his neck with her sharp nails. She rose to her feet and hovered over him.

Chaz felt on fire. His vision blurred. He opened his pleading eyes. Instead of seeing a beautiful creature, the woman before him changed into a hideous hag with a large mouth full of sharp teeth.

He blinked, wondering if one row of teeth had simply blurred into many. It was like looking into the jaws of a shark.

She opened her jaws wide enough to devour Chaz's head.

Chaz tried to speak, but no sound emerged.

Zuma could barely stand, but he saw the danger Chaz faced. He staggered to the chariot and raked the lion's claws down the hag's back, releasing black blood. The monster screamed, but she did not let go of her prey.

Before Zuma could strike again, the lion swept him aside with its paw. Zuma tumbled to the ground next to the outer rim of the platform and rolled onto his back. The lion sprung at him. Zuma could barely see. He held up the severed paw in defense. The lion landed atop him. With a final roar of agony, its head drooped over the platform, its eyes closed and its tongue lolled out of its mouth.

Layla screamed, "Zuma!" She rushed to his side and tried to shove her weight against the dead lion. It didn't budge. She gripped Zuma's hand, which was all she could see of him beneath the bulky carcass that smothered him.

With adrenaline, more than reason, projecting Raj's arm forward, she stabbed Medusa in the stomach, and when the creature dipped her head to inspect the wound, Raj grabbed Medusa by the back of her head and shoved her face toward the wide-jawed creature, leaning down to feast on Chaz.

Medusa kept her eyes tightly closed and shook her head, fighting for freedom.

Raj yanked a snake from her head, then another and another. Medusa's howled and her eyes flared open.

The flesh-eater peered up but for a second. Medusa's orange eyes met her sleepy ones, which widened in defeat before her jaws froze and she turned to gray stone.

Medusa snapped and whipped her snakelike bloody tail, throwing Raj off balance. She grabbed Raj's arms and threw her to the ground and slithered atop her. She pinned Raj's hands against the platform.

Raj slammed her eyelids closed.

Medusa spit into her face. The caustic spittle burned Raj's eyelids and cheeks. Raj shook her head and writhed in agony.

Hearing Raj's cry, Kami turned but for a second. The goat bit into her shield, ripping it from her hand before shooting a final flame of execution, which Kami did not wait to receive. She thrust her sword into the heart of the Chimera. The final flame shot past her and died out, as the creature crumpled to its death.

The noxious effects of the flesh-eater's poison vanished the moment the rest of her turned to stone. Chaz sprang to his feet. He shoved the creature over the back of the chariot. It smashed against the platform and its head rolled away from its body. He leaped out of the chariot and kicked the head into the void. "A secret! Layla, a secret!"

Layla repeated it. "A secret." She felt Zuma's hand go limp beneath hers. "Zuma! Don't you dare die!"

Zuma's hand twitched then went limp again.

Kami raced past Benny, who swung his axe into another of Hydra's heads, leaving one more to fight. As Kami ran toward Raj, she scooped up her shield.

"Look at me," said Medusa, dripping more caustic spittle onto Raj's eyelids. "Before my poison eats your flesh and you will have no choice."

Raj screamed as the acid burned.

The dogs' two black heads lunged at Amir. In unison, they chomped down on his fighting sticks and ripped them out of his hands. They flew into the void. The heads snarled. Drool dripped from their fangs as they leaned closer.

Amir backed away until his feet reached the outer edge and he had nowhere else to go. The heads sniffed Amir's face.

As Amir turned his face aside, he felt their hot, humid breath against his cheeks and neck. One of his feet slipped off of the platform. He grabbed the outer pole that ran up his back to regain his balance.

Amir closed his eyes. Having had sight only recently, he realized he didn't need it. It hindered him by instilling fear, where blindness to the enemy gave him courage, willpower, and the use of stronger senses. Just as he readied his fists for a quick succession of blows to the dogs' necks, one head stopped growling, then the other.

Amir opened one eye to peek. The dogs' noses dipped down to his pocket and sniffed.

"Doggy wants a treat?" said Amir, reaching ever so slowly into his pocket. He withdrew a chocolate chip trail mix bar. He unwrapped it and gave a bite to the first dog. It stopped growling. The other head waited for his share. "Good doggy," said Amir.

Amir gave a second bite to the same dog. The other seemed perplexed but waited.

Amir fed a third bite to the same dog, and this time, the other nipped, trying to vie for the morsel.

The well-fed head snarled and snapped its jaws.

"That's it. Fight over it." Amir had one bite left. He fed it to the first, who ate it greedily, leaving not even a crumb for his brother.

The loser sunk his teeth into his kin's neck and shook his head back and forth.

The other retaliated by biting into an ear and ripping it in two.

As they fought, Amir maneuvered to the opposite side of them. With a running leap and a kick at its flank, he knocked them off their feet, over the side of the platform and into the abyss.

The Sphinx shouted in anger:

> *A double riddle with which to fiddle:*
> *It will stand it up to watch it fall*
> *It holds it back then lets it go*
> *It stops tending it to watch it grow.*

Layla shook her head. "Zuma! Squeeze my hand, Zuma." She didn't want to let go of Zuma's hand, but she had to free him. She rose to her feet, shoved her back against the golden-haired lion and began rocking it, hoping to tip it over the edge without dragging Zuma with it.

Benny was losing. He had to try something new. He raced across in front of the Hydra's last head, which followed him. He swung around a pole, swinging his body out into the void and back again. The Hydra, following Benny's movement without any forethought, wrapped its head around the pole. The moment Benny's feet touched the platform, he sank the axe into the Hydra's head and shoved it over the edge.

Chaz straddled Medusa's orange-scaled body. He gripped the snakes on her head and yanked her head back, as if riding a wild bull.

Kami flew in front of the gorgon and swung her sword, taking aim before closing her eyes. Medusa had not expected an assault from two sides at once. Her eyes flew open as the sword severed her head.

Medusa's body writhed in death. Chaz dropped Medusa's head. He pulled Raj to her feet and into his chest. Raj could barely open her eyes.

"Come on. Zuma's in trouble," shouted Benny, racing past them.

With the sword still dangling from its hollow eye, the Sphinx rose up and strode toward Layla, now joined by Benny, Kami and Amir, who helped tip the lion's carcass over the edge while Raj and Chaz held tight to Zuma.

As the lion's carcass tumbled into the void, the warriors spotted its own claw impaled in its chest.

Layla dropped down beside Zuma and patted his face. "Zuma! Wake up! Wake up!"

Benny sank down, too, and grabbed Layla by the shoulders. "Do you know the answer to the riddle?"

The Sphinx hovered over them.

Riddles bygone and one failed to answer
To save you now, no one has the power.

"What's wrong with you!" shouted Layla. "Help him!"

Benny shook her harder than he wanted to, but he had to get her attention. "You want to save Zuma? Answer the freakin' riddle!"

Layla shook her head. "I don't know the answer." A gasp left her lips. "It's my fault, isn't it? I killed him." She leaned down and whispered, "I'm sorry, Zuma. You're my family, my bro. I . . ." Her head shot up. She jumped to her feet and yanked the sword from the Sphinx's eye. "Parent and child, you spawn of evil! Parent and child. Now die!"

The Sphinx screamed like a wounded banshee. She flew off the platform and into the abyss, followed by her dead brothers and sisters, children of Typhon and Echidna, all losers in the battle.

Zuma remained lifeless.

Chapter Twenty-Eight

Layla wasted no time. She dropped the sword and leaned over Zuma, tilted his head back, placed her mouth over his, and breathed air into his lungs.

Benny knotted his fingers together, locked his elbows, and pressed the heel of his palm into Zuma's breastbone, depressing it enough to squeeze the oxygenated blood out of his heart and into his system. He counted aloud then paused, allowing Layla to force more air into his lungs. "Come on, Zuma!"

Chaz added, "Get up, Zuma! Get up!"

Benny depressed the breastbone again.

Amir fell to his knees beside Benny. He grabbed Zuma's hand and rubbed it between his palms.

Kami said, "*This* can't be for real."

Layla breathed again and again between Benny's depressions. As time passed, the onlookers eyed one another with less hope.

"Dude, wake up!" shouted Amir. "Quit joking around and scaring us."

Layla screamed, "I said we weren't ready! I warned you! Zuma, don't die!"

Benny knew from their basic first aid class that the average time spent on resuscitation in hospitals was sixteen minutes. That time had come and gone.

Chaz tapped Benny out and continued depressions in his place.

Every time Layla sat up, waiting for the count to breathe again, her face contorted, beseeching Chaz to keep trying.

With each passing minute, the onlookers' chins dropped, all but Layla's. Reality had set in for everyone but her.

Raj was the first to turn away, because the horror of watching a friend's death was simply too grim and grotesque to watch.

Exhausted, Chaz nodded to Benny. Benny knelt beside Layla and put a gentle hand on her shoulder. "Layla, he's . . ."

Layla threw Benny's hand off. "Shut up, Benny! No he's not. He can't be. He can't . . ." With both fists, she beat on Zuma's chest again and again. "Don't you do this! Don't leave me, Zuma! Don't leave . . ." She threw her head down upon his chest and wrapped her arms around him as best she could. "I won't let you go. You die. I die."

A second later, her head shot up. "I hear a heartbeat!"

Before anyone had time to verify her claim, Zuma sucked in a deep breath and coughed out. "Am I dead?"

"Not yet, my friend," said Benny. "Not yet."

"Amir?" asked Zuma. "Dude? Are you holding my hand?"

Amir let go of Zuma's hand. "Sorry, dude."

"Looks like we'll live to fight another day," said Chaz.

The roof cracked and peeled away, revealing a red sky and the two giants at the core of the monster-go-round. Echidna—a ravishing, dark-haired nymph from the hips up and a snake from the hips down—squalled at the destruction of her children. She swung a mace. Its barbed ball crashed into the platform.

Typhon, black as night and ten times larger than his mate, bellowed through a gnarled beard and mustache. He coiled his snake legs around his wife in comfort and protection.

Benny said, "Looks like 'another day' has arrived."

Zuma grimaced as Chaz helped him to sit up.

Kami and Raj readied for battle, raising sword and scimitar to protect their friends.

Zuma pulled duct tape out of his backpack and wound it around the slashes on his chest.

"Boy, do they looked piqued," said Amir.

"Piqued," repeated Benny. "We killed their children. They want us dead."

Layla grabbed the sword. "I'm staying with Zuma. He can't protect himself."

"Can too." Zuma rose on one wobbly knee, grimacing the whole time, before sinking back down. "Taken five, dudes. Then I'll be as good as new."

Benny, Amir and Chaz scrambled to find weapons, but, as if he knew their plan, Typhon blew a mighty blast from his lips, sending hot storm winds over the platform. Medusa's head and other loose objects flew into the void. The platform whirled and tilted beneath their feet.

Echidna reached for Layla. Benny rushed to intercede. Layla swung the blade through the air, slashing Echidna's finger.

As Echidna wailed in pain, Typhon roared in anger and reached for Benny with writhing vipers instead of fingers. The vipers coiled around Benny's chest.

Typhon hoisted Benny into the air. Each time Benny exhaled, the vipers squeezed his chest, preventing him from inhaling.

Benny winced. Any more pressure and his ribs would crack and his heart would explode. He couldn't breathe. He could feel himself growing lightheaded.

Typhon bared his teeth, which seemed all the more menacing surrounded by his thickly twisted beard.

With one final effort, Benny grabbed a snake just below its head and rammed its fangs into the fleshy part of Typhon's hand between thumb and forefinger. Another snake lunged forward to strike Benny's face, but before it struck the flesh of his cheek, it flopped down, lifeless. Others wobbled and fell, succumbing to their own venom.

The red storm picked up speed. Benny flopped backward in Typhon's ever-weaker grip.

Crack!

A fissure raced lightning-fast down the middle of the platform directly under Zuma, who rolled to safety, helped by Layla who shoved him away with her feet just before the crack ran between them, leaving them separated.

Despite the widening crack, Layla jumped to her feet. She threw the sword across the divide then leaped over it. Her torso smashed against the deck and her legs dangled in the void. As the platform whipped and twirled, all akilter, she slid over the edge. Zuma passed out. Fueled by her sheer need to protect Zuma, Layla heaved, pulling herself onto the platform. She and Zuma were separated from the others.

Typhon let out a gale-force roar and hurled Benny's body at the platform.

Benny crashed against the center console and dropped to the landing at the contraption's core. His legs dangled in the void.

With a swipe of her hand, Echidna knocked Kami off her feet and toward the abyss. Kami's sword grazed a pole and flew out of her hand as she sailed into the storm. She reached out just in time to hook the pole with one hand. Her body slammed down against the edge of the platform and dangled. Her sword spun to a stop out of her reach, its hilt dangling over the edge.

Kami grunted and kicked as she grabbed the pole with her other hand, but she could not get a leg up. Her body flew out, parallel to the platform. She reached for her sword and almost had it, but another buffet of the platform sent her hand back to the pole, clasping it for the sake of life. The sword tipped and disappeared in the red storm.

The whipping tempest had knocked Amir and Chaz off balance. They slammed against the platform and rolled to the outer edge. They crawled toward Kami.

Amir reached her first. He grabbed Kami's hand as it broke free, but he could not pull her up. Kami's other hand broke free. Amir grunted and held on to her, grimacing from the weight. "Chaz! Help!"

Fighting the wind and whipping twirl and tilt, Chaz crawled to the edge. He reached for Kami's hand, but, buffeted and batted to and fro, he could not reach it. "Raj! Do something!"

Raj hurled her scimitar at Typhon. The tip of the blade drove into Typhon's shoulder, but still the giant fought.

Echidna screamed. She grabbed Raj and lifted her up, squeezing with all her might.

Raj kicked her legs and smashed her fists into Echidna's hand.

"Kami's slipping!" yelled Amir.

Layla jumped to her feet and hurled her sword at Echidna. It struck her in the arm. Echidna released Raj, who plummeted downward, disappearing in the storm.

Typhon snatched Layla in one hand and Chaz in the other.

Echidna reached for Amir.

Typhon inhaled, sucking the red sky in through flared nostrils, filling his chest with enough air to finish the job and blow them all away.

Benny's eyes flew open. He stared into the column of black hands and could see they were, in fact, on the tails of Echidna and Typhon, wound together. He also eyed a golden ring that swung back and forth in the clutch of a hand, larger and more hideous than the others that lined the inner column. Bulbous eyes on the back of the hand eyed Benny warily.

Benny sprang to his feet and climbed the wall of scaly hands, some of which dropped their weapons in order to grip his ankles, preventing his ascent.

The platform spun out of control. The fissure grew. Metal clanged as the last section of roof pulled away from the support poles.

Typhon and Echidna blew in unison. Their breaths combined in a hurricane force.

Kami's hand slipped out of Amir's grasp and she disappeared in the storm just as Echidna's hand reached Amir, but Amir rolled away and leaped into the chariot.

Echidna ripped the chariot from the floorboards.

Amir's ear-piercing scream sent a wave of "nothing left to lose" energy through Benny. Benny slammed his fist down on a hand holding a dagger. The blade impaled the hand below it, and it dropped an axe. Benny swung the axe at the hands holding him. Once set free, he scurried to the top. He raised the axe, ready to slam it down into the bulbous eyes of the hand holding the ring, but its fingers sprung open, releasing the prize—the gold ring.

Benny grabbed the ring. He held on tightly as the platform slowed down and fell. It broke into pieces, which disappeared as he clung to the core.

Echidna and Typhon yowled one last time as the winds sucked them downward. Their fists opened, releasing. Layla and Chaz, who flew into the red-yellow tempest.

The core slammed to the ground, sending Benny flying. After coming to a stop, he lay still long enough to catch his breath. He struggled to sit up. "Anyone else alive?" No response. He mumbled, "Of course, that's presuming I'm still alive."

Lights flashed on and off and bells rang, a carnival-like cacophony announcing a grand-prize winner. Hades' voice broadcast, "Eighth Circle. Watch your step when disembarking from the platform."

Thick blue mist enveloped Benny. The core, not far away, disappeared. "Guys? You out there?" Benny yelled as he put one foot before another, but his voice echoed back at him from all directions.

———

Kami sat up. A body lay across her legs. "Layla, are you okay?"

Layla swept back her long hair and rolled over to face Kami. "I'm not even close to being okay, but I'm not hurt. I think."

"Let's get going," said Kami. "There's got to be a way out of this blue fog."

"Zuma! Benny!" No answer came. "Where are they?"

"Where are we, is the better question. Let's get going."

———

Chaz smelled a sweet scent. A familiar scent that he couldn't place. He stayed on guard as he inched forward in the blue mist.

"Hotter. Hotter," said a soft feminine voice that echoed pleasantly all around him. "You're almost there."

Chaz halted. He sensed a presence. Arms reached around him from behind. He spun and faced the woman in red with the golden eyes.

The mist cleared between them, as if her presence had the force to push it back.

"Inanna," said Chaz. "Or should I call you Ishtar?"

"I have as many names as I have gifts for you." She pressed her cheek against his shoulder and rolled her eyes up into his, but he took a step back to avoid contact.

"And they tell me I move fast."

"My first gift would be immortality. Does that please you, my lord?"

"Hmmm. That sounds like a fairly lengthy commitment for someone I barely know."

Inanna laughed and let enough distance grow between them so that she could eye him from head to toe. "You have your legs."

"In this place, yes."

"Then dance with me. That's not such a long commitment." Before he could refuse, she stepped in and wrapped her arms around his waist and swayed in his arms. Her jewelry tinkled as she danced on bare feet.

Chaz gently took her hands and unwound them from his waist. "Forgive me if I don't trust you, but a redhead tried to skewer me, and a white-haired girl tried to eat me."

"You can trust me. I'll prove it, if you let me."

"Help me find my friends and the items we seek."

"As you wish, my lord." She bowed her head.

"I prefer if you call me Chaz," he said. "And why should I trust you? Why help us? You work for Hades."

"That was before I met you. My plans have changed. I like you."

He leaned down and she titled her chin up. Chaz whispered, "Then bring my friends to me. Now."

She seemed perturbed by his rejection, but eventually said, "Wait here."

Chaz sat down. Despite his appearance of control, his heart still raced from his first slow dance, albeit a short one, with a beautiful woman, a dance, he was well aware, took place on borrowed legs.

———

Kami and Layla joined hands, so as not to lose each other in the mist. "You're shaking, Layla."

"Zuma almost died. Benny, too. And the others?"

"Key word—'almost.' Key point—we're still alive. Look!" said Kami, pointing ahead to a swirling tunnel, a black hole in the blue mist.

"It could be a trap."

"You're kidding, right? We're in the underworld—it's nothing *but* traps. I'm going." Kami bore her gray eyes into Layla's violet ones. "You can stay here."

"No. I'll go, but don't say I didn't warn you."

Kami stopped in her tracks. Her eyes shot daggers. "Warning? Like you yelled out when Zuma was in trouble—that we weren't ready? That you told us so? You think *you* will know when we are ready? Because I trust Minnie more than I trust you. What you really mean, Layla, is that you're not ready. Don't speak for me or anyone else. Got it? Because your negativity isn't helping."

"Okay. Okay. Let's just get out of here."

———

"Anyone there?" called Amir as he crept forward.

"*Woof, woof,*" barked Inanna as she approached him.

"Cerberus? Here doggy, doggy. Please, come help me. I'm quite lost."

"Will I do?" said Inanna, stepping into Amir's path.

"I don't know that face, but I know that voice. You're the girl who was in the car at Hades' castle. The one doing unspeakable naughties with my friend, Chaz."

Inanna laughed. "You mortals are quite amusing."

"He was right," said Amir.

"About what?"

"How he described you. You're beautiful."

Inanna blushed. "I did not take enough notice of you." She stepped closer. "You are most handsome. Your black eyes are irresistible."

Amir leaned down. "Then don't resist."

Inanna turned her face away. "I have a gift for you." She loosened the golden drawstring of a red purse hanging at her hip and withdrew a mirror. "Look how handsome you are."

"Sorry, but I don't trust . . ." Amir pushed the mirror away, but he caught a glimpse of himself in it. He gasped at his own beauty, grabbed the mirror, and turned his face this way and that to catch every detail of his features. "Ooh. I am handsome. More than I thought."

"I see it, too," said Inanna. "Now, tuck that away and tell no one that it came from me, or Hades will punish me severely. And you can use your imagination as to the punishments he can come up with. Come. I'll take you to my lord."

"What lord?" Amir eyed her cautiously.

Without hesitation, she blurted, "My Lord Chaz."

"Since when did he get promoted?" Amir followed her for a short while, waiting for a confrontation. He soon spotted a figure seated in the mist. "Lord Chaz, I presume?"

"Knock it off. She got you here, didn't she? Have a seat."

Inanna blew them both a kiss as she backed into the mist once more.

Benny crept forward one step at a time. He didn't mind the mist or being alone, as alone was a situation he knew all too well.

"Benny."

"Ma!" He saw nothing. "Ma, where are you? Or is that you, Hades?" He raced toward the sound, but found only more mist.

"Go back, Benedito."

He rushed forward again, toward the voice. His mother's voice. He was sure of it. The mist grew red and hotter, more like steam.

"Save yourself," Neeve pleaded.

Benny raced ahead toward the sound, ignoring the sweat that poured from his face. The moist hot air suffocated his lungs, but he stumbled forward nonetheless, calling "Ma!" and gasping.

Kami and Layla had walked for some time in the tunnel, but it seemed like an endless endeavor, a black tunnel behind them and another going forward, yet they felt a draw. A gentle wind urged them forward, until a sudden howling erupted behind them. The winds picked up speed.

"I told you it was a trap!" said Layla. "We're going to die."

"And I told you to shut up," said Kami.

Layla tried to turn back, but the wind stopped her from taking even a step. She leaned hard against it. It whipped her face, pulled the skin of her cheeks tight and howled like a hundred banshees.

The vortex swirled faster, sucking them off of their feet. They flew into the long black throat that had swallowed them whole. Only then did they see long oblong faces circling round them, faster and faster, screaming louder and louder.

Zuma couldn't take another step. His chest hurt. He wondered if he'd broken a rib. He lay down and closed his eyes.

A hand ran over his chest. His eyes sprang open. "Layla?" He saw an olive-skinned woman with golden eyes. "It's you. The girl at the castle."

"Lord Chaz waits for you. Come."

Zuma sat up. "Lord Chaz? Why should I trust you?"

Inanna reached into her red satchel and pulled out a white triangle of what looked like nougat, laced with nuts and specks of color, maybe fruits. "Take a bite. It will give you strength."

Zuma pushed her hand away, but a scent like none other had reached his nostrils, a sweet, savory scent. Better than sugar cookies right out of the oven. Better than freshly caramelized sugar drizzled over cream puffs. Better than a melted chocolate fountain or an apple-fritter stack. "What is it?"

"Ambrosia," said Inanna. "Food of the gods."

"I'm not a god," said Zuma, licking his lips.

"But I am. And I'm giving it to you. Take a bite, regain your strength, then I'll take you to Lord Chaz."

Zuma reached for the nougat. "Maybe just a tiny nibble." He bit off a tiny corner. He didn't even need to chew. It melted on his tongue with a hundred flavors at once, each separate, then combined. His taste buds danced in a frenzy that knocked him back with such ecstasy that he gasped. But it seemed to overpower all of his senses, not just taste. No other food, girl, sight or sound had ever delivered such bliss. He shuddered and groaned as explosion after explosion tantalized every cell in his body, building into a final, intense paroxysm of satisfaction, and a final groan and burp.

"Keep it," said Inanna. "But tell no one. If Hades finds out, I'll be put on a spit and roasted until the end of time."

———

Benny caught a glimpse of Neeve, but she raced away from him. The steam grew hotter. He reached out to stop her, but he could not take another step. The moist air scalded his lungs. He coughed. He watched blisters rise on the backs of his hands. He felt more on his cheeks and forehead. He crumpled to the ground and fell flat on his back. He felt someone grab his feet and drag him forward. He lost consciousness.

———

Kami and Layla shot through the twisting and turning vortex that flipped them this way and that like a hell slide. Layla slammed into Kami and Kami slammed into Layla as they flew, akimbo, in a free fall of limbs.

The tunnel narrowed, grew tighter. The tube pressed in against their faces, like plastic wrap. They couldn't breathe, couldn't reach a hand up to press against it.

Just before they passed out, they shot out of the tube, Kami first, then Layla, and skidded across a black shiny floor, sailing toward a black granite wall. Just before slamming into the wall beneath a sign saying NINTH CIRCLE, a round door rolled open, they shot through it, and it closed behind them.

They flopped to a stop on a dirt floor.

Kami sat up and brushed off the dust. "I think we've just been pooped out."

"I'm sorry I was negative again. I guess it's a habit," said Layla.

Kami stood up and offered Layla a hand up. "The good thing about bad habits is they can be changed to good ones. Wish I knew how, though."

Layla accepted her assistance. "Me, too."

———

Raj saw a red column ahead. She froze. It moved toward her, becoming better defined with each step.

"I'm Inanna. I've come to take you to my Lord Chaz."

"Lord? He's a lord?" Raj scoffed. "Lord of excessively hormonal boys maybe."

Inanna tsked and gasped. "You're hurt." She reached up toward Raj's face.

"Touch me, and I'll pluck out those pretty eyes of yours."

Inanna recoiled her hand. She reached into her red satchel and withdrew a greenish-gold glass pot. She lifted the lid, revealing an iridescent glowing gel. "This will heal the wound down the side of your face and the burns on your eyelids."

Raj hissed and pointed to her face. "This is a birthmark. And this is a wound."

"This heals all. Takes away all imperfections. But if you like your wounds, you may keep them. I'll take you to my lord." She set the lid back on the pot.

"Wait. What do you mean 'all imperfections'?"

"Shall I show you? You have a scar on your wrist."

Raj held out her forearm. Inanna rubbed a little of the glowing gel into it. The scar seemed to ignite in a burst of light that soon faded, leaving no trace of gel or scar behind.

"If it comes back, just use more. When the pot is empty, you will be healed permanently."

"It will fade completely?"

Inanna nodded. "Lord Chaz asked me to prove my loyalty. But tell no one, not even Lord Chaz of this gift, or Hades will punish me—worse than plucking out my eyes, I assure you."

Raj opened the pot and spread some of the gel on her eyelids and over her birthmark. She didn't have a mirror, but her eyelids no longer hurt when she blinked.

"Come. My lord awaits you."

Raj slipped the pot into the outer pocket of her skinny back-pack and followed Inanna.

When she saw Chaz, Zuma and Amir, she raced up and threw her arms around each of them. "Dudes, I'm glad to see you fo-sho!" To Chaz, she added, "But I'm not calling you lord. Not if my life hung in the balance over a pit of lava, and calling you lord would save my skinny butt."

Inanna stepped between Chaz and Raj. "I could find no others, my lord. They've left the mist."

"Inanna," said Chaz. "Do you know where we can find the sybil's books or the key to the first gate?"

"Key, no. But the books are kept in the *kiste mystica*—the sa-cred chest— in the Ninth Circle, but they are well guarded."

"Lead the way," said Raj, pulling her hair back behind her ear.

"Raj," said Chaz. "It's gone. Your birthmark."

Raj raised her chin. "Crazy place, right? Probably won't last."

"Hot damn, girl," said Amir. "You're fine! Almost as fine as me."

Raj grit her teeth. "I was fine before. Guess you never noticed."

"Chillax, Green Goddess. I was blind before, remember?" defended Amir.

"Raj," said Zuma. "He meant it as a compliment."

Chaz stroked Raj's face. "You're flawless, Amir can see, and I've got my legs. Let's enjoy it while it lasts."

Raj put her hand over Chaz's and stared into his cool blue eyes. "Took you long enough to notice."

Inanna gripped Chaz's arm. "This way, my lord."

Chapter Twenty-Nine

Layla and Kami hopped to their feet and dusted themselves off. The stone vestibule in which they stood had nine tunnel openings. A red neon sign above each tunnel cast an eerie glow, and each sign flashed the same word: EXIT.

"Maybe we should split up?" suggested Kami.

"Not a chance!"

"Which way then?" asked Kami.

"Do I look like a freakin' tour guide to the underworld? Look around for clues."

"Good idea. See, you're a tour guide after all."

Layla exploded. "Don't you get it? I'm not like you. I can't do this! My hands are still shaking from the monster-go-round and being sucked through a hell-straw. All I want is a way out." Layla knelt down to examine the soft dirt floor. "There are footprints, human and animal, but they run every which way. All tunnels look equally used."

"There are nine tunnels. Maybe each one leads to a different circle. Takes us back to the start, for example."

"And one is the exit, maybe. But which one?" asked Layla.

"I'm not a freakin' tour guide either."

Squeaks, buzzing sounds and crackling noises neared the vestibule, emerging from each shadowy archway.

"Shhhh. Do you hear that?"

"I don't hear. . . Now I do. What is that?"

As the sounds grew louder, Layla and Kami backed up until they stood at the center of the room, back to back, watching and waiting.

"Anything but more snakes," said Kami.

A single rat scurried into the room and skirted the edge of the wall before sitting on its haunches and sniffing the air. It turned its beady black eyes on them.

"Careful what you wish for," said Layla.

It was like nine plagues rushed out at once from each archway: cockroaches, scorpions, scarabs, giant spiders, frogs and rats all raced across the floor toward the girls. Hornets, gadflies and locusts swarmed the air, diving, stinging and biting.

The girls screamed. With no weapons to fight them off, the best they could do was face one another and huddle up, burying their faces in each other's shoulder, and hoping the vermin disappeared.

The ground moved with a blanket of vermin, which crawled up their boots, their legs, thighs, torsos, arms.

When they twisted in her hair, Kami let out a blood-curdling scream, the likes of which Layla had never heard. "I can't breathe . . . I . . ." Kami tried to break free of Layla's hold. She threw her hands up over her ears.

"No! Don't move," said Layla. "It's a trap."

"They'll eat us alive!" raged Kami, trying to shove Layla away. "I'll take my chances with an exit!" A rat climbed up Kami's back and up to her shoulder. She screamed again. Her knees buckled.

Layla knocked the rat away, dropped to her knees and wrapped her arms around Kami, preventing her from rising to her feet.

Kami's breathing quickened and anger erupted. She threw a fist at Layla.

Layla dodged the blow. It just missed her face. "Hear me out! Footprints go through every doorway. None of them are the exit!"

Kami gasped for air. The insects and creatures crawled onto her head and over her hands. They dangled at her cheeks, where she felt their tiny legs scratching and twitching. "Let me go!" Worse yet, her ears echoed with every crick of beetle crawling over beetle, click of pincer, buzz of wing, croak and squeak.

Layla held Kami tighter, remembering how Zuma had held her in the Abominable Sands. "Close your eyes. Do it!"

Kami complied. She buried her head in Layla's shoulder and washed her friend's neck in heavy breaths.

Layla hummed a song. It came naturally, from somewhere deep inside and long ago. A song her mother hummed to soothe her. Vermin covered their bodies. The girls buried their faces in each other's necks and swaddled together in each other's arms.

The ground rumbled beneath them. Kami's eyes shot open. "Oh, crap!"

As the ground under them opened up and they fell through the floor, Layla shouted, "Poor choice of words!"

———

Something covered Benny's face. As he yanked away a swath of fabric and opened his eyes, he felt more fabric wound around his hands. Bright white light cut into his eyes like shards of glass. He let out a grunt of pain, cinched them shut and turned away.

"Key."

Benny bolted upright. As he ripped the cloth from around his hands, a blurry face, surrounded by a shock of dark wild hair, slowly came into focus. "The key. Where is it?"

"See know key," said the man, scratching his head and nodding excitedly. The man had wild hazel eyes and scraggly hair, scraggly brows, and a scraggly beard. His once-white shirt was shredded and smudged with dirt.

"No key, huh?" Benny rubbed his hands together. No more blisters. He felt his face. Smooth. Pain-free.

The man nodded. "Key know see."

"No see. I get it." Benny observed his surroundings. He was in a cave of light with crystal walls. A fine mist seeped through several openings, and the light that reflected from crystal to crystal created hundreds of arcs of light in soft hues, like a rainbow had split apart. It seemed too pure for the underworld. Benny rose to his feet to search for a way out, which was not apparent. He pressed his hands against the walls to find an opening. "You did fix me up. So, thanks." Even though he could not see it, he knew there must be a way in—and out. He found two fissures large enough to pass through. Benny pointed to the first. "This one?"

The man frantically waved his arms about and pulled at his hair. "Na. Na."

"Not this one, huh?" Benny slid a leg through the other opening.

The man went berserk. He stomped his feet, pulled at his hair and shouted, "Nee! Nee!"

Benny slid his chest through the opening. "Sorry. Gotta go." He ducked to pull his head through.

"Nee! Nee—va."

Benny whipped back through the opening and grabbed the man by his shoulders. "Neeve?"

"Nee—va."

"Take me to her."

The man shook his head and body like a dog shakes off water. He disappeared through the first fissure. Benny followed.

———

Inanna led Chaz, Amir, Zuma and Raj out of the blue mist and into a tunnel system, a labyrinth of volcanic rock, exuding steam in some places, red lava flows in others. She turned down one fork, then another, without hesitation.

"How much farther to the Ninth Circle?" asked Zuma.

Inanna paused long enough to answer. "This is the Ninth Circle. You were falling all the while in the mist. You're as deep as deep will go."

Chaz recited from memory, "A brazen anvil falling from earth nine nights and days would reach Tartarus upon the tenth . . . and if once a man were within the gates, he would not reach the floor until a whole year had reached its end."

"A year?" asked Raj. "Tell me I haven't wasted a year of my life down here?"

"So sayeth Dante?" asked Amir.

"Centuries earlier, actually," said Chaz. "Hesiod in 700 BCE."

"We need weapons," said Raj.

"Just around the next corner," said Inanna. She led them to an ornate marble archway and beckoned them inside. "Choose as you please."

A cache of medieval weapons lined each of five stone walls.

"No guns? No rocket launchers? No grenades?" asked Zuma, grabbing a pair of maces. "Hades is either behind the times or one sick dude."

"He's playing with us, as usual," said Raj, strapping on a sword.

Chaz grabbed a broadsword and shield.

Amir picked up a pair of fighting sticks but reconsidered. "I think I need to step up my game." He shoved the sticks into the outer pocket of his pack and grabbed a scabbard belt, which he fastened about his waist. He withdrew a short narrow dagger from its sheath. "Better."

Zuma grabbed a mace and an axe.

Once armed, Inanna led the small band to a grand door constructed with panels of pure gold, each a relief. A golden grape stalk grew up the center of the door. Golden tendrils ran across the top and down, where a cluster of grapes hung on either side. They seemed to grow from the golden vines. Real grapes. Dark crimson orbs the size of walnuts.

"The inner chamber is guarded," said Inanna. "Pass through a second door, and you'll find *kiste mystica*. Inside the chest, you'll find the sibyl's books."

"How many guards?" asked Chaz.

"I don't know. I've never been inside," answered Inanna. "I must leave you here. Hades must be searching for me. I dare stay with you no longer, my lord."

Zuma plucked a few grapes and secreted them away in his pocket.

"Understood," said Chaz. "Thank you."

"Don't forget me. I won't forget you." Inanna's eyes cast a golden glow upon Chaz's face before she danced away into the labyrinth of tunnels. Her jewelry tinkled long after she had disappeared.

"Chaz-man, you lucky dog." Zuma slapped Chaz on the shoulder.

Raj folded her arms across her chest. "The 'dog' part is right. Lord of all dogs in the almighty doghouse."

"Can we stick to the task here?" asked Amir. "Save the jealous catfight for another time."

Raj huffed. "Oh, right. I'm jealous. Not even!"

"Stop it," said Chaz. "Although it pleases the lord that you fight over him."

"Oh," Raj fake chuckled. "I'm ROFL." She eyed Zuma and Amir, warning them to keep silent. Zuma and Amir stifled a laugh.

"Roll on the floor laughing another time, Raj, and check out the panels," said Amir. "They may be a clue."

"Right," said Amir. "Here's a woman seated on a chest, holding a torch. A girl is kneeling beside her, holding a . . . what is that?"

Raj said, "It looks like a spear tip."

Amir added, "Or a staff, but it's short."

"It's an ear of corn," blurted Chaz. "An ear of corn in silence reaped."

"An ear of corn . . .what?" asked Zuma.

"In silence reaped. Demeter and Persephone, of course."

Zuma, Amir and Raj crinkled their brows.

"You people need to read more," said Chaz. "And take notes when Daniel is lecturing."

"Save the lecture and spill the deets," huffed Raj.

Chaz explained. "Hades abducted Demeter's daughter, Persephone, and brought her here to the underworld to be his wife and queen. Demeter searched for Persephone, and since Demeter is the goddess of the harvest, a drought occurred while she was gone. Crops died. People suffered. Zeus sent his messenger to Hades, requesting he send Persephone home, but Hades had already tricked his wife into eating pomegranate seeds. She had to remain one month in the underworld for each pomegranate seed she ate, but she could return to earth the other months."

Zuma shifted uncomfortably. "What did pomegranate seeds have to do with it?"

"Uh, because everyone knows that eating food from the underworld is a bad thing." Chaz continued. "Demeter searched for her daughter in the underworld. Her torch opened the entrance. It must be the key."

"There's no way in—no handle, nothing," said Raj.

Chaz said, "Let me try something. Hear me out. One day, Raj came upon me in the forest. I had a BB gun in one hand and—"

"Is this some kind of joke?" asked Raj.

"Yes. It is, as a matter of fact. So, let me finish," barked Chaz.

Raj crossed her arms over her chest. "It better be good."

Chaz continued. "As I said, I had a BB gun in one hand and a squirrel in the other. Raj—horrified at my threat to the animal—said 'I'm warning you, Chaz. Whatever you do to that squirrel, I'll do to you.' Upon which I kissed the squirrel's butt and let it go free."

"As if!" scoffed Raj amid the howls of Amir and Zuma.

The door cracked open.

Chaz smiled. "Legend has it that an old woman cracked a joke to Demeter, which made her smile as she mourned the loss of her daughter."

"Whatever you say, Lord Squirrel Butt." Raj bowed.

Chaz peeked through the crack in the door. No guard. He swung the door open. The mosaic floor, strewn with objects and debris, held a central image of grapes, whose vines formed a swirl of eternity symbols.

Another door, wooden and modest, was set in the opposite wall.

"No guards. Let's go," said Zuma, already crossing the floor. As he crossed the grapes, a screech sounded from above their heads. Zuma froze and peered upward. A single bat hung from the rocky ceiling. "That's it. One puny bat? Not much of a guard."

Before their eyes, the bat grew in size. Double. Triple. Man-sized. Double again.

Zuma backed toward the wall. The others circled the room and stood across from one another, ready to fight.

"Puny, huh?" said Raj, sword in hand. "Thanks, Zuma."

The creature spread its wings and dropped to the center of the room on short muscular legs. Its beady red eyes surveyed them; its tall ears twitched this way and that; it snorted the air and puffed out its broad hairy chest. Another screech revealed long vampire teeth. It spread its skinny muscular wings, at the end of which were black hands holding swords.

"No biggie. It's one of him and four of us," shouted Zuma.

"But he's as big as four of us," replied Chaz.

A cacophony of screeches echoed over their heads. A flood of small bats entered the room through a fissure in the roof.

Amir swung his sticks, leaped in the air, and swatted the creatures as they dove toward him. "If these guys grow, we're toast!"

Amidst the diving bats, Chaz and Raj swung their swords to battle the giant bat, which fought both of them at the same time.

Zuma swung his mace into the creature's back. It squealed and swatted Raj with a wing that sent her flying through the air and crashing into a stone wall. Her sword flew out of her hand as she landed upon a pile of baskets and other debris.

Raj winced in pain as she scrambled to her feet and dove for her katana.

The bat swung his swords at Chaz, who worked double time with sword and shield amidst horrendous clangs and clatter. Zuma jumped in to help, swinging his mace, then his axe.

From behind, Amir leaped atop the creature's back and swung his sticks down, which cracked over the head of the beast.

The bat swooshed a sword through the air on a trajectory to cut Amir in half. Raj had already sprung back into action, diverting the sword's path as Amir sprang away, past imminent death and landed on his feet on the tiled floor.

Chaz wasted no time. He thrust his blade into the beast's heart as Zuma flung his axe into the beast's neck.

The giant let out a single high-pitched scream and tottered in death. Chaz yanked his blade free from the creature's chest. It fell backward and died. Before their eyes, the bat shriveled to its original size. The bats in the air darted back into the crevice and disappeared.

Zuma picked up the dead shrunken bat. "Not so tough now, are you?" He flung it at the wall, where it left a splotch before falling to the floor.

Kami and Layla tumbled through a dirt tube, like a giant worm-hole. Each tumble and roll knocked off more bugs and rats. Eventually the chute ended, spurting them out. They dropped to the floor of a volcanic tunnel with dirt floors that seemed to run forever in both directions.

Kami scrambled to her feet, jerked and stomped and shook every part of her body to dislodge remaining hangers-on. "I'm so over chutes and tunnels."

Layla knocked one last cockroach from the top of Kami's head. "Right? Makes you wonder what Alice was thinking when she voluntarily dropped through the rabbit hole."

"Shhhh." Kami closed her eyes, letting her gifted ears reach beyond mortal limits. She signaled for Layla to follow and remain silent. Kami found a fissure just big enough for the two of them and ducked inside. "Izanagi. I'd know that voice any-where. He's mine."

Layla put up a hand. "I remember your threat to destroy him. Focus. Stay calm."

Kami smiled. "And I remember your cowardice."

"Who was afraid of the bugs and rats?"

Kami scowled. "Calm. Got it. Follow me and keep quiet."

The girls slid out of the fissure and crept down the tunnel toward the voices. They crouched beside a vestibule and listened to a heated discussion.

"Where is Hades?" shouted fair-haired Lord Nergal. "I'm tired of waiting."

"He should be here by now!" bellowed Lord Kali, pushing back his mane of black braids.

"Light the torch, Izanagi," said Lord Sharjinn, running a hand over his bald, tattooed head.

Kami motioned a plan to Layla who nodded her understanding. Kami scooped up a rock and threw it down the tunnel. As it made a loud crack, she grabbed Layla's arm and ran in the opposite direction, back to the fissure in the wall.

The room fell silent.

Layla and Kami squeezed into the fissure. They'd barely ducked out of sight before the lords spilled out of the chamber. They had to know how many enemies they faced.

Kami and Layla stared at each other, chests heaving, hoping their beating hearts did not give away their position.

Footsteps grew closer. Layla had a sliver of a view. She hoped the blackness inside the fissure prevented the lords from having any view of her, sliver or otherwise. Izanagi's eyes panned the tunnel. Just outside the fissure, he stopped. "I hate Hades' realm. Nothing but crumbling caves! We'll proceed with him or without him." He turned back toward the vestibule, and the other lords followed.

Layla held up six fingers. Kami nodded her understanding. They had found the lords of the underworld, all but Hades, and the key: a torch that, once lit, would open the first gate.

Kami pressed herself against Layla until their noses touched. Kami whispered, "Ready or not, time to fight."

Layla whispered, "It's two to six, Kami."

"It's now or never."

"It's Izanagi you want. Not the key."

Kami pressed harder against Layla. "Yes, I want him. So, you grab the key."

"Let's wait for the others."

"There's no time."

Layla bit her lip. "I know. I know. Let me think."

Kami moved to exit the fissure, but Layla stopped her. "Wait, Kami. We need a plan. A lay of the land." She stammered. "Look for weapons. Find a way out. I have an idea. Follow my lead."

Kami hesitated. "Your lead?"

"Just trust me, Kami. I have one weapon I never use, but it will give us a few precious seconds. That may be enough to have an advantage over them."

"Oooo, a secret weapon. This I gotta see." Kami waved a hand to let Layla exit first.

Benny followed the crazy man to an archway made of fire. The man pointed at it before running away as if in terror.

Benny stepped through the fire. Oddly, it seemed cool. Perhaps he had been forged by the mist, burned and hardened by it, the same way the tip of a wooden spear is fire-hardened over flames. As he emerged from the flames, he stood on the end of a stone bridge, which arched over a red rushing river. The bridge led to a black stone palace, just like the one on the hill that had sunk back into the earth: Hades' palace.

As Benny crossed the bridge, he eyed the monster statues on

either side that had once encircled the courtyard of his youth —
but they weren't stone now. They were real and menacing. Each
wielded a weapon and eyed him as he crossed the bridge
between them: a frog creature wielding a spear; a fierce crocodile; a two-headed ogre with pink pig faces, hoisting a shield in
one hand, a dagger in the other; a skinny, snarling wolf; a
demented cat, and the mosquito woman with a long hollow
tongue. But for the mosquito women, all held back to let Benny
pass. The mosquito slashed the air with her tongue, which shot
at Benny's chest, stopping his advance. She could have pierced
him but didn't. He could see the displeasure in her large shiny
black eyes. Clearly, he was expected, and they'd been instructed
to stand down. Otherwise, he'd be dead or in the fight of his life.
Still, she provoked him, as if hoping for an excuse to disobey
order, pierce his chest and drink her fill.

Benny stepped forward, and the mosquito woman stepped
aside to let him pass. He climbed the steps. The front doors of
shiny onyx inlaid with gold swung open, and he stepped inside.
The layout mirrored the mansion on the hill but for the opulence,
the likes of which he could never have imagined. According to
Daniel, Hades commanded the underworld and all of the riches
in it: veins of precious ore — gold, silver, platinum — and precious
gems all of which crisscrossed the marble floor beneath his feet.
Gold chandeliers dripped with diamonds and danced with
flames that lit up the veins of emerald, sapphire and amethyst
running through each wall. Ornate platinum bases supported
tabletops cut from slabs of ruby.

Benny knew exactly where to find Hades. He headed to the
library.

The hearth blazed and bellowed with uncontrollable fiery
rage. It seemed twice as large as the hearth of his youth, and he
noticed one other notable exception: the flames did not shoot up

from between charred logs; they shot up through a swelled mound of charred bones and skulls. Benny stepped around the chair, ready to face his enemy at last.

"Ma!" Benny fell to his knees and wrapped his arms around her shoulders.

"Benny! I'm sorry. I didn't know!"

No ropes seemed to bind her. "Come on. I'm getting us out of—"

"At last—a family reunion." Hades filled the doorway. His living ermine coat barked and snapped at the intruder as Hades approached the hearth. "Welcome home, Benedito."

Benny rose, pulling his mother to her feet. "We're leaving."

Hades stuck his hands in the fire and rubbed them together, as if to warm them. "She won't leave the others behind. Will you, Neeve?"

"Others?"

"Come, don't dawdle," said Hades, grinning as he headed to the door. "I've waited a long time for this day to arrive."

Chapter Thirty

Benny locked his mother's trembling hand in his.
They followed Hades, descending the steps to the dungeon. At the far end of the stone corridor, they reached an alcove holding a large cell containing six women. Benny had never seen them before, yet he knew them—each of them.

The women stepped forward and pressed their faces against the bars and mumbled, "Benny."

"Benny," said Neeve. "These are . . ."

Hades waited, but Neeve remained silent. "Oh, good grief. Say it. I hate suspense. No, actually I love suspense. Drag this out—it's delicious!"

Benny approached the cage. A radiant Asian woman with pale skin, upswept black hair and lips the color of cherry blossoms said, "I am Miko. Kami's mother."

The next woman blurted, "Zaria. Amir's mother." Benny remembered Amir bragging about his mother's beauty. Zaria was taller than the others, statuesque. She had pronounced cheekbones, a delicate nose and sable-brown skin. There was a grace about her, yet her soft brown eyes frowned like a deer trapped by hunters.

The next woman had long chestnut hair, parted down the middle, doe-sized brown eyes and a beaded headband. He could see the resemblance to Cookie, Zuma's grandmother, and to Zuma. She blurted, "Zuma's mother?"

She nodded and turned away, putting a hand to her mouth to stifle a sob.

"Tahira. Layla's mother," said the next, a slimmer version of her daughter but with the same violet eyes, timid and vulnerable.

"Amala. How is Rajani?" asked a woman in a pink and gold sari.

"Raj is one tough girl," said Benny. "Don't worry."

"Helga. How is my Chaz?" asked a woman with fair complexion, ice-blue eyes and long blonde tresses. Braids, tied along each side of her face and pulled back, reminded Benny of Friday wearing the flower halo, but this woman was not demure like Friday. Her neck was thick and her shoulders broad. Benny could picture her holding a spear and shield and wearing a Viking breastplate, ready to wage war and plunder a village.

Benny glared at Hades. "You've got me. Let them go."

Hades laughed. "My dear boy, I've got you. And them. And soon, I'll have your friends. And then . . . well, it's not polite to gloat, is it? But I'm not polite, so it doesn't really matter. Soon, I'll have it all—upper world and lower."

Something in Benny exploded like it had the day he fought Dillon. He rushed upon Hades and lunged for his throat. The ermine creatures sank their teeth into his forearms and hands, but he ignored the pain—it was miniscule to the hatred that welled up inside him.

Hades smiled, slow and sinister. With one sweep of his hand, he knocked Benny off his feet and into the air.

Benny crashed down on the stone floor in a heap.

"Benny!" cried Neeve as Hades signaled two minions in black-hooded robes to lock her up.

Neeve struggled to break free. While one guard unlocked the cage, the other two threw her in. Miko and Catori caught Neeve's fall. Neeve caught her balance and threw herself at the bars. "Run, Benny! Escape!"

Benny leaped to his feet and hurled himself at Hades, and again Hades knocked him flat. "You're weak!" Hades threw his coat aside. It ran up the steps barking. Hades approached Benny in a black robe with a fur cowl. "Benny, join me. Rule alongside me."

Benny pulled himself to his feet. He swiped his fingertips across his smashed lower lip. The sight of his own blood on his fingertips fueled his heart, and in turn, his fists. Again, he rushed Hades and pummeled him with blow after blow. But they did no harm. Hades only grinned wider. Benny mustered all of his hate and landed a full punch in Hades' gut just like the one that had sent Dillon flying into his band of friends.

"Oh, I felt that one. A little. Good job. My turn." Hades landed a punch in Benny's gut that sent him flying into a wall. He crumpled to the floor, held his ribs, and gasped for air. He tried to get up but couldn't get his legs under him.

———

Kami and Layla approached the vestibule and listened to the lords.

"It's time," said Izanagi.

Layla strolled straight through the vestibule entrance as if expected. She walked tall and confident, chin tipped downward to open her violet eyes, and held a hand on her hip.

Kami, shocked by Layla's sudden self-assurance, had to rush to catch up.

The lords' eyes turned upon them, and they raised their weapons, until Izanagi raised a hand to quell their aggression.

Layla put her hands on her hips. "I assure you, my lords, we're unarmed. Just wanted to join your little party." Layla eyed Kami before reaching her hands around the back of her neck, scooping up her hair and raising it slowly to the top of her head, where she let it tumble free. Her eyes climbed skyward as one hand rested back on her hip and the other waved before her face, as if to cool herself off. "The underworld is sooooo freakin' hot."

Kami followed Layla's eyes up to a boulder balanced on a ledge. "Super hot," said Kami, jutting out a hip and waving her hand, trying to imitate Layla, but moving more like a spastic flamingo.

Fair-haired Lord Nergal crossed his arms over his sleeveless blue robe. "Hot, indeed."

Lord Apep hissed at Nergal. His eyes swirled, and he whipped his tail into Nergal's chest hard enough to cause him pain.

"Careful, Apep. Do not turn new friends into sworn enemies," warned Nergal, jumping to his feet and stroking his goatee. "I simply meant that I live in a colder clime."

Izanagi never broke eye contact with Kami. "Where are your friends?"

Layla and Kami eyed the room. No weapons, except on their enemies.

"Sorry, it's just us," said Layla.

"Just two little girls," added Kami. "You like the odds, don't you, stinky?"

Layla eyed Kami, shooting her a glance that said, "Good one!"

The comment forced a laugh from Nergal, and from the bald tawny-skinned brute with symbols tattooed across his face and bald head, and from the snake-faced man, and from the no-shirt freak painted like a skeleton and wearing a new feathered headdress and a loincloth, but not from Izanagi, nor from the object of ridicule, the black lion of a beast with a mane of braids swept back from his face. Instead, the stinky one opened his mouth and stuck out his tongue, which dipped down to his chin. He reached for the sword strapped to his back.

As if in some weird competition, the skeleton man also stuck out his tongue and reached it clear to the tip of his chin.

"Dudes, that trick with the tongue. It is sure to wow the girls," said Layla, her comment laced with sarcasm.

Kami added a disgusted, "So not!"

Lord Izanagi reached for the torch and for a stick that burned in a raised fire pit. "Enough! Since you are at the party, you may watch the first gate open before you die."

Kami eyed the swords on his hips. "I expected better manners, Lord Izanagi! To die, I expected; but rudeness, I did not expect, even from an enemy."

Izanagi's eyes narrowed. His anger flared. He threw the burning stick away from the torch. "Rudeness? How?"

"We've never formally met any of you." She eyed Layla, rolling her eyes up to the boulder and back to Izanagi. "Manners have run amuck."

Layla nodded her understanding. "Right? Run amuck."

Izanagi made a slight bow. "Let it not be said that insults preceded your demise but rather you were afforded every courtesy. I am Lord Izanagi. My feathered friend is . . . his name is long, even for me. Just call him Lord of Mictlan. Lord Apep. Lord Sharjinn. Lord Nergal. And, the 'stinky one,' as you call him, is Kali, Lord of Kali Yuga." Izanagi put the flaming stick against the torch.

Kami raced forward and launched herself into the air. She grabbed the hilts of both of Izanagi's swords and whipped them from their sheaths as her foot kicked him in the chest. She flipped in midair, severed the burning end of the stick, and landed on her feet. She tossed one sword to Layla, before pointing the other at Izanagi.

The black lion raised his sword to crash down on Kami, but Izanagi stopped his advance and grabbed the weapon from him. "She's mine!"

"No," said Kami. "You are mine, Lord Izanagi." Their swords clashed. Kami jumped atop the rim of the tall basin filled with burning wood. She leaped in the air to avoid the swipe of Izanagi's blade that threatened to cut off her legs. As she landed, she kicked the burning wood into the air. Glowing sticks and embers rained down on the lords.

Izanagi turned away from the embers that flew at him.

Layla crashed her sword into the peacock's blade dodged fairhaired Nergal's spear. She backed up to the wall, just where she needed to be. She swung her blade full force to push her enemies back and scaled the wall, moving from one ledge to the next.

Kami met Izanagi blow for blow, flip for flip, in a dance that promised to end in the blood or death of one of them. Both fought with such might, it seemed they didn't care about the others, nor about opening the gate, nor about any purpose other than to destroy one another.

Layla reached the upper ledge. The peacock chased after her.

Apep slithered upward just behind Lord of Mictlan. "The party issss not over. Sssstay with ussss." His eyes swirled as he slithered up the rocks.

Layla swung at the snake, nearly decapitating it. Apep whipped his head back and hissed as her sword clanged against the rock. Three quick jabs, born of practice and precision, landed successfully. The first dislodged the skeleton freak's headdress, the second cut away his loincloth, and the third bit into his sword so hard that it knocked him from the wall. He fell, face down, bare buttocks up. Layla made a face of disdain as she ducked behind the boulder and shoved the blade under it. She heaved her weight against the lever to rock the boulder from its perch, hopefully, before the blade broke. The boulder teetered. Apep slithered away to a safe distance.

Izanagi swung his heavy sword downward, directed at Kami's skull, but she ducked. "You've improved."

Kami swung her blade across Izanagi's cheek. "You haven't." The gash made by the sword healed before Kami's eyes.

Izanagi swung the heavy blade down toward Kami's skull.

Kami dropped to her knees and swung her sword overhead. She heard the blades bite. Another blow, one she didn't see, dislodged the sword from her hand and sent it flying. Her eyes met Izanagi's.

Izanagi pointed his blade at Kami, pressing the metal tip into the notch of her neck. "Time for us to live. Time for you to die."

The boulder came crashing down.

Kami saw it first, and Izanagi saw it by the terror in Kami's eyes.

Izanagi eyed the rock over his shoulder. He dove on top of Kami as the boulder crashed into his back, knocking them both to the floor.

"Kami!" yelled Layla, following the boulder's path. She jumped down as nimbly as she'd raced up, grabbed the torch from its perch and raced for the doorway as the lords dove for cover. Sprawled on the floor near the exit, Kali snatched her ankle while Apep blocked her exit with his long tail.

Fueled by a sheer desire to run for her life, Layla smacked Kali's face with the butt of the torch and stabbed the end of it into Apep's tail—noticing that he had regrown the tip. She shot out of the vestibule and into the caves.

Layla raced forward, taking a turn to the right, then left, then left again, with no consideration as to which fork to take. "Get away"—it was her only thought. She even hoped she was lost—which meant they could not find her. Eventually, she slowed her pace, constantly eyeing over her shoulder as much as down the tunnel ahead without knowing if Kami was alive or dead or how to get back to her.

———

Chaz, Amir, Raj and Zuma failed to find a way to open the second door. Neither jokes nor slamming their bodies against it worked. Although the door was made of wood, none of their weapons marred it. No grouping of force budged it.

Raj slammed her fist into the door. "We've come too far to quit!"

"I'm out of ideas, guys," said Chaz, sinking to the floor to sit.

"It's got to be another trick," suggested Amir, pushing debris aside to sit next to Chaz.

Zuma heaved his weight against the door one more time.

"Give it a rest, Zuma. We've tried everything," said Raj, taking a spot next to Amir.

Zuma sat next to Raj.

"What else can you tell us about Demeter?" asked Amir.

"Nothing!" Chaz exploded. He ran his hands through his hair. "I told you what I know. The Eleusinian Mysteries of Demeter and Persephone were kept secret, upon death."

Amir picked up an ear of corn from the debris on the floor. "In silence picked."

"In silence reaped," Chaz corrected, seeing the ear of corn. "That's it!" He jumped to his feet. "You're beautiful, Amir!"

"I know, but how does that help us?" asked Amir.

"This debris. Why is it here? Look, there it is—the basket." Chaz raced across the room and scooped a woven basket into his hands. "Find the top. And grab that corn. What else?"

Raj and Zuma scurried to their feet and pushed the debris aside. "What are we looking for?" asked Zuma.

"Here it is," shouted Raj, holding up the lid to the basket. Chaz grabbed it from her. "The rites. They mimicked Demeter's path: first, her descent, 'a thing done'; second, her search, 'a thing shown'; and third, her ascent, 'a thing said.' The *mystai*, or initiates, put items in a basket. It's worth a shot."

"What things?" asked Zuma.

"I don't remember," said Chaz.

Raj grabbed items from the floor and put them on the grape mosaic in the center of the room. "We'll lay stuff here—maybe you'll recognize something."

"Maybe," said Chaz. As the others collected items, Chaz reached for them, eyed them, and then set them down again: figurines, coins with Demeter's image, red clay pots, a golden viper, husked corn, broaches, branches of laurel, a chalice, an egg, a bust of Hades, a helmet, a lyre, an oar, plates, shells.

Chaz put the egg, the golden viper and an ear of corn into the basket. The door remained closed.

"What if we put them all in the basket?" offered Amir.

"I doubt that would work," said Chaz. "The rites were specific. After all, this was the way to an afterlife."

Chaz kicked the debris aside, whipping piles of it right and left, left and right. He circled the room without luck before bending down to his boot and pinching a tiny object resting atop it between thumb and forefinger. He held his fingers up. "Got it. A seed."

He dropped it in the basket and closed the lid. He set it before the door.

The door swung open. Raj slapped him on the shoulder, Zuma slapped him on the butt, and Amir clapped his hands in delight. Their joy was momentary.

They entered the inner room, a nonagon. Chests, stacked three, four or five high, lined every wall.

"No way!" said Raj. "Where do we start?"

Zuma reached for a top chest, lifted it off of the stack and set it on the ground. "We'll open every one. Let's get cracking."

Zuma raised a lid as Chaz shouted, "Zuma! No!"

Zuma tried to slam the lid back on the box, but a force pushed against him. "It's okay," he said, straining with all his might to reset the lid. "It didn't open."

A black wolf's head shot upward, forcing the lid open. It snapped its jaws, just missing Zuma's throat. Zuma stumbled backward. The wolf sprang from the chest and leaped toward him.

Raj decapitated the wolf, midair, with a single swing of her blade. As its dead body sailed toward Zuma, he caught its massive underbelly and propelled it forward so it didn't land on him. It disappeared, leaving him flat on his back, his arms up. "Thanks, Raj."

"Welcome, bro," said Raj, giving him a hand up.

Chaz showed the others the image carved into the top of another chest he had pulled from a stack. It showed a maiden lifting the lid from a large earthen jar. "She's the first woman, forged by Hephaestus from earth and water, clothed by Minerva, gifted in music by Apollo, speech by Hermes and beauty by Aphrodite. Her name is Pandora. She opened a box and released evil into the world. These boxes could contain the books — or pure evil."

Raj rolled her eyes. "Why do legends always blame the bad stuff on girls? It's sexist!"

"She also released hope," said Chaz.

"That's a good thing," added Amir. "We could use some hope right now."

"Which one do we open?" asked Raj. "We know it's not that one."

"This one has a picture," said Chaz. "Others don't. The rites involved visions of some kind."

"Got an idea. I hope this works." Zuma pulled three crimson orbs from his pocket, shoved the grapes into his mouth and chewed.

"Zuma! No food in the underworld—bad—remember?" shouted Amir.

Zuma swallowed. His eyes turned glassy and unblinking. His lips parted; purple juice and saliva dribbled down his chin. He wobbled on his feet. He turned his head to the doorway, smiled a silly grin and waved. He staggered to various chests, pointed to them, then eyed the emptiness that filled the doorway, as if seeking approval.

Zuma made it more than halfway around the room with no luck. He pointed to the next three chests, starting with the one on top. He shook his head and made a silly face of disappointment. He pointed to the middle chest. Again, he shook his head. He pointed to the bottom chest, and his face lit up. He blew a kiss at the empty doorway.

Chaz raced over and lowered the top chest to the floor. Raj and Amir grabbed the middle one and set it aside. Zuma wrapped his arms over the bottom chest. He kissed it in a lippy, wet, sloppy, long kiss.

"We're trusting our lives to a fool," said Amir. "He better be right."

"Wish I had a camera," said Raj.

As Chaz peeled Zuma off of the chest, his head wobbled like a bobblehead sitting on a dashboard. He rolled off the chest, grinning with a fool's delight.

Chaz lifted the lid. "Got 'em!" Each book was tucked inside a golden case shaped like a book. "I'll get Mr. Happy. You two grab the books."

Raj grabbed two and Amir one.

Chaz lifted Zuma to his feet and put his arm around his waist. Zuma puckered and tried to kiss him. "Persephone is nice. Pretty, too."

Chaz turned away. "You kiss me, and I'll leave you behind."

"Dude, if there's a next time, one magic grape. Just one." Amir held up a single finger.

Zuma held up his hand; all five fingers waved; his head bobbled. "One gape."

Raj led point, keeping an eye out for trouble. They followed the tunnels to a fork in the cave system, where Raj stopped. "Does anyone remember the way we came?"

"No," said Chaz. "But that may not be the way out, either."

"Pick a direction, Raj," said Amir.

"Hey, Happy-man. Know the way?" asked Raj.

Zuma pointed one way, then the other, then back to the way they'd come.

"That's a 'no.'" Raj stared at one black entrance then the other, but neither divulged a clue. She stepped toward the first, but backed up when animal growls echoed from the cave. "Fall back!"

"We can't," said Chaz. "Zuma can't run." Zuma sagged. Chaz pulled him upright. "He can't walk either."

"Then we fight," said Amir, leaning the book against the cave wall and crouching into position, his sticks poised to strike and his dagger waiting patiently in its sheath.

Chaz set Zuma down and raised his sword. "Raj, stay with Zuma and protect the books."

"Totes at your service, Lord," said Raj, setting the books down.

Zuma tried to get up. "Le' me ah 'um."

Raj pushed her boot against Zuma's thigh to keep him down. "Hold the books, Grapehead." She raised her weapon, ready to charge.

Zuma put a floppy arm across the books and let out a hiccup.

The growling grew louder, until it seemed the animal watched them from just inside one of the caves. The growling stopped. Amir and Chaz eyed one another, signaling their readiness to fight.

A small beige blur shot out of the cave and straight for Amir, who dropped his sticks, caught the creature and fell onto his back. Three-headed Cerberus licked and licked and licked Amir's face.

"I missed you, too, you cute thing," said Amir.

"Doggy." Zuma belched. "Wif six heads. And Raj, you haf two. Not good. Do I haf two?" He grabbed his head to check.

Amir scrambled to his feet but held Cerberus in his arms and scratched behind his ears, one head at a time. "Hey, maybe he can lead us out of here."

"Or maybe," said Raj, "he'll lead us right to Hades."

Amir set him down. "Cerberus, show us the way out."

Cerberus barked, lolled its tongues playfully, and wagged its crooked tail before trotting into a cave. He barked as if to hurry them along.

"I can't believe we're trusting a three-headed dog," said Raj.

"Does he—" whispered Zuma as Chaz pulled him to his feet. "Does he have three pee-pees, too?"

Raj rolled her eyes, then said in her most sincere voice. "No, Zuma. But you do."

Zuma stared at the crotch of his pants, then back at her. "Awesome!" He made a move for his fly, but Chaz stopped him. "Not now, Zuma. Keep it holstered."

Chapter Thirty-One

Benny could barely move. He sat up and ran his fingertips over his swollen cheek and cracked lip. He was no match for Hades. He had all too mortal powers. If only he—powers. That's what he needed.

He slid off his backpack and opened it. "Just a quick sip of water, and I'll be right with you, *Grandpa*."

"Join me, Benny. Take what you want—everything you desire. It's yours."

Benny nodded. "Sounds better and better."

"No! Benny," begged Neeve. "You can't!"

Benny uncapped the water bottle and put it to his lips. He had nothing to lose. He downed the bottle, every last drop.

"Silence! Let the boy choose for himself."

Benny felt it. A dark fire within him. The water from the River Styx ripped through his veins, setting his heart ablaze. He could feel it burn, turn to charcoal. Visions of the raging flames of the Phlegethon River filled his skull. He grabbed his head. It felt like fire singed his brain, burning through happy thoughts and leaving menacing ones. His arms tingled. Was his blood boiling within him?

As Benny rose to his feet, the orange flames reached his eyes. The red half turned bright and hot and engulfed the green until only red remained.

Like an unstoppable beast, Benny rushed at Hades. He knocked him to the floor and pummeled him. One blow left a cut on Hades' left cheek. Hades threw his arms up in defense. The black-robed minions rushed forward to help him.

Benny wrapped his hands around Hades' neck and squeezed.

Hades coughed but smiled. His eyes glowed red. He knocked Benny's arms away and shoved him off. Benny slid across the floor. His back slammed into the cage.

"Benny," said Neeve. "What's happening to you?"

Benny jumped to his feet. He grunted as he tried to pull the bars apart. They moved several inches.

Neeve put her hand over Benny's. Green returned to one of Benny's eyes. Benny stumbled back. He felt the fire burn down a notch within him. It must have been his mother's touch. Love dampened his hate. He glanced up in time to see Hades' reach for him and toss him across the room.

With a grunt, Benny tried to get up.

Neeve wriggled through the bars and rushed to Benny's side, but Hades grabbed her by the shoulders and tossed her away.

This ignited Benny's rage. He rushed forward, knocking Hades to the ground.

Helga tried to squeeze through the bars. Her head and chest made it through but her wide hips blocked the exit. She struggled, unable to go forward or retreat. The others urged her back and worked to dislodge her, so they could escape.

Hades and Benny rolled over and over before Hades shoved him off and flew to his feet, roaring in anger.

Benny roared in return and rushed forward again.

Hades caught hold of Benny's shoulders and shoved him back. Benny crashed down at his mother's feet.

Neeve begged him, "If you stay, you'll die. Leave!"

She grabbed his face and kissed him on the cheek. Her tears seeped into his skin. They doused the black fire within him, softened his heart.

"Go!" she pleaded.

Benny pushed her hands away. He needed what strength he had left, and each time she touched him, it seemed to diminish his rage. Once on his feet, Benny ran full speed and slammed into Hades, knocking him into the cage, leaving him dazed but a second.

Benny ripped his mother's amulet from Hades' neck before he raced up the steps.

"Stop him!" shouted Hades.

Benny ran through the castle, out the door, and onto the bridge.

On the bridge, the mosquito woman rushed to halt his progress. Benny held up the amulet, and the ugly mosquito backed away, making raspy hisses. She unleashed her tongue and snapped his cheek, as if to get a taste of him for later. Benny felt the sting and the rising welt, but he raced across the bridge, holding the amulet before him. The monsters backed away.

Benny leaped into the flaming gateway, out the other side and raced through the tunnel system.

Dodging an occasional black-robed minion, who could not keep up with his fire-like speed, Benny ran wildly. Rage and love warred within him still. He spotted a creature up ahead, running away from him. Instinct overtook reason. He roared and hunted it down, ready to tear out its throat in order to get past it.

He grabbed it by the shoulders, spun it around and smashed it against the wall.

"Benny! Stop! It's me. Layla."

Benny focused—or tried to focus. The red flame in his eyes died down and green returned as Layla's face came into view.

"Are you okay?" she asked.

Benny let her go and spun away to let the remaining rage subside at a safe distance.

"Look. I've got the key. Demeter's torch."

Benny spotted the minions in the distance, running toward them. "Let's go!" He shoved the amulet in his pocket and grabbed her free hand, and they raced through the tunnels, one after another, until reaching a fork.

"Which one?" asked Layla.

"Sorry, I forgot to ask Hades for a map," quipped Benny.

A menacing incoherent mumble filled the space around them.

Layla's eyes grew wide upon sight of the shock-haired man, who emerged from one of the tunnels waving frantic hands over his head.

Layla turned. "Run!"

"Wait!" shouted Benny. "He's a friend. I think."

Chaz, Zuma, Raj and Amir stood beside an aqua-blue lake inside an open cavern dripping with black and green crystalline stalactites. Cerberus splashed in the water along the edge of the lake and barked into the throat of the tunnel into which the lake disappeared.

"Can't you shut him up?" snapped Raj. "He's giving us away."

"Doesn't matter. It's a dead end," said Chaz. "We go back."

Raj snapped. "Nice going, Amir. We're trapped."

Zuma waded into the water.

Two figures rushed through the opening from which Cerberus had led the group moments earlier. Chaz and Raj crouched, ready for a fight.

"Benny! Layla!" shouted Amir, dropping his book to greet his friends.

As the pair neared the water's edge, Chaz slapped Benny on the shoulder and hugged Layla. "Good to see you guys."

Benny said, "You, too. My friend here is . . . where did he go? Oh, well. He got us this far."

Raj hugged Layla. "We found the books. Where's Kami?"

"Kami and I found the key," said Layla, holding up the torch. "But . . . the six lords. They were going to light it, open the gate. We had to fight them . . . I don't know. A boulder fell and . . . she . . ."

"Someone stop Zuma!" yelled Raj, setting the books down on the black sand that sparkled with green crystals.

"Let him be," said Chaz. "It might help clear his head. We may need him."

Izanagi and Hades burst through the entrance, followed by Apep, Nergal, Sharjinn, Kali, Lord of Mictlan, and a horde of minions and wretched humans.

Benny added, "Too late for that."

"Grab them!" shouted Hades.

Benny spotted his "friend" in the shredded shirt in the crowd. As he and the hoard ran toward them, arms outstretched, Benny wondered if the man was friend or a foe.

Cerberus bit into Amir's bootlaces and tugged, trying to get his foot into the water.

At the same time, Layla shouted, "Look at Zuma!"

Zuma floated away on the waters of the lake. Although it looked still, it had a current. Cerberus barked. "He wants us to follow," said Amir.

"No other choice," shouted Chaz, grabbing two of the golden books and jumping into the water.

Raj grabbed the remaining book and dove sidelong into the lake.

"I'll take the torch," said Benny. Layla handed it to him, and she dove in.

Benny dove next, the key firmly in his hands. As he bobbed to the surface, he turned back to shore. Amir fumbled with his backpack at the water's edge. Hades closed the distance.

"Amir! Dive!!" Something was wrong. Benny let go of the key and let it float away. He propelled his arms through the water, cranking hard like a water wheel at full speed.

Hades reached out for Amir at the same time that Benny surged up through the shallow water, grabbed Amir by his shoulders and hurled him away, feeling the last of the Styx's power leave him with the effort.

Amir let out a scream and clutched his backpack as he shot forward and plowed into the water.

Hades reached out for Benny.

Benny felt Hades' fingers brush across his back as he dove into the lake and plowed his arms through the water to speed away.

Only when at a safe distance did Benny risk glancing back. The lords and minions and humans didn't follow. Maybe they couldn't for some reason—or the lords had them where they wanted them. He'd find out soon enough.

Benny turned away and swam up to Amir. "What happened? Let me guess. All of that training and you can't swim?"

"I dog paddle well enough," said Amir. "That was close."

"Ya think? Next time I yell 'dive,' dive! Or I'll let them take you."

"Dive. Got it," said Amir, clutching his backpack.

Benny saw the torch floating up ahead. He swam for it.

A current propelled the warriors forward and into the tunnel. The water churned, dipping and tugging them under. The lake became a river; the current, a torrent of force and speed.

Benny gasped for air. Each time he bobbed to the surface, he reached for the key. But it strayed farther from him.

Pairs of green eyes glowed from the walls. Benny caught sight of them as they swooped toward the warriors. They were hairless cat-bats of sorts with long pointed teeth and pointy ears and exceptionally oversized claws and bat's wings and feet.

One cat-bat dove for the key.

Benny kicked his feet and beat the water, racing to get there first. He grabbed hold of the torch at the same time the creature wrapped its black clawed feet around it and began to lift it upward. Benny came with it, surprised that a creature half his size had such power.

All he could do was hold on tight and wait for an opportunity to fight. As Benny's body left the water and rose above it, he inspected the thing for weaknesses. He struggled to hold on to the smooth wood with wet fingers. His grip began to slip. He couldn't lose the key!

The cat-bat hissed. Benny kicked at it, trying to get it to drop the torch and him.

The thing raked the back of Benny's hand with a foreclaw, leaving bloody gashes. Benny cried out in pain and gripped the torch tighter. He couldn't hold on much longer.

A flash of metal flew past Benny's face and sank into the creature's chest, but it only sunk an inch.

Benny glanced down. Amir hung over his pack, which oddly buoyed him up from the water, at least enough for him to have thrown the dagger.

The cat-bat tried to claw the dagger away. It headed toward the rock wall to make its escape.

The torch dipped enough for Benny to get a leg over it. He grabbed the cat's belly fur and pulled himself up in a single effort of movement, where he sat atop the torch. He smashed his fist into the butt of the dagger, forcing it to sink up to its hilt in the creature's chest.

The cat-bat's wings stopped beating, and it fell.

Benny gripped the torch in both hands and plummeted dangerously close to the cliff face. The dead cat-bat fell alongside him. Benny saw a protrusion below. He would hit it.

Just before impact, the dead cat-bat struck the wall and bounced into Benny, pushing him out from the rocks just enough to miss it.

Another cat-bat swooped in to grab the key or Benny, or both, as they plunged into the river. As Benny splashed down, the creature narrowly missed him and swooshed back into the air.

Underwater, Benny wrapped his legs around the torch and held his breath. He swam a few strokes to where the dead cat-bat was sinking. The torch buoyed him up. He stroked harder to propel himself downward enough to grab the dagger hilt then yanked and yanked until it came free. The creature fell to the depths.

Benny swam to the surface. He fought to sit on the torch like a pool noodle to keep it submerged and safe. When he bobbed to the surface, Amir was beside him. He, too, sat on the torch.

"Guess we're even now," said Amir.

"That's if we get out of here alive." Benny stabbed at the creatures that swooped down, and Amir swatted them with his sticks.

Up ahead, the others ducked underwater to avoid being plucked up or, likewise, fended off the creatures using their weapons.

As suddenly as they had appeared, the green-eyed creatures peeled away and headed back down the mouth of the cave. Before anyone had time to rejoice, Raj and Chaz screamed and shouted, but all Benny heard was "all" or "haul."

It took a moment before Benny saw it. The water ahead churned into froth and roared over the edge of what sounded like a long drop, and in this place that could mean miles and miles. Zuma fell first. Then Raj, Layla, and Chaz.

Amir screamed and Benny held fast to the key as they plunged over the edge, separating as they tumbled down the bottomless waterfall.

Chapter Thirty-Two

Benny wrapped his hands and legs around the torch. He struggled to breathe in the wall of water and thick mist. When he broke through to the edge of the cascading falls, he gulped the air. It seemed as tall as the cliff they had scaled down in the darkness, but given the velocity at which he fell, Benny estimated it was several times deeper.

He sputtered and coughed, sure he would die from drowning long before he hit bottom. But bottom arrived in a sudden rush that he had not expected.

Benny shot like a missile into the deep pool at the base of the fall. He didn't feel the impact. It should have killed him. He flailed and kicked to push himself to the surface, but the current pulled him downward, deeper and deeper. It grew darker and blacker, until it was inky and eerie and he had no sense of up or down whatsoever. A rip current, he thought. And no way out.

He couldn't hold his breath much longer. He saw a pinhole of light at the bottom. Too tired to fight, he let the current have him, carry him where it would and the key with him.

The pinhole grew wider upon his approach. The water lightened until it became a bright bluish green. His lungs fought to suck in air. He fought against them, swallowing spit to close off his windpipe.

Benny sailed past a statue of Poseidon holding a trident. He thought he saw a dark-haired woman swim his way but presumed it was a dream of death settling upon him. He closed his eyes to fight against it.

He had to breathe, even if it meant sucking in water. He heard Neeve's voice: "Fight, Benny. You can do this! I'm here, Benny. I won't let you go." Benny felt a shove in his back that propelled him upward.

Benny inhaled a gasping breath just as he broke through the surface. His eyes sprang open, horrified to see the inside of another cave, but he was happy to be alive. He gasped for more good clean air, coughing it out in spurts, then sucking up more. Never had air tasted more delicious.

A small opening in the distance radiated light. Sunlight! He hadn't seen that kind of light in how long?

"Benny!" shouted Zuma. "We're in the Blue Grotto. Home, sweet home."

Benny could not believe his eyes. Zuma, who seemed his normal self, bobbed in the water on the back of a dolphin, its flanks striped with dark gray, light gray and white.

A woman swam up beside Benny. He recognized her. "You're the gypsy from Delphi. Herophile."

"And a sea nymph. You must hurry. My friends will take you to shore."

A dolphin, gray but for slashes of white that painted its hide, swam up under Benny and carried him away. He held tightly to the key as the creature followed Zuma's dolphin out of the grotto opening and into the sunlight. Real sunlight! Blue skies. A blue so bright and blinding it was like seeing it for the first time in his life. Benny spotted Raj, Chaz, Layla and Amir, straddling the back of a whale of some kind with a charcoal-gray back and white flanks.

Benny's dolphin raced away from the Isle of Capri and toward Naples, alongside the whale and Zuma's dolphin. Benny should have been elated and whooping and hollering like Raj and Chaz, but he could only think about his mother—and theirs. And he had questions. If Hades was his grandfather? Then his father was the son of Hades. By whom? His mother clearly had no idea. Where was the next gate? Where was Kami? Was she alive or dead?

Benny eyed his friends. Layla, like him, hung her head low, and he knew why. She felt the loss—not just of a friend, but the loss of the world as she had known it before they entered the underworld.

It became real. All of it. The "truth" hit him in the gut harder than Hades' blows. The underworld existed, thrived below the surface. Marcus Curtius knew it. He rode into it, sacrificing himself and his horse to keep the pathway closed. Hesiod knew it. Dante knew it. Pops and his son, Aeneas, knew it. But now, it was real for him, too. It was here, in his face. And he was a warrior, or at least called upon to be a warrior, and sucked into the fight. The sun no longer warmed his face—that was a perk enjoyed by the ignorant, blissful mortals, who knew nothing more than the idea of what lay beneath the earth's crust. An idea that was far out of reach—or so they thought. As for him, no such ignorance existed. Not any more. Hades' mist had stung him to the quick, seared and hardened him, permanently.

The gentle dolphin dropped Benny as close to a barren stretch of shore as it dared before it made a squall of good-byes and dove back into the sea. Before Benny strode ashore, he checked on the others. There was trouble.

Chaz floundered and Zuma rushed to help him. Benny's heart sank in his chest. Chaz must have lost the use of his legs. Chaz floated on his back and folded his arms over the two golden books balanced on his chest. Zuma wrapped an arm around Chaz's chin and swam him to shore, lifeguard style.

Amir floundered, too, and Layla rushed to help direct him, since he could no longer see. Raj swam to shore on her back, her arms wrapped around the third golden book. She didn't seem to need any help.

"Benny!" shouted a familiar voice from shore.

Benny turned, happy to see Daniel, who was pushing an empty wheelchair toward the shoreline. Minnie and Mike walked beside him. Benny waded out of the water carrying the torch.

"Welcome home," said Daniel.

Mike approached and cleared his throat. "Good job. You didn't die."

Flashes of near death rushed through Benny's mind: the earthquake on the wall, the Abominable Sands, Zuma under the Nemean lion, his fight with Hades, but all he said was, "Not this time."

Mike rushed to the shoreline and scooped Chaz up in his arms. He set him in the wheelchair, which Daniel steadied.

Chaz tried to make a joke of it. "Good thing for you guys we're on a beach with no sand. I'm easier to push around."

"How did you know we'd be here?" Benny asked Minnie.

"Herophile told us where to meet you."

The group gathered around Minnie. Benny handed her the key.

Layla said, "The key. Demeter's torch."

"I should have thought of it," said Minnie. "None of us thought of it, even Demeter."

"How long have we been gone?" asked Zuma.

"Nine days, seven hours and . . ." Mike checked his watch. "Never mind. Too long."

"Where's Kami?" Minnie searched the water for the straggler.

Layla stammered, "We . . . I mean I . . . it's my fault. The six lords had the torch. Izanagi was about to light it. We had to stop him . . . Kami told me to grab the key. She fought Izanagi. A boulder fell on them . . . and I ran . . . I—"

Minnie's voice seemed to admonish Layla for her display of emotion. "It's no one's fault! Kami knew the danger. You all did."

"Don't you have any feelings!" shouted Layla. "She's my friend!"

"And mine," said Raj, followed by the others.

"No!" shouted Minnie. "She is not your friend. She *is* a warrior! You are warriors. You weren't warriors going in, but you are now. If Kami stood here beside us, she'd say the same. We will go on, continue the fight. It's what we do."

"Minnie's right," said Benny. "If Kami's alive, we'll find her. Or she'll find us. And the others."

"Others?" asked Raj, getting in Benny's face. "What others?"

"Our mothers?" asked Chaz.

Benny nodded. "They're alive."

Raj could not contain her emotions. She turned away.

"Mike, you've faced war," said Minnie. "Tell them."

Mike nodded. "She's right, guys. I've seen friends go down. It's hard not knowing, but Kami's tough, and—"

Minnie cut him off. "And there's nothing more we can do for her now. Our job is not yet finished. The sybil needs us. Now."

No one answered. No one moved.

Silence crashed down upon them until broken by a yip. The group turned and inspected the shoreline.

"Sorry," said Amir. "Yip! Yippee! Yip! I'm so glad we're home."

"Zuma," said Minnie, clearly not falling for it. "Grab his backpack."

Zuma yanked it off Amir's shoulders, set it on the ground and opened it. Out jumped Cerberus, but he only had one head. His tail was still as crooked as a lightning bolt.

"Dude," said Chaz. "What did you do?"

"He guards the underworld," added Raj. "This is so not good."

Amir stammered, "Yeah, but think about it. He stops people from going in. But that's silly, right? I mean if people, like us, are stupid enough to go to the underworld, then why try to stop them? Let them in. He helped us, didn't he?"

Minnie rolled her eyes to heaven. "I'm speechless right now. I'm never speechless, but you've rendered me so."

Amir pleaded, "He'll be my guide dog. I'll take care of him. I promise."

"Until he rips your throat out in the middle of the night." Zuma clawed his hands to imitate it.

"Well, what's done is done," said Minnie, turning toward the van. "Our work is not. Follow me."

Benny lagged behind to glare at the shimmering orange-red sun that sank below the horizon and into the sea, leaving them in a new kind of darkness, a twilight between the worlds of good and evil.

Chapter Thirty-Three

Mike drove through the winding dark roads of Naples headed to Cumae. Daniel begged him to drive so that he could hold the three books in his lap. "I can't believe it," Daniel muttered again and again, his fingers tracing over the intricate gold cover of the topmost book. "The Sibylline books, here. In my lap."

"It beats gargoyles and giant frogs," Mike added, but Daniel could hear nothing, see nothing, but the books.

Minnie focused on the road and the task, ahead. "Go faster, Mike. Time is our only enemy right now. She's at the end."

Chaz rubbed his legs.

"Sore, bro?" asked Benny.

"I wish. I can't feel a thing," said Chaz.

Layla and Raj maintained a dour, separate silence. Amir petted Cerberus, coiled in his lap, nonstop.

Zuma began to nod off. Layla nudged him awake. "Sorry, but we're almost there."

Zuma rubbed his face and sat up straighter. "Thanks, bro."

Daniel parked just outside the visitor's entrance, pulling the vehicle well off the road.

"Cerberus," ordered Minnie, after all had hopped out of the van. "Look for guards. If you find any, get them away from the entrance to the cave."

Cerberus barked. Amir grinned.

"Oh, don't gloat, Amir," chided Minnie, staring into the dog's face. "If he's here, he'll work for us. And if he messes up, he's dog chow. Go on then." Cerberus obediently trotted away.

Raj sneered, "Could be a little canine spy."

"You're paranoid," said Amir.

"You're blind," said Raj. "Ha, ha. Get it?"

Minnie shushed them. "Is this the way you behaved in the underworld?"

"Pretty much," affirmed Zuma.

Minnie rolled her eyes. Cloaked in the darkness of a new moon, Minnie led the group forward. All eyes searched for trouble; their ears, for sounds. Raj walked alongside Minnie. Layla helped Amir. Daniel struggled with the three books, but he would not let go of any of them. Benny carried the torch for safekeeping, and Mike and Zuma helped with Chaz's wheelchair.

A menacing growl echoed in the distance, followed by shouts.

"That's our cue," said Minnie. She ducked inside the angled walls of the entrance and shot the beam of her flashlight down the long shaft. She walked fast, just short of running, as did the others.

Before long, they burst through the tunnel and into the expanse of the chamber.

Benny could hardly believe he stood at the starting point of the quest that had begun a mere nine days earlier. No one hesitated. They rushed into the side chamber, all except Daniel and Mike, who shuffled their feet and eyed one another, waiting for Minnie's orders.

Minnie scolded them. "Jump in. No time to waste."

Daniel and Mike no sooner rushed into the alcove than the walls shook and the ground rumbled beneath their feet.

When the earth stilled, an ethereal glow lit the sibyl's room, which shimmered in gold, soft green and violet.

The group spilled onto the mosaic-tiled floor of black and white and saw, again, the familiar fresco paintings of Apollo admiring a fair-haired woman. The marble pedestal in the center of the room sat empty but for Layla's red scarf, untied and draped over it—which held a single grain.

Apollo stepped out of the fresco. "Minnie, sister, you're here at last." He kissed Minnie on both cheeks.

"Brother." Minnie returned his kisses. "Sybil?"

"She's but a grain. I was a fool, sister. She spurned my love, and I punished her for it—but it was me I punished more. I wish I'd given her immortality, so that she could spurn me for all of it. Hurry. Before the last of her disappears." Apollo lifted the single grain from the red scarf and set it in the palm of his hand. He curled a protective fist around it.

"Daniel," instructed Minnie, "put the books on the pedestal."

Daniel set the books atop the scarf. His mouth hung open, his eyes wide with childlike wonder.

Minnie opened the topmost book and flipped to a particular page. She read aloud:

As mighty Zeus commands, and we the gods obey
Give touch to this, the fairest ghostly maid today
Let their love heal a thousand years of dark distance
Let their touch mend and join their hearts with untold bliss.

Lightning struck the books and they disappeared.

"The books!" shouted Daniel. "They're gone!"

Minnie calmed him. "Zeus has them now. He'll lock them in a safer vault than this."

The sybil, in her flowing chiton of sheer white, stepped down from the fresco and strode toward Apollo. A sheer white scarf, secured by a diadem of delicate gold flowers, framed her delicate face. A long twisting coil of blonde hair fell over one shoulder, and her lips formed a confident smile. She stood before Apollo but turned to face the warriors. She placed her hands together and bowed deeply to thank them before turning to face her love.

"I thought," Daniel said to Minnie, "the Sibylline books were prophecies, not spells."

"You're correct," whispered Minnie. "But only the prophecies inscribed in the book and read aloud by a god, demigod or sibyl become true. I inscribed this prophecy just before the books entered the underworld. Never was it read aloud, but even if it had been, the gods' prophecies do not work in the underworld. Thus it became a race against time."

Apollo reached out both of his hands.

The sibyl smiled up at him. She raised her delicate hands and settled them into his palms. A gasp left her lips as she felt his touch for the first time. Apollo bent his face down to press his lips to hers and whispered, "Wife."

"For the rest of my life." As their lips met, they faded away to spend the short time they had before she disappeared forever, leaving only her voice.

Raj and Layla sighed; Benny lowered his gaze, as if to give the pair privacy; Daniel pulled his hanky from his pocket and daubed his eyes, and Mike and Minnie raised chins up, resisting any sign of emotion.

"Deets," said Amir. "What happened?"

Chaz replied, "Apollo got the girl, Amir. He got his girl."

"And she got her man," added Zuma. "She's hot. Not sure I'd have waited a thousand years though."

Daniel blew his nose and stuffed his hanky back in his lapel pocket.

Mike cleared his throat, his usual sign of stifling his emotions. "If you loved her, you'd wait, Zuma. You'd definitely wait."

Zuma puckered his face, "Whatevs."

Chaz answered, "I'd totally marry her, even if she only had a day or two left."

Raj scoffed, "Ha! You'd marry her because she only had a day or two left."

"Not true," said Chaz, eyeing Layla, who blushed and turned away from his gaze.

Kami added, "Minnie, can't you do something? Give them brains like the Wizard of Oz could?"

"Sadly, not one god in all the heavens can speed up maturity. If they could have, they would have," said Minnie, heading to the alcove. "Come. It's time to head to the hotel. You've earned a rest."

Mike added, "And some medical attention. They're pretty banged up. I can help there."

"Of course," said Minnie. "We'll make a stop by the pharmacy in Delphi."

"Food," said Zuma. "I'm too tired to sit down to a meal, but I'm starving."

"Same," said Benny, and the others followed.

"Bandages and sustenance," said Daniel. "You shall have both. Delivered to your rooms."

———◆———

No one said a word on the way back to the hotel. Daniel and Mike made the rounds to each room, checking the wounds, while Minnie remained in the lobby making arrangements for the plane.

Benny had a banged-up knee, a gash across the back of his hand and a triangular cut that he called a "flapper" on the other, not to mention a split lip and swollen cheek and sore ribs. Zuma was the worst though, with gashes across his chest. Mike wrapped him up and helped him into bed, where he had difficulty finding a comfortable spot, one that didn't hurt.

———

"Mi scuzi, signorina?" said the desk clerk, coming up beside Minnie as she finished her phone call, whereby she ordered the pilot to have the plane ready for flight in the morning.

"Yes," she responded, tucking away her cell phone.

"Flowers arrived for you while you were out." He pointed to an arrangement that sat on the counter.

Minnie crossed the lobby to reach the red spider lilies in a black crystal vase. "Izanagi," she whispered, reaching for the card whose face was black with a single red lilly. She opened it and read the haiku aloud:

> *Deaf. Mute. Blind. And wise.*
> *See within to see without.*
> *Time for one to die.*

"Shall I put them in your room?" asked the clerk.

"No need. I'll take care of them." Minnie tucked the card away, lifted the vase and walked outside into the warm night air. Upon passing the first trash bin, she dumped the vase. It clunked as it fell. An owl screeched overhead.

———

Layla jumped into her nightclothes and curled under the sheets and blanket. She turned on her side, facing the wall.

"No shower?" asked Raj.

Layla made no response.

Raj paused before adding, "We'll find her, Layla. I trust her. And I trust that you did all you could. Sleep well." She walked over and pulled the covers up over Layla's shoulders that heaved in silent, guilt-ridden shudders.

Raj jumped in the shower and cranked up the hot water until it scalded her clean. The room filled with comforting steam. She took her time before stepping out of the shower and drying off. She wrapped herself in a towel and dug through her backpack for toothpaste and a toothbrush—she hadn't used them in the underworld—but who knew toiletries were not needed? "Note to self. Leave toothpaste. Bring baby powder to sprinkle on invisible wall walkers." She dug again, felt an odd shape and pulled it up. She eyed the greenish-gold pot—Inanna's magic gel.

Raj opened the pot. The gel shimmered and enticed. Raj stepped to the mirror, which was coated in steam. She used a hand cloth to clear a circle in the center. She pulled her hair aside and ran her fingers down the purple spike that raced angrily down the side of her face. It had reappeared. But her eyelids showed no sign of burns. The ocean waves must have washed the healing gel away, but it had worked on the burns better than on the permanent stain. She thought of applying more, but she didn't trust Inanna. "Flawless or chinked?"

Raj capped the pot and let it fall into the trash. It clanged against the metal pail. She hurried to toss on her pajamas, turned out the bathroom light, and jumped under the covers and into bed.

In the next room, Amir and Cerberus snuggled nose to nose on the pillow. Benny, reluctantly, slept in the same room after losing a coin toss. Zuma and Chaz—the winners of the coin toss—occupied a room across the hall. The coin toss had come about after Zuma whined, "I'm not sleeping with the hellhound. He might tear my face off as I sleep."

Benny had a quick shower and fell into bed. As he lay there, he gobbled a fluffy pastry filled with meat and spices. His eyes closed as he chewed bite after bite, until his mouth opened and waited, but his arm dropped to his side, letting go of the pastry, which fell silently to the floor.

Cerberus leaped off of Amir's bed and gobbled up the treat, then returned to Amir's side.

Amir held up the mirror that Inanna had given him without expecting to see a thing. He let out a small squeal. To his delight, his face smiled back at him. "Cool! I may be blind, but at least I can see myself in this mirror. Mirror, mirror, who's the fairest of them all? Me! I know!"

Amir kissed Cerberus three times on his head—in case he still had three heads but he was only able to feel one. He checked the mirror once more. "I wonder how I'd look with a mustache and a goatee. Dashing, I think." He tucked the mirror in his pack, which lay beside his bed. He settled in, dropping an arm around Cerberus and drifted off to sleep.

Across the hall, Chaz sidled out of his wheelchair and into bed.

"What was the offer, bro?" asked Zuma, chomping into a cream-filled pastry and speaking through a mouth full of food.

Chaz stared at the ceiling. "Inanna wants to marry me."

Zuma had to swallow before he could speak. All he could do was wave a hand at Chaz to signal he had something to say. At last, he blurted, "Dang, dude! The goddess of love. You and

Pops." Zuma shoved the last bite of his eighth pastry into his mouth. He still felt hungry, but there was no more food in the room.

"And Pops was scortched. Besides, eternity is a long stretch, bro, even with a beautiful goddess."

"Good point."

"You get enough to eat?" said Chaz, shifting the conversation.

"In defense, I offered you one."

"I'm not hungry. Good night, Zuma." Chaz turned off the bedside lamp.

"Must be tough."

"What?"

"You could walk. Then . . . poof."

A long pause ensued.

"And dance," Chaz whispered. "Night, Zuma."

Zuma tossed and turned while Chaz let out a rhythmic purr moments after he closed his eyes. Still hungry, Zuma dug in his pack and pulled out the ambrosia—the only food left in the room. He nibbled a tiny chip from the corner of the cube. It melted on his tongue. He could not see that as he swallowed, his throat glowed purple, as if he had eaten a light bulb. It was all he could do to stifle his moans of pleasure. He slapped both hands over his mouth to hush the sounds he wanted to make. It was hot in the room. He shoved the covers off. He rubbed his stomach in satisfaction. He fell into a gentle, peaceful sleep. His belly glowed purple. A shape rose upward and stretched Zuma's belly and the fabric of his nightshirt, forming a lump. As it rose higher, it took the shape of a spindly hand that reached out as if to stretch before sinking down to sleep. The purple glow subsided.

In a fitful dream, Zuma clutched his belly.

Raj flipped this way and that and finally sat up. She saw a faint glow emanating from the bathroom trash can. She eyed

Layla, who was fast asleep. She pushed the covers aside, walked softly to the bathroom and reached for the pot. Her hand shook as she set the pot on the sink and uncapped it. The pot slipped from her hand, falling less than inch, but the smack of glass against porcelain rang out. Raj spun around and eyed Layla, whose head jolted upright from the sound, but rested back down again.

They had become attuned to danger, to sounds that made them jump, but deep sleep and a deeper need for respite prevailed.

Raj closed the bathroom door and faced the mirror. "Chaz said I was flawless. He noticed me." She reached for the pot, tempted to throw it away and be done with it, but she noticed that in the short fall a drop of gel had left the pot and landed along the side of her finger. She raised her finger to the top of the purple dagger that marred her face. She touched her skin and slid her finger downward. Her eyes closed. She breathed hard.

"Probably doesn't even wor—" Before finishing her sentence, she opened her eyes. The gel had erased a finger-width of the birthmark. Her trembling fingers dipped again into the gel and again down her face, until she saw an unmarked face, clean and lovely. She held her hair back. She turned her face right and left, time and again, before gently lowering her hair.

Raj screwed the top on the pot. "It probably won't last 'til morning." Before she turned off the bathroom light, she glanced once more in the mirror and smiled.

———◆———

The council surrounded Hades' hearth.

"Did you send the . . . invitation?" asked Hades.

"Flowers and a clue. They'll come," replied Izanagi.

"And you, Inanna, did you deliver the gifts I gave you?"

"Yes, my lord," she confirmed.

Hades warmed his hands in the roaring fire of the hearth. "It has begun. Our time is near."

Coming Soon

Other books in the series:

#3 Evil Sees
#4 Evil Touches
#5 Evil Feeds
#6 Evil Deeds
#7 Evil Desires

Other books by S. Woffington

Literary/Multicultural/Historical

"Unveiling is an excellent story and compelling read."
–Judge, Writer's Digest SP e-book awards

What would you sacrifice to fulfill your destiny?

Sara—a spirited, young Saudi woman—is passionate about preserving and expressing her ancient heritage through her art. But this seemingly simple goal puts her at odds with her prominent family and the traditions of her heritage, which demand she veil her artist's eyes. Forced to choose between her two greatest passions, Sarah escapes to America, only to find that unveiling entails far more than the removal of a black piece of cloth. This act of defiance thrusts Sara into a perilous triangle involving family, government, and a relentless suitor. Only by finding the courage to unveil her own heart can she paint her destiny.

For more, please visit swoffington.com.

An Interview with S. Woffington

You grew up in Bakersfield, California. What was that like?

I can't imagine growing up anywhere else. We called it Nashville West, since Buck Owens and Merle Haggard were topping the country charts. I still go back to visit friends and stop by Dewar's for ice cream and taffy.

You married and moved to Riyadh, Saudi Arabia in 1979. Did you have to veil?

Not at all, and I didn't cover my hair, but I dressed in modest kaftans. Saudis were welcoming and hospitable. I fell in love with Saudi Arabia: with the people and the desert landscape and the Red Sea! It was like going back in time, except it changed daily. Mud-walled palaces came crashing down and new shiny marble ones rose up because of the money flooding in from the Oil Boom.

And this adventure planted the seed for your debut novel *Unveiling*?

I just had to capture this time of upheaval, the time when oil money and mechanical cranes threatened to destroy more than buildings— they erased heritage and culture. It was also a time when Saudi women spoke up and called for change, which led to sections of the university opening to women and protests for the right to drive, but change takes time. My middle grade students don't understand that, until they learn about the civil rights movement. I tell them about my mother (b. 1919), who was dissuaded from a professional career of substance. She wanted to be a doctor, but her parents forbid it. After raising three daughters, she returned to college. Back then, there was also age discrimination. The college would not accept her into the nursing program due to her age, but she found a back door and became a nurse. She graduated at sixty, and that taught me that it's never too late to pursue your dreams. And never give up! I returned to college in my forties.

Would you say Saudi Arabia is more resistant to change than in the West?

I would say it takes longer there, but it does happen. Despite the Kingdom's progressive stance, each step forward incites protests. I was in the Kingdom when the Grand Mosque in Mecca was taken over by zealots who saw the Saud family as too progressive and friendly with the West. Unveiling traces the history of two such groups of religious zealots. Such groups threaten peace today, and they thwart women's advancement. But women have always found a way, and courageous men have supported their growth—the largest women's university in the world opened in Saudi Arabia in 2011, thirty women were seated on the Shura Council in 2013, and women were allowed to vote in municipal elections and run for office in 2015. That's incredible change!

The main character of *Unveiling*, Sara, struggles to pursue her passion for art and follow traditions that demand she veil her eyes. But she cannot sketch what she cannot see. I understand that the main character was inspired by a real Saudi artist:

Yes, Safeya Binzagr sparked the idea for my character, Sara. Safeya has worked tirelessly to capture her country's heritage in art. She opened a museum, gallery and school in Jeddah to promote art in the Kingdom. I can't say enough about her. I admire her so much.

What makes *Unveiling* literary? Was that a conscious decision?
It's what the novel demanded. I wanted to capture the feel of *1001 Arabian Nights*, so there are stories within stories which make it literary. The ancient stories of the family ripple forward and affect Sara in the present day, which I believe history can do. History touches us like ghosts from the past, which is why *Unveiling* incorporates real historical events where Sara's ancestors appear. And I included three pieces of calligraphy in Arabic. Since my character is an artist, I really wanted this art form to be part of the novel. It's an art of words, which is a powerful concept. When I worked on these pieces, I let Sara do the work, something like an actor assuming a role. I don't consider myself an artist when it comes to drawing, nor am I Saudi. It's demanding to write about a culture that you're not born into, and I took that challenge seriously. If I couldn't get it right, I was willing to scrap the novel. Besides massive research, I was fortunate to find Lina Karmouta, who earned her MA in Arabic Literature from King Saud University, Riyadh and who taught in the Kingdom. She critiqued the novel, and I can't thank her enough for her valuable advice which led to numerous changes of the final draft of *Unveiling*. I've had positive feedback from the Arab community, for which I'm grateful.

The inspiration for the *Warriors and Watchers Saga* hits closer to home. After completing your double masters at Chapman University, you accepted the position of lead middle school instructor at a Montessori school. Do you enjoy teaching?
I love it! Every morning, I barely set one foot outside of the car

and someone shouts 'Good morning, Ms. Sandy!' You can't have a bad day with that kind of a start. Each child's needs are unique, and I love helping to prepare them for high school, but it's about more than academics. Middle school is two or three compact years fraught with physical, social, emotional and hormonal changes. It's angst and joy, a time when boy sees girl and vice versa, and I try to help my students through it, fostering social skills and a strong sense of self. Each year ends with my feeling that they gave me as much or more than I gave to them.

You teach math, English, and History. Which is your favorite?
All of them in some way, but I love history and mythology. I tell my students that history is so cool, because it's real stories about real people. Since my Saudi experience, I've thirsted to travel and meet people around the world. I don't intentionally interject history or mythology into my novels, but they always seems to creep in, so it's clearly a part of me.

The *Warriors and Watchers Saga* is about seven teens, ranging in age from fourteen to eighteen, but some of them have physical challenges: blind, deaf, paraplegic. How did that come about?
I once helped out at a Special Olympics type of event, and I was amazed at the joy, talent and fortitude of the athletes. Talk about heroes! When writing a series with teen heroes, they stepped forward in my mind and leaped onto the pages, and they continue to raise their voices and be heard.

Do you use any of your students as characters?
I'm asked that a lot. No. I can't write about people I actually know, but sometimes a real person is a jumping off point to creating a character.

The seven-novel Warriors and Watchers Saga is an Epic Mytho-logical Fantasy. What do you love most about this genre?
Anything goes! I can let the creative mind explode. Some of the characters and places in *Evil Speaks* have blown me away. I didn't see them coming, which sounds odd, because I outline the plot points and scenes, but sometimes a scene changes course and the ideas flood so fast that my fingers have a hard time keeping up. And I type fast. *Evil Hears* is plotted and the writing has begun. It, too, is a wild ride!

Read more about the author or visit her website at **warriorsand-watcherssaga.com**. Sandra encourages you to leave a comment or ask a question or otherwise engage in a discussion. You can also find her on the following sites:

Facebook Author's Page: www.facebook.com/sandrawoffington
Twitter: twitter.com/swoffington
LinkedIn: www.linkedin.com/in/sandra-woffington-4450675b

Also on Google Plus and Pinterest

CPSIA information can be obtained
at www.ICGtesting.com
Printed in the USA
LVOW10s1433240217
525372LV00001B/97/P